MW01146740

By Gretchen Craig

NOVELS

Always & Forever: A Saga of Slavery and Deliverance
(The Plantation Series, Book I)
Ever My Love: A Saga of Slavery and Deliverance
(The Plantation Series, Book II)
Evermore: A Saga of Slavery and Deliverance
(The Plantation Series, Book III)

Tansy
Crimson Sky
The Lion's Teeth

SHORT STORY COLLECTIONS

The Color of the Rose
Bayou Stories: Tales of Troubled Souls
Lookin' for Luv: Five Short Stories

Theena's Landing

Gretchen
Craig

Published by Pendleton Press.

www.GretchenCraig.com

Kindle e-book edition available from Amazon.com.

ISBN-13: 978-1511990646
ISBN-10: 1511990643

Theena's Landing

Chapter One

Biscayne Bay, Florida

Summer, 1886

Theena stilled her broom and watched Jack Spode pole his dugout into the landing. His sun bleached hair caught the light, almost like a halo, but Jack was no saint, at least not the kind that swore off women. She checked that her top buttons hadn't popped open, not that Jack would notice if they had.

Theena glanced at her sister's bent head. "Jack's here."

Hera spilled peas across the weathered porch floor in her hurry to set the bowl down. Holding her skirt up, she ran barefoot across the sand to the landing, then rushed full tilt into Jack before he was ready for her.

"Damn, Hera." The two of them tumbled off the low bank into the crystal clear shallows of the Miami River.

Theena didn't mean to spy, but she was there on the porch. She couldn't not see Jack on his back, little wavelets washing over his bare shoulders, Hera on top of him, laughing. She planted a wet sloppy kiss on his face before he held her off by the arms.

"Hera." Jack nodded his chin toward Theena.

Theena felt the heat rise in her face and knew she was tomato red.

Hera tossed her curls and made sure she spoke loud enough for Theena to hear. " 'Spect there's no law 'bout kissing in the full light of day."

Jack shifted Hera off and pulled her up the bank. He reached into the dugout for his shirt, his bare back as bronzed as his arms.

Hera walked him to the cabin, her hands wrapped around his arm. Her skirt clung to her thighs and the wet bodice plainly showed her bosom. All they'd been through with Mama and still Hera threw herself at a man like a wanton, no shame in her at all.

Theena leaned against the porch post, arms crossed, and kept her eyes on the sun glitter of the river.

At the bottom of the porch steps, Jack slapped the water out of his palmetto hat. “Hey, Shrimp. How’s your daddy doing?”

“About the same.”

He nodded, a worry line on his forehead. “Worse than hell being sick in the summer.”

Hera reclaimed Jack by squeezing his arm to her breast. “Jack and I’ll walk down to the bay to let the sun dry us off. You finish shelling the peas?”

Theena picked up Hera’s bowl and made a point of not looking at Jack and Hera strolling through the sand. Now a damned scorpion poised under the rawhide chair, its spiny tail raised to do battle against some unsuspecting bare foot. Well that was one battle Theena could win. She lifted up the chair, aimed the tip of a leg, and squashed the damn thing.

She cradled the bowl in her lap and ran her thumb up the seam of a pod. For weeks now, Hera had been making a point of keeping Jack away from her. Theena didn’t know why she bothered. His eyes on Hera’s wet bosom, he’d already forgotten she was there. And she, Theena Theophilus, had no business thinking it should be otherwise.

It’s not like Theena didn’t have a beau of her own. A handsome man, refined, educated. What he wanted with her, a barefoot Florida cracker, mystified her, but she meant to live down the reputation Mama had painted her daughters with. She herself would be a proper wife and mother some day, blameless and virtuous. She wouldn’t be found crawling all over Randolph Chase with no more than a spindly palm tree for a sliver of privacy.

But it was hard not to notice Jack, the way the sun streaked his brown hair and tanned his skin so that he already had smile lines around his eyes. She’d never seen a man so at ease with himself, a man who slouched against a porch post or threw a net with equal grace. Theena had been lanky and prone to adolescent awkwardness when Jack first came to the Miami River. A Conch with salt water in his veins, he had sailed up from Key West to start a citrus grove and quickly became an object of fantasy for half the women in their little fishing village. But he’d fastened his eye on the middle Theophilus sister. Sweet-faced, curvy, cuddly Hera.

The door swung open and Dite, the oldest of the three, came onto the porch and sighed herself down into the rawhide chair.

“Mind your foot,” Theena said.

Dite glanced down at the crispy, gooey remainders of Theena's kill and rubbed her hands over her face. She had dark circles under her eyes, her skin as pale as a bleached petticoat.

"Did you get any rest?" Theena asked her.

"On toward morning, I did."

Dite glanced toward the river twenty yards across the sandy yard, frowned, and put a hand to her brow. "That sun on the water spears you right in the eye."

Theena stilled her hands over the pea shelling and admired her river. This is how she liked it best, sunbeams raying through the trees, glittering on the water. Dite wasn't usually immune to beautiful sights. She was worn down with nursing Daddy. Theena offered again. "I'll sit with him tonight."

"I'd rather sit with him myself, Theena. I can't rest when he's bad, anyway."

"All right then."

Dite shaded her eyes with her hand and peered toward the river at Jack's dugout. "Jack's here."

"Uh-huh." Theena nodded her head toward Jack and Hera headed for the beach.

Dite squinted at them. "Is her dress tail wet?"

Theena lowered her voice so Daddy couldn't hear. "You'd think after what Mama did, she'd take more care."

"It's not the same, Theena. You don't remember."

Theena gouged out a row of peas from their pod. She remembered the nights she cried herself to sleep wondering how her mother could have left her. She remembered the whispers and mean looks at the store and at the little schoolhouse on the bay. Shame had curled in her belly as heavy as loss.

"Neither of them is married to someone else," Dite said. "Besides, we aren't all little miss saints in training like you." Her voice held no spite, just weariness and a hard view of the world. After Mama ran off, Dite had hired on at the Peacock Inn, working four days a week cleaning rooms, then coming home to see to the family. Dite wasn't the least bit motherly, but she'd seen that Theena kept her face washed and her hems clean. "And we don't all wait for life to just happen to us like you do."

"I don't wait . . . ." Theena glanced at the door and leveled her tone so Daddy wouldn't hear. "Anyway, you wouldn't do that." She nodded toward Hera draped around Jack's arm.

Dite's lips curved in a disdainful half-smile. "Not my style."

Dite, as beautiful as Daddy had thought she'd be when he named her Aphrodite, drew men like flies on honey. With her fiery red hair and eyes green as a sycamore leaf, she could have any man she wanted. But she didn't mean to settle for a cracker destined to spend his life living fishing in the bay and fighting the jungle for a little garden space. She meant to use her looks to find her a rich man to take her away from South Florida forever.

Hera was as pretty as a girl with soft strawberry blonde curls and pink cheeks and a ready smile could ever be. Theena knew she was the not-so-pretty one. She had her Daddy's Greek coloring, dark brown eyes and heavy dark hair with only a hint of wave in it. Dite was petite, her figure a perfect hourglass. Hera had curves top and bottom, a much fuller hourglass. Theena was tall as Daddy, slender and long-waisted. She knew she suffered in comparison.

She fingered the buttons at her neck and wondered for the hundredth time if what Mama did meant there was a taint in her daughters' blood. Of the three of them, she seemed to be the only one who made an effort not to be like Mama. Surely her sisters knew what men were thinking when Dite arched her neck just so or Hera shoved her chest out. Theena chose to keep her bodice buttoned to the neck and loose enough not to outline her breasts. She didn't want men looking at her like that, thinking she was cheap or easy.

She waggled her foot at a fly tickling her ankle. It lit on her again and out of the corner of her eye she caught a blur of pink. She wheeled around to catch a young man dressed in Seminole finery with a flamingo feather in his hand.

"Billy, I swear. You got nothing better to do?"

"Hi, Dite." To Theena he said, "Come on down to the store with me. I'll buy you a penny candy."

Theena squinted at him. "You got smelly hides in the dugout?"

"Nope, just feathers."

"Go on, Theena," Dite said. "Give me the peas, and don't wake Daddy getting your shoes."

Daddy was already awake when she tiptoed in. "How you doing, Daddy?"

"That Billy I hear out there?"

"You want to talk to him?"

Daddy took Theena's hand. "Not now, baby. Think I'll sleep some more."

She kissed his stubbled cheek and touched his chest to feel for fever. Dite had just bathed him, and he was cool to the touch, smelling of soap instead of the sick scent that lingered around him. "I'll be back for dinner, Daddy."

She retrieved her bonnet and her shoes from under the bed. Once she settled in the dugout, Billy shoved the boat into the stream and let the current catch them. Theena trailed her fingers in the cool, clear river and admired the rosy spoonbills covering up a custard apple tree.

Under that same tree, Billy pulled over to the bank and the birds flew up in a mass of whirring pink wings. "Be a minute," Billy said and disappeared into the underbrush.

Theena lay back in the dugout and watched the clouds scud overhead. Billy would be marrying his Rosa soon. He wouldn't have time for her anymore. She'd miss him. First time she met Billy, they were eight years old. While Daddy and Sam Yoholo talked about hunting gators, Theena had sidled up to Billy and whispered, "I got puppies."

They crawled under the front porch where six little black mutts snuggled, their soft bellies bulging. Theena slid her hands around a pup and gently handed him to Billy, who buried his nose in puppy fur. Billy's pick was an ancient dog now, privileged to laze and dream under the palmetto-thatched roof of the Yoholo chickee.

Billy emerged from the deep green shade with three frothy white egret plumes held aloft to show his prizes. At Brickell's General Store landing, Billy tied up his dugout next to a dozen other boats. On a Saturday, this was the busiest spot on the coast from Fort Pierce all the way down to Key West. Here Seminoles and Crackers alike brought gator hides, pelts, feathers, and coontie starch to sell. Brickell sold them sugar and flour, salt and lard, calico, matches, fuel, fish hooks and shot gun shells – most anything a man could use in the Florida wilds.

Billy traded in his feathers for everything on his mother's list and had credit left over to buy two strings of red beads for Rosa. He gave Theena a sheepish smile. "She won't marry me 'til you can't see her neck for all the beads. That's what she says."

They took their candy out to sit on the porch, their legs dangling over the side, saying hello to neighbors going in and out. After what Mama did, Theena had been miserable coming to Brickell's, everybody in the settlement knowing. But Dite had showed her how to brave it out with her chin up until it seemed like folks had forgotten. Now, with her best friend at her side, this porch was another home, the bay bluer than the sky, pelicans diving, gulls crying. She savored the candy and smirked at Billy's tongue stained strawberry red.

Billy nodded his head toward the man at the horse rail. "That your beau?"

Under the palms, Randolph Chase dismounted and tied his horse. The high polish of his brown leather boots caught the light. His starched white shirt gleamed bright in the shade. Randolph was blond, and therefore usually a little red from sun burn. Not tall, not short. But he always looked very fine, Theena thought. She put her candy away and hoped her lips weren't purple.

Randolph stopped in front of her rather grim faced. Where was the happy-to-see-you smile she'd come to expect? Her dress was faded but it was clean. She'd put her hair up, and she even had her shoes on. Presentable enough. She glanced at her lap where Randolph's eyes lingered. Her skirt with just one worn petticoat underneath did allow a suggestion of legs under the thin fabric. She felt her face go scarlet.

"Good morning." Randolph tipped his hat. He eyed Billy's calico turban, the tunic belted at the waist, the knee-high moccasins, but he did not speak to Billy Yoholo.

Ah. He doesn't like my sitting here with Billy. "Mr. Chase," she said formally. "This is my friend, Mr. Yoholo. Billy, Mr. Chase."

Billy hopped down, changed the candy to his left hand and held out his sticky right to shake. Theena silently counted to three, her throat closing -- surely Randolph couldn't refuse to shake Billy's hand. Then Randolph displayed the gentlemanly manners Theena admired. He offered his hand and looked Billy in the eye. "How do you do?"

Billy beamed idiotically and shook hands with great enthusiasm. "You be my good friend. We be good friends together." Billy had learned to read before she had, and she wondered if Randolph would see past Billy's simple savage act to read the intelligence in his eye.

Billy was an awful tease. Poor Randolph. Theena granted him her most winning smile. The stiffness left his shoulders and the line between his eyebrows eased. There, that was when he was most handsome, when he smiled at her like that.

"I'll call Sunday evening, if I may."

"That'll be nice," she said, meaning it.

His gaze flicked over her lips, and his own almost quirked into a smile. "All right, then. Sunday."

Randolph raised his broad-brimmed hat, nodded to Billy, and went on into the store.

"You got a mean streak, Billy Yoholo."

"Yeah." He grinned at her. "It was fun."

"Are my lips purple?"
"Purple as plums. You ready to go?"
Back at the Theophilus place, Theena waved good bye to Billy at the landing and hurried up to the house, hoping Dite had finished shelling those peas. It was going to be hot as three hells in the cook shed, but Daddy needed a good dinner.
Before she set foot on the porch steps, she heard him coughing again, coughing till his lungs had no breath left in them. Her hand on the latch, she squeezed her eyes shut and gathered her courage. She the door, prepared to be cheerful for Daddy's sake, but the smell of blood and sick sweat rolled over her. Then Dite moved aside and she saw the bloody handkerchief at Daddy's mouth, the deep red speckles on his shirt. She pressed the back of her hand to her mouth against the fear bubbling up in her throat.
Dite turned swollen eyes on her. "Get some water."
Without a word, Theena hurried to the river, but her hands trembled so she could hardly draw the bucket up. Back inside, she helped Dite clean Daddy and the bed and laid him down on the moss-filled pillows. He was gray-faced and exhausted, but his breath came a little easier.
"Daddy," Theena said, "how you feeling now?"
He turned sunken eyes on her and nodded his head slightly. "Don't worry, baby," he said, and closed his eyes.
Hera sauntered back in just before dinner, her hair amuss and her lips swollen and pink. The buttons on her bodice were all off one hole so that the neckline zigzagged. Theena turned her eyes away from Hera's obviously sated state.
"Hera, you slut," Dite hissed.
Hera's rosy glow did not diminish under Dite's hostile gaze. "You can waste your life pining for some rich man to rescue you," Hera began, "but I --."
"Daddy's worse," Theena interrupted and held a hand out for Hera to come closer. Their father slept, his breath thin and labored. His skin had become pale the weeks he'd been in bed, and the fever had made him thin and blotchy. At sight of the bloody foam bubbling on his lips, Hera pressed a hand to her heart.
Dite motioned toward the door. On the porch, Hera turned on her older sister. "We have to have a doctor. Right now."
"Daddy said no doctor," Dite told her.
"Why not?"
Her face haggard, Dite shook her head. "It won't do any good."
"I'm going to send for the doctor," Hera said and went inside for her shoes.

Relief eased the tightness in Theena's chest. She had yielded to Daddy when she herself had suggested a doctor, but Hera wouldn't yield. At Brickell's Hera could send a message to Fort Pierce. The doctor could be here as early as tomorrow evening.

The rest of the afternoon, Theena sat with Dite to watch their daddy sleep. They ate a bit of cold supper, but Daddy wouldn't have any. "Water, just water," he said when they urged him to eat half a banana.

Hera came home looking ragged and weary. "Mr. Brickell's relaying word up the coast. Doc Moses will come soon as he can."

"All right," Dite said, her voice flat.

At twilight, Theena closed the shutters over the cheesecloth-covered windows. It'd be stifling hot in the cabin, but cheesecloth was no challenge to the evening mosquitoes. They took on a meanness and determination that sunshine mosquitoes didn't have the energy for.

"Not tonight, Theena," Dite said softly. "Daddy needs a little breeze."

The resigned note in Dite's voice scared Theena more than Daddy's pallor. She hugged her elbows to her ribs. If even Dite had lost hope . . . .

Stavros Theophilus woke when Hera lit the kerosene lantern. His dark eyes took in his three girls, soon to be orphaned and alone in the world. He'd named Hera thinking of Zeus's queen, but she hadn't turned out to be queenly. Not a pretentious bone in her, his Hera knew what she wanted, life here on the river, and she would see to it that's what she got. Jack Spode was a good man. Even if he'd already had her, he'd marry her, and he'd provide for her. Hera he didn't have to worry about.

His gaze rested on Dite, as beautiful as her mother. He'd been a fool over that woman. How had he thought he could keep a beauty like her on a hardscrabble dirt farm? And then he'd got sick. Dite had her soft spots, and he was glad of that, but she was like her mother in more than looks. Tough, and selfish, but that meant she'd take care of herself. Looking like she did, she probably would snag a rich man, just as she said she would.

But Theena. *I've spoiled her, I know that.* His baby was so winning, so generous with her affection. Not as striking as Dite's red-haired beauty, but pretty. Big brown eyes, cream colored skin, and a head full of heavy black hair like his mother had had. He'd hoped for wisdom for his youngest when he'd named her Athena, but Theena was a dreamy, sensitive child. She'd took it the hardest when her mother left. *Who will take care of my Theena?*

"I want to talk to each of you girls," he rasped. "Dite."

Theena picked up the bottle of home-made citronella and followed Hera out. Dite pulled her chair closer to the bed.

Alone with his first-born, Daddy gazed into her green eyes, so like her ma's. "You're a beauty, Dite. I reckon you know that."

Dite squeezed his hand.

"You've done fine by me, Dite, and I'm proud of you. You can always make a living nursing, it comes to that."

He watched her smooth forehead scrunch into a scowl. "I take care of you because I love you, Daddy. I don't aim to be a nurse."

He shook his head. "You got to think twice about using your looks to get on in life, sugar. Looks don't last."

"I know that, Daddy."

Her voice was tired. Tired from staying up nights with him, tired of hearing all this before. Since she was fifteen, he'd been saying this, but he had to say it one last time. "You meet up with one of those rich yachtsmen, that's all right. But you be sure he wants you for more than pretty hair and a pretty face. You get you a piece of paper before you run off with him."

"Don't worry about me, Daddy. I'm going to be fine. You know it."

He patted his beautiful girl's hand. "I believe you will be, honey." He nodded toward the door. "It's Theena I worry about."

"Randolph Chase has money, a name. Everything."

"You think he'll marry her?"

"He'll marry her if she'll let him."

Theena just had to get over this juvenile crush on Jack Spode. She thought she hid it from everyone, but the only one who couldn't see it was Jack himself. Her baby sister's lack of good sense irked, but she tried to soften the disdain in her voice. "I'll talk to her, Daddy."

Probably should have straightened her out before now, Dite thought. All Theena knew of men were the cracker boys whose first declarations of interest involved exploring hands. And Miss Theena would have none of that. Because of what Ma did, she thought she had to be virgin-pure like some Catholic saint, all the time lust running as strong in her as it did in any healthy woman, whether she acknowledged it or not. And Theena didn't understand Chase. Theena thought his reserve meant he was cold, but Dite had seen glimmers of fire in his fine blue eyes. He was no cold fish under all those fine manners.

Dite kissed her father's hot forehead. "I'll send Hera in."

As soon as Hera closed the door behind her, Dite lowered herself next to Theena on the top step and accepted the citronella to keep the mosquitoes from carrying her away. Theena offered. Lantern light from the window cast a yellow glow over Theena's face. Only five years younger, but she still had the soft cheeks and rounded chin of a girl. It was time for Theena to grow up.

"I want you to listen to me." Dite dabbed her neck with citronella and screwed the cap back on the bottle . "You have to face up to Daddy leaving us."

"Daddy's been sick before. It's just so hot now, but when --."

Dite held a hand up to stop her. "That's just what I mean. Daddy's worse this time, worse than he's ever been. You have to quit your dreaming and figure out how you're going to live."

"But the doctor is coming. He could be here late tomorrow, or the next day."

"And what do you think Doc Moses can do?" Dite snapped. "Put a tourniquet on Daddy's chest?"

Theena leaned her face into her knees.

"Look at you. Hiding. Daddy won't be here to take care of you anymore. You understand that?"

Theena looked at her with those soft, sad eyes. Dite wanted to pinch her. "You'll be the death of Daddy, you and your dreamy secrets."

Theena jerked back as if she'd been slapped, her eyes shocked.

God, I'm so mean. And so tired. "I didn't mean that." Dite put her hand over Theena's. "It's not your fault Daddy's sick. But you have to grow up and forget about Jack Spode."

Theena pulled her hand away. "I don't --."

"Hera may pretend she doesn't see it, but it's plain enough. And I know you. You get your heart set on something, and it's like your head turns to wood. For Daddy's sake, be practical. You can't have Jack Spode, ever, so just make up your mind to it."

"Don't you think I know that?" Theena's jaw tightened and she tipped her chin up. "I would never --."

Hera stood in the door and looked from one sister to the other. "What were you saying about Jack?"

"Nothing," Dite said. "Go on in, Theena. Wipe your face before Daddy sees you."

Inside, Daddy's eyes were huge and dark across the room. Crickets chirped under the house, but the silence in the cabin felt heavy as fog. Theena sat down in the chair next to the bed and took his hand. "You haven't coughed for a while, Daddy. You feeling a little better?"

"Honey, I'm not going to feel better. You need to understand that."
Theena rested her forehead on the bed next to her father.
"I'm sorry, baby. I wish I could take care of you a little longer." He stroked her hair. She swallowed, trying not to choke on the heavy lump in her throat. "I want you to hear me out, Theena. Sit up here and look at me."
Theena wiped her face and sat up straight.
"You like this Chase boy well enough?"
"I like him."
"I want you to marry him. I know he hasn't asked you yet, but Dite says he will, if you just give him some encouragement."
She did like Randolph, very much, but he hadn't said anything about marrying her. He'd been courting her since the winter, and still . . . they'd barely held hands. "Daddy, I--."
Daddy coughed and lay back gasping for air. She propped him up on his pillows and wiped his face with a damp cloth. When he could, he said, "Theena, the world is a hard place for a woman alone. You got to have a man, and I want to rest easy you'll do as I say."
"Daddy, I know life is hard. I can fish and make starch – or take in sewing."
Daddy shook his head. "You're not cut out to be alone, and I can't stand the thought of you getting poorer every year till your elbows poke through your sleeves." He stopped to breathe a minute. "You hear what I'm saying? I want you to marry Chase. You do that for me?"
Theena nodded. "All right, Daddy. I will."
"You be a good wife to him, and he'll be good to you." Daddy closed his eyes.
Theena kissed his hand and laid her cheek against it. His breath came fast and shallow, and his hand was hot and dry. She dipped the cloth in the basin and bathed his shrunken arms and chest to take the fever down.
"I love you, Daddy," she whispered.
The three girls sat the night next to Daddy's bed. He'd doze a while, then be seized by another coughing fit, soaking yet another handkerchief, the blood a deeper red with each spell. His weathered face paled to ash.
Theena prayed for Doc Moses to come. He had a bag full of medicines. Something would make her father well again. Her hands knotted in her lap, her chest ached at the rattle in her father's, and her own lungs strained for breath as his did.

Before the sun rose over Biscayne Bay, Stavros Theophilus passed away.

Chapter Two

Randolph Chase joined the men and women filing into the unpainted clapboard structure that served as city hall and clearing house and church. He found a little standing room at the back and searched for Theena. She sat with her sisters on a bench at the front, only a few feet from the closed casket.

Her black bonnet, nearly purple with age, shielded her face, but the trembling of her bent shoulders told him she was crying. If he'd only come earlier, he could be sitting beside her, offering her his handkerchief. But, ever the dutiful son, he'd stopped to explain yet again why he meant to attend the funeral of Stavros Theophilus, a mere fisherman whom his mother had never heard of.

Randolph's mother disapproved, of course. She'd come with him to Florida without fully appreciating the changes it would mean in her life. Lemon City was no more than a village. No society, no theater, no visiting back and forth with quality ladies of her own sort.

All the things Mrs. Chase missed about Philadelphia were the very things Randolph was glad to leave behind. He cared nothing for the endless round of dinners and balls and lunches at the club. He was more than tired of the games he was meant to play with the young ladies on the hunt for a well-to-do husband.

Randolph had found what he wanted here on this narrow strip between the Glades and the ocean. A sense of purpose. Up at dawn and out in his groves, a measure of physical labor, and plenty of intellectual occupation in building this new enterprise. And then he'd found Theena.

He fell in love with her the first time he saw her, sand-crusted and smelling of salt air. Her father was out in the water, hip dip, casting his net for mullet. Theena waded in the shallows, picking up shells. Barefoot and windblown, she moved with the grace of someone completely unselfconscious. The bottom half of her skirt was sodden, and the dress faded, but when she saw him riding along the beach, she'd raised a hand at him, a stranger, and called out, "'Morning."

He'd slid off his horse, pleased at the open friendliness he often found down here on the lower coast. And, he admitted, drawn by her loose black hair and her obvious lack of a corset. She looked a little prim in her high necked collar, but the bedraggled dress did not hide her willowy figure. Seeming unaware of both her disarray and her charms, she'd held out her hand for him to see the tiny white shells in her palm. "Angels' Tears," she told him.

Now, sweltering through the minister's eulogy, he knew his first impressions of Theena's qualities had not nearly done her justice. She wouldn't know how to address a kitchen staff or plan a supper for fifty, but she could row a boat, throw a net, or wring a chicken by the neck and have it plucked and on the table in an hour. There was no artifice in her. No missish simpers. She had a quiet demeanor and a quality of reserve, the way she often touched her top button to be sure it was fastened, but then -- Theena's laugh shook her whole body, her whoop loud enough to frighten the birds out of the trees. He'd never heard anything so artless and whole-hearted, and if he'd been poised on the edge of falling in love with Theena, that laugh had shoved him over.

The minister's sermon about heaven, about a life well-lived, about faith and trust in God came to him as a buzz, like some droning fly trapped in the house. When the mourners moved outside to the gravesite, Randolph shuffled through the crowd and managed to find a place just behind Theena.

Positioned at the head of the grave, Dite, the oldest one. As beautiful a woman as he'd ever seen, but the first time he'd met her, he caught something cold, maybe calculating about her. There was fire there, but ice, too. Not now, though. Here at her father's grave, her face was drawn and pale, her green eyes huge. Opposite Theena, Hera, pretty with her strawberry curls and peach and cream complexion, now marked by bright red blotches. A careless woman, Randolph thought, lacking any grace. And on this side of the grave, Theena. Her hands tightly clasped, she stared at the black and blue flies lighting on the pine box, looking for a way in.

With her dark hair and eyes, her trim figure and natural ease, he thought Theena might pose as a Greek goddess for an ancient sculptor. Yet she had none of the regal pride of a goddess. Her sweetness belied her name. Even barefoot and windblown, hers was a spirit of grace and gentleness.

The afternoon sun scorched Randolph's neck and bore down on the back of Theena's dress. He stepped so that his shadow protected her from the direct rays.

The service ended. People moved away. He touched Theena's elbow so she'd know he was there. She turned her pale face to him. "Randolph."

"I'm sorry, Theena. I know Mr. Theophilus was a good man." He unfolded his linen handkerchief and passed it to her.

"Yes, he was a good man."

He followed her gaze to the other side of the grave where her sister Hera was turned into Jack Spode's chest, her shoulders shaking. Jack had his arms around her and his cheek on the top of her head. Randolph wished he could hold Theena like that, but not here, not now. It was too soon. And he, he was well aware, was too hide-bound to show his feelings like that.

Theena turned back to him, her breath shuddering, her big eyes wet and grieved. He took her hand, as intimate a gesture as he could allow himself.

He should at least give her some hint of how he felt about her before he left. He took a deep breath. "Theena, I have to go to Key West. Maybe to Guatemala. Looking at stock for oranges. And bananas." *She doesn't care about that*, he told himself. His thumb stroked the back of her hand. "A couple of months, maybe ten weeks. When I come back, I want to talk to you."

"All right." Eyes closed, she pressed her first hard against her mouth, holding it all in. *She needs me to hold her*, he thought. *Why can't I do that?* He reached for her, his hands on her shoulders.

"Theena," Dite said. "You coming?"

Randolph dropped his hands. "Take care of yourself. I'll be back in a couple of months."

Theena fed the chickens, collected the eggs, hoed in the garden, cooked the noon-day meal, all the time cradling a fragile heart in her chest. She felt brittle and light, as if she might break like a twig underfoot. As much as she had struggled not to cry at Daddy's funeral, now she couldn't.

Even with two sisters, Theena grieved in loneliness. Dite spent Wednesday through Monday at the Peacock Inn in Cocoanut

Grove doing light housework. The sisters needed the cash, but mostly Dite wanted to be visible when the rich sportsmen visited the resort.

Hera was no company either. If she and Jack were around, she lived up to the reputation of her namesake goddess, jealous as Zeus's nagging wife. She guarded Jack's attention, clinging to him like a strangling fig. Theena thought it was wasted effort. As far as she could tell, Jack still saw her as a baby sister.

But it didn't matter what Jack and Hera did. Dite thought she should put her future in Randolph Chases's hands. Daddy did, too, and she'd promised him. It was no hardship. When he got back, she would be glad to see him.

Coming in from cutting okra Saturday morning, Theena found Dite shining her shoes with lamp black and lard. "I didn't think you'd be home for another three days."

"Soon as I've finished these shoes, I'm off."

"Off? What do you mean you're off?"

"I'm going away on Mr. St. Claire's yacht."

A foggy sense of loss crept over her. "How? I mean, are you to cook? What?"

"Mr. St. Claire heard me telling some of the children the Cyclops story. He wants me to nanny for his two boys back in Philadelphia."

Theena sat down heavily. "So you're really going."

"I always said I would. I'm not spending my life in the backwoods of Florida." She buffed the toe of her shoe with vicious strokes. "And I'm not going to be a nanny to somebody else's spoiled brats for long either."

"But you said that's what you're going for."

Dite scrubbed the polish off her hands in the basin. "Mr. St. Claire admires more than my story-telling." Her voice crackled with determination. "I'd have to be blind not to see how he watches me. And he's a widower. I mean for him to marry me."

Theena let out all her breath in a sough. "You're really going."

Dite put her shoes in a burlap bag and picked up her satchel. "I've left half my wages and Mr. St. Claire's address on the mantle. You remember what I told you, Theena. I want to hear you've married Randolph Chase by Christmas."

Theena bent over her lap and covered her face. "Oh, Dite."

Dite hesitated at the door. She set the satchel down to hug Theena's hunched shoulders. "You'll be fine. Tell Hera I said good bye. I'll write when I get to Philadelphia." And she was gone.

Theena sat in the empty house listening to the quiet. Someday Hera would be gone, too, and she'd be alone. Didn't people who lived alone go crazy, like the hermit who lived across the bay?

The sun poured in the west window, and Theena bestirred herself. No use moping. Hera and Jack would be back in a few hours from digging coontie roots. Mr. Brickell was paying good money for ground starch and they'd need to start saving to pay the preacher when he came.

Theena caught a mess of catfish from the river. Then she dug a few sweet potatoes out of the ground. Daddy had never cleared much of the 160 acres of government grant land, but he had dug a big garden patch. Maybe Jack would stay for supper and the house wouldn't be so quiet. Jack liked to talk, loved to tell tales. If he caught a two foot fish, he'd tell it up good so it was a four footer that ate a half a boat-load of bait before he wrestled it on board. He told it all with a gleam in his eye, not expecting anybody to believe him. He told his stories to entertain, not to boast.

By the time Hera and Jack pulled into the landing, Theena had the potatoes cooked and the fish dredged in cornmeal ready for the pan. She slid the first ones into the hot oil and watched the fat sizzle around the edges. Then she shoved the fish over in the big skillet to make room for the corn cakes.

Hera, dirty and sweaty, joined her under the shade of the shed. "We had a good day," she said as she ladled a drink from the bucket. "Must have close to a hundred pounds of roots in the boat."

"Where's Jack? Isn't he going to stay for supper?"

"He's washing up at the river." Hera narrowed her eyes over the dipper. "Why?"

Theena wiped her hands on her apron. "Well, it's just that I cooked more than you and I can eat. I thought . . ." She faltered under Hera's sharp look. "I thought he'd stay to supper, is all."

Hera wiped her mouth. "I 'magine he will. I'm going to the house to clean up."

Under a spreading live oak, Daddy had built a sturdy table from teak boards washed on shore from a shipwreck. Jack straddled a bench and sat hunched over his hands on the table.

Theena left him to his thoughts as she fetched the salt and the pepper vinegar.

Unguarded, not even thinking about her top buttons being open to bear the heat over the cook fire, she shoved the hair off her hot face with the back of her wrist and placed a platter of fish on the table. She glanced at Jack and he was looking at her.

He held her gaze for a moment. Then his mouth twisted in a smile that didn't reach his eyes. "How was your day, Shrimp?"

She'd always smiled when he caller her that, she, the tallest sister. Now she forced a smile as awkward as the one he had given her. "Billy stopped by. I'm going to start peddling catfish at the farms along the river, and he said he'd show me the best fish holes out in the glades."

"The glades? That's no place for a woman."

"It'll be safe with Billy."

Jack's eyes were on her again. The absently fond look he usually gave her was gone. *He sees me*, Theena thought. *For the first time, I think he really sees me*. With trembling knees, she sat down on the bench opposite him and met his steady gaze. She'd never tire of looking at that face.

It wasn't that Jack was handsome. Not in the usual sense. But Jack's maleness surrounded him like a cloud. The angular face, the way his sunburned hair swept over his forehead, even the rough power of his hands – his very aura more than made up for his lack of fine looks.

Jack dropped his gaze. "What does Randolph Chase say about your spending so much time with Billy Yoholo?"

Theena tilted her chin. "Randolph hasn't said anything, and he needn't. Billy is my friend."

Jack thought for a minute. "He's not going to let you see him when you're married."

Loneliness washed over her. Was she to lose everyone?

Jack read her face and reached for her hand on the table top. "I'm sorry, Theena." For what he wasn't sure. That she had to give up Billy, that he had only just this day seen that behind the buttoned up collar, Theena hid the graceful curves of a beautiful woman? All this last year, his mind and body saturated with Hera's charms, Jack had hardly noticed the prim little sister. But what he saw in her now zinged right through him. Her mouth was lush and wide, her face dewy and flushed, and her eyes bottomless.

His gaze flickered over her breasts, and he cursed himself for a scoundrel. *You are a damn fool, Jack Spode.*

Jack heard the door slam behind Hera as she came out of the house and withdrew his hand. He hoped Hera hadn't seen him touch Theena. He was no cad, bouncing from one woman to another with every change in scenery, and he wanted Hera to know that. Especially today.

When Hera glared at her sister and slid onto the bench so close to Jack he had no elbow room at all, he knew she'd seen. Time would show her she'd got no need to doubt him, he thought, and shifted the fork to his other hand.

After they'd talked over Dite's likely fortunes with Mr. St. Claire, Jack patted the hand Hera had wrapped around his arm and then looked at Theena, fully in control of his himself now. "July's near gone, and we haven't had a big blow yet. Brickell has a good sturdy building, on as high ground as we've got around here. If you see signs of a storm coming, Theena, don't stay here by yourself. Head down to the Brickells and wait it out with them."

Theena looked at Hera, a crease between her brows. "You won't be here?"

Hera hugged Jack's arm against her breast. "I'm moving in with Jack."

Theena's mouth gaped. "But the preacher won't be here for weeks."

"And when he comes, we'll get married. But since I'm already pregnant, I can't see any reason to wait, can you?"

Theena stared at her. "You're pregnant?" She looked at Jack, but he kept his eyes on his empty plate. The old tide of hot shame rose from her chest into her tightening throat. "Hera, what will people say?"

Hera laughed. "Let them talk. As soon as we're married, they'll gossip about somebody else."

For an ugly moment, Theena wondered if Hera had done it on purpose, to ensure Jack Spode would be hers. That would be . . . shameless. Hera certainly betrayed no sense of being ashamed. But Theena felt it. The same sick feeling she'd had when word got around her mama had run off with Mr. Alnot, leaving not only his wife and three kids to fend for themselves, but Daddy and her own three daughters. Theena fisted a wad of her skirt, hot tears gathering at the corners of her eyes. Mama, and Hera. Theena felt dirtied.

"It's going to be a boy. Jack Spode, Junior." Hera beamed up at Jack and he patted her hand again.

Such a heaviness in her chest she wondered how she could bear it, Theena looked at Jack again, but he slid his gaze away from her. It was irrevocable now. Jack belonged to Hera forever. Well, hadn't she known that? Didn't she know, too, that people had babies all the time before they got married? Dite was right. She was a fool and it was past time she grew up.

"Aren't you going to congratulate us?" Hera said.

Theena forced her lips to curve. "Congratulations. I hope it's a boy, too."

Jack stood up. "So, if a storm comes, you'll go to the Brickells."

She didn't look at him again. "All right."

Theena collected the forks as Hera had trapped Jack's arm again. He cleared his throat. "Theena, you don't have to keep this place up by yourself. As long as you're still here, I'll stop by and see the roof shingles are good, whatever needs doing."

"Theena has Randolph, Jack. She doesn't need you doing for her."

"She's your sister, Hera. Till she's married --."

Theena clattered the forks into the wash bucket. "Don't worry about me. I'll be fine."

"Of course you will. I'll get my bundle, Jack, and we'll be off."

Theena's head jerked up. "You're leaving tonight?"

"Might as well be tonight."

Theena realized suddenly that for the first time in her life she would be alone all night.

"Don't be so glum, Sis. You'll be fine." Hera stood on tiptoe to kiss Jack's jaw. "Just be a minute." She went in the house to get her things.

Jack stood with his arms folded, his feet spread apart. He looked at the sky. "We'll just make it before dark."

"Yes."

The easy, brotherly manner was gone. Jack seemed to look everywhere but at her. "I don't like leaving you here alone at night."

"I'll be all right."

Jack's gaze flickered over her, and then away. No smile on his lips, no teasing twinkle in his eye.

It would have been easy to believe in the old gods at that moment, Theena thought. A Zeus or a spiteful Aphrodite, goddess of love, laughing at her: just as Jack Spode seemed to recognize her at last, he was caught, good and surely. If Dite were here, she'd laugh at her for the fool she was.

Hera bustled out of the house with her pack and gave Theena a peck on the cheek. "We'll probably see you at Brickell's on Saturday."

Theena waved as Jack poled the dugout into the river. She cleaned up her outdoor kitchen, then she trudged back to the house. Inside she lit a smudge pot against the mosquitoes.

The house was quiet. Empty. Outside, she could hear palm trees creak in the breeze. Inside, she could hear the very silence.

Every ghost story Theena ever heard came to mind. She glanced into the shadows and then away, shuddering. "I should get a dog," she said. Since old Sugar died of snakebite early in the summer, they'd lost three chickens to something or other, probably a big cat. A dog would disincline a panther from coming around. More important, Theena needed another living creature to keep her imagination from populating the shadows with furtive shapeless phantoms.

She took stock of what was left in the little house. Daddy's bed. His hat on the peg by the door. Dite's narrow cot under the window. The bed Hera and Theena had shared. The table and chairs, two of them hung on the wall out of the way. One chifferobe, a drawer for each of them.

Theena opened her drawer and pulled out the drawstring bag Mama had made for her. She had saved egg money to buy blue velvet and ribbon and had made her girls these special keepsake bags the last Christmas she was home.

Theena untied the black ribbon around her neck and pulled a cowrie shell from between her breasts. Smooth as porcelain, a rich deep spotted brown, the shell had been one of those Jack picked up on an idle Sunday evening on the beach, the family wading and digging for scallops in the bay. He'd tossed it to her, casually. She'd worn it this year and more, as big a fool as Dite said. Worse, she'd been disloyal to her sister. Maybe she had some of Mama's meanness in her after all.

She didn't want any part of being like Mama. She dropped the shell into her velvet bag and pulled the ribbon tight, flushed with shame. She wanted to be the woman Daddy expected her to be, virtuous and respectable. Wise as Athena.

Mama had insisted on calling the girls by their Christian names long after Daddy and the girls themselves used only Dite, Hera, and Theena. Mama had chosen Hephzibah, Urijah, and Hilkiah from the Bible, awkward, ugly names no one else had ever heard of. Mama was trying hard to be Godly, Theena thought. She just hadn't tried hard enough.

Over the mantel were the family's three books -- Mama's Bible, and Daddy's dog-eared copies of *The Iliad* and *The Odyssey*. After Mama had led them through evening devotionals, Daddy read to the girls every night from his books. At first Mama had objected. Theena couldn't keep the bitterness from creeping into her thoughts. Mama was uncommonly Godly for someone who'd run off and left a sickening husband with three girls to raise. "Those are heathen gods, Stavros -- that Zeus and Apollo, Ares and Poseidon." But Daddy had convinced her there was no soul on the planet who still believed in the old Greek gods. *The Odyssey* was just stories, adventure stories, and Mama had relented.

Theena pulled the mildewed *Iliad* off the shelf and lit the lantern. She thumbed through the book and finally settled on a page at random. Her eyes ran over the passage where Odysseus attempts to persuade the great Achilles to put aside his anger and rejoin the fight below the walls of Troy. Achilles' proud reply pierced Theena: "For as I detest the doorways of Death, I detest that man who hides one thing in the depths of his heart, and speaks forth another."

Theena drew a deep breath, her conduct with Randolph suddenly clear as a cloudless sky. Dite would have her lead Randolph on, pretend she felt more than she did. She shook her head. She herself would be just such a liar if she told Randolph Chase she loved him. She couldn't say those words and be an honorable soul. She liked him, but she didn't love him. She didn't know him, not well, and Randolph didn't seem to know who she really was either.

A gallant romantic, Randolph brought Theena little presents, like the first sweet blossoms from the citrus trees or a bouquet of ripe guavas. *Which is very nice,* she thought, *but why doesn't he touch me?* He had read a great number of books. Maybe his notion of womanhood was influenced by those novels – she'd read two from Miss Brickell's collection -- in which women, pale and delicate, were given to swooning. Theena knew herself to be a physical woman, neither pale nor delicate, and she certainly had never swooned. Neither was she like Hera with no concern for appearances. She meant to be in control of her passions, to hold herself back until marriage.

That didn't mean she denied feeling the pull of a man when Randolph was near. She wanted him to hold her in his arms, his lovely sweet mouth on hers, his starchy shirt collar scratching her cheek. She wouldn't give him more than she should, but everyone thought kisses between sweethearts were allowed.

One evening, weeks before, after the sun had punished everyone all day, Jack and Hera, Randolph and Theena had walked down to the beach to enjoy the cool breeze. Jack and Hera strolled barefoot along the shoreline, their feet in the shallows of the warm water. Randolph in his fine trousers and polished boots settled Theena and himself on a driftwood log. He pulled out the tiny volume of sonnets he kept in his pocket and found the page where they'd left off last time.

" 'How do I love thee?' " he began. Theena expected another dreary account of spring days after a death. So many of the poems Randolph chose either bored or befuddled her, but this one she understood. When he finished, she asked to hear it again. *Yes*, she thought. *"To the depth and breadth and height my soul can reach." That's love.*

Hera and Jack wading hand in hand down the beach drew her gaze. *Jack doesn't read poetry to Hera*, she thought. *He shows her with his eyes, his hands . . . .*

Theena looked at Randolph's fine hands, at the golden hairs on his wrist. Here she sat with a man who seemed to care for her, the balmy ocean breeze cooling them, the lowering sun lighting the sky in orange and violet, yet Randolph sat on one end of the log, she on the other, his hands busy holding a book instead of her. His eyes perused the sonnets rather than her.

If only Randolph would touch her. Passionate kisses, that's what she craved. She wanted her hair to fall loose and her lips to swell up from hot kisses. Instead, she merely twisted the button at her throat. When Randolph had pecked her on the cheek to say good night, she'd consoled herself that this was what respectable sweethearts did.

Theena closed the book about the mighty Trojan battles and considered being Randolph's wife. No heroic battles to be fought along the Miami River, yet there was honor in ordinary people's lives too. *People say you grow to love one another after marriage. I'll learn to love Randolph. I will.* She liked his handsome face, his full mouth, his long-fingered hands. She liked *him.*

He meant to please her; it could be that his restraint in touching her was merely the mark of a gentleman. So should she tell him she loved him when he returned from Key West? No. She wouldn't lie. The day she did love him, she would speak the words.

Theena snuffed out the smudge pot and the lamp, changed into her thin muslin nightgown, and climbed into bed under the mosquito bar. There she lay listening to the weathered little house creak as the boards cooled off. An owl hooted in the tree tops and complained about the full moon. The crickets chirruped loudly for what seemed like hours. She willed herself to think of pleasant things -- the clumsiness of big turtles on the shore and their exquisite grace in the water, the saw grass of the glades moving like waves on the ocean when the wind blew. Finally she fell into an uneasy sleep, her first night alone in the world.

Next morning, Theena opened the door onto the porch and nearly stepped on a black snake.

"Damn!" she said under her breath. She got her broom and swept the lazy snake off the rough weathered boards and called Daddy's old sow. "Soo wee," she sang.

Short Ribs emerged from the woods at an amble, but she picked up speed when she saw the snake in the sand.

"Short Ribs, you're going to end up bacon yet you don't keep the snakes eat up around here." Theena closed her eyes as the sow began to gobble at the writhing snack. "And now I'm talking to pigs."

She meant to keep herself busy. This time of year, the garden needed lots of attention or else it'd turn into a jungle of beans and peas and tomatoes and okra, all tangled together with invading vines and full of sheltering critters. Once she'd done all the picking and hoeing she could do out there, she lit a fire under the iron wash tub. While the water heated, she stripped the beds and pillows, collected every stitch of clothing she wasn't wearing, and started in on the laundry. Once she had the sheets flapping in the wind, she took her scrub brush to the porch. Then scrubbed the floor in the cabin and cut straw for a new broom. About sundown, she wiped the damp hair from her face and thought maybe she'd tired herself out enough to fall asleep without all that staring up at the ceiling.

She washed and changed into her sun-smelling nightgown. By the light of the lantern, she read a few pages in Daddy's beloved *Iliad*, but her eyes kept drooping. She went to bed and was drifting off when a sound pulled her back.

Was that a step on the porch? Had she locked the door? There it was again. It could be a man's step. Or a panther's.

She tiptoed to the smoothing iron and held it raised. "Who's there?" she tried to shout, but her voice had no air behind it. She tried again, and a snuffling grunt answered her. She relaxed her grip on the iron. It was Short Ribs trespassing on the porch. She opened the door. "Shoo," she said. "You're too heavy for these old boards. Git." The huge sow lumbered down the stairs into the moonlit night.

Theena climbed back into bed and listened to her heart beat slow down. What if it hadn't been Short Ribs? There were plenty of other animals attracted by the chickens or the garden. Next time she saw Billy, she would make him show her how to use Daddy's shotgun. Dite had learned how to load and shoot, but somehow Daddy had never gotten around to teaching Theena and Hera. *And I definitely need a dog,* she thought again.

Next morning, with a clean frock on, she pinned her hair up and checked herself in the little mirror over Daddy's shaving shelf. Good enough, she thought. She untied Daddy's skiff and oared downstream to Brickell's.

It was easy to lose a whole hour in the general store looking over all the things there were to buy. Why Dite thought she had to go north Theena didn't know. Except, of course, to save herself from the relentless sun. That was no small thing for a redhead. But Theena couldn't think of a thing she'd ever need that wasn't right here in Brickell's store.

She checked the cork board where people left messages to see if anyone had a litter of puppies ready to wean. Miss Alice came out from the back carrying a bolt of calico.

"What you looking for, honey?" she called.

"A dog, Miss Alice. To keep the critters away, and to keep me company."

"So you need two dogs?"

Theena smiled. Miss Alice was known to be literal minded and a bit eccentric. As postmistress, she was responsible for sorting and giving out the mail that came up from Key West once a week. But sometimes she didn't feel like it. So she didn't.

"One dog will be plenty," Theena said. "Know anybody wants to be rid of one? I have chickens for trade."

"Well, my stars. You are Johnny on the spot, Theena Theophilus. One of Henry's bitches whelped a few months back. I'll let you have one of the pups for . . . oh, say, a hen and a half dozen setting eggs."

Theena beamed. That was more than generous of Miss Alice.

"Take her 'round back, Charley," Miss Alice told her little hired boy. "Pick her out a good mutt. Maybe that little tan and white." She turned back to Theena. "Bertie's her name, but I reckon you can call her whatever you want."

Behind the store, Henry Brickell kept ten or twelve dogs for himself and the sportsmen who came up from Key West or down from the Northeast. Eager to bag a gator or a bear or a panther, the men of leisure kept the taxidermists in heavy pockets.

Charley led Theena to the sandy shade where the dogs lolled. "This here one is Bertie. Come here, girl."

A long legged pup, nearly grown, frisked over to Charley. Theena knelt and scratched behind her ears and the back of her sleek head. "How's about you come home with me, Bertie?"

When the dog wagged her tail and licked Theena's face, she let out one of her ridiculous laughs.

Charley grinned at her. "Well, looks like you two is a match. I'll tell Miss Alice you taken her on home with you."

"I'll be back with the chicken and eggs. Come on, girl." Bertie fell in at her heels and when they reached the skiff, she jumped in readily.

Back at the homestead, Theena gave Bertie a tour of what was theirs. The dog surveyed the perimeter, sniffed every bush and bug, and claimed the place as her own.

The plan had been to put the dog out after dark to chase off chicken-stealing cats and coons. Instead, Theena climbed into bed and held the mosquito net open. She slept soundly with Bertie curled up at her feet.

Chapter Three

Six miles from the bay, the river of grass, *pay hai okee*, Billy called it, supplanted the mahogany trees and scrub palmettos. The men told tales of the glades – of alligators so thick you could walk across their backs, moccasins so plentiful they roiled by the score in the gator wallows. Why, they said, you had to designate a man just to keep the snakes knocked out of the boat. The women's tales were the ones that frightened Theena the most. Accounts of exactly how the body liquefied after half a dozen moccasin bites. Tales of being bit by skeeters till you bloated up and split.

But Theena knew men who spent half a day in the glades and came back with boatloads of huge, sweet catfish to sell to the farmers up and down the river. Her daddy had made her an accomplished fisherwoman, and she could earn some cash peddling fish.

Billy hadn't wanted to show her where the catfish ponds were. "It's easy to get lost out there. It's dangerous, and . . . ." He listed all the ways she could imperil her life alone in the swamp, but she eventually wore him down.

"All right then," he said and threw up his hands. "But I have something out there to show you."

Since she wouldn't see a soul all day long out in the glades, and saw grass tore at sleeves and fish slime left trails across your skirt, she changed into her oldest calico dress, threadbare at the elbows, and tied on her faded pink bonnet. Billy slid his boat up at the little landing and Theena stowed her pole, her hooks and lines and bobbers, and the bucket of bait she'd caught that morning.

"Stay, Bertie," she said and climbed into the dugout.

Between the ocean and the Everglades, people lived on a narrow strip of land made out of coral and sand and zones of rich black dirt. A few planters, like Randolph Chase, had carved room for orange groves out of the jungle. Some, like Jack, acted as guides to the sportsmen who came down on their yachts. Most people, like Theena's daddy, made a living fishing, hunting, making charcoal, and farming.

To get to the Glades, a man could cut his way through brush and vine, fighting for every yard. Or he could step into a boat and take the Miami River from the bay directly into the swamp.

Billy poled them upstream and into the vast inland sea of grass. Except for the occasional sink, the water was shallow, but no one ever tried to wade out here. Leeches, snakes, gators, mucky bottom. No, people kept to their boats unless they found one of the larger hummocks, spongy dry land a couple of feet above water level that might afford a little tree shade.

No place else smelled like the glades. Breezes off the Atlantic kept the shore fresh and salty smelling. Theena's beloved river smelled green and new. Her garden smelled of earth and tomato leaves and oregano. But out here, heat raised up the smells of gator wallows, rotting vegetation, grass and mud. And under all that, the clean smell of sweet water.

Billy poled the dugout through the saw grass to a wedge-shaped hummock and pulled them ashore. The little island was no bigger than a large garden patch, but it offered shade and dry ground. Once Theena spread more camphor on her arms and neck, Billy put brown hands on her shoulders and turned her back the way they'd come.

"All right. See where we came out of the river?" He pointed a little to the north. "What are your landmarks?"

"Well, there's a gumbo limbo right there."

"Must be ten thousand gumbo limbos on the edge of the glades."

Theena raised a hand to her eyes to peer toward the morning sun. "There's another tree across the bank full of white cranes."

"And, Miss Theena Thickhead, if the cranes don't happen to be home the day you come out here?"

Theena sighed, but she got it. Multiple points would be required. Just north of their hummock she could see a string of small tufts where the mud had piled up and a palmetto or two had taken root. To her right, she counted three distant smaller hummocks with patches of cypress anchoring them in the muck.

"And to the west?" Billy prompted.

Nothing in sight that way but a sea of grass. Theena knew there were more hummocks out there, lots of them, for that's where Billy's village was, due west. But from here, she might just as well be looking at the trackless sea.

"What if I just paint an X on the side of the boat right here?" Laughter burbled out of her and erupted into her silly guffaw.

"Yeah, you're a funny girl. Now try to keep your bearings. We're going north to the fishing hole I told you about."

They shoved off and Billy poled them through the razor-edged grasses. Theena knew to keep her hands in her lap lest she be cut, and she kept a sharp eye out for ambitious snakes and gators. Every one she saw, though, chose to slide away from them.

It was sweltering among the saw grass. Billy standing in the boat could see where he was going and at least sniff the wind, but the grasses towered over Theena's head and closed in behind the boat as they passed. Finally Billy poled them into an open pond and Theena gulped in the breeze.

Easy together, they baited their hooks and hauled in the fish, feeling no need to chat at each other. An hour later, Billy held up their catch for Theena to admire. "We got ourselves a string of the sweetest catfish south of the Okeechobee."

"Hope Rosa forgives you for bringing home fish instead of beads."

Billy grunted. "Probably not." Then he smiled. "But I know where her tickle spot is."

Theena smiled, too, but it was an effort. Everyone seemed to have a someone, everyone but her. With Dite gone north and Hera at Jack's house in Lemon City, sometimes she feared she'd lose herself, forget who she was without someone else around – someone to define her as sister, daughter. Sometimes she stood stock still in the little house, trembling, nearly overcome by the enormous silence.

Theena still had not cried since Daddy died. She couldn't seem to feel much anymore besides the loneliness. She hurt, and yet somehow she was numb, too. She yearned for something, someone, to break through the icy daze that had come over her at Daddy's graveside.

In the afternoons, when the insects droned and the humidity lay like a heavy blanket on her chest, she succumbed to feeling friendless, forlorn, lost. She did not go to Brickell's store on Saturday. She didn't want to see Hera hanging on to Jack, claiming him in front of everyone on the bay. She chose to keep her solitude, but now the days dragged on, and Theena's life became burdensome.

Fishing with Billy brought Theena around. She was herself when she was with him. Even when she and Billy didn't speak, there was the comfortable thrum of being with a friend.

Billy strung another fish on the string. "We bout got enough, don't you think?"

"Plenty," she said.

Billy had punched holes in a tin pail to let the water circulate and to keep the turtles from getting their catch. He returned the string to the bucket and picked up his pole. "Which way?" he said.

Theena stood up in the boat and looked around. They had entered the pond from over there, or was it from over there? "Oh dear," she murmured. Whether she looked left or right, ahead or behind, it was all water and grass and an occasional hummock overgrown with trees and brush. She chose and pointed. "I think we came from that way."

Billy turned the boat and pushed them in the opposite direction without comment. She scowled at him and tried to figure out where they were.

Half an hour later, he said, "You keeping your eyes open for the river?"

"Not there yet. I thought you said you had something to show me."

"Getting pretty close to it, I'd say. So which way is home?"

Theena looked for the row of tufts. She scanned the horizon for the string of hummocks, the gumbo limbo, the tree full of white cranes. She did see a good sized hummock off to the right, but it was the wrong shape, and she didn't think it was in the right place either.

Billy waited. Theena stood up carefully to see farther and gazed all around. Feeling clever, she checked the shadows for direction. "Over there," she said confidently. She pointed to the eastern edge of the swamp marked by an outline of trees.

"Over there by that tree with the osprey?"

Theena nodded and then breathed out in relief. She'd been afraid she wouldn't be able to find it.

"Listen, Theena. This is what I wanted to show you."

She looked around her. "What?"

"We passed the river a good mile back."

Theena sat down hard, deliberately rocking the boat, and gave him a nasty, red-faced glare.

Billy skillfully walked the length of the dugout to sit in front of her. He touched her hand with one finger.

"You see now? I know you can fish as well as anyone, but you can't fish out here. Not without me."

She didn't relent, her mouth set and her eyes still fixed on her betrayer like he'd stolen her best fish hook.

Billy gave her a chuck under the chin. "Next time I'd come to town, the neighbors would have given you up for gator bait. I'd have to go looking for a lady alligator wearing your pink bonnet."

She wanted to curse. She wanted to curse really bad. When it came it was explosive. "Damnation!"

Billy held his hands up as if to protect himself. "Whoa. Don't think I've ever heard anything like that out of your mouth." He grinned at her. "Say it again."

"Damnation," this time without much behind it.

Billy's laughing eyes were still on her. She relented, a reluctant smile stealing over her face.

Then Billy turned sober. "Do you promise? You won't come out here by yourself?"

She stared at the confusion of grass, water, mud, and trees under an empty sky. Her shoulders slumped. Billy was right. She had no idea how she'd find her way home by herself.

"I promise."

"Good. How long you planning to stay mad at me?" Billy said.

Theena glared. "I'm going to count to at least a hundred before I forgive you."

"I guess I can wait that long."

He picked up the near end of the pole and walked his way back down the boat. After they entered the Miami proper, the current pulled them along nicely and Billy sat down to enjoy the ride until they came to a clearing above what passed for rapids in southern Florida.

"Let's eat," Billy said.

Theena built a fire on top of the black ruins of earlier fires while Billy cleaned the fish. They ate two beauties along with some of the congealed *sofkee* Billy had brought from home. Theena loved Seminole grits, especially fried in a little bacon grease. As it was, they ate their fish stick-roasted and their *sofkee* cold.

They sat in the sand, shoulder to shoulder against a fine old live oak and finished off the plums she'd brought. Theena felt the tension ease from her shoulders. Her river, the bright blue sky, and nearby, saucer-sized magnolia blossoms perfuming the air. When they'd been quiet a while, Theena said, "What are you thinking about? Getting Rosa to marry you?"

Billy gave her a funny look. He shifted so he could see her face. "I was thinking about you."

"Me? What about me?"

"How you going to get by with your daddy gone, and your sisters, too?"

"I can take care of myself," she said. "I may not know my hat from a teacup in the glades, but I'll have the chickens and the eggs, all the fish I can catch in the bay or the river." There were oysters and scallops, too. She'd get by just fine. If only the days weren't so silent.

Billy shook his head. "You'll need flour and coffee, shoes, thread, cloth. You don't have a cash crop like the planters around here." He looked back at the sun sparkles on the river and shook his head again. "Fish and field peas aren't all it takes to have a life."

"Don't worry about me." She forced a smile. "I'm supposed to marry Randolph Chase, didn't you know that? I told Daddy I would." She laughed. "I just have to tell Randolph."

"I thought you were mooning over Hera's beau."

Theena blushed so hot she felt the roots of her hair burn. "Well, that was nonsense, of course," she said. "I'm over that."

"So it's to be Chase, then," Billy said flatly.

Theena nodded. "He has wonderful manners, and he's read so many books he can't count them. And I've always been partial to blue eyes." She didn't dislike Randolph at all, not at all, and yet . . . .

"He reads poetry to me when -- ."

"Shh, shh." Billy thumbed her wet cheek. He put an arm around her shoulder and pulled her to him.

They so seldom touched anymore, not since they'd left childhood behind them. All the fear and the need she'd been fighting to keep down the last weeks bubbled up. She wanted to climb into him, to shelter in his arms.

He kissed her forehead. Her arms trembled as she buried her face against his chest.

He caressed her hair, her back, her waist, stroking and petting. She shifted her face, her lips level with his chin. He dipped his head, his mouth closing on hers, the taste of salty skin and tears mingling on their tongues.

Billy lay her down on the sand. “Theena?”

The gray numbness, the fierce emptiness of the last weeks, gone now with Billy's body pressed to hers. She wrapped her arms around his neck and raised her mouth to his. His sure hands ran up her thigh. Her body loosened, her knees shifted. He made love to her, loved her. At the moment when violent waves of need shook her body, her lungs convulsed in all the sobs she'd suppressed since Daddy's funeral. Billy held tight and let her cry it out.

Exhausted, she lay still against Billy's solid warmth in the shade of the live oak. When her breath slowed down, she hid her face in his shirt. All her fine resolutions, her pride in not being like Hera. “Oh, God, Billy. What have I done.”

He laughed. “You don't know?”

She slapped at his chest. “You know what I mean.”

Billy held her at arm's length so he could see her face. “We did nothing wrong, Theena. You are my best loved friend in the world. It's okay.”

“But --.”

“Theena, it's all right.”

They rolled themselves upright against the tree. Billy brought her to his side and let her lean against him, his arm draped over her shoulder.

Theena closed her eyes and breathed deeply, allowing herself another minute of touch, of warmth. *It can't be all right. For now, though, for just this moment, I can let it be. Just for now.*

A deeply pink spoonbill stalked its dinner in the reeds along the river's edge, moving its flat beak from side to side in the water. They watched it grab a minnow and shake it down its throat. “That's the prettiest bird out here,” he said.

“Billy, what about Rosa?”

“Hoo boy. I'm not going to tell her.”

Theena smiled. “I won't mention it either.” She squeezed Billy's hand and sat up straight. “Thank you. For holding me.”

Billy pushed a strand of hair off her forehead. "You're welcome."

"I love you, too."

"You ready to go?" Billy said.

They slipped downstream through the lush growth on either bank, cranes, spoonbills and anhinga keeping them company under a perfect blue sky. At the landing, Billy handed Theena her string of catfish. They held hands a moment. "See you soon," he said and shoved off.

Theena stood on the bank and watched him go. How very strange. After all the promises to herself that she would be a virgin on her wedding day, she'd given herself to Billy, just now, today. Where was the guilt and the anguish she was supposed to feel? Where was the shame for committing the same sin as Hera? It hadn't felt wrong under the oak tree. It didn't feel wrong now.

She put her catch in a bucket with a lid on it to keep the critters out. In the house, she walked directly to the mirror set into the chifferobe. Her hair was a mess and her cheeks and chin reddened where the sun had slipped under her bonnet. That didn't interest her. Shouldn't she look different? She'd lost her virginity today. She was a woman now. A sinful woman. She shook her head. The same eyes stared back at her as on any other day. No, she decided. Not really the same. She looked, she felt, calm and at peace for the first time since Daddy died.

That's what making love did to people? Made them feel lighter? She tilted her head and looked at herself again. Not a virgin, anymore. A woman who's known a man. Not what she'd expected. What she'd felt had not been the passion her imagination conjured up when she dreamed about making love. It had been tender and kind, not flaming, not . . . ecstasy.

Maybe because she and Billy were not in love with each other. She had never thought about the shape of his lips, had never noticed whether the sun glistened on his hair, had never wished he'd touch her. They had made love, she and Billy, yet she still felt untouched, somehow. She opened the buttons of her bodice till her cleavage showed. She didn't want to be untouched. She wanted – more. She wanted Randolph to come home.

Chapter Four

Hera would be needing curtains on the windows, sheets on the bed. One chair wouldn't be enough anymore. And the little one. Jack had no idea what a little one would need, but he'd see to it that Hera had everything she wanted for him.

Jack walked through his small grove. He'd come to Biscayne Bay to take advantage of the government's free hundred and sixty acres for homesteaders, and he'd cleared nearly a fifth of it through stubborn hard work. Only waist high, the trees already bore fruit. Jack wrapped his big hand around one of the hard green little oranges and felt its weight. Another three months, he could start picking.

Heading back to the house, he tried to think what to do about Hera. *Just no need of her getting all worked up over nothing like she does.* That time he spoke to Tom Dalkin's daughter at the store, she'd been in a snit the rest of the day. And if he mentioned going over to see about Theena, she turned into a harridan. Hardly seemed the same sweet girl when she got like that, and there Theena was fending for herself.

Now he and Hera were next thing to married, Theena was family. He wouldn't let her do without. Yes, he admitted to himself, he was aware of her in a way he hadn't been a few months ago. He'd been too wrapped up with Hera to notice she'd grown up. Well, he'd noticed. But he was going to be a father, and a husband. No way he would mess that up.

Jack scraped his feet on the bottom step of the house.

"Just in time." Hera met him at the door with her face turned up. He gathered her up and gave her a squeeze and a kiss.

"What's for supper?"

Hera fed him string beans and fried chicken and biscuits with guava jam. "I talked to Alma Jenkins today," she said as he finished up the biscuits. "She and Joseph stopped by on their way to the bay, and I asked Alma about Mrs. Collins, the midwife I told you about."

"Uh-huh?"

"Alma said she's had Mrs. Collins for her last two younguns, and paid her a dollar each time. She was real pleased with her."

"A dollar?"

"That's what she said. Is that too much?"

"No. I've got two dollars, as a matter of fact. But that's about all I've got."

Hera walked around the table and sat in his lap. He wrapped his arms around her and nuzzled her neck. "Don't worry about it," he said. "I been thinking it's time I got some cash together anyway. I can go back to work for Mr. Lindberg on his sponge boat."

"But you'd be gone all the time."

He didn't want to go, but he hoped to buy more trees come spring. And Hera would be needing things for herself and the baby. "I'll come back for a spell every layover, how's that?"

Hera laid her head against his chest. "I'll miss you."

He rubbed his hand over her belly. She barely looked pregnant, but he looked forward to her getting round as a melon. "Why don't you get Theena to come stay with you while I'm gone?"

Hera looked around the cabin. It wasn't any smaller than the one she'd grown up in, but it was newer, and he guessed she figured it was hers now. That pouty mouth told him she didn't mean to share it with her little sister.

Jack hitched a ride down to Key West on the mail boat, paying for the passage with his strong back and his store of outrageous yarns. Once on the island, he looked for Mr. Lindberg at the spongers' wharf. The odor here was nothing like as powerful as the stink on the boats where freshly harvested sponges turned slimy and stinky. These piles of sorted sponges on the dock had already been beaten of their mucilaginous animal remains, washed, and strung in the sun to dry.

Mr. Lindberg spotted Jack winding through the piles of sponges. "Spode! Over here," he called. They shook hands and Mr. Lindberg offered Jack a cigar out of his pocket. "Hope you've come to join on," Lindberg said. "Got need of a good man, Jack."

They shipped out at sunrise the next morning, sailing east northeast into the shallow waters of Florida Bay. Jack relished being on the water again. The vibrant greens and blues of the sea, the warm breeze, the gentle rocking of the schooner.

The smaller boats were put over the side and Jack and his mate Juan oared over to a promising smudge on the sea floor. Here the water was clear and calm, yet the glare on the surface of the water made it hard to tell what lay below – the near-worthless loggerhead sponges or a patch of prime sheep's-wool.

Jack, the designated eye of the team, leaned over the side of the boat with the water-glass, a wooden bucket with a glass bottom held a few inches below the surface. He knew, later in the day, after hours spent peering over the side of the boat, his back and shoulders would stiffen and cramp, but for now he marveled at the brilliant little fish, yellow and orange and a startling blue, playing among the sea-fans and anemones. Rich red coral branched and twisted into exotic trees; lush purple sea weed waved its fronds in the current.

Off the stern Jack spotted a rich lode of grass sponge, first quality it looked like. "Back her up a bit, Juan." Jack reached for the long pole behind him and maneuvered it overboard. Here is where the expert sponger distinguished himself from the less skillful man at the oars. Jack plunged the long sponge-hook into the water and automatically compensated for the weird effect of refraction as the submerged part of the pole seemed to dart off from its above-water part.

Wielding the three pronged hook at the end of the pole, Jack raked sponges from the sandy bottom and pulled them up into the boat. Again and again he dipped the thirty-foot shaft until he'd harvested nearly the entire colony. The sponges would grow back from the bits left on the sea floor, and in a couple of years, Mr. Lindberg or some other enterprising sponger would be back.

Blessed with a body uniquely suited to the shoulder and arm work of sponging, Jack still found that by day's end his back ached, and his skin, in spite of a Florida man's perpetual tan, had burned right through his calico shirt. It had been too long since he'd worked on the bay like this, and Jack remembered why he'd quit the sponging business.

Had to be an easier way to earn a living, he'd decided. But here he was. Not many ways a man could pick up cash money as quickly as he could sponging. The challenge was not to take his hard-earned dollars to the taverns and their temptations when he hit Key West again. Which Jack would not do, not now he had a wife, soon-to-be, and a baby on the way.

Day after day, Jack labored. His back reaccustomed itself to the work, his skin toughened, and he could wield the heavy long poles from sunup till sundown. The monotony of the labor gave him plenty of time to think.

When Hera had told him she was pregnant, Jack had been shocked. *Damn fool,* he told himself. *What'd you expect?* Marriage hadn't been on his mind, not before he'd got his orange grove producing an income. He'd left the life of the Conchs, the life his father and grandfather had led, for the chance to make a living on the land. He wanted to build something, have something, not just live from one shipping-out to the next.

But he'd let himself lose sight of his long-term aims for the pleasures of Hera Theophilus's soft, sweet body. *A Conch through and through,* he told himself with disgust. Hera had assumed her being pregnant meant they would be married. He'd accepted that as the rightness of things. He would not be like his old man, a woman in every little fishing village. Jack figured he had a dozen half-brothers and sisters scattered over the Caribbean.

"You don't mind?" Hera had said. "Of course not." He'd kissed her and held her tight so she couldn't see him swallow around the lump in his throat.

These last weeks, he'd warmed to the idea of a son beside him fishing for jack or planting orange trees. He imagined Hera big with their second child, a strawberry blonde little girl, and then a third. He counted off the days before he could get home for a layover.

"Jack," Juan called, and pointed to the schooner. "Lindberg's got the flag up."

They rowed back to the ship, tossed a line to the man on deck, and climbed aboard. Jack stretched his back, then followed Juan's gaze toward the peculiar color of the eastern sky.

Chapter Five

Theena spent her days working the garden, fishing the bay, and re-reading *The Iliad*. She began a letter to Dite, but gave it up. What was there to write about? The sun glinting on the water like a thousand diamonds, the fresh smell of the bay in the early morning, the feel of the clean sand squeaking under foot? Dite had seen it all and left it far behind.

It was easier to be out in the bay than to be alone at the homestead. The open water, the birds, the clouds, the smell of the sea were a sort of company. But she carried her aloneness with her, and the prospect of returning to the empty cabin at day's end filled her with dread.

She did have Bertie, and she was a good listener. "What do you think, Bertie? You want to go pick some beans?" Bertie would tilt her head, cock an ear, and look at her as if she seriously considered Theena's offer. When Theena tried reading to her, though, she rested her head on her paws and went to asleep. Still, she was company, and though she sometimes disappeared to satisfy her hunting instincts, she always came back by dusk.

One night, however, Bertie didn't come home. When the sun sank below the tree tops, Theena walked into the yard and called for her. "Bertie, come, Bertie."

The sun set. Theena retreated to the porch. From the top step, she hollered, "Bertie! Come, girl. Bertie!"

She sat on the old rawhide chair, watched the woods, and listened for Bertie to come crashing home through the underbrush. Red eyes glowed from the edge of the clearing -- a coon, a polecat -- a panther? The bushes rustled, and Theena stood up and hollered for Bertie again. The creature moved off through the woods. Theena took herself inside and barred the door.

She lit the lantern, then took the shotgun down from the wall, looked at it carefully, and discovered how to open it. It was empty. She pulled the trigger a couple of times, trying to figure out how the inner mechanism worked. The box of shells was under Daddy's bed, and she pulled out two. Looked like there was only one way for them to go in. She guessed she could use it if she had to.

Heavy steps on the porch. Even as spooked as she'd been by the red eyes among the bush, she knew these steps were too heavy to be Bertie, or even a big panther. Short Ribs again. If she didn't break that old sow of coming up on the porch, she'd likely crash through the floorboards one of these days.

The shotgun over her arm, pointed at the floor and all but forgotten, Theena jerked the door open. "Shoo, now," she said, and then she saw the looming shape on the porch.

Theena and a black bear stared at one another, both of them paralyzed with surprise, and then Theena screamed. The bear startled, turned in a tight circle, then ran down the steps into the darkness. Theena slammed the door shut.

It took a while for her to calm down. "A lot of good it did me to have a gun," she muttered, pacing up and down. "Talking to myself again. I've got to stop this." She wondered if she were going crazy like the old hermit on the island.

She hadn't spoken to another soul, excepting Bertie and Short Ribs, in days and days. The last two Saturdays, Theena had chosen not to go to the store when most everyone on the bay would stop by. She'd wanted to think, to get used to the idea of herself as a fallen woman. Not as bad as Mama – Theena hadn't hurt anyone. She'd simply let loneliness overcome good sense, that day with Billy. She wouldn't do it again.

She knew herself better now, understood Hera better. That didn't mean she'd be comfortable running into her sister at Brickells. Hera's tummy would be showing by now, the ladies leaning their heads together about her. Even worse, Theena didn't want to see Hera's glowing face, her arm attached to Jack's like a tick on a dog. And Hera hadn't troubled to come see about her, either.

But the solitary days weighed her down. *Tomorrow,* she decided, *I'll go to Brickell's store. I'll sit on the porch the live long day and talk to everyone who comes in or out.*

Next morning, the sky was gray and overcast. The wind was picking up and it felt like rain. Bad weather or not, Theena couldn't bear to spend another day alone. She put on her best dress and tied her shoes up in an oiled bag. "Here, girl," she called to Bertie, who'd wandered in after breakfast, and the two of them boarded the skiff and headed down stream.

At Brickell's, Theena went inside to visit with Miss Alice while Bertie went round back to romp with her pack.

"Land sakes, child, what you been doing with yourself?" Miss Alice said.

"Fishing, mostly. And reading Daddy's books."

"You ought to be wearing your bonnet more, Theena Theophilus," Miss Alice said. "You getting brown as your daddy was."

Theena walked over to the little mirror by the hat rack. She had been leaving her bonnet off in the mornings out on the bay, enjoying the breeze through her hair, on the back of her neck. She surely didn't look like the milky-white girls in Miss Alice's magazines. She touched her face. "Well," she said. "It's too late now. I'm a brown-faced fisherwoman, and that's a fact."

"Dark as an old Seminole woman," Billy Yoholo chimed in.

Theena whirled around to catch Billy in her arms. She hugged him tight and when he stiffened, she looked up and followed his eyes to the young woman at his side. Her black eyes flashed, and Theena quickly released Billy.

"Rosa, this is Theena Theophilus," Billy said. "I told you about her."

Rosa nodded her head, lips drawn tight and eyes narrowed.

"We're married, Theena," Billy told her. "Last week."

"Married!" Not once since she and Billy had lain together had she worried about seeing him again, about feeling awkward. All she felt was delight to finally meet his beloved Rosa. "Congratulations!" Her face split into a broad grin as she held her hand out. "Or maybe I should be offering condolences now you're stuck with him."

Rosa took her time reading Theena's face. Gradually, the tightness around her mouth eased. She took Theena's hand and greeted her properly. "Hello, Theena. I am happy to meet you."

Rosa's English was heavily accented, but it was correct. She was a tiny young woman, as beautiful as a doll. Her blue-black hair was elaborately coiffed, and in the style of her people, she wore pounds and pounds of beads around her neck.

"When Billy comes to town, Rosa, all he talks about is you."

"He does?" Rosa said, all her reserve lifting.

Mr. Brickell stomped into the store, shaking the sand off his boots. "How you doing, Billy?" he said. "How's your dad?"

"Doing good. He's got himself a new hunting dog and gone up toward Okeechobee to hunt bear."

"He'll be out of this mess then. You notice the haze in the air? I come in to check the barometer." They walked over to a polished mahogany device mounted on the wall.

"My papa said he watched it drop four millibars in an hour one time. That must have been a bigger blow than any I've seen." Mr. Brickell tapped the glass tube gently and shook his head. "It's lower since I looked a couple of hours back. Reckon we're in for a storm."

"How soon?" Billy asked.

"Can't say with any certainty, but likely plenty of time for you to get on back to your people, if that's what you want. Or you and your missus are welcome to stay here."

"Thanks, Mr. Brickell."

Billy walked outside to look toward the southeast. That's where the biggest storms came from, all the way from Africa he'd heard. There was a mass of white clouds in a sky the color of brick dust. Smaller, lower clouds scudded overhead.

He walked under the palm trees to join a group of men standing at the shoreline. Whitecaps marked the waves where the wind had kicked up further out. Here in the bay, the storm signs were not so clear as they were out in the ocean, but there was a distinct swell even here in the shallows, and the water pushed in past the high tide mark.

A man in dungarees pointed to a frigate bird flying northwest, ignoring the shore line and heading inland. "There's you a sign," he said.

"My wife told me this morning the butterflies that hang around her flower garden – they's all gone."

"Yeah, I heard they do that when there's a storm coming. They know something we don't before we know we didn't know it."

"You Sam Yoholo's kid?" an old Cracker asked Billy.

"That's right."

"Uh huh. You aiming to get back before this storm hits, you best get going. Looks like a good one."

Out a hundred yards from shore, a water spout swirled up and a rain squall blew across the bay right for them. Before the men could take shelter, the squall dumped huge stinging drops. By the time Billy got back to Rosa at the store, he was drenched.

Shivering in his wet shirt, he checked the barometer again. Down almost another millibar.

"We got to get back, Rosa." He grabbed her hand and headed for the front door, urgency in every step. He stopped and turned back to Theena. "You stay here, understand?"

Theena clicked her heels and snapped a salute at him. "Yes, sir, General Yoholo, sir."

Rosa laughed, but Billy was not amused. He walked back to her and poked a finger in her chest. "I mean it, Theena."

"All right, then. I'll stay."

Billy let his breath out. "Good. Rosa, let's get going. Your mother will need help with the little ones."

"Good-bye, Theena," Rosa said.

"Stay here," Billy called back at her through the wind, and they were gone.

Theena walked around to the back porch so she could see the bay. The wind blew her skirts and pulled her hair loose. It'll be like a party, she thought, with the dozen or so people staying at the Brickells. They'd listen to the wind howl, talk, and eat all the goodies the wives brought in.

Then she realized how unprepared she'd left the homestead. Her best pot and all her knives were out at the cook shed. They'd wash away or blow away one. And her fishing gear lay out in the open on the front porch. Irritated with herself, she gripped her skirts in the wind and wondered what to do. Then she thought of her chickens pecking around loose. They'd either drown or blow off into the glades where the gators would get them. She couldn't afford to lose those chickens.

She studied the sky. She'd been in a couple of blows before. There was plenty of time.

Theena whistled for Bertie and ran down to her skiff. She took a minute to take her shoes off and wrap them, then rowed with her back in it to get home as quickly as possible. With the wind behind her, she made good time.

She pulled the skiff on shore and hurried to the chicken coop. She dragged the coop, about three feet by six, over to the house and hauled it up the porch steps, bumping and scraping it all the way over the boards. Then she rounded up the chickens, skittish or hiding, none of them cooperative. She finally got them in their coop inside the cabin.

"All right, that takes care of you."

It was raining now. Theena put on Daddy's old slicker and headed for the garden to harvest as much as she could. Some of it she'd take with her back to Brickell's; the rest she'd leave inside the house. The cabin was built on stilts, so she didn't have to worry about flooding.

Her fishing gear, the hoe and the spade, the knives, the pots – all these she put inside. She found Short Ribs and her shoat sheltering under the house. That was as good a place as any for them to hide from the wind and rain. It wasn't likely the water would come up this far from the shore line, and couldn't pigs swim?

Theena took another look around the house, closed all the shutters and bolted the door. She whistled again for Bertie, who'd taken off as soon as they'd landed the skiff. The wind whipped the breath out of her mouth. She hollered and whistled, but no Bertie.

The wind was definitely stronger. The rain drops were heavy and warm, then stingingly tiny and cold. She ran to the far end of the garden. "Bertie, Bertie!"

Bertie poked her head out from behind the shed. She whined, but when Theena insisted, she crawled out and tried to shelter herself in Theena's billowing skirts.

"Come on." She tugged at Bertie's scruff and pulled her toward the landing. The rain slanted into her face so that she could barely see the river from ten feet away. She sheltered her eyes to look for the skiff, but she must be upstream from it. She turned to her right and skirted the bank, one hand on Bertie's neck.

She struggled against the wind till she was in the weeds at the east edge of the landing. Where was the damned boat? She turned around and retraced her steps. She must have walked right past it without seeing it.

Wind lashed at the trees overhead. A helpless snake whipped by inches from her head. The rain was now nearly horizontal, and she could see no more than a foot or two in front of her. One hand out like a blind man, she retraced the few yards of cleared landing. The skiff was gone. The rising river had taken the boat.

She allowed herself a single cuss word. "Damnation, Bertie." Billy would be plenty mad when he found out she'd left the Brickells and got herself stuck at the cabin.

Bertie wriggled free of her grip and dashed off into the storm. Theena stumbled toward the house. After she'd begun to think she might be lost, she put a blind hand on the wall of the shed. She'd missed the house altogether.

Rain water covered her feet, and a current began to pull at her ankles. Where did so much water come from, and where was it to go? She didn't trust being in the shed in so much water. It simply sat on the ground, no foundation, no stilts. She cupped her hands around her eyes and tried to see the house. She could just make out a gray mass through the torrent and pushed against the wind to get to it.

A gust blew her to her knees and she crawled the rest of the way. Bertie emerged from under the house and Theena wrapped her arms around her neck. Together they climbed the steps.

Her earlier irritations slid into real worry. When she opened the front door – would she be able to close it again?

Once inside, she put all her weight and strength behind the door to push it to, but the wind threw her back as if she were a ragdoll. The chickens squawked and rioted in their cage; every loose thing in the house fluttered and flew. Just as Theena despaired of shutting the storm out, the wind veered away and she slammed the door. Seconds later, the wind attacked again, pounding the door so it creaked and shook against the bar. But it held.

She stood gasping for air in the middle of the room. Water streamed from the mack, from her sodden dress, from her hair. Sooty rivulets ran down the chimney and across the boards. The windward windows rattled and leaked, and water seeped under the sills.

As the storm moved in, the sun might as well have been somewhere over China. Bertie whined in fright. Theena sat on the floor and held her, both of them trembling. The chickens all had their heads under their wings. They didn't make a sound, but the little house smelled of wet dog, wet feathers, and fear.

Theena let Bertie slink under Daddy's bed in the alcove. Shivering, she changed into dry clothes, then crawled into her bed and listened to the hurricane rage.

The wind shrieked and shook the house. The rain pummeled the walls, the roof, the windows. Hours or minutes passed, she didn't know which. The whining and the howling seemed to go on forever. She would be mad if it didn't stop soon. She clamped the pillow over her head, but then she couldn't be sure where each wind-driven missile on the other side of the thin walls landed, and she had to know. She had to feel each moment of the storm as if she could somehow prevent the worst by straining every nerve.

Huddled in the bed clothes, Theena jumped when something careened into the roof. Then other, larger missiles made direct hits. She clasped her hands behind her head and pressed her forearms against her ears.

Roof shingles had to be blown clean off. Cold, cold water dripped insistently over her bed, soaking the quiltlet and the mattress. The drip turned into a steady stream. Heart thundering, Theena dashed across the room to Daddy's bed in the alcove.

A cocoanut – something -- bombed against the side window and popped the shutters free of their hinges. Theena clutched the pillow and stared at the quivering panel of glass. If it broke, the storm would be here, inside the house. Lightning flashed and illuminated trees bent to the ground, cocoanuts flying, whole palms hurtling. The window glass could not survive such a wind.

Trembling so she could hardly use her hands, Theena groped on the mantelpiece for the hammer, knocking the can of nails over. She hardly registered the pain when she stepped on the nails stumbling to the chifferobe. Frantic, she jerked a drawer out of the chest and knocked it apart with the hammer. She felt on the floor for nails, her fingers numb with cold. She slammed a board against the window frame. Pouring all her strength through the hammer, she pounded nails into that board. Then another board and another.

She had only a five inch swath near the top to cover when another projectile smashed into the window. The boards protected Theena's face, but above the boards, the wind propelled a thousand glass shards into the room.

Theena barely felt their stinging impact on her scalp, her attention on the boards now taking the full force of the wind. She tried to nail the last slat at the top, but the wind tore it out of her hands and knocked it against her forehead. She collapsed on the floor, stunned.

As Theena staggered to her feet, the first nail popped out. That board loosened, the other nails popped as if they'd been shot from a gun. The storm shoved into the house, the wind and the rain driving in horizontally. Debris flew in, battering the other windows, the walls, each blow shattering and loosening. The pressure punched upward until a quarter of the roof tore away near the chimney and water poured in with the volume and velocity of a river. Continuous lightning blazed in the blackened sky.

The wind muscled and roared through the window and out the top. Every loose object in the room became airborne, sucked up through the gap in the roof. Chunks of the house flew away, enlarging the gap.

Stunned by the pandemonium, by the force of rain and wind on her skin, by the thunder and the shrieking of the wind in her ears, Theena hardly knew the fear that clawed at her. She scrambled underneath the big bed where Bertie huddled. The dog snapped at her and growled. Theena pulled her body to the other end of the bed and curled into a ball. Her eyes screwed shut, Theena prayed. It was up to God now.

Chapter Six

Someone called her name, or maybe she dreamed it. Bertie, curled against her body, raised her head, too, and perked her ears up.

"Theena!"

Watery sunlight pierced the darkness through a crack in the wall. Theena tried to sit up, but she was still under the bed. "In here," she called.

"Where?"

It was Jack. Jack had come for her. Joy suffused her, but then she heard Hera's voice, and she realized this was no dream. The storm was over. She was alive.

"Where are you?" Hera shouted. "Yell out so we can hear you."

"I'm under the bed. Daddy's bed."

Hera and Jack called out over each other. "Are you hurt? Are you okay?"

She'd had a blow to the head, she remembered that. But she was fine. She must be fine. Just bruised and sore and wet. And oh so cold.

"I'm all right."

Theena tried to make sense of what had happened to the house. She could feel the floor tilting toward the front porch, but from the one crack admitting light, there were only jumbled shades of gray. "I think I can crawl to the door."

"No! Don't do that, Theena. Stay where you are."

"What's wrong?"

"The house fell in," Jack said. "Sit tight. We'll get you out."

They were close. Theena heard Hera say, "Where do we start? The whole thing could shift."

Jack didn't answer for several minutes. "Over here," he said quietly. He was very near now. "Go slow, one board at a time."

Bertie growled when she heard the disturbance of her lair. "Shh, Bertie." Another board slid away. Then another. They were so slow.

"Not that one," she heard Jack say. "Hera, let me do this."

Painstakingly, cautiously, he pulled the debris away. Theena smelled fresh air and caught a glimpse of Jack's hand.

"I see you!"

Hera put her face near the opening. "It's coming. Be patient."

Oh so carefully, Jack enlarged the gap. Theena held on to Bertie to keep her from dashing through the maze of fallen roof timbers between them and freedom.

Jack tested the resistance of a timber, and then pulled on it. The mass of tangled roof shifted and slid, creaking and groaning.

"Don't move," Jack yelled.

The broken roof settled and the opening Jack had made was closed again. Theena smelled rain. A mild wind blew in at her feet.

"Jack?"

"I'm here."

"Try around the other side."

Hera got there first. "Look! Right here. A new opening." She leaned her face into the gap. "Theena, you see me?"

Theena moved to get out from under the bed. Jack said, "Wait! Let's take our time."

Bertie couldn't wait. She squirmed free, scooted out from under the bed and wiggled through the gap. Outside, she ran around in circles and barked at the wind.

"All right, Theena. I'm going to move one more chunk, and if everything holds, you can come out."

Theena held her breath as Jack made the opening just large enough for her shoulders. Nothing moved. She crawled from under the safety of the bed and wiggled under the timbers a few inches above her head. She got her shoulders and arms through and Jack pulled her the rest of the way out.

He set her on her feet. When she swayed, he grabbed her.

"Let go. I'll take her," Hera said.

Hera's voice seemed distant and her face blurred. Why was that?

Theena's arms and legs began to tremble so that Hera couldn't support her.

"It's the shock," Jack said. He took her back and sat her down on the wet ground. Heedless of the mud, her wet hair and dress, he sat down behind her and pulled her between his legs.

Jack's body stilled the trembling. Her breathing slowed and she became aware of the puffs of tropical air, the scrubbed sky. And of her sister, hands on hips, scowling at Jack Spode.

"She's fine now," Hera snapped.

"Can you stand up?" Jack said into her ear.

Theena nodded. She felt light as smoke, brittle as straw. Hera held out a hand and heaved her to her feet.

"What's that in your hair?" Hera said. She touched a shiny bit, and Theena sucked in a gasp. "My God, your head is full of glass."

"That's a good knot on her forehead, too," Jack said.

Hera pulled Theena's head down for a better look. "What a sticky bloody mess. I'm going to need the tweezers, maybe a needle and thread," she said.

"Let's get on home," Jack said. "It'll be dark in a couple of hours."

"You seen Short Ribs?" Theena figured the chickens were battered and drowned, but pigs were tough.

"She's probably got her brood out in the woods, snuffling out dinner. Don't worry about her."

Woozy, Theena grabbed hold of her sister's arm. Hera held her steady back to the boat.

Jack shoved off into the river, generally slow and clear, now a swift, muddy current. Theena's trembling started up again. Hera handed her a flask of water and wrapped a shawl over her wet shoulders. At the mouth of the river, Jack pulled them into the shallows of the bay. With hardly any chop left, he made short work of the two miles north to Lemon City.

Hera and Jack's cabin stood intact. The yard was littered with branches and driftwood and shingles, but Jack's carpentry had withstood the storm.

While Jack checked out his orange trees, Hera got Theena some dry clothes. "You were supposed to be with the Brickells," Hera accused her. "I got there just in time and then spent all night worrying about you. Your head so thick you don't know to get out of that tumbledown shack ahead of a blow?"

"You and Jack went to the Brickells?"

"No. Jack just got back from the keys a couple hours ago. First thing he picked me up from Brickells, we had to push upstream to see about you. You should have been at the store, Theena."

"I'm sorry," she said, shivering as she pulled a dress over her head. "I meant to be, but the storm came up so fast."

Hera heaved out a sigh. "Well, you're all right. Here, let me button that. You're still trembling like a leaf."

Every stick of wood sodden, Hera fixed them a cold supper. Theena hadn't eaten since breakfast the day before and embarrassed herself reaching for the dried fish and the slabs of grits. Jack smiled at her. "I guess you got a right to be hungry after all this."

Theena caught Hera's tight-lipped glance, first at Jack, then at her. Hera's thoughts were as clear as if she'd spelled them out. She would as soon not share her husband's company. Theena felt it keenly, loneliness so heavy it filled her chest. Dite gone. Billy married. She had no one. Grow up, she told herself. Other people in the world got through their days without friend or family. Besides, Randolph would be home soon.

Hera lit the lantern and gathered her tweezers and needles. "Sit here on the floor where the light's on top of your head."

Theena sat at Hera's feet and winced as Hera picked at the glass in her scalp, eyes squinted in concentration. Blood dripped over Theena's face, and Hera handed her a cloth. "Try to keep the blood off that dress," she said.

Tears stung Theena's eyes from the pain, and it was hard not to cry. She felt fragile, listless, spent. When Hera probed a particularly deep splinter, Theena shuddered.

"I can't see it for the blood, and it's really in there," Hera said.

"Let me do it," Jack said. "I see better than you do."

Jack took Hera's place in the chair, his knees on either side of her. She was keenly aware of his body, of the intimacy of sitting between his legs. She wondered that Hera would allow it, but Hera really didn't see small things well, Jack's manner was blameless, and all Theena felt at this moment, besides fatigue, was gratitude.

He delicately plucked a sliver from her scalp. "I told you to go to Brickell's."

"I was there. I just went home to see to the chickens, get things put away. Then I got caught. I never knew a storm to come in so quick."

"Me neither."

At Theena's sharp intake of breath, Jack apologized. "I'm sorry, but it'll fester if I leave it in there." He reached for the knife at his waist.

"Wait a minute!" she said. She'd seen that knife before. It was eight inches at least, and sharp enough to slice through gator hide.

"Theena, I'm just going to use the tip to flick it out. You'll hardly feel it."

Theena reached for Hera. Her sister sat down on the floor next to her and gripped both her hands. "Okay," Hera said, and nodded to Jack.

By the time Jack was satisfied he'd gotten every splinter of glass, Theena was trembling again. Hera gave her cold coffee left from yesterday morning. It was bitter, and gritty dregs floated in it, but Theena drank it down. Then Hera leaned her over a basin and poured vinegar over her head to cleanse the wounds.

"Good God in heaven," Theena gasped. It felt like a thousand needles pierced her scalp as acid ran over the cuts.

"I know it hurts," Hera said. She wrapped a towel around Theena's head, sat her on a chair, and pulled warm socks on her feet. " It's all over now."

Jealous of Jack's attention or not, Hera treated Theena tenderly. She made her a pallet on the floor and gave her the best pillow. "You'll feel better in the morning," she said, and pulled the extra quilt up to Theena's chin.

The crickets had survived the storm with no seeming loss of numbers, and their chorus filled the night air, announcing the day was over. Fear had drained Theena's body and mind of all reserves. She slept.

Next day, Walter Simms came by to see how they'd weathered the storm. He'd been to Brickell's for the news. "Not much damage there," he reported. "This warn't nearly the storm we had back in '78. You remember that one, Jack?"

"My daddy and I were fishing down in Cuba when that one blew through. We didn't get the worst of it like you did."

"Still, this one's bad enough. You hear about old man Gunnerson? Found him up in a tree, deader'n dead."

"Where's his wife then?" Hera said.

"Hasn't nobody seen her yet. They had bad flooding down in that hollow. Gunnerson, he had a cracked head. Likely got hit by a flying cocoanut or some such. They was snakes hanging from every branch, but he don't seem to have been bit, leastwise not when he was alive."

Theena shuddered. The Gunnerson place was right on the edge of the glades. If Mrs. Gunnerson was blown out into the saw grass where the gators were . . . "Mr. Simms, you heard anything from the Seminoles?"

"Yes'um, I have. Old Sam Yoholo come by, said they didn't lose more than a few chickens. Some of the chickees blew down, but the folks all stayed safe in those storm shelters they throw up. Work good, they do."

Then Billy and Rosa were safe too, thank God. Tears sprang to her eyes. Embarrassed, she bent down to scratch Bertie's ears. She'd made friends with Jack's dog Gator and seemed as happy to be here as anywhere.

"I'm heading on over to Widow Thompson's place to see what needs doing," Mr. Simms said. "You want to come along, Jack?"

"Yeah, I will. Let me get my tools."

While Jack was gone, Hera and Theena cleaned up the yard, stacking the debris the other side of the garden. The plants were all torn up and drowned. Rations would be short until they got another crop growing.

It felt good to be doing something. Theena still had the urge to cry now it was all over, but she kept her hands busy and tried to ignore the images of the storm that flashed through her mind.

Hera went in the house ahead of Theena. After Theena finished clearing the brush away from the yard, she went inside, expecting Hera had prepared them a meal. Instead, she found Hera on a chair, stretching a blanket across a cord she'd strung, making a curtain around her and Jack's bed. Irrationally, Theena was hurt. She knew she had no right to be, but she felt excluded and unwelcome at sight of the orange striped divider.

She didn't belong here, but she had no place to go.

Chapter Seven

The second day after the storm, Jack found Theena's skiff, mostly intact, tangled in a thicket of mangroves on the bay shore. He towed it back to his place and looked it over for leaks. The little boat was remarkably fit considering what it had been through. Theena wished her shoes had been inside, but she gratefully rubbed her hands over the boards and cleaned the mud out of the bottom.

The third day, Theena tied an old bonnet of Hera's on, picked up one of Jack's smaller nets, and headed for the skiff. The path to the bay took her past the woodpile where Jack was splitting kindling. He had his shirt off, and Theena's eyes ran over his bare shoulders and back.

Stop it, she told herself. *You ungrateful, disloyal . . . . I will stop this mooning. I'm not going to be that kind of woman.* The unwelcome image of what she'd done with Billy flashed in her mind. But that was . . . that was just comfort from a friend. She was *not* that kind of woman.

"Where you going?" Jack wiped the sweat out of his eyes and rested the axe on his boot top.

"Down to the bay, get a mess of mullet for supper."

"You don't need to do that."

"I don't want to be a burden," Theena said.

Jack's glance flicked to the porch behind her. Theena turned to see Hera, watching them as she shook out a rag rug. Even from the woodpile, she could see Hera's plump lips thinned into a frown. Theena's face flushed and she dropped her gaze to her bare feet.

"It's too soon for you to go out alone after that knock on the head," Jack said. "Stay on shore, Theena."

He leaned his axe against the stump. Slowly but purposefully he walked toward the porch. He climbed the steps, took Hera's elbow, and escorted her inside.

Theena hung the net back on its hook and wandered over to the edge of Jack's grove to give him and Hera some privacy. She didn't know what to do. Not about this particular moment, but tomorrow and the next day. She'd have to figure out something. There'd be a job board at Brickell's.

She picked up a green orange off the ground and tossed it in her hand. Someday, Jack would have a flourishing plantation, but now immature fruit littered the ground, storm-sent fodder for the squirrels and coons and rats.

Jack reappeared on the porch and headed for his wood pile. Theena nodded at him across the yard, just to be polite. He strolled over, hands in the tight pockets of his dungarees. "What a mess," he said, looking at his trees.

"Looks pretty good. Just broken branches, no uproots."

He nodded. "Could be worse," he said. "Hera says ask you if you'll come in and help her with dinner. Some of the wood's near enough dry if you don't mind a smoky fire."

Here was another reason to admire Jack Spode. He was determined to make her, a burdensome younger sister, feel part of their life here. She wondered what he'd said to Hera. Kind as it was to make her feel welcome, it didn't change anything. Hera had a suspicious nature, always had had, and she didn't want her here.

"I'll go in then," she told him.

Theena hung the bonnet on a peg. A little woozy, she sat down at the table. She'd been having short spells like this ever since the storm. Likely a concussion, according to Jack. She'd get over it in a few days.

When Theena laid her head on the table, Hera said, "You dizzy again?"

"When did you set the room to spinning?"

"You lie down. I'll get dinner."

Hera helped her settle on the pallet. Theena closed her eyes, and Hera brushed the hair out of her face. "Sleep if you want to," she said.

The following days it appeared that whatever Jack had said to Hera, it helped. She sang in the evenings when she washed the dishes, and she didn't watch Theena every minute Jack was around. Theena found it easier to breathe, easier to accept her sister's food and shelter.

She counted up how many days Randolph had been gone. She wanted to hear about Key West and how the storm hit down there.

She even wanted him to read to her, his voice wonderfully alive with a poet's words in his mouth.

She missed him. But what if he hadn't missed her? Maybe, all those weeks down in Key West, he'd met a girl like the young ladies he'd known in Philadelphia. One who'd know how to talk, how to act in polite society. One without calluses on her feet and hands, one whose creamy skin wouldn't be wind burned and suntanned. She'd know all those poems he loved.

Theena wished Daddy were alive. No other soul would understand how she could be genuinely fond of Randolph, could wish he'd kiss her and make love to her, and yet still think about Jack Spode. What was the matter with her? Was there something in the blood that made a person capable of such duality of the heart? She hated herself for it, hated any notion she was like Mama. What mattered, she thought Daddy would tell her, is not what you feel, but what you do about it. He used to caress the top of her hair and tell her, "You're my good girl, Theena." She'd give anything to hear him say that again.

Theena hiked to the Peacock Inn a couple of hours' walk down the beach. Even if they could only use her half days, she wouldn't feel like such a drain on Jack and Hera. No, sorry, Mr. Plum said. Maybe when the winter tourists come down. Maybe after Christmas.

She dragged her feet through the surf on the way back, Hera's shoes slung over her back, Bertie frisking along beside her. The sun was high, and she regretted not wearing Hera's old bonnet. Miss Brickell was right, she'd be brown and freckled like an old hen. She didn't much care.

Seagulls squawked overhead, white as sea foam. A mullet jumped in the shallows, landing with a soft plop. She loved this beach, this water, this sky, these birds, these fish. She loved the smell of the bay, even at low tide when the seaweed and the oyster-crusted roots of the mangroves stank in the sun.

She picked up a stick and threw it for Bertie to chase. With her toes, she dug into the wet sand for the yellow and blue and purple coquina shells she and Hera used to string into necklaces.

But even her beloved sun, sea, and sand couldn't keep the worries away. She had promised Daddy she'd marry Randolph Chase, if he asked her, but he wasn't here, and he hadn't asked her.

With a quick glimmer of hope, she realized she hadn't taken a good look at Daddy's place when Jack and Hera pulled her from under the fallen house. Maybe the shed was still intact. No reason she couldn't stay in the shed. There'd be plenty of lumber from the cabin to patch it if need be. She could plant a winter garden and sell greens at the Inn or in Lemon City. She could take Daddy's skiff into the bay and come back with a boat load of fish to sell, too.

Half a mile down from Hera and Jack's, Theena heard hammering. That'd be Jack patching the roof with the cedar shingles he'd made. When she reached the path, she whistled for Bertie and walked into the clearing. Somebody was up there with Jack.

She put her hand up to shade her eyes. Randolph Chase straddled the roof ridge, a mouth full of nails, a hammer in his hand.

She felt her grin spread ear to ear. "Hello up there!"

So quickly she feared he was falling, Randolph slid down the slope to the ladder, descended the ladder nautical style, and strode across the ground toward her. Suddenly shy, and very aware of Hera's ill-fitting dress and her bare feet, she held out her hand to greet him.

Randolph ignored the hand. He grabbed her up, bent her back, and bestowed a loud, smacking kiss right on her mouth.

Surprised, startled, thrilled, Theena hung on when he pulled her upright. He kept his arms around her waist.

"Hi," he said, his grin showing white against his tanned face.

What had gotten into Randolph Chase, the man who'd not even kissed her goodbye? Her hands still on his shoulders, she sunk into those bright blue eyes.

Randolph touched the fading bruise on her forehead. "I should have told you to go to my mother if a storm came," he said. "You'd have been safe there."

"I'm fine, Randolph."

Jack climbed down from the roof. "Hera made sassafras tea this morning. It'll be cool by now."

Theena regretted the loss of his hand on her waist when Randolph stepped away, but he touched her briefly on her lower back as they followed Jack inside.

Hera brought in the jug she'd had cooling in the creek and served up tea cold enough to make beads on the outside of the glasses. All the pleasantries and first news out of the way at last, Randolph stood up.

"Would you like to ride along the beach?"

Daddy hadn't kept a horse. Like most folks around here, he did his traveling by foot or by boat, so Theena had seldom ridden. "I'd love a ride."

Randolph fetched a bucket of water for his horse while Theena let the mare lick her fingers. Once the horse had drunk her fill, Randolph cupped his hands for Theena's foot.

"I'm barefoot," she said, a crooked, embarrassed smile on her face. "As usual." She knew her face had gone red.

"No reason not to be, out here." He gave her a cocky smile. "And I've seen your naked feet before, Miss Theophilus."

He readied his hands for her sandy foot and lifted her into the saddle. He stepped onto a log and seated himself on the horse's broad rump, then reached around Theena for the reins.

She loved the feel of his arm around her waist. He'd always been tentative about touching her, but now -- he seemed to have brought a new assurance home with him. Whatever had happened in Key West, Theena liked this new Randolph Chase.

With white sand ahead of them as far as they could see, Randolph spurred the mare and they loped along with the horse's hooves splashing through the shallows. The sun bathed them in late afternoon light, and the breeze blew Theena's hair loose. Randolph himself gathered the thick black tresses and lay them to leeward over her shoulder.

When they approached a thicket of mangroves blocking the beach, Randolph dismounted and held his hands up for Theena. As she slid into his arms, Randolph caught her to him and held her close. She smelled the sandal wood and citrus scent he used, and under that, she smelled a man who'd been hammering shingles. She breathed it in, breathed him in. He bent to her and kissed her lips, softly, tenderly.

Theena had never been kissed like this. She pressed herself against him and wrapped her arms around his neck. This was what she'd longed for, a man's touch, a man's heat. And it was Randolph, quiet, shy Randolph, who gave her that intense heightening of senses, at last.

His lips moved to her eyes, to her neck. She tipped her head back for him to take her throat. Her breath slowed and deepened.

She felt drunk and weak in the knees as if she'd had too much elderberry wine.

Randolph pressed her against him, her belly hot against his hardness. She yearned to surrender her body to him. All tension left her, signaling her readiness to yield to him, to take him in.

He breathed hard against her neck, one arm around her waist, his other hand holding her steady. "We'd better go." he said huskily, "before I forget myself."

Her lips swollen, her heart thrumming in her ears, she wasn't sure she'd heard him. "Go?"

"I'm sorry." He hugged her, this time without kissing her. He laughed. "I'm getting ahead of myself."

He moved his hands to her shoulders and delivered a chaste kiss on her forehead. "I missed you, Theena."

She looked into those beautiful eyes. There was a lightness there, unlike the solemn, rather humorless depths of the Randolph she'd known. "Kiss me, Randolph."

He laughed again. "Believe me, I want to. But there's only so much a man can take." He pushed the hair off her face. "I'll get you home."

Randolph called to his horse and got Theena back into the saddle. When he'd climbed up behind her, they followed the shoreline back to the house. Theena touched the buttons still fastened at her neck. In a few more moments, she thought, they would have been open.

Mingled with the desire that still heated her body, at last Theena felt shame. She was supposed to be the one who said wait, slow down. She was supposed to be virtuous – and virginal. And Dite had called her Saint Theena.

What would Randolph think of her if she knew she'd had relations with Billy? Could he understand it had not been love, not passionate love, but simply loving comfort? In fact, she realized, she still felt virginal. Emotionally, she'd never plumbed those depths she expected of passion. She'd never felt that rising tide of desire flooding her senses, never felt like a hot tropical flower trembling at the first brush of the hummingbird's wings. Not until now.

In every way that matters, she realized, *I am a virgin.*

Chapter Eight

Theena pushed her chair away from the table and ran for the back porch. Hera caught up with her there and held her forehead while Theena heaved.

"Now you know how I feel every morning," Hera said with a laugh. She patted Theena's back and handed her a damp dishcloth to wipe her face.

Jack stood in the door. "She okay?"

"It's just nerves. She'll be fine."

"Don't let the old bitty get the best of you, Theena."

That "old bitty" was Mrs. Harlan Chase, Randolph's mother. Mrs. Chase had invited her to take tea. Her hostess would probably be dressed in silk, have tiny satin-clad feet, soft white hands, and impeccable manners. Theena would be in a calico dress, Hera's scuffed and too-tight shoes, and a faded blue bonnet. She had a blister on her knuckle from tending the fire carelessly, and her face and hands were sun-browned.

At one o'clock, Theena checked her hair one more time and declared herself ready. "I wish you were coming with me," she said to Hera.

"I don't think sight of your pregnant sister with no wedding band would do you any good with Mrs. Chase."

Jack leaned in the back door. "Ready?"

Theena tied her bonnet on. "Ready as I'll ever be."

Jack was home for the week before shipping out with Mr. Lindberg again, and he'd volunteered to walk Theena the hour or so to the Chase homestead. He'd wait around, take a nap under the palm trees, then walk her back. Mrs. Chase had thoughtlessly – or deliberately -- chosen a day when Randolph could not escort her; he was in Ft. Pierce for a week on business. Theena certainly felt herself capable of getting there and back, but Jack wouldn't hear of it. Even Hera agreed she shouldn't go alone, though Theena felt her sister's green eyes on her back as she and Jack left the yard.

The northwesterly path to the Chase house turned from white sand to black loamy dirt the farther they traveled from Lemon City. The strip of land between the glades and Biscayne Bay was no wider than six miles along here, sometimes a lot less. Wildlife abounded, some of it so beautiful it stopped your breath, like a flock of snowy egrets with the sun on their wings.

Once they were on the path through the woods, Jack told her, "You'd be in a pickle if you ran into a mean old she-bear out here, her thinking you were just the tasty morsel she'd been looking for. That's why you need a hero along."

"I declare, I believe you're right," Theena exclaimed. She batted her lashes at him and he laughed.

"So that book you and Hera always talk about is full of heroes, right? Who's your favorite?"

"Hmm. I like Hector. He only wanted to defend his home."

"Odysseus is my man. The smart one."

With the easy banter they used to enjoy when Jack still called her Shrimp, the hour passed quickly. When the big frame house came into view through the trees, Theena brushed the sand off her bare feet and put on Hera's shoes and stockings. "We're not late, are we?"

Jack's only timepiece was a clock in the house. He took a look at the sky. "I reckon not. Close enough, anyway."

"Do I look all right?"

"Theena, she's not the Queen of England. I'll be just over there, see that shady spot? Wake me up when you get finished. We'll go on home, and you can tell Hera all about the fancy cups and spoons."

Theena approached the prettiest house she'd ever seen. It was painted white and had gingerbread carvings on the eaves. So this is where Randolph lived with his mother. Where Theena would live, until he built them a house of their own.

Not that Randolph had proposed yet, but she was sure now that he would. He had been to see her nearly every day for the past three weeks. And each of those days, he took her riding on the beach, his hand pressed against her middle, her back pressed against his chest. They kissed until Theena thought she'd tear the shirt off his back to get closer to him. Then they'd cool off, holding hands and wading in the surf, until Randolph drew her into his arms again and turned her mind and body into a throbbing, aching mass.

Still Randolph held back. That he expected his bride to be virginal on their wedding night crossed Theena's mind, but she didn't dwell on it. She'd put that incident with Billy out of her mind. Didn't she learn something new about desire every time he took her down the beach? She *was* virginal.

Theena stepped onto Mrs. Chase's wide porch, wiped her hands on her skirt, and knocked. Quick footsteps tapped across the pine floor and Walter Simms' granddaughter came to the door.

"Susan!" Theena said. "What are you doing here?"

Susan opened the door with a finger to her lips. She winked at Theena and whispered, "I work for Mrs. Chase. You come on in and act like you don't know me. That's the way she'd like it."

"But of course I know you . . . ," Theena began. She and Susan used to share an orange crate for a seat when the itinerant preacher came around.

"Susan, is that Randolph's young friend?" a voice called from the next room.

Susan raised an eyebrow at Theena in collusion. "Yes, ma'am."

"Well, show her in."

Susan took her bonnet and said, officiously, "Right this way, Miss Theena."

Theena followed her to the front parlor where the rare scent of roses drifted from a bouquet in a crystal vase. Sheer white curtains billowed softly with a gentle breeze. A vagrant sunbeam gleamed on the polished furniture.

On a plum brocade sofa sat Mrs. Chase, her dainty feet squarely in front of her on the Turkish carpet. "Forgive my not getting up, my dear. It's the lumbago, I'm afraid."

Mrs. Chase held her hand out toward Theena. Was she to curtsy? Shake the hand? Or simply sit in the general direction of the gesture? Susan stood just behind Mrs. Chase and pantomimed a single handshake, and Theena gratefully followed the hint.

"Let me look at you, Miss Theophilus. My Randolph has told me so much about you."

Theena continued standing for her inspection, aware that her garments could not measure up to the fine linen frock Mrs. Chase wore. But she could do nothing about that, and in truth, now that she was here, she didn't really mind her dress. It was the best she had.

She inspected Mrs. Chase as thoroughly as her hostess did her. The older woman's thick blond hair was streaked with white and carefully arranged on top of her head. Her composure admitted not a hint of unease or doubt. Her blue dress showed nary a wrinkle, and her long white fingers rested in her lap.

"Why, you're a lovely girl, Athena. May I call you that? I know my son calls you Theena, or is it Theenie, but I believe your name is actually Athena, is it not? Do sit down, Athena.

"Susan, I believe you should be seeing to the tea?"

"Yes, ma'am." Behind Mrs. Chase's back, Susan smiled and put her thumb under her chin to wish Theena luck.

"I can certainly see your father's Greek ancestry in you. The dark hair, the rather olive skin. And yet I believe your sisters both have red hair? How fortunate for them."

She resisted the urge to touch the bun at the back of her neck. *Well, Randolph likes my hair*, Theena thought, remembering the feel of his fingers tangled in her tresses.

Mrs. Chase tilted her head, waiting.

"Yes, ma'am. My sister Dite has dark red hair, rather fiery, actually. Hera's is more of a strawberry blond."

"Dite? Is that short for another goddess? Let me think. Of course, Aphrodite. How quaint. And does your sister live up to her namesake's beauty?"

"I imagine she does," Theena said. "Most everyone declares her the prettiest girl they've ever seen."

"Hmm. And now you're all orphans. How very sad. I hear you weathered the hurricane all by yourself in a little shack on the river. You must have been terribly frightened. Of course you could have sheltered here, with Susan. We're on relatively high ground, and a ridge to our east redirected a bit of the wind."

Daddy's cabin had been much like the other settlers' houses, gray and weathered and no bigger than it had to be. Not a shack. A home. *Can a body be that insensitive, or does she make insulting comments on purpose?*

Theena decided right then that Mrs. Chase would never be a friend. She allowed her chin a little rise and waited for the next barb.

"You're a quiet girl, I see," Mrs. Chase said. "My Randolph is rather quiet himself, as I suppose you know." She patted her perfectly coifed hair and tilted her head to the side, her sideways gaze on Theena.

Theena endured her speculative look, feeling as if she were a piece of merchandise the grand lady had come across on the remnants table.

"Most often a quiet man looks for a woman with the social gift, someone who can help smooth the waters in society, whose charm can open doors for him."

Theena's heart sank deeper into her chest. Randolph had said nothing about social duties. Did he expect this of her? To pour tea with polished nails and a smug smile? She gave Mrs. Chase what she hoped was a confident response. "I'm sure charm is a great asset in a wife."

Susan entered with a china tea service on a tray. Mrs. Chase poured. "Do you take sugar, Athena?"

"Two lumps, please."

Mrs. Chase raised an eyebrow, but added the second lump without a word. So, Theena thought, another gaff. Who knew one should only ask for one lump of sugar? Her backbone strengthened at the pettiness of a woman counting sugar cubes.

Mrs. Chase passed Theena a delicate wide-mouthed cup so thin she could see the sunlight through the lip. She balanced the saucer carefully on her lap and sipped the most fragrant, full-bodied tea she'd ever drunk. Where did one come by tea like this?

"Randolph thinks the social graces don't matter down here in the wilds of Florida," Mrs. Chase said as she stirred her tea, "but I assure you, running a plantation is a business like any other. Buying and selling so often depends on personal relationships, and a wife who knows how to entertain her husband's contacts is essential."

When Mrs. Chase raised the cup to her lips, her smallest finger raised itself up like a flagpole.

Theena sipped her tea, eyeing Mrs. Chase over her cup. She let a little deviltry sneak out and raised her little finger. It felt absurd, but the subtle mockery felt like getting a little of her own back. She was tempted to declare herself an excellent hostess, a person who knew how to please men and put them in mind to do business with her husband, but she didn't imagine she'd be very convincing. She obviously was short on conversation here in this parlor.

"Were you in Key West with your son, Mrs. Chase?"

"During the hurricane? Oh, yes. We thought we'd be blown all the way to Texas, the wind was that hard. And when it was over, Randolph searched frantically to find an undamaged sailboat to come back to the Bay. The fruit trees, you see. He had to see what the storm had done to his fruit trees."

Theena's sunken heart rose back up to its rightful place. The woman's clumsy lie gave Theena power, for Randolph had already told her the truth. *Frantic to find a seaworthy boat, yes, but it was me he hurried home to, not his groves.*

"Well, I'm glad we've had this little chat," Mrs. Chase said. "Randolph will be spending more time in Key West as the groves become productive, of course, and you understand there will be many suitable girls whose attention he will attract. I don't like to be blunt, but I did want to spare your feelings, my dear."

Theena placed her cup back on the tray. "I understand you perfectly, Mrs. Chase. Thank you so much for the tea."

Mrs. Chase rang a little bell for Susan. "It was my pleasure to meet you," she said. "Susan, Miss Theophilus is leaving now."

The two women in Randolph's life nodded at each other, and Theena walked from the room with all the dignity she could muster. At the front door, Susan squeezed Theena's arm. "You did fine," she whispered. "The old sow is tough, but you didn't give her an inch. No chinks in your armor, Theena."

Theena shook her head. "I think there may be a few."

The little bell rang again. "Don't worry. True love conquers all," Susan said and hurried off to see to Mrs. Chase.

Theena's stomach was unsettled again as she walked down the oyster shell path and out of the yard. Did Randolph mean to teach her to be the fine lady? He'd have a job cut out for him. She wanted his arms around her right now, her nose buried under his chin, breathing in his scent. If this is what he wanted of her, she'd do her best to become a proper Mrs. Chase.

Jack lay propped against a toppled palm tree, his straw hat over his eyes and his arms crossed over his chest. Theena studied him for a moment. Everything about him seemed so right. She guessed a part of her would always admire him, but it was Randolph's kisses she wanted now.

Theena picked up a pebble and tossed it at Jack.

He caught it.

"Now how did you do that?" she demanded.

"Special order hat. Got eyes in the brim." He grinned at her. "How'd it go?"

"Wasn't much of a party. I'm not good enough for Randolph. My hair, my skin, my house – not good enough. Let's see, anything else? Oh yes, my name."

Jack fell into step beside her. "Well, you are plug ugly. What's wrong with your name?"

"It's quaint, I believe were her words."

"But no tears, no furrowed brow?"

"I wouldn't mind using a few of those words Mama would wash our mouths out for saying."

A little smile on his face, Jack said, "I won't tell on you."

Theena grinned wickedly. "Damnation." A flicker of memory, of the last time she'd said that word, flashed in her mind, but she pushed it away. That day didn't matter anymore. It never happened.

"Naw. That was lame," Jack said. "Try it again."

"Damnation! Hellfire!"

"That's more like it. Puts the old lady in her place."

They walked on for a spell, Theena thinking through the prospect of living with a mother-in-law who looked down on her. Finally she announced her resolve. "I'm not going to let her get to me. It's Randolph I'm going to marry, not his mother."

The next morning, Theena again rushed from the smell of bacon on the table to throw up over the back porch rail. "Must have been that tea yesterday." She wiped her mouth with the back of her hand. "The old witch probably put poison in it."

Hera tilted her head, a speculative look in her eye. "Did you and Randolph --?" She looked away. "Never mind."

Again the following morning, and then later that same day, Theena threw up. "I don't know what's the matter with me."

"Don't you?" Hera said.

"I guess I've got something. I'm nauseous half the time for the last week or so."

"And likely you will be for the next few weeks, too."

Theena groaned. "What do you think it is?"

"You really have no idea?" Hera's snide tone finally penetrated Theena's misery.

"What?" Theena said.

Hera shook her head in disgust. "You're pregnant."

"I can't be pregnant."

"Are your breasts swollen? Sore?"

Theena didn't answer her.

Hera narrowed her eyes. "They are, aren't they?"

Theena's eyes grew wide. She shook her head and put a hand to her mouth. "I can't be pregnant. It was only the one time." The slow horror, the awful injustice rolled through her. One time. She ran for the back rail and threw up what little was left in her stomach.

Hera's raised voice came out strident and harsh behind her. "So help me God, Theena, if that's Jack's baby, I'll throw you out. I'll see you rot in hell before I let you -- ."

Jack's steps shook the front porch. He stomped the dirt off before he opened the door. Before him stood Theena, white as the sand on the beach, and Hera, red and furious.

Poor Theena, no one in the world but Hera and him, until she married Chase anyway, and here Hera was at it again.

Fury twisted Hera's pretty face into an ugly mask. He'd never seen her as mean-looking as this.

Hera spat it out. "Theena's pregnant."

Theena's ashen face suddenly flushed red and she turned her face from him. How could she be pregnant? he thought stupidly. Chase had only been back a few weeks.

Hera marched up to Jack, hands on hips. "I want to know the truth, Jack Spode. Is this your baby?"

Jack looked at Hera as if she might be speaking to someone else. His baby? He was slow to understand, but when he realized Hera accused him of getting her little sister pregnant – at the same time he was getting Hera pregnant – anger flooded him like a rising tide.

His carefully contained voice might have been an arrow aimed at Hera's heart. "You have insulted your sister, and you have insulted me. I don't know if Theena's heart is big enough to forgive you where you stand, but mine isn't, not this time."

He put his hat back on his head and left the house. The quiet click of the door sounded like cannon fire.

For a moment, both women might have been statues. Then Hera's face seemed to fold in on itself, her mouth an ugly sobbing square.

"Go after him," Theena said.

Hera pushed the table aside and knocked a chair over on her way to the door. She ran across the porch and down the steps calling "Jack! Wait, Jack!"

Theena sank into a chair. She put her face in her hands and rocked back and forth. What was she to do?

Chapter Nine

Jack picked up his machete and hacked furiously at grass and weeds on the way to his grove. When Hera came running out of the house, crying and calling his name, he kept walking.

"Jack," Hera sobbed. "Wait."

He didn't even turn around. Like the other times she'd been in a jealous huff, she wanted him to tell her it was okay, that he forgave her. But he couldn't do that. Not this time. Not yet.

"Go back to the house, Hera," he said without waiting for her to catch up.

"Jack. Please."

"I don't want to talk to you. Go back to the house."

He heard her sobbing, heard her steps falter. Let her cry, dammit.

He raised the machete for a vicious swipe against the first broken branch in a row of orange trees. *Never been so insulted,* he fumed as he wielded the machete with the full force of his formidable strength. *Never. And with no cause at all. Haven't even touched her.* A rat darted past his feet and he hurled the machete at it, then kicked the decapitated carcass out of his way. *She's got nobody else, not yet, and that makes her my responsibility. A sister-in-law, soon enough. A sister, same thing.*

Jack slashed the broken branches off the trees and shoveled the rotting fruit into mounds. *And who the hell got her pregnant?*

Anger exhausted him far more than the two hours of hard labor. He walked down to the bay to plunge into the water and wash off all the sweat, to clear his head.

The path opened up onto the sandy beach and there was Theena, sitting on the broad bow of her skiff, watching the clouds gather over the bay. A school of mullet were pocking the water nearby, advertising their presence to the hungry pelicans.

Jack didn't know whether to join her or not after what Hera had said to them. And maybe he had over-reacted a little. Maybe there was just enough truth to Hera's suspicions that Jack felt a little guilty. He could admit that. Innocent of the deed, yes, but not of the desire.

I'm going to have my swim, he decided. *She'll be gone when I get out of the water.*

Theena turned around when she heard his steps in the sand. "I'm going in," he said and pulled off his boots. He splashed into the shallows until the water came up to his thighs, then dove in and traveled under water five or six yards before he surfaced for air. His long arms pulled him out with sure strokes until he was a quarter of a mile out in the bay.

He stopped and looked back to see if Theena was still there. The low sun was in his eyes, but he could see her silhouette on the skiff. She was going to wait him out then. Just as well. If she was going to be in his house, they had to find some ease between them, in spite of Hera's suspicions.

Jack dove and swam underwater till his lungs were near to bursting. He broke through with a splash and shook the water out of his eyes. With leisurely strokes, he swam back to shore.

In the shallows he waded through the gentle bay surf on to the beach. He stood dripping in front of Theena. She looked up at him, but the light was behind her and he couldn't read her face.

Theena scooted over and he sat down on the bow next to her. He left a good two feet between them. Uneasy in their silence together, they watched the sea gulls wheel and dive.

"I'm sorry about that, earlier," Theena said.

"Not your fault."

"They're not hiring at the inn, Jack, but tomorrow I'll go to Brickell's and put up another notice. I'll find something."

There wasn't anywhere else for Theena to go. All that was left at the homestead was the shed and they'd been through that. He wasn't going to let her live in a shed. "You're family, Theena. This is your home as long as you need it."

The evening off-shore breeze kicked up and Jack shivered in his wet trousers. He didn't move to go in, though. Finally he said, "Do you want to talk about it?"

She was quiet so long he thought she wasn't going to tell him anything. That was all right. She didn't owe him an explanation. None of his business. But maybe she needed him to have a word with the fellow, to help him see -- .

"I didn't know it could happen like that. I mean . . . I didn't know it only took one time to . . . I just didn't think . . . ."

If it was Randolph, Jack felt confident he'd do the right thing. But what if it wasn't Randolph? What if it were some no-account she'd met up with, some Cracker who took advantage of her after her daddy died. Theena might be grown, but she wasn't one to let her head tell her what to do.

"I need to talk to him? Make him see how it is?"

Theena shook her head. "No, Jack. It isn't like that."

Jack looked at her. "What do you mean, it isn't like that? Has he already said he'd marry you?"

He tried to see her face, but she kept her head down. "He can't."

Jack's hands on the edge of the boat tightened till they were white. He'd like to smash the man who'd done this. Probably had a houseful of kids, and a wife.

"Jack?" Theena said. "What am I going to do about Randolph?"

"It's not his."

"No."

Jack got up and paced the stretch of beach in front of the skiff. Would Chase want her and her carrying another man's child? It was a lot to ask of a man. Who knew if Chase had it in him?

"Theena, you'll have to tell him so he'll know what he's getting into."

Theena nodded.

"Does he love you?"

"I think so," she said.

"Well then." He looked at his feet and then up the path toward the house.

"You're chilled, aren't you?" Theena said. "We'd better go in." She stood up. "Maybe you should go first. I'll come along in a few minutes."

"No," Jack said. "We're not going to do that."

They headed up the path in the twilight. His hand brushed hers accidentally. Theena folded her arms across her chest, and Jack stepped further over to the side of the trail.

As they approached the porch, Jack stopped. Whether he felt like it or not, he needed to make peace with his wife. "Maybe you could give us a few minutes after all," he said.

"All right."

Jack found Hera sitting at the table. Supper was laid out, cold by now, and her face was puffy from crying.

He sat down and put his hands on the table, unfriendly closed hands.

"I'm sorry," Hera said.

He looked at her a long minute. "No more of this, understand?"

"Yes, Jack."

He barely heard her. She didn't seem to have any air in her lungs.

"It's you I'm going to marry, Hera, and it's you I'm going to make my life with. You and our children."

"Yes, Jack."

He looked at the cold field peas in their oily broth, the corn pone next to it, and his stomach clenched. He didn't see how he could eat tonight.

"Hera, I want you to welcome your sister in this house. We're all she's got."

"I will."

"She's outside, waiting for you to ask her in. Can you do that?"

"Yes." Hera stood up. "I really am sorry, Jack."

She hesitated next to his chair, and he took hold of her hand. "All right," he said.

Jack followed Hera to the door and watched as she walked across the yard in the last light. Under the banyan tree where Theena waited out of the wind, Hera opened her arms and wrapped them around her little sister.

Jack went inside and broke off a hunk of corn pone. Tomorrow, he'd catch a ship sailing down to Key West and sign on with Lindgren again for a few weeks. He needed a lot more cash to support Hera and their baby, and now, very likely, Theena and hers.

He tossed the corn pone on his plate. *God, what a mess.*

Chapter Ten

Theena took long walks on the beach tormenting herself with guilt and doubts. Randolph was due back from Fort Pierce. What was she to do?

Mama, with all her faults, had read the Bible to her girls every day, taught them to pray, taught them about sin and salvation. But some sins were worse than others, weren't they? Randolph assumed she was a virgin, and Theena had already decided it was not such a very bad sin to let him think so. She almost was, anyway, from one point of view.

But being pregnant. That was a secret sin of a different magnitude.

She had always been taken care of except for the few weeks leading up to the storm. Now she had no house, no one to help her with the baby. Was it right that she should be loveless and alone all her life?

Why couldn't Randolph be expected to love another man's child? Women did it all the time. They married widowers with half a dozen kids and raised them like they were their own. Why couldn't a man do that?

No. No use trying to pretend this situation was the same. Those women knew ahead of time whose children they'd be raising. Randolph did not know she was pregnant. What would he do if he knew?

And what if he knew the baby would not be full white? She hadn't told Jack that. It was worse than he realized.

She needed Randolph. She wanted him. *What am I going to do?*

Bertie splashed in and out of the shallows, then sniffed a dead jellyfish on the beach. Theena picked up a stick and threw it in the water for Bertie to retrieve. They played their game over and over as they wandered toward the mangrove thicket.

With Bertie's joyful splashing and barking, Theena didn't hear Randolph's horse until he was nearly on them. He rode in so fast and so close, Theena held up her hands and stepped back into the surf. With a fierce sort of grin, Randolph leapt from the mare, splashed into the water in his fine leather boots, and swept her into his arms.

"I missed you," he said. He caught her hair in his fingers and pulled her mouth to his.

His lips were hungry and demanding. His kisses plunged deeper. His hands signaled a new possessiveness, a taking. He palmed her breast, ran his thumb over her nipple.

God, Randolph. Theena couldn't breathe, her senses overwhelmed with his salty smell, his hands, his mouth. *Please.*

In one quick move, he lifted her from the water and carried her ashore. Behind the first row of dunes, he set her down among the sea oats. Theena raised her arms to him, and he lowered his length along hers and pressed her into the sand. She moved her knee to touch him, to show him she wanted him.

He pulled her wet skirt away, ran his hand up her thigh. "I'm going to marry you," he said.

She should tell him now. She should tell him. But he covered her mouth with his, opened her bodice, ran his tongue down her neck, and bared her breast. She was on fire, ready, eager.

When he entered her, she gasped his name. Her hips met his thrusts, the rhythm quickening, the urgency overwhelming until waves of joy rolled over and through her, answering his every shudder.

She pressed her face to his chest, her body still shaking.

"Did I hurt you?" he whispered.

She shook her head. "I love you."

He rolled his weight off her and kissed her tenderly. "Will you marry me, Theena Theophilus?"

Her voice came out with a hiccupping sob. "Yes." *Everything's going to be all right.*

He gently moved the hair out of her face and kissed her eyes.

"I forgot my book of sonnets," he said. "Do you mind?"

She laughed. "This was much better than poetry."

"I believe you only humor me when I read to you."

She kissed him lightly on the lips. "You are correct."

He goosed her, and she snuggled closer.

Theena heard a note of wariness in Randolph's voice. "Mother told me you had been to tea," he said over the top of her head.

"Your mother has the most wonderful tea. And the cups, I could see right through the cups."

"You don't have to pretend, Theena." He hugged her tighter. "I know she was god awful to you. She told me herself what she said to you."

"She's disappointed you're not marrying a society girl."

"She'd be disappointed in King Solomon's daughter."

"I can understand that. You're her only child, and I'm -- ."

"And you're wonderful. It won't take her long to see that, and then she'll love you, too." He ran his hand down her arm and took her fingers in his. "It'll be fine. I promise."

Randolph fastened his trousers and helped Theena shake the sand out of her hair. They walked back along the shore, Bertie and the horse trailing along behind, Theena's hand held firmly in his.

When Theena first realized Randolph did intend to marry her, she'd been weak with relief. She wouldn't have to bear the shame of waddling around Lemon City, big-bellied and man less. She wouldn't have to face life alone, struggling to take care of herself and a child. She wouldn't have fight poverty and loneliness and disgrace. But over the last few days, conscience had reasserted itself. Her deceit gnawed at her constantly.

I should just tell him. Jack is right. He deserves to know.

But what if she lost him? Theena couldn't rest, the argument in her head going round and round, morning and night.

When he comes tonight, I'll tell him.

Randolph rode over after supper and they strolled barefoot along the beach, arm and arm. "I've brought news," he said.

"What's that?"

"Miss Brickell has had a letter from Reverend Ragsdale. Said he's been laid up for weeks with an episode of gout, but he's better. And he'll be in Lemon City at the end of the month."

Randolph pulled her around in front of him and took her hands. He smiled down at her, his beautiful blue eyes full of love. Full of trust. "We can be married in ten days time, Theena."

"Randolph." She dropped his hands. He might despise her for a slut after this, might never touch her again. "Randolph, the day we ... the day we lay in the dunes."

She read his eyes. He had no idea what she was about to say.

"We can do it again anytime," he teased.

"Randolph, I lay with a boy once before."

His eyes lost their adoring gleam. He looked away from her, staring out over the bay. In a moment, he took a few steps into the shallows, his gaze fastened on the clouds low in the sky.

"Randolph?" *Oh God, please don't let him hate me.*

He crossed his arms and looked down at the water lapping over his bare feet.

Please, God.

Randolph glanced at her and, arms still crossed, turned his head from her and walked away. Theena yearned to follow him, to reach for him, to beg him to forgive her. She still had a remnant of pride, though, and acknowledged a man had a right to be disappointed when he found his beloved was not a virgin. She sat down in the sand, wrapped her arms around her knees and bent her head. Her chest tightened so that she could hardly breathe. Today, he would forgive her, or he would despise her. Her life would be wonderful, or miserable for evermore.

Randolph walked up the beach, unaware of sea smells, birds, glaring sun. Theena, his Theena, so sweet, so pure, had lain with another man. He could hardly grasp how wrong he'd been about her. She'd always been open, and friendly, but there was no flirtation in her, no forwardness. Her sisters flaunted their charms, but not Theena. Her loose dresses and buttoned up bodices, he'd thought, meant a girl who held herself apart from the open sexuality of the flirty girls in town.

She hadn't said how long ago she'd let herself fall. It must have been years ago, before he even came to Florida. Maybe she'd had a school girl crush. And her mother being gone, she'd not had the guidance she needed. He could swear she'd been faithful since he'd started calling on her. He couldn't imagine the Theena he knew being loose with her favors, being unfaithful to the man who courted her.

Theena hadn't had the advantages of the girls he'd known back in Philadelphia who had governesses or chaperones surrounding them from birth till marriage. How many of those proper young ladies would remain pure if they lived here on the edge of the Florida wilds where society's niceties were scarce? At least Theena hadn't pursued him in a relentless campaign to marry a wealthy man like several of the belles he'd known. It wasn't fair to expect her to meet the standard for chastity when she exceeded the standard for true character.

Randolph raised his head and pushed his fingers through his hair. He was going to have to accept this. He loved her. He would forgive her.

He smiled a little at himself. Hadn't he committed the same sin, worse actually? He'd been so wrapped in propriety, ever since he'd been caught nuzzling a kitchen maid and humiliated to the roots of his soul, that he'd become a man of lead. Afraid of his own fire, afraid to express the least tenderness to a woman. He hated that in himself, this steel encasement of his heart and his loins.

And so he had sought a woman in Key West, and found Viola Villiers. She knew men. In the first minutes of their acquaintance, she knew him. She took him to her bed, cracked the hated shield, and helped him reclaim his manhood. It hadn't been love, neither of them thought that. But his weeks with Viola had released him from his self-imposed frigidity, and he was a better man for it.

He'd made love to Theena, out here in the dunes, before he'd proposed to her. And like him, her buttoned- up persona hid a sensual response that gave him joy. It just didn't matter what she'd done before he knew her. They made each other happy. He turned back to her.

Theena closed her eyes, her face buried in her arms. Too frightened to think or hope, she waited in a limbo of dread. She didn't hear Randolph's footsteps in the sand. When he touched her hair, she looked into his smiling face. The sun broke through the gray haze of fear, lit his golden hair, and chased away the chill around her heart.

When he reached down a hand for her, she grabbed hold of it like it was a lifeline. He pulled her to his side and wrapped his arm around her shoulder. Still, he didn't look at her. He watched a lone pelican splash into the water and scoop up a mackerel before he spoke.

"I met a woman in Key West, Theena," he said. "After your father died." Randolph tightened his grip on her shoulder. "I was already in love with you, but I took her to bed. I don't want you to think it's something I'd done before, but I needed to --. Theena, I slept with her for all the weeks I was down there."

And she changed you, Theena thought. *You came home a different man, as if she'd opened you up.* "Randolph, I never --."

He put a finger on her lips. "After the hurricane, I left her. Not that she minded much. She already had her eye on the next conquest, I think. But, Theena, I'd be a hypocrite to condemn you when I've committed the same sin."

It's not the same, though. There's more. Theena clutched his shirt in her hands. She opened her mouth to tell him, all of it, but he didn't want to hear anymore. He kissed her, his mouth taking the words from her, silencing her confession until she no longer had the will to finish it.

In the end, she simply lacked the courage to tell him the rest. She wasn't brave enough to risk losing him. She would marry Randolph, have Billy's child, and pretend forever that it was Randolph's. Until her last breath, she would protect him from this secret.

To pass the nervous days until the preacher came, she washed and ironed every scrap of clothing in the cabin. She mended every sock, shirt, and skirt, then made a rag doll for Hera's unborn child, and then another. She didn't allow any time for thinking.

Sunday morning, gray clouds scudded across the sky. They'd have rain later in the day. Randolph drove a wagon to Lemon City to collect Theena, Hera and Jack. They rode on to the combination storage and meeting house where Reverend Ragsdale waited with the Bible on his knee.

Everybody for miles around came for the weddings, the memorial services, and the reverend's preaching. Afterwards, if the rain held off, they'd all picnic on the beach.

Reverend Ragsdale didn't cotton to the idea of marrying everybody in one fell swoop. Another couple, June Wilson and Harold Ickes, marched down the makeshift aisle first. Folks sat on salt barrels and citrus crates, and everyone together hummed the wedding music to the accompaniment of Mr. Simms' jaw harp. An interminable oration later, the reverend pronounced, "You may kiss the bride." June's mother cried, her daddy shook Harold's hand. They were married.

Hera and Jack stood up next. Only a few months ago, seeing Jack in front of the preacher with Hera at his side would have broken Theena's heart. But now, with Randolph beside her, she relinquished Jack to a happy life with her sister.

The preacher went on and on, covering most of the same speech he'd just delivered for June and Harold. Randolph squeezed Theena's hand and smiled into her eyes. He was so handsome, so happy. Gratitude and guilt, admiration and desire filled Theena's heart. She called it love.

"You may now kiss the bride," Reverend Ragsdale intoned. Jack bent down to Hera, blushing to kiss her in front of all his neighbors. Hera glowed with pride to be Mrs. Jack Spode. The two of them walked the aisle between the well-wishers and out into the salt air as man and wife.

"Come on up here, Randolph," the reverend called. "And bring that pretty gal with you. You the youngest of Stavros' girls, as I recall. Miss Athena Theophilus. Very well." He was about to proceed when he stopped. "Where is your lovely mother, Randolph?"

Randolph shifted his shoulders. He was unaccustomed to lying. "She is unfortunately indisposed this morning."

"Nothing serious, I hope?"

"She'll get over it," he said grimly. He wrapped Theena's arm through his. "We're ready, Mr. Ragsdale."

The third time through the ceremony, Rev. Ragsdale cut out some of the flowery passages, but he still managed to consume ten minutes of everyone's life expounding for the third time about the sanctity of holy matrimony. Theena tuned him out. Her mind was on the firmness of Randolph's grip as he held her hand, on the fact that they would sleep in the same bed tonight, that she wouldn't have to be alone ever again.

Everyone cheered when Randolph kissed her, then Mr. and Mrs. Chase walked through the congratulating congregation to join the other newlyweds outside.

A dark cloud hovered over head and the wind had picked up. "We're going back inside for the preaching," Harold Ickes said. "You folks coming?"

Jack and Randolph exchanged glances over their brides' heads. "No," Jack said. "You go on in, Harold. I think we'll try to beat the rain."

Randolph drove up to Jack and Hera's house just as the first drops began to fall. "Ya'll come on in," Hera said. "I'll make us a pot of coffee and put a chicken on to stew."

Theena kept her seat, her eyes on her lap. She didn't see how she could tolerate sipping coffee and waiting for the rain to let up, not when her whole life opened up before her, a new life as Mrs. Randolph Chase. Her husband spoke for both of them. "Thank you, Hera. But I have slickers for us. We'll drive home before the lane turns to mud."

Randolph urged the horse along. The clouds let go and every inch the slickers didn't cover was sodden. Theena didn't mind. She had her arm through Randolph's and admired his handling of the wagon in the muddy ruts.

Mid-way to the plantation, he pulled up under the protection of a live oak. She tilted her head, wondering why he stopped. He turned her shoulders toward him and wiped the rain water from Theena's face. "Mrs. Chase," he murmured. He put his hands on either side of her face and kissed her. Long and sweet and slow.

As if there were no rain in the world, the sun shone and the birds sang in Theena's soul. "Randolph, you take my breath away."

He held her hand to his chest. "I give you my every breath, Mrs. Chase." He kissed her again, rain and acorns falling through the oak leaves.

At the barn, Randolph left the wet horse to be tended by the stable boy. He swept Theena off her feet and ran with her through the rain. On the back porch, he kicked open the private outer door into his room and carried her across his threshold.

Theena's arms around his neck, he closed the door with his foot and crossed the floor toward his bed. Then he thought of the sopping rain slickers and how much better she would feel under his hands if he got all those wet things off her.

He stood her on her feet, the two of them dripping water in the middle of the floor.

He shed his slicker and pushed hers off her shoulders, eased it down her arms, then tossed it. His eyes on hers, he slowly untied her bonnet and let it drop. Theena loosened his silk cravat. He found her pins one by one and let her hair tumble loose. She slid the cravat from around his neck. Smiling, he reached for her top buttons. She worked at his. Unhurried, they shed their clothes layer by layer until there was nothing between them but warm air.

He looked at her, his glorious Greek goddess. She raised her arms to him and he lifted her so her legs came around his hips. All sense of patience and leisure evaporated in an urgent need to have, to possess. He crushed her lips to his and took her to his bed.

Rain darkened the windows. Thunder from over the bay rolled through the house. Theena knew only the fever in his hands, the heat rising in her belly, flooding her mind. His body pressing against hers, into hers. Pulsing, blind pleasure turned her into a creature of sensation and need.

Tension rose to an unbearable peak. Randolph thrust into her, fierce, quick, mindless. Theena soared, crested, and on a cry she was falling, her body gripped by rolling, consuming waves of surrender. Randolph swallowed her cries, his mouth devouring hers, at last yielding to the demand to pump, to push, to release.

Their breath easing, Randolph rolled her over with him and held her close.

"My goodness," she whispered.

"Indeed," he sighed.

Theena woke with her head cradled on Randolph's arm. A ray of sunshine found them on the bed, lighting the golden hair on Randolph's chest. She ran her fingers across his breast, then over a small scar under his left nipple. She'd have to ask him how he got it.

He stirred, murmured in her ear. "Do I get equal privileges?"

Lazily, this time, they explored each other's body, taking time to taste, to savor, to stroke and caress. Never had she felt so close to another human being. Never had she felt so cherished, so safe.

Spent and happy, she snuggled under her husband's arm. "I'm never leaving this bed."

Randolph kissed her nose. "I think I smell pork chops. And cinnamon apples."

Theena sniffed. "Well, for pork chops . . ."

"I thought so," he said. He grinned and flicked the light quilt off her. "I get one more look before we get dressed."

She felt only a little embarrassed at his study. "And I get equal privileges?" she said. He grew hard again under her gaze, and she reached for him.

Randolph groaned. "Later," he promised. "Mother will be waiting for us."

Theena slipped her shift over her head and picked her dress up off the floor.

"Wait." Randolph pulled his pants on and then laid a large box on the bed. "Open it."

She unfolded layers of gossamer tissue paper to reveal a dark blue taffeta gown. "Randolph!" She held it up in front of her, the fabric rustling, and then twirled around the room with it. "It's the most beautiful dress I've ever seen."

He helped her with the buttons up the back. She turned and held her arms out to be admired, her heart swelling at the smile on her husband's face. He reached for her, and joy bubbling through her chest, she brought his face down and kissed him. "Thank you, Randolph."

"There's more," he said, but he didn't let her go. He nibbled at the corner of her mouth. "Lots more."

"How? There's nothing like this in Miss Brickell's store."

"I bought them in Fort Pierce."

"You mean, before you even asked me to marry you?"

"Exactly." He pulled at her ear with his teeth.

"That sure of yourself, were you?" she said, poking him in the chest. Then she clasped his hand. "Randolph, your mother does know we're married?"

"Of course. Right now, she's no doubt counting how many minutes we're holding up our wedding supper." He stroked her cheek with the back of his fingers. "Supper can wait. Open your presents."

On the dresser were three more boxes. Inside the first, Theena found a silver brush and mirror. A set of tortoise shell combs for her hair nestled in the next box. And in the third and smallest box, a necklace of jet beads winked in the last light from the window.

As Randolph fastened the necklace around her throat, Theena said, "I didn't bring you anything."

He nuzzled her neck. "I'll let you make it up to me tonight." He turned her in his arms and kissed her. Finally he pulled back. "You'll have me back in the bed, and I'll miss my pork chops."

She let out a single guffaw and clapped her hand to her mouth. God, he loved that completely unlady-like laugh.

Grinning, he held an arm out and escorted her from his room, through the study and the parlor and then into the dining room where his mother sat regally at table, her rope of pearls glowing in the candle light. *Mother*, he thought. *Trouble in a pale green gown.*

Mother sipped her wine. "Good evening, Randolph, Miss Theophilus," she said.

He heard Theena's long intake of breath beside him and squeezed her hand.

"Mother, don't be rude, please." He pulled Theena's chair out for her. "Theena is now Mrs. Randolph Chase. Please welcome her into our home."

"Congratulations, Athena." With tilted head, his mother ran her eyes up and down Theena's length, appraising the beautiful taffeta gown. "You've made quite a match for yourself."

"Yes, ma'am. I have." His bride smiled sweetly, bestowing a smile his mother did not deserve. "And I remember what you said, about helping Randolph with his business associates. I hope you'll teach me what I need to know, Mother Chase."

As Randolph help Theena with her chair, he whispered in her ear. "Well, done, my dear."

Chapter Eleven

At the first call of the mockingbird, Theena woke to Randolph's hands wandering hands. He kissed her where her eyelashes curved against her cheek. "You have the thickest, darkest eyelashes I have ever seen."

Theena fluttered them at him and smiled.

"Do that again and we'll be late for breakfast." She batted her lashes furiously.

Thirty minutes later, both of them a bit red-faced, they were greeted in the dining room with a frown from Mother Chase, who rang the bell for Susan before they had taken their seats.

"The eggs will be rubbery now," she complained.

Theena saw Randolph flush as he unfolded his napkin. Poor Randolph, caught between his bride and an angry mother. "Oh," she said, "you shouldn't have waited for us, Mother Chase."

Mrs. Chase's mouth turned down. "Of course I waited for you. Randolph and I always sit down together for meals."

Susan came in with the coffee pot. "Eggs will be ready in just a minute. I cracked them in the pan when I heard you come in." Mrs. Chase sniffed, and Theena covered a smile with her napkin.

Once breakfast was on the table, Mrs. Chase asked, "What are your plans for today, Randolph?"

He put his fork down and turned to Theena. "How would you like to ride over the plantation today?"

"I'd love it."

He took her hand over the table and beamed at her, pleased. "Then that's what we'll do."

Theena warmed, her confidence soaring with her husband a happy man. *She'll see,* she thought. *I'm going to make her son happy, and she'll come around.*

After their last cup of coffee, Theena began to collect the plates to take into the kitchen.

"What are you doing, Athena?" Mrs. Chase said.

"Why, I'm clearing the table."

Mrs. Chase huffed a sigh. Theena looked from Mother Chase to Randolph, whose eyes were on his coffee cup.

"You are Mrs. Randolph Chase now," Mrs. Chase said with exaggerated patience. "You do not clear the table."

Theena felt the flush rising up her neck into her face. She'd embarrassed Randolph. She knew she would. She had no idea how a lady of means was supposed to act. She swallowed hard not to show how awful she felt.

"Nor do you make beds or wash linens. Those are jobs for the hired help."

"Yes, Mother Chase." Theena glanced at Randolph from under her eyelashes. Folding his napkin, his manner indicated this little matter was no concern of his. Well, at least he didn't scold her, too.

She returned to the bedroom to get her hat, her spirits drooping. Randolph followed her in and embraced her from behind.

"I'm sorry, Randolph."

"Forget it. You'll get it fast enough." He nuzzled her neck and felt her breasts through the thin calico dress. "We'd better get out of the house, or I'll spend the whole day in bed with you."

She turned her neck to give him a crooked smile. "And that would be terrible."

He kissed the end of her nose. "Some of us have work to do, Mrs. Chase."

And what kind of work am I to be allowed to do? Theena wondered. What did women like Mrs. Chase actually do all day?

"Now," Randolph said. "While I speak to the manager and see to our horses – ," Theena raised her eyebrows " – yes, you may ride your own horse today – ask Susan to come in and take your measurements. Be thinking about what you need, and after lunch we'll send an order to Key West."

She was to have a new dress! Except for the blue taffeta, Theena had never had a dress she or her mother hadn't made. Randolph exited the house through his private door onto the porch; Theena went to the kitchen in search of Susan.

Back in the bedroom, Theena stripped down to her shift for Susan to measure her with a tape. "I have no idea what to order," Theena said. "How many dresses can a girl use?"

Susan considered, smirking. "I think you should have at least as many as Mrs. Chase. Only fair."

"What does Mrs. Chase do with herself all day, Susan?"

"Well, she reads her magazines. A book sometimes. She does a little sewing, embroidery mostly. She writes letters. Let's see, what else? She makes me dust twice, do a perfectly clean stove top over again, hand-dry her china cups. Is that what you mean?"

How boring, Theena thought. She'd never be content sitting in the parlor all day. She wanted to be on the bay in her little skiff, feeling the breeze and the sun and the salt spray. But not now. First she had to learn to be a lady.

"You writing this down?" Susan said. "Waist, twenty-one inches."

In the spring when Theena had last made herself a dress, she'd been only twenty in the waist. Her belly still looked flat, but if she was already gaining weight, she would have to watch what she ate if she wanted to avoid showing as long as possible.

She put her hand on her belly. A wave of nausea swept up toward her throat. She hated deceiving Randolph. Hated it. But it was too late now. She swallowed the bile in her throat. She'd chosen her course.

"So," Susan said. "Mrs. Chase has seven every-day frocks, two dining gowns, and one fancy-dress gown. You'll need something to ride in, too. Ms. Brickell has one of those split skirts that let you ride astride. And you'll need a blouse or two to go with that."

"Nobody needs that many dresses," Theena protested.

"Susan Simms and Theena Theophilus don't need that many," Susan said. "But Mrs. Randolph Chase does. What about your small clothes? How many shifts and step-ins do you have?"

By the time Theena tied her bonnet on, Randolph had two horses saddled and ready at the back yard. The warm autumn sun burned off the morning mist as they ambled along the dirt trail through the orange groves. As with Jack's tiny stand of citrus, a lot of the fruit had blown off the trees, but Randolph's groves were further inland. He would still have a crop to sell this winter.

Men in kerchiefs and shortened pants touched a hand to their foreheads in salute to their boss. The workers, some of the older ones ex-slaves, had picked up the naval greeting from sailors who came ashore for a more settled life. Randolph nodded his head at the men and spoke to the ones he knew.

The plantation went on and on. Orange trees gave way to grapefruit and then to lemons. Theena's seat was sore long before they reached the far side of the groves. On the way back, Randolph took her past the vegetable gardens, the pig pens, the chicken coops, and a stand of cane. "Next year, I'll put up a sugar refinery. Nothing grand, just big enough for our own use. Nothing better than molasses on your biscuits at breakfast. Assuming we make it down to breakfast." He winked at Theena, and she nudged her horse close to his.

"Shameless," she whispered, happier than she had any right to be.

Theena and Randolph joined Mrs. Chase for a lunch of fried chicken, black-eyed peas, sliced tomatoes, and corn bread. For dessert, Susan brought in a bowl of peach preserves and a pitcher of cream. Theena's family, not keeping their own cows, had seldom had cream, and she eyed the pitcher greedily. Then she remembered her waistline and passed the creamer on to Randolph.

Mother Chase looked at her with a raised eyebrow. "Surely you are not watching your figure at your age?" she said.

"No, ma'am. I just don't care for cream."

She blushed at the lie. Randolph apparently didn't notice as he poured cream on his peaches, but Mrs. Chase continued to eye her.

After lunch, Randolph begged to be excused from ordering Theena's new wardrobe. "I need to see about the fencing and talk to the manager about the fertilizer shipment. Mother, you'll help Theena, won't you? Order a whole wardrobe, whatever you think she'll need." He kissed the top of Theena's head and left the ladies to their task.

Susan fetched the paper with Theena's measurements. Mrs. Chase copied them on to her stationery with an order for four frocks in cotton, two in linen, one in wool. A dozen drawers and three shifts. "You already have the taffeta for fancy wear," she reminded Theena.

Pointedly, Mrs. Chase looked at Theena's bare feet. She'd worn Hera's old too-tight shoes to go riding, but she'd shucked them off as soon as she was in the house.

"What size shoes do you wear, Athena?"

"I have no idea, Mother Chase. A six? Or a ten?"

"Those are dress sizes, Athena, not shoe sizes. No lady ever had feet that big." She pulled out another sheet of fine stationery from her desk drawer. "Susan, trace Mrs. Chase's feet, if you please. We'll let the cobbler worry about the size."

The order completed, Mrs. Chase decided to retire. Her back ached, and she needed a nap.

Theena wandered through the house, picking up a curio here, examining a bit of lace there. In Randolph's and her bedroom, she took stock of the furnishings. The big chair near the lamp showed wear, but the leather glowed a comfortable reddish brown. The bed cover was an ugly yellow. Her own favorite blue coverlet had blown away in the hurricane. This one reminded her of the droppings in the chicken yard. When she was in her confinement, she'd have nothing better to do than sit and sew. Then she'd make a new quilt. Mama had always said she sewed better than anybody else in the family, but that meant straight seams and simple darts and pleats, not fine embroidery like Mrs. Chase did.

She pushed the bedroom's outer door open to find Bertie lazing in the yard. Somewhere the dog had found a length of rope and was happily chewing on it. Theena grabbed the other end. "Come on, Bertie." Theena tugged, Bertie tugged back. In all-out war, Bertie growled and Theena laughed from deep in her belly.

"Come on, Bertie. Pull!"

Theena caught sight of her mother-in-law's disapproving face at the upstairs window. The laughter died in her throat, and she let the rope drop. *Good Jesus Christ, I've done it again.* She felt like she had when she was six and Daddy had gotten on to her for laughing in church.

Mother Chase disappeared from the window. Sick of herself, sick at heart, Theena paced down the road to the front entrance of the plantation, Bertie at her heels with the rope trailing.

She felt like a fool, playing with the dog like a child. Mrs. Chase had one more reason to think she was a rough country girl.

Then common sense snuck back in and bolstered her spirits. *Well, in fact, I am a rough country girl. And I'm the girl Randolph Chase chose.*

Bertie put her paws on Theena's waist and begged for a kiss. "You like me just fine, don't you Bertie?" Bertie licked her face and Theena scratched behind her ears.

Back at the house, the only sounds inside came from the kitchen where Susan toiled. Theena stepped in, just to lend a hand at whatever needed doing. Judging by the snoring coming from upstairs, Mother Chase was safely asleep.

Susan was rolling out a pie crust. Theena sat down at the table and started shelling pecans for the pie.

"How long have you been here, Susan?"

"A year ago last May."

Theena nodded. She herself might have looked for just such a job if Randolph had not wanted her. "You like it here?"

"It's all right. Once I got over being homesick. But it's not the same as cooking and cleaning for your own. Someday, though."

They got the pie in the oven. Theena looked around. "What next?" she said.

Susan smiled. "I'm going out to cut collards. But you, Mrs. Chase, better stay here. Your mother-in-law will expect to find you cool and clean and fresh when she gets up."

"You mean she expects to find me idle."

Susan gave her a cautionary look. Theena held her palm up. "Very well. I shall be a lady the rest of the afternoon. Lucky you, getting to go out in the sun and cut greens."

"Poor little mistress," Susan agreed. She tied her bonnet on and picked up a basket. "See you later."

In the parlor Theena found a few books and chose one to take back to the bedroom. She piled the pillows on the bed, got comfortable, and opened the leather-bound volume. "It was the best of times, it was the worst of times," she read. "It was the age of wisdom, it was the age of foolishness, it was the epoch of belief, it was the epoch of . . ." Theena's eyelids fluttered. She laid the book aside and closed her eyes.

Her prince wakened her with a kiss. "You're a vision lying there with your hair down, your lips as red as wine."

"I need another one of those wake-up kisses," Theena said sleepily.

"Only one?"

"Depends. How much time before supper?"

"Susan is ladling it up right now."

Theena's eyes flashed open. "I'll die of shame if we're late for dinner again." She put a hand to her hair.

"Then get hopping," Randolph said. He sat in the rocking chair to watch her put herself together. When she was tidied and straightened, he offered her his arm and walked her through the house.

As they entered the dining room, Theena caught Mrs. Chase checking to see whether her daughter-in-law had worn shoes to supper. She had. "Good evening, Mother Chase."

Is the old biddy never going to give up looking for faults? Maybe I'll give her a conniption fit. Eat with my fingers. Slurp my soup. Smack my lips.

When Susan served soup before the main course, Theena picked up the spoon laid crosswise above her plate, resolved to eat daintily.

"Athena," Mrs. Chase began, "I'm sure you won't mind my helping you with the niceties society expects, will you, my dear."

Theena looked up sharply. What had she done now?

"One always begins the meal with the utensil farthest to the left, farthest from the plate, you see."

Theena's daddy had always told his girls you catch more flies with honey than you do with vinegar -- to which Dite had always said, "Who wants to catch a bunch of flies?" Theena had every intention of using honey to win over this particular fly. Still, she couldn't help the sudden urge to stick her finger up her nose.

Bolstered with secret amusement, Theena replied with the docility suitable to the occasion. "I declare, I never saw so much silverware at one person's place. Now I understand, Mother Chase. Thank you."

She glanced at Randolph to see if he caught her insincerity. He nodded and smiled. Proud of her. Such a sensible girl, he seemed to signal, missing the bite behind her sweetness.

Maybe she and Randolph didn't know each other very well, after all. She realized she'd never shown him the side of her that could be sarcastic, even caustic. Billy and Hera, Jack too, had always thought her wry comments were funny, but maybe Randolph preferred her to be meek and mild instead.

Well, she thought. They had a life time ahead of them to work it out, once she had won Mother Chase over so there wasn't this constant tension in the air, this expectation that she was about to make a fool of herself.

A week of rainy weather confined Theena to the house. She embroidered in the parlor with her mother-in-law, but Mrs. Chase disdained her efforts. "Can you not make smaller stitches, Athena? Perhaps a finer needle?"

While Mrs. Chase took her afternoon nap, Theena slipped into the kitchen to sit with Susan, to shell peas or mix a cake. Mostly, though, Theena waited for Randolph's return to the house with her mound of pillows, a book, and a nap. After supper, he sometimes read to her and to his mother, usually poetry, and Theena fought to keep her eyes open.

Finally, a day broke with no rain clouds in the sky. After breakfast, Theena returned to the bedroom to change into her oldest dress. She was going fishing today. It was only a mile or so to the river, and the path was straight and broad. She'd bring home a string of fish for Susan to cook.

Randolph popped into the bedroom to get his hat before he headed out onto the plantation. "What are you doing? That old thing's your fishing hat, isn't it?"

Theena put her hand on top of the hat and twirled around for him. "It is indeed. The finest fishing hat on the river."

"Theena, we can't go fishing. I have work to do."

"That's fine. I'll meet you back here at dinner time."

Randolph shook his head. "Theena, you're not going to the river by yourself. And I don't have time to take you today."

"Randolph. I don't need you to take me. I've been fishing a hundred times on that river, all by myself. And I can swim, though if I fell in, I'd likely just wade ashore. But why would I fall off a bank?" She stood on her toes and gave him a loud sloppy kiss.

He didn't kiss her back.

"Really," she said. "I'll be fine." She tied the strings of her lucky straw hat and ignored the frown on his face. She did not intend to spend another day sleeping her life away.

"Theena. Be reasonable. You can't just go walking around the Florida wilds by yourself. There must be forty different kinds of snakes in these woods, gators, bears, cats. Leeches, have you thought about leeches?"

"You're sweet to worry about me, but I'll be fine." She wrapped her arms around his waist. "I grew up here, remember?"

He pulled her hands away from his back. "No. No," he said. "I can't allow it. It's unseemly, and risky, too. I want you here at the house, where you belong."

"But Randolph -- ."

"I insist."

His face was stern and unsmiling. Could he really command her to stay home? He was her husband, yes, but her father had never taken that tone with her mother, nor did Jack tell Hera what she could and couldn't do.

Randolph tucked her head under his chin. She allowed him to hold her, but she kept her body stiff. "I'm sorry you're lonesome while I'm out," Randolph said, "but I do have a business to run. Why don't you and Mother do something together? A puzzle, maybe. And after supper, I'll take you riding. How's that?"

Theena's feelings were a boiling confusion. Her jaw clamped so tight it ached, she seethed that he presumed to order her to do anything. She had a brain, a will, two arms and two legs.

But hadn't she sullied her soul so that Randolph would love her in this very way? So that he would protect her and take care of her? Randolph was her husband. He loved her. And her sin nullified any right to complain.

Theena loosened her body and leaned into his chest. In a small, dispirited voice, she said, "I'd love to go riding tonight."

"There's a good girl."

No, that was not her. She'd once been a good girl, but now she was a deceitful woman.

Randolph tilted her chin up and kissed her. "I'll see you later."

Theena sat down in the chair and rocked.

Chapter Twelve

It was time to tell him. They'd been married two months, and she was more than three months pregnant. She really didn't show yet, not really. If the baby were small, if she didn't deliver early, if Randolph simply didn't think to count the months – everything would be all right.

She turned out the lantern and climbed into bed. He held his arm up for her to snuggle in close. With her fingers curled in the pale hair on his chest, shielded from the tribulations of the world, she'd never felt so loved. Surely he would love her forever.

"Randolph."

"Hmm?"

She twisted around so her chin was on his chest and she could see his face in the moonlight."You're going to be a father."

He raised himself to his elbow and peered into her face. "Are you sure?"

"Uh huh."

He kissed her mouth, tenderly, lovingly. "That makes me very happy." He pulled her back against his chest and held her close. After a moment, he said, "I don't care if it's a boy or a girl, the first one. Do you?"

"No, Randolph. As long as you're happy." And she meant that with all her heart. He deserved to be happy.

If she thought her husband had been protective before, now he forbade her to stand on a chair to reach a box on top of the wardrobe. He wouldn't allow her on a horse. He wouldn't even let her stroll the lane too far from the house unless he or Percy, the stable boy, accompanied her.

"Women in your condition have to be careful," he said.

Theena rolled her eyes. She'd known women who plowed and hoed and bent and stretched right up until time to deliver the baby. She'd seen Mrs. Armstrong out on the bay, three fishing lines over the side, and her eight months pregnant.

Randolph cupped her chin in his hand, not amused. "I mean it, Theena. Promise me you won't go climbing on chairs or running around outside with Bertie."

With an exaggerated sigh, she conceded. "All right." She took his hand and kissed it. "I promise."

As her pregnancy progressed, Randolph's restrictions became less frustrating. She mostly wanted to sleep anyway. Eat and sleep.

Randolph ordered her a dozen novels when he discovered she had a taste for Dickens though she could only read fifteen minutes before her eyes closed. He complimented her when she put her hair up in a new way. He told her every day that he loved her, and he urged her to eat more, to rest – and to enjoy his mother's company.

When she couldn't keep her eyes open for Robert Browning, Randolph found her a book of bawdy, silly verse and challenged her to write her own. In the mornings, then, when she felt bright-eyed, she made up limericks.

"There once was a gator named Bucket," she began, counting syllables on her fingers. She had written a few that were suitable for reciting in front of Mrs. Chase in the evenings, but the ones that were the most fun to write were unfit for polite company. Those were the ones Randolph howled at, too.

As she continued her patient campaign to win her mother-in-law's acceptance, she saw Mother Chase's chronic back ache as an opportunity.

As she usually did after lunch, Mrs. Chase announced, "I'm going to retire for the afternoon."

"I'll be up in a few minutes, Mother Chase. I've made an ointment like the one my Mama used on Daddy's back."

"That isn't necessary."

Theena ignored the stiffness in her manner, the frost in her voice. "You'll sleep better after a back rub. I'll be right there."

Mother Chase was as prickly as a thistle at having her sanctuary invaded. Theena made allowance for her being unaccustomed to disrobing in front of anyone else, and unused to being touched. Patient as a saintly horse trainer, she handled her mother-in-law like a wild colt, coaxing and reassuring as she rubbed the ointment into Mother Chase's sore back, massaged the corset-weakened muscles, and kept up a steady stream of chatter.

"Mr. Brickell told Mama if she'd bottle up some of her ointments, he'd try to sell them, but nothing ever came of it." That had been just before Mama ran off. Theena was fairly certain Mrs. Chase knew nothing of that. And she was not going to tell her.

Even as Mrs. Chase sighed with relief at Theena's thumbs working the soreness from her spine, she continued her high-handed, insidious remarks. "People like you," she said as Theena's fingers probed for tight spots, "have strong hands. All that hard labor, but of course you're born to it." She stretched her own hand out to admire the aging but still graceful, slender fingers.

Determined never to lose her temper with the old shrew, nor to let the barbs pierce her hide, Theena smiled grimly over her mother-in-law's back. "You're right about that. I killed a bear cub with my own hands when I was barely six. I could crack a cocoanut when I was three." Mrs. Chase's back muscles tensed at the lie, but Theena merely dug in more deeply with her thumbs.

They didn't speak again until Theena wiped the ointment off her hands and helped Mrs. Chase fasten her clothing. Then the thanks offered was a mere, "That will do, Athena."

The massages became an afternoon routine, not that Mrs. Chase ever asked to have the knots in her back eased. "I'm fine. I just need to lie down," she'd say. Theena graciously offered the persuasion required, accepting the ill grace Mrs. Chase showed in accepting. *As if she's the one doing me a kindness*, Theena thought. But there were fewer evil looks over dinner now, fewer scowls when Randolph touched her in front of his mother.

Theena could not decide if Randolph was oblivious to his mother's lack of kindness, or if he simply thought his wife should be able to handle a few cranky comments. Certainly he found his mother interesting company. The two of them could chatter on about the plantation, the overseer, the news from Philadelphia for long spells before Randolph remembered to include her in the conversation.

The best part of Theena's day came in the evenings when Randolph would discreetly raise an eyebrow at her, and the two of them would say their goodnights to Mother Chase. Leaving the bedside lantern lit, Randolph would unbutton her slowly, teasing her, tracing fingers over her breasts until she shoved him on the bed, dug her teeth into his neck, and made him laugh. After they made love, they cuddled in the soft bed and talked about the house they'd build someday, how they would have running water piped directly into the house, how many bedrooms they'd need for the children.

"I'm going to keep you pregnant all the time," he told her.

"And bare foot, too?"

"You don't fool me. You'd rather be bare foot anyway."

Theena spent hours imagining the baby. She even indulged herself in the fantasy that the baby might have blond hair and blue eyes like his father, like Randolph. The fantasy never lasted though.

Fear. It all came down to fear. She'd always thought she was more courageous than her sisters, than the other girls along the river. She didn't shudder at the mice and ever-present roaches that found their way into the house; she didn't panic when a small rain squall caught her and Daddy in their boat on the bay; she hardly flinched when Dite had to dig a splinter from her foot or stitch a gash.

But this sin, this pretending another man's child was her husband's – it grew out of a loneliness so deep she had feared she'd forget who she was. *I'm not brave at all. I'm selfish, and I'm a coward.*

She tried to push her offense away, to recapture the happiness Randolph offered her. But the weight of shame and conscience bore down on her.

Randolph's Bible, leather bound, a little mildewed, lay on a shelf of his wardrobe. Theena took to reading it after lunch when she retired to the bedroom. She avoided those early pages in which God frightened his people, threatening them with fire and brimstone for their mistakes. She turned to The Psalms. God loved the sinners in the world, too.

Dear God, I'll never tell another lie, she promised.

Once Theena's belly began to show, she caught Mother Chase's suspicious glances. She had only the one son now, but Mrs. Chase had lost two girls to diphtheria years ago and another baby boy had died soon after birth. Four babies of her own. Theena figured she would know a thing or two about what pregnancy does to a woman's body, and when.

Still, she's only guessing, Theena told herself. *She can't know, not really*. But Theena continued to resist the temptations of the table, passing the cream pitcher along without indulging herself.

The seamstress in Key West had constructed Theena's new wardrobe with the slenderest of seam allowances to let out, so Theena soon needed cloth for her confinement wardrobe.

"Order whatever you like," Randolph said.

"I want to make them myself, Randolph. I have little enough to do. Will you take me to Brickell's?

"All right. Saturday."

Theena hadn't left the grounds since her wedding night. Hadn't been to the store, seen the bay, visited with Hera. She counted the days till their excursion.

Saturday morning, Theena buttoned up a too-tight linen dress from the Key West tailors and fixed her hair with eager fingers. After a quick breakfast, she mustered up enough charity to sound sincere. "Mother Chase, you're sure you won't come? We'd hate for you to stay home alone."

Her chin tilted up as if Theena had insulted her. "I'm perfectly capable of staying home alone." Her voice changed to a sickly sweet tone. "Randolph, dearest, do excuse me. My back, you know. I'll be quite content right here with my needlework and a cup of tea."

"All right, Mother." Randolph stooped to give her a quick kiss. Over the top of her head, he winked at Theena. "We'll be home by dark or a little after."

Winter in south Florida was cooler than July and August, but not by much. Theena tossed a shawl in her day-bag for the drive home in the evening, and she was ready. She settled herself on the padded seat, Randolph climbed in beside her, and they drove off down the rutted, canopied road.

The shady lane to Lemon City was dry and easy traveling. No gators sunning in the road to spook the horses this time of year; they'd retreated back to the wetter swamps. No brigands daring to molest a man who had a rifle and a pistol to hand, even if one should find it to his profit to loiter on such a seldom-used road.

Wild honeysuckle tantalized the air, hints of ocean spiced the morning breeze, and birdsong filled the sky. The crispness of the morning, having Randolph to herself, seeing Hera – it was going to be a wonderful day. But she had to admit a measure of anxiety underlay her heightened spirits. She hadn't outright said to Jack or Hera that she'd told Randolph everything, but she feared Jack would guess that she hadn't. He might take one look at her guilty face and know she deceived her husband. She dreaded seeing disappointment in his eyes.

But Jack was no mind reader, she reminded herself and took an easier breath. And it really was none of Jack Spode's business. Everything was going to be just fine between her and Randolph.

Randolph drove them in and around the dozen or so buildings of Lemon City, out the eastern end, and on to the Spode place. Theena hallooed at first sight of the house. Randolph put a hand on her knee to keep her in her seat until he'd stopped the buckboard.

Hera appeared on the front porch. "That you, Theena?" She wiped her hands on her apron and lumbered down the steps. She looked every bit of eight months' pregnant as she hurried across the yard in a rolling gait.

The sisters grabbed hold of each other and then pulled away to take stock of the other's girth. "I swear, Theena, you don't hardly look pregnant at all." She realized her mistake immediately. She wasn't supposed to know Theena was pregnant yet. She looked over at Randolph, who was talking to his mule. He hadn't heard.

Theena hugged Hera's enlarged girth. "You feeling good?"

"Hello, Randolph," Hera called. "Nice to see you." She took Theena's arm and turned her back to the house. "I never been so miserable in my life," she told her sister. "I can't hardly get around anymore."

"Half an hour, Theena. Then we better be on," Randolph called after her.

"Nonsense," Hera said. She turned back to Randolph. "You'll stay to dinner." Randolph began to speak, but Hera held up her hand. "I insist."

"Please, Randolph. I'll be as quick as ever I can be at the store. I promise."

Randolph yielded with good humor. He'd anticipated this and padded the time they'd need to get their stores and ride home again. Theena, he figured, knew it. He'd have to quit babying her, he told himself. She was going to be a mother in a few months. And she was even sharper than he'd given her credit for.

He grinned to himself as he gave his mule a bucket of water. Some of those limericks she came up with. He shook his head. Who'd think his sweet little Theena had such a bawdy streak?

She just had to learn to take better care of herself, to accept her role in life as a plantation mistress. Her days of wandering up and down the river with bare feet and a sun-browned face were over.

He left the mule under a live oak. As he entered the house, Theena was saying, “How long till Jack comes back?”

“Jack's gone? Where's he off to, then?”

Hera patted her belly. “He'll be back any day.” She looked to Randolph. “Jack's down in the Keys. Sponging again, because of the grove. Wait'll you see it. He's been gone so much, the brown rot got into it, and there wasn't enough crop to pick.”

Randolph put his hat back on his head. “I'll have a look at it.” He left the sisters to their talk and went out the back.

Hera watched the door till Randolph was well away. “Does he know?”

Theena shook her head.

“You're not going to tell him? What if the baby looks like. . . the father?” Hera looked hard at her sister. “It's Billy's baby, isn't it? Has to be.”

Theena avoided Hera's eyes. “Randolph will love the baby.” The fingers at her mouth trembled. “He wants this baby.”

Hera sat back in her chair. “I'm just saying you have to think ahead. It is Billy's, isn't it? What if the baby looks like Billy? Randolph is blond.”

“But I'm not. It'll be all right. You'll see.”

“Wishful thinking.”

The forced cheer drained from Theena's face. “It's too late. I can't tell him now.”

The clock on the mantel ticked on. Here at Hera's table, Theena could not pretend all would be well. It might be that nothing would ever be well again after the baby was born.

Hera stood up and walked over to the mantel to fetch an envelope. “A letter from Dite came last week. I'm going out to kill a chicken for dinner.”

Theena opened the heavy paper and read Dite's scrawling script. *My mind is at ease to hear you've married Randolph Chase,* she wrote. *He'll take care of you, just like Daddy wanted.* She described the wonderful cool weather in Philadelphia, the colors of the fall leaves, the museums and theaters and libraries, the absence of stinging insects. *By the way,* she said, *I'm no longer with Mr. St. Claire. He has married a chit of a girl with no breasts, but a large fortune. He was perfectly willing to keep me on for his children, and for his own amusement, but I've found another opportunity. Alex Bronson has hired me to be his mother's companion. He's very wealthy if a bit old, but he's not shy about his admiration. We'll see. Hera, have you arranged for Mrs. Collins to midwife you? She's supposed to be better than Sara Mills.*

Not a sign of homesickness in her letter, no mention of heartache or disappointment.

Hera came back in with a plucked chicken. "Sis seems cheerful enough, doesn't she? I can't see she was much attached to Mr. St. Claire or his children. But then, Dite ever was a cold fish."

Randolph stomped the sand off his boots. "You've got a mess out there. Fruit's already got the white coat, the rotten odor. Even where the fungus hasn't gone so far, the leathery brown spots on the peel make them unmarketable."

"That's what Jack said. He'd been hoping for a small crop this year." Hera poured Randolph a cup of coffee and made room for him at the table.

"Tell you what. I'll send a couple of men over to do what they can. Won't save this year's crop, but they can improve the health of the grove with pruning and cleaning up."

Hera wrapped her arms over her belly. "You'd do that for us?"

"We're family now." He reached across the table for Theena's hand and smiled at her.

Theena clasped his hand as if she just held on tight enough, she could keep him this happy always.

.

Chapter Thirteen

Jack had been home three weeks when Mrs. Collins banished him to the porch. He paced out in the yard for a while, sat on the porch and whittled for a while, then paced for another while. Every time he heard Hera groan, he thought his heart would stop. When she screamed, he had all he could do not to run off into the grove.

He was standing on the porch, kneading his fist, when he heard his baby cry. He drew in a huge breath and rubbed his hand over his mouth. He took two steps toward the door and thought he couldn't go in there yet. He was about to bawl. He leaned his forehead against the post and closed his eyes. *Breathe, just breathe.*

With his lungs working again, he poked his head in the door. "Can I come in?"

"Jack!" Hera said, her face pale, but smiling. She held her hand out for him and all the tension drained out of his body.

"You've got yourself a baby girl," Mrs. Collins announced from the pine table where she had a bundle of blankets, as far as Jack could see.

He knelt beside the bed and took hold of Hera's hand. "How you doing? You all right?"

Hera touched his face. "Now it's over with, I'm all right. Next one, you have."

He laughed, but the idea of carrying a watermelon in his belly all those months was more than he could contemplate with any real humor.

Mrs. Collins reached around him and placed a snugly wrapped baby in Hera's arms. Hera peeled back the blanket enough to see her face. Jack leaned over. Red downy hair covered his baby's head. Her blue eyes were wide open and he could swear she looked right at him. *This is the best day of my life.* He swallowed hard and touched the pink cheek. *The best day.*

"I'm sorry you didn't get your Jack Junior," Hera said. "But from the smile on your face, I don't think you mind."

"I don't mind. Does she have to be wrapped up like that?"

Hera scooted herself up to lay her baby across her legs. Carefully, she unwrapped the blanket to show a perfect child, two arms, two legs, ten toes, ten fingers.

"She's beautiful," he said.

"Jack Spode, are you going to cry?"

He laughed. "I might. Give me a minute."

Hera squeezed his hand. "Priscilla. After your mother. All right?"

All Jack could manage was to nod his head and grin like a fool.

That night, when his baby girl cried, Hera stirred. "No, don't get up." He padded barefoot across the floor to the drawer that served as a crib and gently, oh so gently, slipped his big hands under Priscilla's little body.

Hera said, "You can do that tomorrow night, too."

He knew she was teasing. No man he knew of got up in the middle of the night with his babies. But he was going to. "It will be my pleasure."

He got up three times that night, four the next and the next. The interrupted sleep left him a little bleary-eyed during the day, but he didn't mind. After Priscilla had nursed, he rocked her and crooned to her, long after she'd gone to sleep. He didn't want to unwrap those tiny fingers from his.

On a fine day in April, Hera declared herself strong enough to walk to Theena's. She wanted to show off her baby, and Jack had been waiting for the opportunity to thank Randolph Chase. When he'd returned from sponging, he had enough cash to last them through the year, but he'd been anxious and deflated about his hopes to become a planter. And there, on his return, was his grove, pruned, swept clean, and on the way to recovery. He owed his brother-in-law a great debt, one which he knew he was meant to repay with only his thanks.

Jack chose a hen to carry in a bag over his shoulder. Hera bundled Priscilla in a soft blanket she'd knitted herself and strapped the baby across her chest with a shawl. They hadn't walked ten minutes on their way to the Chase homestead when Jack suggested Priscilla was surely too heavy for Hera to carry such a long way.

Hera smiled. "I swear, you're like a boy with a new puppy." He walked the rest of the way with his daughter cradled in his arms.

Jack spotted Theena on the front lawn with her pup. He hallooed and she met them with her arms out for the baby before she even said hello.

"Oh, look at her. She's beautiful!" Theena's sincere gushing praise confirmed what he already thought.

He admired how pregnancy rounded out Theena's face. *She looks happy.* He'd worried about that, those long hours on the sponging boat. He didn't know Chase well, didn't know if he'd be good to her. But she looked like everything was fine.

"Hello to you, too," Jack said.

Theena laughed. "Sorry. Hello, Jack. Hello, Hera. How are you?"

Hera dipped a deep curtsy to gibe at her. "Very well, thank you, Mrs. Chase."

"That's Priscilla you've got there," Jack said. "Priscilla Hera Spode."

Theena stroked Priscilla's cheek, and she promptly opened her mouth and turned her head toward the finger. "Is she hungry?"

"First thing you learn about babies," Hera said. "They're always hungry."

Reluctantly she handed her niece back to Hera. "Come on in."

She led them into the parlor where Mrs. Chase sat with her embroidery. She looked at them over her glasses, the half lenses winking in the light. "Who's this, Athena?"

"Mother Chase, this is my sister Hera and her husband, Jack Spode. They've come calling with their Priscilla."

Hera sat down next to Mrs. Chase on the settee to show off her baby. Mrs. Chase thawed as if a warm wind had blown in.

"What a beautiful child. Priscilla, is it?"

"Yes, ma'am. Would you like to hold her?"

Theena marveled to see the old woman's face crinkle into a smile as she took Priscilla into the crook of her arm. "Are you the sweetest baby?" she crooned. Theena's eyebrows rose as far as they could in astonishment. This was a woman she'd never seen.

"What lovely golden hair. Reddish like yours, Mrs. Spode. And fair skin. So much like Randolph's coloring when he was a baby."

Theena's breath stilled. She put a protective hand on her belly, and caught Jack looking at her. *He knows. He knows I didn't tell Randolph.* She lowered her gaze and turned her head. *Jack sees me for what I am, now. A liar.* She felt as if a hot rock lodged under her breast bone.

"Oh, Mr. Spode, excuse my manners. Sit down, please."

Jack lowered himself into a lady's brown horsehair chair, his knees rising above his hips. Theena thought to direct him to the larger chair Randolph preferred, but she couldn't bring herself to look at him. Not yet.

Mrs. Chase admired Priscilla and reminisced about each of her babies. By the time Susan wheeled in the serving cart, Priscilla squirmed and fretted. Hera raised an eyebrow at Theena.

She took Hera into her bedroom and moved a book off the rocking chair for her to nurse the baby. Alone with her sister for a few minutes' talk about babies settled Theena. Nothing had changed. Not really. She'd be able to face Jack now.

In the parlor, Jack listened to Mrs. Chase's excruciatingly proper chat, his expression one that at first glance might indicate his conversant fascinated him. Theena caught the rigidity of his smile, though, and took pity on him.

"Randolph's likely out to the barn just now," she said. "Or if Percy says he's on the land, he'll saddle you a horse and take you out to him."

Jack picked up his hat immediately.

"Unless you'd rather sit with Mother Chase and me and have tea?" She quirked a smile at him.

Jack kept his face impassive, as she knew he would. He dipped his head to the senior hostess. "I hope you'll excuse me, Mrs. Chase. Business prevents my enjoying your company at the moment."

With his back to Mrs. Chase on the way out of the room, he cocked an eyebrow at Theena in gratitude.

The men came in for noon dinner after riding over the plantation, discussing the merits of lemons, oranges, and grapefruit. Both of them were a little dusty, but presentable. Mrs. Chase, Theena thought, but would be pleased to have two fine looking men at her table.

Over fried ham and turnip greens, pineapple and sweet tea, Mrs. Chase enquired about the sponging business. "The newspaper from Key West describes a thriving industry," she said. "But is it not very dangerous?"

"Not so dangerous, if you keep your head when you're under water. Mostly, though, we use long hooks instead of diving. The hardship comes from being away from home for weeks at a time, till the ship's got its hold filled. That and the smell."

"Yes, I've been to the sponge docks in Key West," Randolph said. "I wonder you can stand it."

"Well, you have to breathe. You just get used to it. But I admit I stopped at the bay and scrubbed up with sand before I presented myself at the house."

"And I thank you for that," Hera said.

After dinner, Mother Chase retired for her nap. Hera returned to the bedroom to nurse Priscilla. Randolph excused himself to confer with his manager for a few minutes. That left Theena to entertain Jack.

"Let's walk," she said. "I'm not to go even as far as the gate without an escort, and I'd love to get out."

"You? A cracker girl like you needs an escort?"

"It seems my cracker days are over." With a shake of her head, as if she imparted terribly sad news, she said, "I'm in training to become a lady like Mrs. Chase."

"And how's that coming along?"

She looked up into his face, not surprised to see a glint of fun in his eye. He knew she was no shy, proper lady. "Just about like you'd think." She did a mean imitation of Mrs. Chase's snooty manner. "I have learned, however, that when at table, one does not stick peas up one's nose."

He snickered, and they strolled on down the lane, Theena in the expectant mother's smock loosely covering her figure, Jack in his best trousers and starched white shirt. Theena appreciated his shortening his stride to accommodate her big-bellied pace. When they reached the white-washed gate, she leaned her elbows against the rails and looked down the rutted lane toward the river. Jack crossed his arms and looked back at the house. "A pretty place," he said.

"Randolph says he'll build us our own house in a few years, when the groves start making money."

He looked down at Theena's belly, at her rounded face. "You look good," he said quietly.

She held his eyes, trying to read his face. Did he despise her for her deceit? *I can't bear it if he despises me. I love him too much* --. She stopped herself mid-thought. She was past her school girl crush on Jack Spode. She admired Jack. She liked Jack a great deal. She loved Randolph.

She dropped her gaze, confused. Ashamed.

They walked toward the house, the three feet of space between them an impassable chasm. Theena's steps felt too heavy to cover the hundred yards to the porch, her heart thudding with the realization that nothing had changed. She loved Randolph, she desired Randolph, yet still she wanted Jack Spode. Every fear she'd had that she might have somehow inherited her mother's traitorous nature reared up and chewed at her heart. She clamped her jaw tight. She was her father's child, too. Even if she had a perfidious heart, she would never betray Randolph. *Though haven't you already, you with your secret?* She wiped a hand over her brow, suddenly tired beyond bearing at the bite of that sharp sneering voice of conscience

The party gathered in the parlor again. Mrs. Chase handed Hera coffee in a bone china cup. "Such an exciting time in a woman's life. I wish I'd been in church for your wedding. It must have been early last spring, when my lumbago was too bad for me to drive into town."

The room was very quiet for a moment. Then Hera put her china cup in its saucer and looked directly at Mrs. Chase. "Actually, Jack and I married in October, the same day as Randolph and Theena."

"Is that right?" Mrs. Chase's demeanor betrayed hardly a hint she could count the months since then, or would even think to. "How very nice, sisters getting married together. I'm sure your poor mother would have loved to be with you on your special day."

Theena's hands fisted. She'd told the old woman months ago that Hera and Jack married the same day as she and Randolph. And Mrs. Chase never forgot a thing. She'd figured it out during her little naptime. She had been so friendly, so kind, and now she'd reverted to type: rude, spiteful, purely mean.

Hera, however, did not rise to the insult. Theena admired how she held her chin high and answered the obvious barb with civility.

"Yes, ma'am," she said. "Mama, and Daddy, surely would have been there if they could."

Mrs. Chase seemed not to see the hard look Randolph gave her and serenely poured a cup of coffee.

"Jack," Randolph said, "Percy will bring the wagon round. No need for Hera to walk all that way back."

"I'm sure she'll . . ." He looked at Hera's pale, tight-lipped face. "Are you done in?" he asked her.

"I am, Jack. I'm sorry."

"No need to be sorry," Randolph said. "Percy is through for the day, and I think he's got his eye on a girl in Lemon City. He'd love to drive into town."

Theena hugged her sister. "I'm sorry about the old bat," she whispered.

Hera shook her head. "Don't be. It's nothing." She handed Priscilla to Theena and let Jack help her into the wagon.

Jack shook Randolph's hand. "I thank you again for what you did with my grove."

"Glad to do it."

Theena handed Priscilla up to Hera and stepped back from the wagon wheels. Randolph draped an arm over her shoulder and she leaned into him.

Jack gathered the reins. For an instant, his glance flicked over her and her heart went still. Then he touched his hat in farewell and twitched the reins for the mule to move out.

The last weeks of Theena's confinement, her ankles swelled and she felt restless and huge and lumbering. In day after day of fine perfect weather, she'd sit on the porch, praying for the baby to hold off another day.

Theena sat embroidering at the window in the early morning sunlight when she suddenly doubled over with pain. Mrs. Chase observed her coolly. When Theena straightened up again, white faced, her mother-in-law said, "Should you like some water, Athena? It's only false labor, you know. It's far too soon for you to have the baby, however large you've become."

Theena ignored the insinuating tone. Plenty of babies were born earlier than nine months. She wouldn't satisfy the old woman with an answer. Mother Chase surely knew the truth anyway. It'd been obvious by March that she was far along in her pregnancy.

Randolph didn't seem to notice, but Mother Chase's narrowed eyes had taken her measure often enough.

But so what? If Randolph and she had made love before the wedding, it was a common lapse. It was none of her mother-in-law's business. She was married to Randolph, not Lavonia Chase.

Theena calculated she had lain with Billy four weeks and three days before Randolph made love to her on the beach. Not so very many weeks for a baby to be considered early. Plausible. Theena refused to think any further than that, refused to worry now about what the baby would look like.

Randolph had thought little about Theena's pregnancy. He enjoyed sliding his hand across her belly when the baby kicked out with a foot or an elbow, but otherwise, there wasn't much to see. He thought there were weeks yet to take care of . . . whatever she'd want him to take care of. So he was unprepared when he came in for noon dinner and found Theena on the bed, mid-contraction, panting with wide, scared eyes.

He grabbed her hand. "Good God, Theena. You're in labor? Why didn't you send for me?" He left her to go to the side porch and holler for Percy. "Go get Mrs. Collins. And hurry!"

Randolph stayed with Theena, wiping her forehead, holding her hand. When Mrs. Collins arrived two hours later, she bustled him out of the room.

Adrift, feeling useless, Randolph wandered into the parlor. His mother sat by the window attending to her endless embroidery.

He leaned against the doorway for a moment, watching her. "Why didn't you send for Mrs. Collins?"

She tied a knot and broke the thread with her teeth. "It's likely to be false labor, Randolph. Athena is nowhere near her due date, even if I count from the very day of the wedding." She began to rethread her needle. "I would expect her to carry several more weeks."

"Even I know babies can come early," Randolph snapped. *Her and her damn counting. Even to insulting guests in our home.*

"Of course. First babies, however, are more often rather late."

His mother's imperturbable air infuriated him, but he was not in the habit of yelling at his mother. He took himself to the porch to pace and smoke and brood.

Theena labored ten hours to deliver her child. In the early twilight, even in the parlor, Randolph could hear Theena's groans, could feel her pain. He kept his fists so tight his wrists began to ache.

"Do sit down, Randolph," his mother said. "Theena is from strong peasant stock. She'll have no trouble delivering a baby."

He was too distracted to address yet one more insult to his wife. He paced to the window to stare into the darkness, then moved to the next window. Theena was in there, in pain. And he helpless to do anything for her.

When he heard the midwife's spank and the newborn's cry, tears flooded his eyes. He knocked at the door, impatient to hold his child, to see Theena.

Mrs. Collins let him in. "It's a boy! A fine healthy boy."

Theena's eyes were dark wells, the skin around them bruised and sunken. His heart pinched in fear as he knelt at the bedside and reached for her.

"I'm all right, Randolph," she said, an exhausted smile on her face. He thought he would weep in relief.

Mrs. Collins handed Theena her bundled babe and Randolph sat on the edge of the bed to get a look at his son. The baby gazed at them from alert blue-gray eyes. His hair was a thick black thatch, and his fingernails needed trimming on this first day of his life. He was a fine, healthy boy. A big boy.

"Even with his little face red and scrunched up, he looks like his mama," Mrs. Collins said.

Randolph beamed at his son. "He surely does. Look at that hair," he said.

Theena turned her face to him. Her eyes, already brighter in just these few minutes, reassured him she was going to be fine.

"Randolph, Junior?" she said.

"Nathanial Randolph, for my father."

"Nathanial, then."

Mrs. Collins touched Randolph on the shoulder. "Mr. Chase, sir, if you wouldn't mind."

He kissed his wife and son, his hand lingering on the baby's head. All the tension of the last hours drained from him. He felt as if a light glowed inside him, Theena safe, a fine son for them to raise together.

"I'll check in later," he said and returned to the parlor.

"Well?" his mother said.

"It's a boy." Randolph ran a hand through his sandy hair, a grin on his face. "A boy, Mother."

She nodded once. "Nathanial, of course."

"Yes. Nathanial Randolph Chase."

Randolph wandered out to the yard, to gaze at the night sky, to count the blessings God had sent him. His heart was full, and he could have sung full throated to the moon.

Chapter Fourteen

As with any new mother, Theena's days and nights were a confusion of joy and sleep-deprivation. No matter how deeply Theena slept, she woke instantly whenever Nathanial stirred. As he nursed, he gazed at her somberly with his beautiful gray eyes, the lashes thick and curling. Theena thanked God for this perfect child, and tears fell at the wonder of Nathanial Randolph Chase.

Theena recovered quickly, and she didn't see how she could possibly last the prescribed two weeks in bed. By the fourth day, she was restless. By the fifth day she was determined to get up, but yielded to Randolph's insistence she stay in bed. On the sixth day, she rebelled. When he came home for dinner, Theena sat fully dressed on the porch with Nathanial in his fine walnut cradle at her side.

Just as she expected, Randolph greeted her with a scowl. "What are you doing out of bed?"

"Have you ever lain in bed for six days, Randolph Chase? I was ready to go mad in there. So don't fuss at me." She reached for his hand, and he relented.

Randolph moved the blanket away from Nat's face for a better look. "Every time I see my son," he complained, "he's asleep."

Theena picked up the baby and handed him to his father. "Nat can sleep anytime."

Nat squirmed and stretched. His tiny mouth yawned wide, and he opened his eyes. "He woke up!" Randolph said.

"Talk to him. He'll look at you if you talk to him."

"What does one say to an infant?"

"Try Coo. Or Hello Mr. Chase. Or ask him what he thinks of the price of grapefruit."

He gave Theena a smiling glance and turned back to his son. "Hey, there, Nat. How's my boy?"

Randolph sat on the stoop and cradled Nat against his chest. When Nat grabbed his finger, he turned to her, grinning. “Look at that.”

Theena sat back in her rocker. God must have forgiven her. She didn’t deserve this happiness.

Nathanial slept, ate, and grew. Soon he was smiling and cooing at his mama and daddy. Never was there a brighter, sunnier, more beautiful boy. And yet his grandmother showed little interest in him. Theena remembered how her granny had fussed over her and her sisters, how she taught them songs and made dolls for them. Mother Chase, though, continued her needlework for new chair covers.

Mrs. Chase might for a moment set her work in her lap and gaze at her grandson waving his rattle and babbling, but she didn’t speak to him. Instead she eyed him as if she suspected he might be a changeling brought to them by some devilish imp.

In those moments when Mrs. Chase’s beady eyes fastened on Nathanial, Theena felt her heart rise in her throat. What was the old woman thinking behind that hard gaze? That he was too dark? That he didn’t look like a Chase?

It was as natural for a child to look like his mother as his father, Theena reasoned. She’d remind Mother Chase of that. In the parlor as Nat played with his toes, Randolph beside her for courage, Theena interrupted her mother-in-law’s reading. “Maybe the next baby will be a little blond girl. You’d like that, wouldn’t you, Mother Chase?” When Mrs. Chase didn’t answer her, Theena nervously fussed with Nat’s cradle pad. “I mean, Nat looks so much like me, I thought you’d like the next one to look like Randolph.”

The expression on Mother Chase’s face was unreadable. “It’s far too soon to know who this child will look like.”

“Look at that hair and that little nose,” Randolph said, shaking Nat’s fist to make the toy rattle. “He’s the very picture of his mother.”

Mrs. Chase turned her attention back to her book.

As Nat grew, sweet baby-fat buried his cheekbones and made his face round and jolly. Theena delighted in every milestone of his growth. Already he rolled over and back again in his crib. He’d be sitting up before she knew it.

One evening, Theena excused herself from the parlor to put Nat to bed. A few minutes later, as she crossed the hallway to return to Randolph and Mother Chase, she heard her mother-in-law's venom-filled voice.

"You've only to look at him," she hissed. "He's brown as a bear. And you tell me that's your child? Wake up, Randolph."

Theena's vision blackened. Her body trembled from knees to jaw. She groped for the wall lest she fall into the chasm at her feet. All these months of happiness, and now black, inevitable despair.

She stumbled against the door trying to get away, to flee, somewhere, the barn, the grove, the swamp. Randolph opened the door. Lantern light flooded in, yellow, blinding. She shielded her eyes, gripping the jamb to keep herself upright.

Fear thrumming louder than heart beats, she looked for final condemnation in Randolph's face. He was flushed, and his eyes flashed blue anger. But . . . he held his hand out for her.

"Come in, Theena. You might as well know what Mother is saying about you. It isn't pretty."

"I heard," Theena said with a voice squeezed small in her chest.

"Well?" Mrs. Chase said.

Randolph had taken her hand. Every hope and chance of happiness flowed from his hand into hers. God forgive her, she would fight, steal, cheat, and lie for that chance.

She looked the threat of ruin in the eye, her chin held steady and her vision clear. "I'm sorry Nathanial isn't the tow-headed child you think he should be, Mother Chase, but he belongs to Randolph."

"All right, then, Mother, there's the end of it. No more of your insinuations. Theena is my wife, and I expect you to treat her with respect." He took Theena's elbow and steered her toward the door. Over his shoulder, he said, "If you choose not to love your grandson, Mother, that's your loss."

Gripping her hand, he led Theena outside into the night and pulled her down the lane at his side. He was so angry, Theena could hardly keep up with his brisk steps, but her spirit soared as if she rode the wind. He believed her. He loved her. Whatever sacrifice he asked of her, to her last breath, she would gladly give him.

They reached the gate. Randolph put his hands on the rail and lowered his head. When he had his breathing under control, he pulled Theena into his arms.

Her head pressed under his chin, she felt his breath on her cheek. She wrapped herself around him, the thudding of his heart loud in her ear.

"I'm sorry, Theena." He lifted her face to kiss her forehead. "Don't let her hurt you."

"As long as you love me, Randolph, nothing else matters."

He kissed her cheek, tasting tears. He captured her face in his hands and bruised her mouth with kisses. "I do love you. Don't ever doubt it."

"Kiss me again, Randolph. Always kiss me like that."

The next days and weeks, Theena see-sawed between relief and guilt. The worst was over. Mrs. Chase had raised the ugly fact that Nat looked less and less like a Chase, and still Randolph had chosen Theena, and his son, over his mother. All would be well.

But in every quiet moment, dread circled her heart like a poisonous fog. *I promised God I would not lie, ever again. And I did.* The weight of sin pulled at her day and night.

But she could not take the risk that Randolph would forgive her, that he would love Nat, if he knew. She was more frightened of losing Randolph than she was of God.

But wasn't it the same lie, not another lie? No, God wouldn't accept such quibbling. She would have to live with this guilt for the rest of her days, and bear the burden of it to her grave. She would make it up to Randolph. She would make him happy. But the shadow of the lie was on her.

Near summer's end, Randolph asked her to go to Brickell's with him. Theena eagerly accepted, glad to get away from the house, away from the tension between her and Mrs. Chase. As she bustled to get a sleeping basket and mosquito net ready for Nat, she stopped mid-stride, leaned over Randolph in his chair, and planted a sloppy kiss on his cheek.

Watching her tie her bonnet on, he teased, "You sure you want to go? It'll rain for sure, you know."

She flashed him a smile in the mirror. "I'm sure it will."

He left his chair and stood behind her, his arms around her. He eyed her in the mirror as he tasted her ear. "The mosquitoes on the way through the woods are fierce."

Theena turned around and poked him in the chest. "Nat and are I coming, Randolph Chase, no matter how many bears or gators or skeeters you conjure up."

"So I see." He bent to get under her bonnet and kissed her. "Let's get going."

On the way through the woods, she dabbed camphor on the three of them and kept up a steady stream of chatter. It was wonderful to be alone with her husband. No mother-in-law, no interruptions from the manager, no demands on Randolph's attention. To surprise him, she recited a poem he particularly admired. "We two will lie 'i the shadow of/That living mystic tree/Within whose secret growth the Dove is sometimes felt to be."

She thought she must radiate happiness as bright as the sun when Randolph turned admiring, adoring eyes on her. "I had no idea you'd been reading Rosetti."

She looked at him sideways, tweaking him. "I like limericks better."

He laughed at her. "All right. Fair's fair. 'There was a young fellow named Chick/Who fancied himself rather slick./He went to a ball/Dressed in nothing at all/But a big velvet bow round his prick.'"

Theena let out her maniacal guffaw and clapped a hand to her mouth. "You devil," she said at the grin on his face.

"Now your turn."

The breeze brought the smell of the bay as they drew in to Lemon City. When Randolph drove the wagon into the Spode yard, Hera walked out onto the porch with Priscilla on her hip. "My stars, I thought you were never coming to town again. Come on in."

Hera sat Priss down on the floor with a wooden spoon and a tin pot. "Let me see this boy," she said and reached for Nat. "What a big fellow you're getting to be."

Nat babbled back at her, delighted to be admired. Theena knelt down to Priss and tapped a rhythm on the bottom of the pot. Once Randolph came in from seeing to his mule, he entered a house of babble, song, and spoon on pot.

Over the clamor, he asked, "Where's Jack?"

"Working down in the keys so he can buy more orange trees."

"Why don't you and Priss come to the store with us?" Randolph said. "We'll picnic under the palms."

Theena smiled up at him. He couldn't have done anything better to please her than ask her sister and another noisy baby to come along.

Hera touched her hair. "Give me two minutes."

Randolph put a hand to his ear and cocked his head. "I think I hear the mule calling me," he said over the racket. Theena laughed and waved him off to wait in the shade of the banyan tree.

Hera tidied her hair and bent down to Nat. She tenderly smoothed the hair out of his face. "He's a lovely child, Theena. Is . . . everything all right? I mean. . . ." Hera glanced at the door. "He doesn't look anything like Randolph."

"Yes!" Theena swept Nat into her arms. "Everything is wonderful."

After their picnic, Randolph went in the store to get started on his mother's shopping list. Theena lingered outside with Hera, talking with old acquaintances, both of them happy to show off their babies.

Squinting in the sun, Theena peered toward the river at a large dugout pulling into the bank. "It's Billy!" She hurried ahead of Hera to meet him at the landing.

Behind her, Randolph came down the steps with a package in his arms. He spotted Theena heading for the river. As soon as he put his package in the wagon, he cut across the ground to meet her at the landing.

Theena should have felt something, some prickling or premonition, but she was focused only on the pleasure of seeing Billy and Rosa. Her happiness with Randolph and Nat filled her mind and her heart so that all she saw on this glorious day were bright skies and good friends.

Billy's face split into a big smile when he spied her coming toward them, a baby in her arms. He said a word to Rosa, gesturing toward Theena. Rosa waved.

From his vantage twenty yards away, Randolph recognized Billy Yoholo getting out of his dugout. He nodded to a group of men smoking pipes in a patch of shade and returned their how-are-you's on his way to join Theena and her friends.

Theena didn't notice Randolph approaching from her right. She shifted Nat to face Billy and Rosa. "Say hello, Nat. Can you say hello?"

Billy reached a finger out for Nat to grab. "Nat, is it? I'm your Uncle Billy, Nat."

But Rosa. Rosa took two steps back. She stared at Nat, at his black hair, his round cheeks, his smile so like Billy's. Her open face revealed everything – surprise, then comprehension – and bitter hurt.

"Rosa," Billy said, "have you ever seen such a . . . What's the matter?"

Rosa's eyes bored into Billy. She might have shouted what was in her heart, so plain was it on her face. Betrayal!

Abruptly, she ran toward the bay.

Billy's confusion kept him mute for a moment as he watched Rosa running, running away from him. He looked at Nat, at Theena, and then he too understood. "Theena?"

Blood pounded in Theena's ears. She held Nat too tightly, but his whimper hardly penetrated the whirl of black horror in her mind. She opened her mouth, but she couldn't speak, couldn't say the words to take back what she'd done.

Billy's eyes left her face to search for Rosa. He touched Theena's arm. "I have to find her."

He left her rooted in the sand. And then Randolph stepped before her, pale faced, his eyes on Nat.

He had seen it all. He knew.

Chapter Fifteen

Randolph walked away, leaving Theena's world in ashes. Her eyes followed him as he strode silently to the wagon. He tied a canvas over the boxes and kegs, then mounted to the driver's seat.

Hera and Theena, as wordless as Randolph, took their places in the buckboard with the babies, and the party proceeded back to the Spode place.

Theena reached for her sister's hand and gripped it. She felt bloodless, as insubstantial as a leaf in the wind, and dizzy, every trembling breath too shallow. She dared a glimpse at Randolph. He had no color whatsoever and he clamped his teeth so tight the muscles stood out in his jaw.

At the Spode place, Hera climbed out the wagon and reached up to take Priscilla. "Do you want to stay with me?" she whispered.

Theena's throat too constricted to speak, she shook her head, but she couldn't bear to take her eyes from Hera, her last friend in the world.

Randolph drove the mule through the woods. Nat slept in his basket on top of the flour bags. A foot of space separated Theena from Randolph, an impassable, unbridgeable foot.

That moment -- Theena relived it over and over. Rosa's shocked face, the hurt in her eyes. Billy's slow recognition as he looked at Nathanial. Worst of all, the dawning certainty in Randolph's face that he knew his child's true father.

I should have laughed it off, Theena thought. *'What ever is the matter with Rosa?' I might have said. 'Silly Rosa.' Or ' Isn't Rosa feeling well?'*

Not saying anything was as good as a confession. Why didn't I say something? Theena pressed her fingers over her mouth. *Guilt – guilt stopped my tongue.*

God must know she would have lied again if she had had the wit. And so He had at last punished her for her sins.

What happens now?

It was nearly dark when they drove onto the Chase plantation. Theena found a little courage, a little hope. “Randolph?” she said softly.

He shrugged her hand off and wouldn’t look at her. Theena thought her heart would burst.

Randolph drove the wagon into the barn, jumped down and strode to his gray mare’s stall. Theena remained on the wagon, her hands clutched together, watching him, silently begging him to say something to her, anything.

He saddled his horse and rode out into the growing darkness.

Percy came in to unload the wagon. Theena took Nat into the house. Mother Chase had retired for the evening. Theena put Nat in his crib and washed the grime off at the washstand. Then she adjusted the mosquito netting and climbed into bed, her back against the headboard. Immediately she shoved the netting aside and rushed to the porch and vomited.

Shaking as if she were fevered, she climbed back into bed. Her breathing came shallow and labored. Wide eyed, she listened to the crickets. She waited for his step on the porch, dreading, hoping. She felt she might cease to breathe if he didn’t come.

Hours passed. Theena waited, too tense to sleep, too frightened to cry. Each time she allowed her mind to touch on how deeply he must hurt, she felt the bile rise in her throat. She did this to him. Her selfishness, her weakness, her treachery had pierced his heart as surely as if she’d stabbed him.

At sunrise, Nat woke, demanding to be fed. Theena nursed him, but he fussed and bit at her nipple, the milk hardly flowing. “You can eat at the table, sweetheart.” She bathed him, then handed him a favorite toy.

She would begin the day as she would any other. She would wash, dress, fix her hair, present herself at the breakfast table. Everything would return to normal if she just kept to her routine.

She couldn’t look in the mirror, couldn’t face what she’d see there. With wooden fingers, she twisted her hair into a knot at the back of her neck. Where had he spent the night? He couldn’t have ridden all those hours. She handed Nat the toy he dropped.

He would have to come home. He’d see she was still his wife, the same person he’d loved all this year and more. Their life together would go on. It had to.

She carried Nat into breakfast and sat him in his high chair.

"Good morning, you two," Susan said. She held a biscuit out for Nat, who reached for it with both hands. "We've got a hungry boy this morning."

Susan looked at Theena's ravaged face and frowned. "Are you sick?"

"I just need some coffee." While Susan poured, Theena heard Randolph's boots on the side porch that led into their bedroom.

Her throat felt full of gravel. She couldn't swallow. She gripped her cup with both hands, but they shook so she couldn't bring it to her mouth. She buried her hands in her skirt and waited in a private white hell.

Mother Chase joined Theena at the table. "Good morning," she said with her usual frosty formality. She looked long and hard at Theena, but she said nothing about her appearance.

"I see Randolph has been out early. Stopping along the way for you to visit your sister yesterday put him behind in his work."

"I'm sure it did," she murmured.

Randolph at last entered the room. If he had given her the merest glance, she would have leaped from her chair and thrown herself on him. But he did not look at her or Nat or his mother. He pulled out his chair and unfolded his napkin.

Hollow eyed and pale, he wore fresh trousers and a white shirt. He'd shaved and wetted his hair back from his forehead. Normal. He was going to act normal, just as she was. But oh how she wanted one look, one word.

"Good morning, son," Mrs. Chase said. "You must have been out before dawn. How was Miss Brickell?"

Randolph watched Susan fill his cup. "The magazines you ordered were in, and I got everything on your list."

Theena busied herself feeding Nat his scrambled eggs, aware of Randolph's every gesture. He managed to keep up the conversation with his mother, telling her the local news, the price of sugar and meal. A less astute woman than Mrs. Chase might have thought all was well.

Theena lifted the coffee pot. "Can I refill your cup?"

Randolph stilled. Theena froze, pot in mid-air. A moment of great danger had arrived. Even if he couldn't look at her, if he would just let her do this one small thing for him, it would give her hope.

Randolph put his napkin on the table. He rose, and then, then he met her gaze. The pain she saw seared through her and burned her heart to ashes.

"I have to get to work." He strode out, his footsteps quick and loud on the floorboards.

Randolph didn't come in for noon dinner. Theena hadn't eaten since yesterday's picnic, but she only pushed the food around on her plate.

Mrs. Chase deigned to speak to her, a hint of satisfaction in her voice. "You look as though you hadn't slept in a week. You'd best lie down when Nathanial takes his nap."

"Yes, I'll do that." But she didn't sleep. She stared at the ceiling, a taut wire running from her throat to her belly, tightening with every hour his boots failed to strike the floor.

He also failed to appear for the prescribed six o'clock supper hour. Mrs. Chase insisted that Susan serve supper. "I'm sure my son is still trying to catch up after that little outing to your sister's yesterday. He'll be in when he can."

After that longest of days, Theena put Nat to bed and sat in the parlor pretending to read. When she heard him come in at the back door, her heart beat so hard it fluttered the bodice of her dress.

Susan clattered some silverware and plates. He'd eat in the kitchen. Twice she moved her feet to go to him, but courage failed her. She listened, and waited.

The back door slammed and she heard his footsteps on the little porch off their bedroom. Their bedroom. He had to see her, look at her, speak to her in their bedroom. Theena glanced at Mother Chase, took in the bright eyes of a hawk watching its prey at last emerge from cover. She closed her book with clammy hands. "Good night, Mother Chase. I'm going to bed."

Randolph had not lit the lamp in the bedroom. In the gloom, Theena at first didn't find him. He wasn't in his chair, nor in the bed. A glimmer of moonlight showed him on the floor, on his bedroll from the tack room. He lay on his side, his back to her.

Theena approached him slowly. She knelt down and touched his shoulder. "Randolph?"

His body stiffened. He didn't turn to her. Didn't take her in his arms. Didn't tell her that he loved her. That he loved Nathanial.

"Go to bed, Theena," he said.

The next day set the pattern for the months to come. Randolph rose from his bedroll on the floor at first light. He dressed quickly and left the room without looking at Nat in his crib, without patting his back or smoothing his hair as he slept. He didn't speak to Theena nor look at her in the bed where she sat up, hoping for a word from him.

Theena's days began with tears and remorse. Even words of blame, recrimination, or accusation from Randolph would have been better than this silence.

She wanted so much to tell him why she had deceived him. That she was weak, not cruel. That she would never ever hurt him again. But she imagined how Randolph would look at her with cold hatred in his eyes, with withering unforgiveness, and her words died unspoken. If he despised her, she deserved it.

She awaited every meal, eager to see him, yet dreading it too. Their only contact was at the table when he would occasionally speak to her about some impersonal matter like letting her know his annual delivery of guano would be arriving and she would have some of it for her garden. She yearned for him to say a word to Nat, too, but he never did.

In the first days of the estrangement, little Nat had smiled and reached for his father. But as the days and weeks wore on with no returning smile, no acknowledgement from Randolph, Nat became indifferent to the cold man's presence. An aching sadness for Nathanial's loss added to Theena's own sorrow.

And how awful for Randolph. He had loved Nat, and now he felt he had lost his son.

Getting through each day took all Theena's grit. The parlor clock ticked off the hours, the days dragged by. The world lost its color. She had no appetite, no ambition. She took care of Nat, but the joy she'd taken in him every moment he breathed was muted. She survived the constant, twisting grief only by desperately clinging to hope that, someday, they would be a family again.

For Theena, the after-supper hours alone with Mother Chase in the parlor were interminable. The women read or sewed, neither of them making any effort at conversation. Theena had no illusions that Mrs. Chase was ignorant about the rift between her and Randolph. It seemed to Theena that Randolph's mother kept alert for some unnamed moment, but her vigil seemed perversely cheerful, even smug. Glad at last for her son to see Theena for the low, common thing she was.

Whatever she thinks, Theena told herself, *I'm still Randolph's wife.*

In the shorter days of winter, Randolph took to his pallet earlier. More hours for Theena to gaze at his back where he lay on the floor, exhausted by all the labor he could find for himself during the day.

The full moon lit the bedroom where Theena sat up in bed, listening to his steady breathing. Big and low and silvery, the moon reminded her of the night she and Randolph had sat on the porch steps and watched it rise a year ago, holding hands, her head on his shoulder. They'd talked of the future, of filling the house with children. She lay her head on her knees and choked back her sobs.

She thought he'd been asleep half an hour or more, his back turned to her as it was every night. She wrapped her shawl around her and crept to his pallet. Quietly, she lay on the floor alongside him, careful not to touch him. He didn't stir.

She shifted her body closer and timidly put a hand on his hip, just to feel his warmth. She moved her hand to his ribs, and he sighed in his sleep. She wanted so much to touch him. She dared to press her forehead against his back.

The slight sound of his breath stopped. She didn't dare move. She heard the clock ticking in the other room.

"No," he said.

That was all. Theena rolled away, humiliated, stifling her sobs. She knew he needed to punish her, but this was too cruel.

I deserve it, though, she thought. *God knows I do.*

Chapter Sixteen

"You had no right!" Randolph stood over his mother's chair where she sat with a letter in her hand. "You had no business discussing my marriage with anyone, not even with Mr. Merrill." He clenched his fists, so angry he wanted to smash something, anything.

"I am not blind, Randolph. This is not a marriage, not any more. I simply see no reason you must live on like this. Get the annulment, as my lawyer suggests, and you'll be free again."

"You never welcomed Theena into this house. You never did."

With perfect self-possession, his mother adjusted a loose curl. Unbidden, a vision of his fist smashing into his mother's face came to him. The image startled him, and he stepped back.

"What I'm trying to say to you, son, is there are more suitable girls in Key West. Or Philadelphia. We could go north for a few weeks. Put all this behind you."

"You will stay out of my affairs, Mother. My marriage is none of your concern." His nails cutting into his palms, he strode from the room.

Outside he swung himself onto his horse and spurred her down the lane. His heart was fractured into so many pieces, he didn't know if he would ever be whole again. His only respite from anger and hurt was on the plantation. He did the work of two men, pushed himself to keep going until he could bear the thought of entering the bedroom where Theena and Nat slept only ten feet away. There he would collapse in exhaustion, fatigue the barrier that kept regret and longing at bay.

He saw very little of Theena or the boy. That's how he thought of Nat now. The boy. Losing him had been as painful as losing his wife, but he'd cut him from his heart. These days he encountered his wife and the boy primarily at supper; Randolph thought that was the necessary minimal contact.

In the early days of the estrangement, hearing Theena crying in the bed moved him not at all. Let her cry. His own grief welled up like water threatening to overspill a dam, but he gave it no voice, no outlet. She had betrayed him in the worst possible way, had lied, had tricked him. She'd never loved him at all.

If she still cried in the night, he didn't know it. He slept hard, and he didn't want to know it. For the first time in years, Randolph missed his father. He wished he could talk it over with Pa, let Pa tell him what to do. But Randolph was entirely alone with his pain.

He rode through his groves, the oranges nearly all picked by now. He'd been busy through the winter hiring pickers and packers and wagon drivers. Almost busy enough to grant him a little relief from grieving over what Theena had done. But at moments, sometimes when he thought he was safely engaged in adding a column of figures or writing to his distributor, the hot searing pain of loss wracked him. He missed her. He wanted her so keenly he'd take a first step toward the door, toward her. But memory held him back. The pain of her betrayal hurt far more than missing her.

Chapter Seventeen

Mr. Lindgren shook Jack's hand. "You change your mind, you come on back down. I'll take you on."

"Thanks, Otto, but I think I've pulled my last sponge."

"Ya, it's hard for a family man. Good sailing to you."

Jack threw his knapsack over his shoulder and boarded a sloop headed up the coast. He'd been gone six weeks, this time, and thoughts of taking Hera to bed when he got home had occupied a good bit of Jack's waking hours, but most of all, he'd dreamed of his Priscilla. She probably walked all over the house now, had new teeth, had smiled a million smiles, and he'd missed it all.

For two days, Jack watched the sloop's wake stretch out behind them. He was a paying passenger, this trip, and the unaccustomed idleness left him moody. He watched the gulls and frigate birds hunting, speculated on the clouds coming over the horizon to the east, admired the old salts' skill at the helm. Nothing to do but think.

He and Hera were good together. She'd tamped down that jealous temper ever since he'd got her good over the Malone girl. After church, Louella Malone had sidled up to him and asked him did he like orange marmalade. She made the best marmalade on the coast, she said, and fluttered her eye-lashes at him. She wasn't more than sixteen, just a kid. Practicing on somebody safe, a married man, a friend of her brother's. But on the walk back home, Hera had been prickly and sulky.

"Reckon I ought to tell you," Jack said, sauntering along home beside her. "You saw me talking to Louella Malone?"

"I certainly did." He could hear her teeth grinding.

"I sure do admire a full-figured woman like her, I sure do." Louella's figure resembled a cane stalk more than it did an hour glass. "I invited her to come stay with us a few weeks. I'll just move back and forth between your bed and hers. Give you a rest. That'll be all right, won't it?"

Hera's face turned red and her mouth tightened into a straight line. Building up a good head of steam, she was. Then in a flash, she burst out laughing. She socked him in the chest a couple of times, but she didn't put any mean behind it. He'd put his arm around her and they ambled home, sweetness restored.

Yes, he and Hera were good together. His thoughts turned to his little plantation. He reviewed all the steps he'd taken to get the brown rot out of his grove. It should be in pretty good shape by now. And he had the cash to order another fifty or sixty trees. With any luck, this was his last sponging expedition. He'd take on as a guide and work closer to home from now on.

He did worry about Theena, though. Jack had taken Hera and Priscilla to visit again before the orange trees blossomed. Randolph kept bee hives throughout his groves, and Jack wanted to know what breed they were. He had a lot to learn, and his brother-in-law was a generous source of information. When they'd gone back to the house and the ladies, however, it wasn't hard to see things were bad between Randolph and Theena. They basically were not speaking to one another.

And no wonder, Jack thought. *Hard thing for a man to find out, and in public like that.*

It had hurt Jack to see Theena that day, thin and pale, her smile brittle. She did her best to be cheerful, but there might as well have been a pall of black smoke hovering over her. *Wouldn't have fooled anybody.*

While everyone was admiring a foal in the barn, Jack had hung back with her. He'd touched her hand and she'd pulled back as if he'd burned her. Then she laughed, as harsh a laugh as he'd ever heard. "Guess I'm just not used to being touched, Jack."

"Things are that bad?" Jack had said.

"I can't blame anybody but myself," Theena said. "Maybe, later on, he'll --." The others headed out of the barn, and Jack started talking about Alice Brickell and her whimsical ways.

Oh, Theena. How he'd wanted to comfort her. As a brother. Not that brotherly feelings were what Theena had wanted from him back before he married Hera. He knew that. And he hadn't always felt like a brother to her either. But that's what they were now. In the eyes of the law, and in Hera's and Randolph's eyes too, they were brother and sister.

Taken ashore not far from Brickell's, Jack found his land legs and whistled as he strode home. Gator met him coming, and Jack stopped to rub behind his ears. "How's aboy?"

There was washing on the line, baby naps and aprons and a row of ladies' drawers. He smiled at the sight, at the thought of getting Hera out of hers.

"Hello, the house," he hollered. Hera stuck her head out the door, spied Jack and hustled down the stairs. He whirled her around, squeezed her tight and kissed her right in broad daylight. *A glad thing, when a man's wife is happy to see him.*

"I'd begun to think you weren't ever coming home again," Hera said into his chest.

"Well, tell you the truth, there was a mermaid asked me to stay awhile, but old Lindgren, he took her for himself."

Hera slapped his chest. "Come on in. You hungry?"

"Like a starving man. Where's my girl?"

Inside, Hera stood beside Jack and together they lifted the mosquito net to watch Priscilla sleep. She had Hera's pink skin and reddish blond hair. Too soon to know if she had inherited Jack's long bones or Hera's short ones. Either way, she was the most beautiful baby they had ever seen.

"How much longer you think she'll sleep?" Jack whispered.

"I just put her down. Can you let her be till after you eat?"

"I guess. But maybe I got better things for you to do than cook." He pulled Hera gently away from the crib and then drew her toward the alcove where the big bed stood.

An hour later, Jack carried Priscilla and walked all over his little plantation. When they returned, Hera had supper on the table, the crickets were tuning up, and the sun was going down. Jack was home, and the three of them were a happy family.

Chapter Eighteen

As February passed, Randolph noticed Theena's color return, though when he allowed himself to glance at her, he saw the haunted look still shadowed her eyes. Three quarters of a year had passed. He was glad she still suffered.

Randolph began to watch for her around the plantation. She'd given up trying to be the lady, he noticed, out in the garden without her shoes, hands filthy, skin darkening in the sun. He saw her on the lane, walking toward the river with a cane pole on her shoulder, her hand holding the boy's. Wearing that disgraceful hat he used to tease her about.

From his horse, he would spy her through the orange trees, walking with the boy through the groves. She'd see him. She didn't hale him, she didn't raise her hand to him. She only looked at him, still as a statue, her heart-broken eyes deep and dark, until he broke even that contact and spurred his horse on.

On a day filled with the scent of orange blossoms, Randolph walked out among his trees. The leaves were glossy green and judging by the spring blossoms, there would be a good crop next winter. Bolton's voice came to Randolph over the murmur of the bees, no doubt directing a crew further on.

As he approached, however, he saw there were no hands anywhere about. Bolton's horse grazed as he stood talking to Theena. The boy toddled in the grass nearby. He'd gotten so big, hardly a baby anymore.

Randolph stepped in among the branches of the nearest tree, to listen, to watch.

Bolton had his back to him, but Randolph could see Theena clearly. She pushed a strand of hair out of her face, and then she laughed. Bolton said something else, and she laughed. Not that crazy-woman guffaw he loved. He hadn't heard that in a long time.

Randolph thought Theena and Bolton had barely been introduced, and here she was alone with him. Her ease with his manager hurt him like needles in his palm. Theena had no sense of right and wrong, no sense of – she shouldn't be talking to another man at all. His hand fisted around a cluster of orange blossoms.

Theena swung the boy on her hip and walked toward where he hid in the deep green branches. Over her shoulder, she called, "Nice talking to you, Mr. Bolton."

"You too, Mrs. Chase. Take care." Bolton mounted his horse and rode off farther into the grove.

Randolph stepped out from the tree into Theena's path, the miasma of cloyingly sweet fragrance choking him. A gust of wind whirled orange blossoms into the air and released them in a flurry of white all around her, in her hair, on her shoulders.

She stopped, her eyes deeper, darker, more beautiful than he'd ever seen them. He tried to read her face. *Has she been meeting him behind my back all this time?* Or, as hope surged in spite of his determined renunciation of it, *Is she glad to see me?*

What he saw was loneliness. The yearning in her eyes pulled him closer. How he wanted to fold her into his arms, to crush her to him. He looked at his son, so big now. *He's not my son.* Anguish washed over Randolph fresh and sharp. He could step no farther.

Theena approached him slowly, wary as she might be of a wild animal. When she stood ten feet away, she halted. Tears spilled over her cheeks, but she showed no sign of knowing it.

"How long, Randolph? How much longer?"

Misery coursed like lead in his veins. He tried to memorize her face, her brow, her mouth, for all the days he wouldn't be able to look at her again. When he spoke, his voice seemed thin to his own ears. He managed to give her the only answer he could. "I don't know."

She lowered her head, the sun glinting on her beautiful black hair. She walked away from him without looking back.

If she had only held her hand out, he told himself. *If she'd said she loved me. If she'd touched me . . . .* Would it have all been over? Could forgiveness come to him so easily as that?

Three days later, Randolph led his weary horse through the twilight. As he entered the barn, he heard voices in a stall glowing with lantern light. His pulse picked up. Theena's bitch was about to deliver her litter any day. She was here, in the barn, with Percy.

He dropped the reins. The need to see her grew with every step as he approached the stall. But it wasn't Percy with her. Bolton. Bolton knelt with six or eight new puppies around him.

Theena sat in the straw with Bertie's head on her lap. "What a good mama," she crooned, stroking her dog's sleek head.

"What are you doing?" It was out of Randolph's mouth before he could reign himself in. It was nearly dark, and here was Theena alone in the barn with Bolton. His voice was too harsh, he knew it, but he couldn't stop himself. *New puppies, is all*, his head cautioned him, but he couldn't listen. He could hardly see for the fury and fear he felt. Theena . . . with another man?

He grabbed her arm and pulled her up roughly. Bolton stood. "Mr. Chase!"

Randolph ignored him. He hauled Theena out of the barn and across the yard, gripping her upper arm, his blood a roar in his ears.

Theena offered no protest, no explanation. Mindless, hardly knowing what he meant to do, he pulled her into the bedroom, kicking the door shut.

He whirled her around to face him. He expected anger, outrage, even fear on Theena's face. But there was a peculiar light in her eyes, almost a smile on her lips. The stream of invective he'd been about to whip her with died in his throat. He grabbed her to him and mashed his mouth against hers. All these months, the anger, the longing – he punished her lips and when she leaned her body against his, he threw her on the bed.

He wanted to hurt her, to force her, to show her she was *his*. He tore at her clothing, ripping and tugging. She wrapped her arms around him, accepting the violence. No, receiving, embracing the fury in his hands, the force of his mouth on hers. She opened her lips, taking him in. He thrust himself inside her and she dug her fingers into his back. He rammed into her again and again, and she met his every lunge with her hips. Pain or pleasure, he could not tell the difference.

He climaxed on a staggering, shattering sob. He buried his face in her hair, his body quaking, his tears hot on her neck. She held him, she stroked him. She loved him, her own tears wet on his face and in his hair.

When they lay spent, boneless with the ferocity of their release, the silence pressed in on Randolph. Who would speak first? And say what?

Confusion dominated his mind. He'd been savage. Had he hurt her? Did she hate him? All he wanted in this world was to make love to her again, softly, tenderly. But would she want him to touch her after he'd taken her so brutally?

Then God sent him His blessing. Theena put her hands on his face. She kissed him, carefully, gently, insistently. Randolph felt a loosening in his chest, a hint that the rawness in his heart might heal. He wrapped her in his arms, held her tight as if he could fuse her body to his. He made love to her, this time without the fierce pain, this time with a tender passion.

When he at last yielded to all the intensity of his sex in a pulsing, depleting climax, he lay in Theena's arms, no longer caring about her sin, or his pride. He cared only for Theena.

Chapter Nineteen

Theena and Randolph grabbed every opportunity to be together in bed, their bodies entwined. They spoke very little. Touch was the healing agent they trusted most.

Yet Theena wondered if such wounds as theirs could ever heal completely without more than the intimacy of their bodies. They needed to know each other, to understand what had happened to them. She thought she knew Randolph's pain, his need to punish her, but he showed no sign of including Nat in his forgiveness. That she could not understand.

Touch alone could not heal to the bone. Randolph seemed satisfied with their renewed ardor, but Theena, after months of suffering, wanted a true reconciliation. She wanted her husband to know her, to accept her weakness, not to have simply yielded to his lust. And her sweet Nat -- Nat had never sinned against anyone, and he needed a father.

And what of the need that had led to her own sin? When she began to speak of it, lying in the bed with her head on the same pillow as Randolph's, he put his finger to her lips. He didn't want to know how afraid she'd been of losing him, why she had wronged him so.

In the early morning when dawn let a little gray light into the room, Theena slid out from under Randolph's arm to go to the crib. Nat had been babbling to himself the last half hour, the happiest sound Theena had ever known. She spoke to him softly and picked him up. Back in the bed, she nestled him between her and Randolph and let him play with her hair.

Randolph was more awake than not, she thought, but his eyes were still closed. She leaned over Nat and ran her hand across Randolph's bare chest. He grabbed her fingers and pressed his lips against her palm. Then he rolled over, away from her and Nat.

Her mouth quivered, but she would not cry. There had been so much hurt. Neither of them could heal overnight. *Patience*, she told herself. *He's not ready yet.*

The mildness of spring yielded to the trials of summer. More mosquitoes, sand flies, and heat. During the longer days, Theena took every opportunity to put Nat in Randolph's path, so when she saw Randolph heading for the barn, she took Nat out to look at the puppies, grown big and noisy now.

She took him into Bertie's stall and set Nat down on the straw. Randolph put his tackle aside and leaned on a post, watching him frolic with puppies as big as he was.

"Which one you think we could keep for Nat?" Theena asked.

Randolph stepped over the make-shift gate and the puppies jumped up on his legs to investigate. He knelt and gently tussled with the little white and tans, finally choosing a plump female. He held her up and endured a lick across the mouth.

He was about to offer the pup to Nat, but Nat lost his balance and fell in the hay. Three pups converged to crawl on his back, to kiss him and devour him all at once. Nat laughed, and then one of the pups nicked his ear with its sharp baby teeth and Nat wailed.

Theena scrambled over to him and pushed the puppies off him. She pulled him into her lap and held her hand over the bloody little nick, rocking and crooning to calm him down. She looked up at Randolph, hoping this might bring him to a moment of tenderness toward Nat.

Instead, Randolph said, "Don't baby him, Theena. It's just a scratch."

Quick as wildfire, anger surged through her. "And he's just a baby, Randolph."

Randolph's head went back as if she'd slapped him. He stood up and brushed the straw from his pants, then left her and Nat with the puppies. Theena closed her eyes, her forehead on the back of Nat's head. *What have I done? At least he showed some interest, and I ruined it. Stupid, stupid, stupid.*

The rest of the day, and the next and the next, she felt he'd rebuilt the wall between them. The old pain would have crushed her except that he still turned to her in the night. But if they couldn't talk to each other, how were they to go on together?

Just before dawn, she felt him leave the bed. He pulled his pants on and looked for his shoes.

"Randolph?"

"Hm?"

"I'm sorry I snapped at you, about the puppies. You were right. I baby Nat too much."

He sat on the bed with his back to her. She waited, the bed shaking as he pulled his shoes on. Was he not going to answer her? What if he said 'he's *your* son.' *God, don't let him say that.*

Randolph tucked his shirt into his pants. He stopped at the crib for a moment, but Nat was still sleeping.

"See you at breakfast," he said.

Theena lay back on the pillows. Randolph had looked at Nat as he slept. How long had it been since he'd done that? She got out of bed with a smile on her face. *He loved Nat once. He will again. I just have to be patient.*

She didn't know how much longer she could believe in patience, but she had no other strategy. She often thought of forcing Randolph to sit down with her and have it all out: *I'm sorry. I wronged you. You had every right to hate me. But Nat,* she'd tell him. *It's not his fault. He'll love you, if you let him.* But it wasn't only Nat she wanted to save. *Randolph*, she wanted to say, *you need to open your heart for your own sake. Let go of the anger and the resentment. Just let it go.*

A fine thing for the sinner to say to the sinned against. *Just let it go.* No, patience would do its work. She'd win him over in time. This very morning Randolph had leaned over Nat's crib.

Theena washed and dressed and by then Nat was ready to get up. She held his hand as he toddled into breakfast. When they entered the dining room, Susan was pouring coffee for Mrs. Chase.

"Look at that boy," Susan said. She put the pot down and held her hands out for Nat to come to her. His face the picture of joy, he took two steps and fell into Susan's arms. She raised him up and smacked him loudly on the cheek. "That's my big boy," she said. "You want a biscuit?"

Mrs. Chase occupied herself with stirring sugar into her coffee as if she were unaware there was a beautiful child in her dining room. Theena expected nothing more from her and tucked Nat into his high chair. She heard Randolph scraping the dirt off his boots on the back porch and then coming in through the kitchen.

"Good morning, Mother," he said. "Theena, your rose bushes are nearly head high."

"Full of blooms too. It's the chicken manure --."

Nat dropped his spoon off the side of his tray and leaned over to watch it hit the floor. Theena picked it up and handed it back to him. "It's the chicken manure that makes the blooms so big."

Delighted with this new game, Nat dropped it again. When Theena bent for it, Randolph said, “Wait, Theena.”

Randolph picked up the spoon and placed it next to his own plate. “Don’t let him play games at the table. He has to learn to behave.”

The smile died on Theena’s face, and the wonderful feeling of lightness she’d felt this morning blew away like smoke.

“Yes, you’re right,” she said. Nat fussed and reached for the spoon, but she distracted him with a piece of bacon.

Theena breathed in. This was progress. Their fractured family was having a normal breakfast, as long as Theena didn’t mind Mrs. Chase’s continued frost. And she didn’t. The old woman had never offered her love, and hadn’t earned Theena’s, so none was lost.

Randolph folded his napkin. “I’m off to the salt mines.”

As he passed behind Theena, he gently placed his hand on her shoulder. That one small touch, and joy washed over her. Everything was going to be all right.

As she left the breakfast table, she felt a little sick to her stomach, but she shrugged it off and took Nat into the garden to pick crookneck squash. When she smelled the manure she’d spread around the plants, nausea conquered her, and she retched between the rows of okra. Her mouth tasted foul, but she smiled to heaven. *God, let it be true,* she prayed. Another baby, this one Randolph’s, and he’d be whole again. *He’ll love us all, and be the father he’s meant to be.*

Chapter Twenty

Winter 1878

The nine months, every one of them, brought Theena and Randolph closer. She felt wonderful, no morning sickness, no anxieties. No more doubts or sorrow. She loved it that he touched her whenever he passed by, her shoulder, her neck, her hair. She loved it that he put his ear to her growing belly to listen to the life thumping around inside. And most of all, she loved her husband for becoming, slowly, a father to Nat.

Then Elizabeth Lavonia Maria Chase was born, and the birds sang.

Theena was content to lie abed in the days after Liza's birth, tired, sore, and a little blue. That was normal. At Liza's first cry in the mornings, Randolph hopped out of the bed, eager to pick up his baby girl, his love child with the deep blue eyes. Before he handed her to Theena to nurse, he rocked her in his arms, crooning, entranced when her little fingers wrapped around his.

He crawled back into bed to watch Liza nurse, to stroke the downy hair, to kiss Theena's fingers. When Nat toddled into their room, Randolph scooped him up with one arm and settled him between himself and the baby.

"How many, Nat?" he said, gently touching each tiny toe on Liza's foot. "One," he said, prompting Nat to count his sister's toes.

Theena thanked God every day for forgiving her and bringing Randolph back to her. They were a family, now. Theena had everything. Two healthy, beautiful children, and a happy husband. But she could not find her own way to happiness.

After Nat was born, she'd chafed to be out and about. This time she could not bring herself to leave the bed. Randolph hired a girl to help, and Theena lapsed into deeper lethargy.

After two weeks, she forced herself to get up in the afternoon. She couldn't be bothered to wash her face or comb her hair, but she was up. She sat on the porch and watched Nat play. In the cradle next to her, Liza slept wrapped in the lacy blanket Grandmother Chase made for her.

She was up, but she was not herself. Theena put a hand to her forehead. *What's the matter with me?* She took no pleasure in anything, not even in the way Randolph welcomed Nat into his lap now. She wanted only to sleep.

Randolph found her weeping, Liza sleeping peacefully beside her, Nat playing nearby. "You're up too soon, Theena. You need to be in bed." He called Julie, the wet nurse, to sit with the children and led Theena inside. He tucked her in and wiped the stringy hair out of her face.

At his tenderness, she cried like a child, sobbing, wretched and confused.

"What's wrong, Theena? Have I done something to upset you?"

She shook her head, burying her face in the pillow.

She felt his weight leaving the mattress, and she quickly turned, grabbing for his hand. "Don't leave me, Randolph."

He squeezed her hand and then waggled it to be let free. "I have work to do, Theena. You get some sleep."

At the Spodes' place, Hera propped her heavy legs up on the opposite chair and sat on the porch darning socks. Jack would clomp into her kitchen soon and want his noon dinner, but right now she needed some time off her feet.

"Daddy's home!" Priss called and ran to be swept onto her father's shoulder. He didn't disappoint her. *He never disappoints her,* Hera thought, thinking how her daddy had been like that.

"Brought mail." Jack handed her an envelope.

"Make it out loud, Mama," Priss said.

"It's from your Aunt Dite. *Dear Hera and Theena*, she says. *It snows half the time here. It's pretty but it seeps in your boots and the cold wind whistles down your neck.*

Hera stopped to explain to Priss what snow was. "Though I've never seen any myself," she added. Dite asked about Theena and her family, about Hera and hers, about Miss Brickell and other people they knew. Then she got down to it. This latest gentleman had disappointed her, and she was leaving him. *I'm coming home. Just for a while, till I'm over being heartbroke.*

"Pocketbroke, more like it," Hera muttered. *I'll arrive on the twenty-fourth, weather permitting. They'll drop me off at the south end of the bay, just below The Inn. Can you have Jack meet me?*

Hera narrowed her eyes at Jack. She looked for him to light up because her sister was coming – she knew what Dite did to men. But the grim look on his face surprised her. "You don't look happy."

"Sure, I'm happy. She's your sister. She's welcome." He got up from the step where he sat with Priss. "What you got for us to eat, Mama?"

Hera fed her family, turned her cheek up for Jack's kiss on his way out the door, and put Priss down for a nap. All afternoon she imagined Dite in the little cabin with them. It was one room, actually, with their bed in an alcove. She could string the blanket again for some privacy, but it wouldn't stop the noise of the bed creaking or of the little cries she made when Jack made love to her.

And the way women eyed Jack, Hera didn't really want another woman around the place day in and day out. Especially not a woman like Dite.

Plain and simple, Hera did not want Dite in her house. But she was family. What could she do?

Hera was hanging wash on the line, the white sheets flapping in the wind, when a solution presented itself in the form of Randolph Chase.

Priscilla hid behind her mother's skirts when the big man got down from his horse. *A far bigger man than any of us expected,* Hera thought. *Not every man could have forgiven what Theena did to him.*

Randolph knelt and smiled at Priss when she peeked at him. "Did you forget your Uncle Randolph?" He held his fist out, then opened his palm to reveal a hard red candy.

"Go ahead, honey." No more coaxing needed, Priss eased out from behind her mama to claim her candy.

"Everybody okay at your place?" Hera said. "Theena and Elizabeth?"

"Liza's fine. I came to talk to you about Theena."

"Come on in. I'll give you a cup of coffee."

Hera sat at the table and heard Randolph out. She'd never known him to talk this much, but she could see he was scared.

"I know the baby blues happens to lots of women," he said, "but not like this." He turned his coffee cup round and round in his hands. "She doesn't even take care of Nat anymore. She lets Julie get him up in the morning and put him to bed at night."

Hera tapped her fingernails on the rim of her cup. She could hardly imagine Theena letting someone else see to her boy. "Mama said she had it bad with one of her babies. Theena, I think."

Randolph gripped her hand across the table. "Hera, will you come home with me, stay a while?"

He looked like a lost little boy, at that moment, a boy who'd lost the world. Hera patted his hand. Of course she'd come. *I know just what she needs. I'll make her stay up from dawn to dusk, get her washing the curtains or hoeing the garden, or something. Theena will get over all this a lot faster if she's busy.*

Hera was about to tell Randolph she would gather a few things and let Jack know. Then she had another thought.

"I tell you what, Randolph. Jack needs me here now he's got so many trees in the ground. But Dite is coming. She should be here in a day or two."

"Dite?"

"You could give her a couple of days to recover from the boat, then come get her." Randolph didn't seem enthusiastic. He had his hands on his cup again, slowly twirling it round. "You know she's been nursing up north since she left here. She'll be good for Theena."

Randolph nodded his head, his eyes on his empty cup.

Hera certainly couldn't leave Jack alone in this house with Dite. "Theena will be thrilled to see her," she said. "They were always real close." *Now, God, that's only a little white lie.*

"Well." Randolph scraped his chair back and stood up. "You talk to your sister when she gets here, see if it's all right. I'll ride over on Friday with the wagon."

When Randolph got home, he found Theena's face red and puffy. She'd been crying again. *For God's sake, what's she got to cry about?* But even Mother acknowledged she was ill. What Mother had actually said, he remembered, was "I've known it to happen to some women. If they're given to that sort of thing, self-indulgent, spoiled. You know the type."

If he'd been inclined to sit Theena down and tell her to snap out of it, to make an effort, his mother's spiteful tone changed his mind. Theena was not self-indulgent nor spoiled. He took from his mother what he needed: This happened to some women after a baby. Randolph resolved to be patient.

"What's wrong now, sweetheart?" he said, pushing the hair out of her face.

"You've been gone for hours, and I didn't know where you were."

"Since when did you ever need me around?" he teased. "You always have a thousand things to do during the day." Not lately, she hadn't though.

Theena reached for him. "Don't leave me, Randolph. Don't ever leave me."

"Now you're just being silly." But he said it kindly. He shucked his shoes off and climbed on top of the covers to hold her for a while. Maybe she'd go to sleep.

They had had nearly a year of happiness. Because they had earned it. And they appreciated what they had all the more for the pain it cost them. Surely when her sister came, he'd have his Theena back.

Chapter Twenty-One

Dite lay prostrate with sea sickness most of the voyage down the coast. By the time she disembarked at Biscayne Bay, she had lost five pounds she didn't need to lose, her hair was greasy and matted, and her face was pasty white. When she'd boarded the boat in Philadelphia, she'd enjoyed how the sailors vied for her glance, but after days of hearing her retch and emptying her slops, they'd lost the yen for her.

I need a bath. And a meal.

The men rowed her ashore and unloaded her trunk onto the sand. Dite gave them each a coin, her last coins, and her thanks. They knuckled their foreheads to her and rowed back out to the ship.

All right. Empty purse, reeking of travel, hungry – but I'm here. And where's Jack? Dite took off her shoes and washed her face and neck in the brackish water of the bay. Then she sought the shade of the flimsy structure built to shelter travelers using this inlet for embarkations and debarkations.

By the time Jack arrived, Dite had dozed, fretted, and dozed again. When she heard the jangle of the wagon and mule, she shielded her eyes from the glare. "Hey, Jack."

"Hey, yourself. Been waiting long?"

"A while."

Jack hopped down from the wagon. "Sorry about that." A pause, then Jack offered his hand and they shook. "You a little worse for wear, it looks like." *Thank you very much,* Dite thought. "If you want," he offered, "we can stop at the Peacock Inn for you to freshen up."

"Lord no. I don't want anybody to see me like this." She touched a hand to her hair. "I know I'm a sight."

"Just the one box?"

'Just the one box'?_Well, Jack never was one for pretty speeches. Don't know why I thought he'd changed.

Jack wrestled the trunk, which held everything Dite owned, into the wagon bed, then helped Dite climb aboard.

"Did you happen to bring anything to eat with you, Jack?"

"As a matter of fact, I did. Biscuits and bacon in that sack at your foot." Without further discussion, Dite gobbled every bite of the lunch Jack had brought for the two of them. "Jug of water behind you," he told her.

"Thank you," she said and wiped her mouth daintily. When Jack smiled, she laughed. "I know, I'm a pig. I don't think I've eaten that much in weeks."

"Not much of a sailor, eh?"

They passed the hour pleasantly, Dite full of stories about the cities up north, the way rich folks lived. She didn't volunteer any information about the men she'd pinned her hopes on, or how she had found herself nearly destitute and friendless in Philadelphia. And Jack didn't ask. *Jack's no fool,* she thought. *Well, I won't be down and out for long.*

The Peacock Inn attracted wealthy men by the dozen in the season. Hunters and fishermen, yachtsmen and convalescents – all of them rich. *Give me time to put back some weight, and I'll find myself another lonely, lusty rich man.*

They passed by the store and Jack waved to Henry Brickell. Dite figured it was Brickell's wagon she was in. Even so, she kept her head turned so the bonnet hid her face. She didn't want old acquaintances seeing her like this, the defeated high and mighty Miss Theophilus returning bedraggled and poor. When she was more herself, she'd go to the store with her head held up. But not today.

At the house, Dite stood in the shade of the porch and watched Jack manhandle her trunk off the wagon. *God, he's strong.* She shook her head a little. *Smart, manly as they come, and happy to live his days out here in this godforsaken place.*

Jack set her trunk down inside the cabin.

"Where's Hera?"

"She went over to Theena's yesterday morning. Should be back this afternoon." Jack got him a cold slab of ham out of the safe.

"Theena okay?"

"No, she's not."

Dite watched his face as he set the ham down, as if he couldn't eat after all. "What's wrong with her?"

Jack shook his head. "I don't know what it is. Cries all the time, Randolph says. Won't take care of herself. Or the children."

"That's not like Theena."

"No, it isn't." Jack stood a minute, nothing to say. Then he picked his hat up off the table. "I got to get the wagon back to Henry. I'll be gone a while if you want to get you a bath."

"I'm that bad, huh?"

Jack grinned at her. "Just a suggestion."

"Here. Take your ham. I know I ate your biscuits."

Alone in the cabin, Dite looked around. Hera kept a clean house. No clutter, no mess. Small though, very small, for the three of them. Plus the baby. *What is her name? Prudence? No, Priscilla.*

Small and rough as it was, this place would have to do for now. Dite found the wash tub on a nail on the back porch. She set water to heat and laid out fresh clothes. She still had the expensive lavender soap she'd taken from Mrs. Glenellen's lavatory. The old lady had boxes of the stuff.

Dite was on the porch drying her hair when Hera drove up with the child and a young fellow, must be one of Randolph's men. Dite eyed her sister's round figure. *Lord, she's fat as a pig.*

Hera lumbered down from the wagon with the little girl, then rushed over to grab Dite in a big hug. "My stars, Dite, you're skin and bones. Say hello to your Aunt Dite, Priss." The child gazed up at her and grabbed a handful of her mother's skirt.

"She looks like you," Dite said. *Pink all over, like a piglet.*

"Except she's a skinny little thing."

"You were, too, when you were little. Jack's taking the wagon back to Brickell's." Dite sat down again. She eyed the kitten the child pulled into her lap. *Probably full of fleas.*

"So tell me what's going on with Theena."

Hera eased herself into the other chair. "She's got what Mama had after Theena was born. Remember her talking about that? After that Mrs. Smythe had twin boys, then took herself out in the bay and knocked a hole in the bottom of the boat with an axe?"

Dite's head snapped back to Hera. "Theena tried to kill herself?"

"She's not that bad. I don't think. But you'll need to keep her up and busy. Keep her working. Talk to her, that kind of thing."

"Me?"

"Well, you don't have any other obligations at the minute, and I do. And at Theena's, you'll have a room. With Nat, but he's a good boy; he won't bother you."

"So you've got it all worked out, have you? Still careful of your Jack."

"You have other plans, do you?"

"I certainly do. I'll be going back to the Peacock Inn when I've got my feet under me. Did you think I'd come back for good?"

"Not if you can find another rich man to pay your way."

Dite had perfected a glower that made old men tremble and young maids cry. She used it on her sister. It made Hera at least flush, embarrassed at what she'd said.

Hera started over, but her pique still came through plenty loud. "Listen, Theena is your sister, too, and she needs help getting through this. Could you maybe think about that instead of your precious self?" She stomped inside, leaving Dite with Priss and the kitten.

Dite folded her arms, her lips and jaw tight. She'd sworn she'd never nurse another day in her life, and now this. The child had her eyes on Dite's white feet. "Stop staring," she snapped. She left the porch with quick steps and walked barefoot down to the bay.

This was a beautiful place, if you liked to look at scenery. Dite liked her scenery in small doses so she could go back to a nice hotel and room service afterwards.

Jack delivered the wagon to Henry and ambled home along the beach, in no hurry to join the women in the cabin. It'd be crowded for one thing. And Hera would probably turn into that monster with a thousand eyes, watching him, watching Dite, and he'd have no peace, no peace at all.

She's a beauty, no doubt about it. Even half green from sea sickness, she makes a man remember he's a man. A beautiful woman, and six kinds of trouble.

As Jack approached the path to his house, he spotted Dite sitting on a driftwood log. Her red hair caught the fire in the sun's rays, and even from twenty paces, Jack could see her complexion had recovered. Her skin was milky white, but there was color in her cheeks. She turned her green eyes on him, and he had to remind himself, *six kinds of trouble.*

"Well, Jack," she challenged him. "You man enough to sit with me awhile, or has Hera got you hogtied?"

Jack folded his arms across his chest and stared down at her. A hell of a thing to say to a man.

Finally, Dite lowered her eyes. "I'm sorry. That was nasty."

Jack sat in the sand. "You and Hera at it already?"

Dite picked the hair up off her neck – a slender, long neck -- and spread it across her back to finish drying. "I'm just tired. Worn out, really. And now Theena -- I didn't expect to be nursing again soon as I got my feet on shore."

"That what you've been doing? Nursing?"

Dite's eyes narrowed. "I've done some nursing."

Reckon it's none of my business. He admired her profile as she looked out over the bay at the pelicans catching a last meal before sunset.

"What's left over at Daddy's place?"

"Not much. The house collapsed. Folks took a lot of the timber to patch up their own places. The garden is grown over. We divided up the chickens, the few pigs. Your daddy's tools are in the shed here."

"Well, maybe my share will pay for my living on my sisters for a few weeks."

Jack shook his head. "You know you're welcome in your sisters' houses."

Dite snorted. "I know I'm not. At least not in this one."

Jack stood up and beat the sand off his dungarees. "It'll work out." He led the way across the beach back toward the house.

"Damnation!"

Jack turned around. Dite leaned against a palm tree looking at a gash on her foot. "An oyster shell," she said. Her foot streamed blood, a lot of blood.

Jack took her foot in his hand to have a look. "It's a bleeder all right." He hadn't seen a foot that soft and that white in years, not since he'd been with a girl down in Key West, a blonde gal who wore her shoes every day. "Let's get you back and wrap it tight, put your foot up high." Dite took a step, but obviously she was going to have trouble walking. Jack swept her up easily and carried her down the path.

She smelled good. Her face was just beneath his own, and he felt her breath on his neck.

"I don't believe I've yet to meet a rich man as gallant as you, Jack."

"Yep, I'm a gent all right." Jack felt her bosom against his chest and tried to remember he was a married man.

"Why didn't you ever try for me, Jack? Why was it always Hera?"

Now how can I answer that? Beautiful, yes, but there was a hardness about her even then. A discontent, a cold place inside somewhere. That's what I thought, and I think I was right. "Plain and simple, Dite -- not man enough for a girl like you."

She scoffed, but mercifully she dropped it. Jack flirted with the willing ladies at the store or after church often enough he knew how, but when the female was in his arms, and she was as desirable as Dite Theophilus, and his wife stood on the porch waiting for them with arms akimbo, well . . . he'd rather wrestle an alligator than banter with this woman.

"My stars," Hera eyed the trail of bloody drops across her scrubbed floor. "What'd you go and do?"

"Get a pan, you want to save your floor," Jack said. He set Dite in the chair and wrapped a dish cloth around her foot till Hera set a basin down.

"That's my best dish cloth, Jack."

"Sorry to have inconvenienced you by gashing my foot open," Dite said.

"I'm just saying --."

"I think this is going to need sewing up, honey." Jack interrupted and turned his head up to see Hera's lovely mouth twisted into a scowl. "You going to do it or you want me to?"

Hera crossed her arms and took her time answering. "I'll do it. You get the turpentine."

The sight of the blood soaking quickly through the cloth made Dite light-headed. Her foot hurt like the very devil, and the stitching would too, especially in Hera's resentful hands.

"Do you have any whiskey?"

"Oh, don't be such a baby." Hera's voice dripped with scorn.

So Hera means to get her licks in while I'm down. Dite leaned her head over the leg extended across the chair. *Don't want to faint.*

"That's it. Keep your head down and your foot up. I'll get the jug," Jack said and patted Dite's back as he left her.

"You can forget the branch water," she called after him.

By the time the bleeding stopped, Dite had downed a second cup of shine. It might not be as good as the single malt Scotch she'd become accustomed to, but it was better than nothing.

She let Hera settle her torn foot in her lap and watched her poke the black silk thread through the needle. The kerosene lantern hissed noisily and a solitary fly buzzed over head.

"Oh!" The needle might as well have been a blade it hurt so bad. "Hera if you smile, I swear, I'll . . . ."

"Not my fault your feet's too tender for the beach."

Dite breathed in hard. "Lord that hurts."

She reached for Jack's hand and thought better of it. The most jealous woman she knew was sewing her foot.

"Tell me one of your stories, Jack," she said, trying not to watch the grisly business.

He poured a little more moonshine in her cup. "You tell me one."

"All right. I'll tell you about old Fitz and his racing horse."

Dite took him through the finer points of horse racing in Pennsylvania. At last, Hera tied a knot of black silk and snipped the thread with her tiny sewing scissors just as Dite finished her story.

"And so my poor old nag with the hitch in his hip sailed right on by Fitz's fine thoroughbred, and my ticket paid off at sixteen to one."

Jack laughed, but Hera said, "Seems to me you made a stupid bet. The odds were against you."

Mama always fussing over Hera, while it was Dite do this and Dite do that, and Hera thick as a cocoanut.

Dite exchanged a look with Jack. She could trust him to catch even a whiff of irony. What Hera caught was that look. Her piggy face went red and her mouth drew into a tight line. *She certainly has lost her looks.*

Well, let Jack handle this. He's the one has to live with her long after I'm gone.

"I just don't get --."

"Let me see your handiwork," Jack said.

Dear Jack. He really is the best of all of them. Too bad he's poor. And married to a dumpy frump.

When Randolph showed up on Friday morning with the wagon, Jack was mightily relieved. No more tip-toeing around in his own house to keep from making Hera more snappish and prickly than she was, no more sleeping on the edge of the bed to keep Hera and him from making embarrassing married noises.

Dite tried to be a good guest, he'd give her that. She was lively and witty and stimulating -- in more than one way – but Priss didn't much like her and she spoiled the peace of their little family. *Not her fault, I reckon, but the woman strains a man – like being half-starved with a fried chicken leg dangling just out of reach all the time. Glad to get my house back to normal.*

Jack watched with amusement as Dite turned the full force of her charms on her second brother-in-law. She'd been walking around fine on her cut foot all morning, but with Randolph to lean on, she found need to limp. "I'm afraid I require your assistance," she'd said, looking at him from under her lashes.

Jack had not hidden his smile very well, and Dite shot him a glance full of vinegar. She placed a delicate hand on Randolph's arm and crossed the dirt yard as if she were walking on a red carpet at the palace.

Jack leaned in his doorway watching Randolph help Dite into the wagon. Hera stood beside him, her arms crossed and her mouth mean. He snuck a squeeze of her bottom and whispered in her ear. "Bout time for Priss to take a nap?"

The grim line of Hera's mouth softened. She bumped her hip into his, waited till Randolph got the wagon turned round and Dite waved goodbye. Then she turned her pretty smiling face up to Jack. *Here's my girl,* he thought.

As the wagon bucked along the rough road, Dite kept her arm around Randolph's. Much as she'd like to crawl into bed with Jack Spode, she had to admit Randolph Chase was a handsome man, if a little florid. South Florida was hard on blonds and redheads.

Dite expected to entertain Randolph on the slow journey through the woods. She had a repertoire of charming little stories about her life in Philadelphia, and also about the few months she'd spent in New York City. He wanted to talk only of Theena and Liza.

Dite crossed her arms under her breasts, propping them up slightly so that any red-blooded male ought to be enthralled every time the wagon went over a bump, but Randolph droned on about Theena. Handsome or not, Randolph was a bit of a bore.

But Randolph's description of Theena's melancholy sobered her. She uncrossed her arms and pressed her hands on the bench. *So Theena really is ill,* Dite thought. *Another good reason never to have a baby.*

In spite of Randolph and Hera's accounts, she was stunned at first sight of Theena, the blank look in her eyes, the lank hair, the clothes hanging loose. *Poor baby.* Dite hugged her little sister.

"You're going to be all right, honey. You'll see." *God in heaven, I hope I can do this.*

Dite agreed with Hera. Keep her out of bed, build up her strength. Find some work she was capable of doing and keep her at it. No more lying about. If she had to suffer, she needed to do it on her feet. Then in time, she'd get over this. Women did.

That night, after Randolph put Theena to bed, she sat with him in the dining room. She finished her cup of cider and propped her forearms on the table. "Tell me again what Doc Moses said."

"He gave me a packet of goat weed. Hypericum, he called it. And he's sent more since then." He stared into his cup. "Susan's been making a tea out of it for a couple of weeks now. Can't tell it's helping."

"I'll make it stronger."

The next morning, Dite threw herself into getting Theena up and around. She insisted she walk with her to the gate. That exhausted her, but Dite wouldn't let her lie down.

The rose bed needed tending, so Dite dragged her out there. Once Theena's pride, the bushes carried dozens and dozens of dead blossoms. She sat on the stool with her hands in her lap, the pruning shears at her feet.

"Theena?" Dite leaned over to see her face. She handed her the shears. "You have to try, honey."

Theena's dull eyes and slack mouth appalled her. Dite had been told she was a natural born nurse, more than once, in fact. She'd despised them for fools. She didn't have more than an ounce of compassion in her. She just knew how to bully her patients into taking their medicine, and she was good enough at it they thought she was the sweetest thing. But here was Theena. If she couldn't get Theena well, what use was she at all?

In the mornings, Dite brewed the goat weed tea herself and watched Theena drink it down. Gradually, Dite observed with relief, Theena yearned less for her bed though her eyes still looked out on the world with little interest.

As for Theena's mother-in-law, Dite had seen worse. She had expected a shriveled, sour old woman, but Mrs. Chase was charming. She'd read extensively, was full of good conversation, and showed a flattering interest in Dite's years in Philadelphia.

"Have you met the Bakerfields, Miss Theophilus?"

"Please, call me Dite. Yes, I do know the Bakerfields."

Mrs. Chase ruminated or reminisced, whatever old women did when their bodies sat right there but their minds seemed to leave the room.

"And did you visit the Liberty Bell?"

"As a matter of fact, it was Bobby Bakerfield who showed it to me."

Not as bad as she could be, Dite thought. *But then I'm not her daughter-in-law. And thank heavens for that. No mother-in-laws for me, ever. Not after Mrs. Fitzgerald.*

She liked men, oh yes, but there were other ways to have a man and all the advantages he could give her without marrying him. Of course, if he had enough money, wasn't too big a fool, and had no mother, well, she might enjoy the security of a wedding band.

Dite sat on the porch to dry her hair. In a miasma of sweet jasmine from her hair rinse, she combed her fingers through the heavy waves and watched Theena from the corner of her eye.

Theena stared at Nat playing in the dirt, but Dite read the unfocused, beclouded eyes. Theena had turned in on herself again so that she was hardly aware of what happened around her. Unless Dite insisted she stir herself, Theena would sit immobilized like this for hours.

Dite's eyes lit on the child. Nat's hands and legs and face were filthy. He wore yesterday's shirt. His hair fell into his eyes. "That child needs a bath."

"I suppose he does," Theena answered, her voice flat.

"Go tell Susan to heat some water. I'll sit here with him till you get back."

Theena continued to look at Nat.

God, can't she what a mess he is? "Theena, you hear?"

Theena went inside. While she was seeing to the water, Randolph Chase strode from the barn toward the house. Dite watched his long legs in the buff trousers, so much more an active man than the gentlemen she'd known in the cities. His legs were taut, his hips were slim. And she did like a flat belly. And that look in a man's eye.

If Theena should see that look in her husband's eye directed at her sister – *well, maybe it'll stir her up.*

Dite smiled at Randolph. She always smiled at him. Women who played the game by pretending to be aloof – well, Dite's ploys were much more direct.

The gleam of sun on Dite's red hair lured Randolph to the porch where she sat. He'd never seen her hair down before, spread out and swinging over the back of her chair. Glorious hair, gold and red and full of fire. He itched to grab a handful of it and wrap it around his wrist. Pull her head back, and take that lush mouth.

"You going to catch a cold out here with wet hair?"

She laughed. "In this heat? Anyway, I'm not inclined to be sickly."

He caught the gleam of green eyes as she looked at him from under her thick pale lashes.

"How about you?" she said.

He settled himself on the porch floor, his back against a post. *Jasmine,* he breathed. He could reach out and touch her slipper, her white foot, if he dared.

What was that insinuation in her voice? *Am I man enough for her? Is that what she's asking?* His smile was brief. "I'm healthy." *Able to grab you, Aphrodite, and take you -- .*

"I'm glad to hear it," she murmured in that sultry voice.

She's out here in the middle of nowhere. Nobody else for her to flirt with. Randolph had known well-brought up young ladies like that in Philadelphia. Professional flirts, that's what he and his pals had called them. Knowing that, though, Randolph still felt her murmur vibrate through his core. *She knows what she's doing to me.* His eyes ran over her, over the white skin of her neck, over the fabric strained across her breasts, the tapering midriff and the tiny waist.

His breathing deepened. She made him aware of his own body, his limbs, his skin, his manhood. He felt tall, strong, and virile around her. She made him so, those looks she gave him. She even dared to look at his trousers, watching to see him come alive because of her.

His gaze rose to her eyes. He knew she was aware he'd been scanning her body, seeing her beneath the calico dress. But no missish blushes from Dite, no pretense of offense or of not understanding. Her eyes were frankly knowing.

Theena pushed the porch door open. "The water's ready," she said.

Randolph dropped his gaze. *What the hell am I doing?*

Theena looked at Randolph a moment. She saw the flush on his face, how he avoided meeting her eyes.

He wants my sister, she realized. She leaned against the door she held open. Randolph hadn't made love to her in such a long time. Since before Liza was born. He was kind to her in the bed; he held her and made her feel safe. But he hadn't wanted her, and she had been grateful to simply be held, to go to sleep with his arms around her.

Theena was so tired. *I can't think about this now.* She straightened up a little. "Nat, come on. It's bath time."

Nat turned his chubby face up, ready to assert himself. "No!"

Randolph was on his feet and swatted him once on the behind. "Don't say no to your mother, young man."

Nat wailed, and Theena closed her eyes. Her boy ran to her and cried into her skirts. She laid a hand on his head, all the comfort she had to give. She wanted to be in her bed with the curtains closed, her arms around a pillow.

"I can't do this," she whispered, staring at Nat's thick thatch of dusty hair.

Dite shook her long red tresses out once last time and sighed. "Nat, let go of your mama. Come on, we'll bathe him together."

Theena swallowed the tears that welled up at the least little thing these days. If Dite helped, she could maybe stay up another hour or two. She took Nat's hand. Before she went in, she looked at Randolph, but his eyes followed the back of her sister's skirt.

On a Sunday evening, after Theena and the children were put to bed, Dite sat in the parlor with Mrs. Chase and Randolph. Mrs. Chase smiled on them as Dite and Randolph played cards, and

Dite was at ease, fairly sure Randolph's mother was as yet unaware of the undercurrents beneath Randolph's pleasantries.

"You didn't get too much sun this morning, I hope?" Mrs. Chase's eyes were on her sewing.

Randolph's gaze warmed the skin of Dite's neck and bare forearms. His eyes swept over her bosom and then, filled with the smoke of desire, lingered on her mouth. Finally he took her with his eyes.

Dite laid down a card and accepted his gaze, smiling, acquiescent, inviting.

"Fair skin like yours and mine," Mrs. Chase went on. "Too delicate for this sun."

"I wore my bonnet, Mother Chase," Dite said as she met Randolph's eyes across the card table. She relished the stirring in her own body, responding to the want in his look.

She dealt the cards again. The old lady would retire soon, and then . . . . *Just how interesting is this going to get?*

Finally Mrs. Chase wound her sewing into a ball and put it into her basket. "I'm going to bed, children," she said. "I'll see you in the morning."

Alone in the parlor, the overhead lantern hissing quietly, Randolph and Dite finished the round they'd begun. Dite counted her points, knowing Randolph's eyes were on her, feeling the heat radiating from him across the table. *He's had enough of flirtation, I think.*

Dite began to stack the cards, but Randolph put his hand on hers.

His need, his desire, flowed down his arm and into her body. The heat in his veins transferred into hers. Her breath stilled.

Randolph scraped his chair across the floor as he rose. Dite tilted her head at him. *Will he?* He hesitated for the merest moment – *Will he really go through with it?* -- then he seized her arms and raised her roughly from her chair.

Thrilled at the animal lust in him, his power and command, Dite closed her eyes and let him crush her against his body. Willingly, eagerly, she yielded to Randolph's brute strength and the heat of his mouth. *Ah, yes.*

Chapter Twenty-Two

No stranger to sin, Dite found the stolen moments with Randolph Chase among the most invigorating of her liaisons to date. *Guilt,* she thought, *is a most piquant sauce.*

They exchanged quick hot kisses on the porch before breakfast. Randolph ran his hand up her leg and cupped her through her skirt. She raised her knee to rub her thigh against him. Then Susan's or Nat's or someone's footsteps approached and they broke away, breathless. Stolen moments, quick and fiery, at every opportunity.

In the night, they made love on the musty parlor carpet, stifling their breathing and their groans.

"Randolph, my love," Dite breathed into his ear when they lay spent on the parlor floor. "We can't do this anymore."

He jerked his head back to look at her in the dim light.

"I mean we can't do this in here again."

He let his breath out. "Too much noise?"

"Yes. And I like to make noise," she whispered, nibbling his ear. "Let's use the stable." Just thinking of fresh straw and a rough blanket under her, Randolph on top of her, in her, the two of them rutting like beasts in a stall next to a sleek black stallion – Dite was roused again.

She pressed against him and filled his mouth with her tongue so that he understood her. *Now. In the stable, now.*

Next morning, she found straw in her hair and idly wondered if Randolph had taken the trouble to check his own hair before he retired to Theena's bed.

Randolph no doubt expected them to remain undetected. Dite took care never to touch him, never to give him one of those want-you looks in Theena's presence nor in Mrs. Chase's. But Dite knew their prolonged desire could not long be hidden from discerning eyes. Mrs. Chase now darted uneasy looks at her over dinner and had less and less chat in the evenings.

And Theena? She wondered if Theena had known all along. Whether because of the goats' weed tea or the weeks of urging Theena to eat, to work in the garden, to take longer and longer walks, she had improved steadily. The lethargy had left her. Her eyes had brightened. She even laughed out loud at Nat's shenanigans, that silly, infectious laugh of hers making them all smile.

She's found herself again, Dite thought. *She'll want her husband back now. Maybe the knowing is what's helped her pull out of this. Well, good on me.* Dite laughed at herself, appreciating the irony, well aware her motives in having Randolph were not charitable.

Randolph was a fine lover. Urgent, but controlled. Ardent, but tender. And big. She liked a big man, a man who could fill her completely. He revived her from the weeks of privation since Fitz's mother had at last pried her darling from Dite's grip.

Yes, Randolph was a lovely man. *But not what I'm looking for, and of course I wouldn't take Theena's husband away from her.* And, Dite thought, he's determined to live in this jungle, so Theena was welcome to him.

Anyway, Dite wondered how long she, the touted beauty, would be able to entrance Randolph Chase with Theena's looks restored. *Clearly, the man needed a woman when I came along. Half-starved for it, he was.* Theena's hair again a glossy black, her cheeks rosy, her step light – wouldn't her revival be followed by a renewed ardor for the marriage bed? Yes, Randolph would soon find his wife ready for the heat he now lavished on her.

Dite sincerely celebrated her little sister's return to health. Besides, she had plans of her own to make.

Sunday morning over eggs and fatback, Jack said, "Let's invite ourselves to dinner over at Theena and Randolph's. While you women gab, I want to talk to Randolph about shipping the fruit."

Hera hesitated, and Jack supposed she was marshalling her usual indignations. *Dite this, Dite that,* he thought. *I guess that's what sisters do, resent the prettiest one.*

"I expect Percy will drive us home," he coaxed.

Hera yielded. "I've got some new honey. Mrs. Chase likes my honey even if she doesn't like me."

"I wouldn't worry about it. Far as I can see, she doesn't like any of us."

"Oh, yes she does. She likes Dite."

It was a fine morning. Jack adjusted his long stride to Hera's waddling gait and pondered his grove. All summer his orange trees had sucked in the sun and the rain, and they were weighted down with a multitude of hard little green orbs. He was pleased. With any luck, he'd make a profit next winter.

Once they were in the woods and lost the breeze, the heat bore down on them. Priss, straddling his neck, had grown quiet, her chatter all used up, and her head slumped on top of his. "She asleep?" he whispered.

Hera nodded.

It was warm, and Jack's hands on Priss's legs were damp, but he worried at the rivulets pouring from Hera's forehead and neck. She'd grown stouter with every year. He didn't mind. She still had the prettiest baby-doll face. But it was hard to be so fat in the heat. "Just another mile," he told her.

The Chase home looked the picture of Sunday morning ease, not a soul bustling around the place. Jack woke Priss, put her on her feet, and rapped on the front door.

Theena herself answered it, her face bright. She laughed and clapped her hands, hugged Priss, then Hera.

Thank the Lord, she looks like her old self.

"Come on in!"

Hera took Priss by the hand and went inside to get the weight off her feet, leaving Jack smiling down at Theena.

Without thinking, Jack opened his arms and Theena entered his embrace. The first time he saw Theena hollow eyed and laid low, he'd wanted to take her in his arms like this and cradle her. Now he kissed the top of her head, inhaled the sweet fragrance of her hair. *I've missed you* – he almost said it aloud, but bit it back. He hugged her tight, then made himself let her go.

He heard Mrs. Chase inside the house saying "Do come in. Oh my. Mrs. Spode, you're flushed. I think she needs a footstool, Randolph."

"You're all red and puffy." That was Dite's voice.

"Get her a glass of water," Mrs. Chase commanded.

Hera had had a harder time of it than Jack had realized. He followed Theena into the parlor. Dite gave them the eye, but Jack ignored her. He knelt down next to Hera. "You all right?" he said quietly.

"Mr. Spode, how nice to see you," Mrs. Chase said. "Won't you sit here next to me?"

Jack gave Hera's hand a squeeze and then joined Mrs. Chase on the settee. Jack kept up his end of the conversation with Mrs. Chase, but he detected a something in the room, he didn't know what.

He attuned himself to the tension in the air. Mrs. Chase spoke a little too brightly, maybe, tried a little too hard to entertain him. But she wasn't the cause. Randolph Chase lazily rocked Liza's parlor cradle with his foot. Theena played blocks with the children in the corner.

Dite seemed perfectly at ease entertaining Hera with some talk about dress sleeves, but Jack caught Hera's glance. *She feels it, too*, he thought.

Mrs. Chase was saying. "Do you know this Javier Guevara making all the fuss in Cuba?"

With only half his attention on his hostess, Jack told her, "Sailed with him out of Havana for a season when I was a kid. Before he took up politics."

It's Randolph, Jack realized. Randolph lolled in his chair, but there was a readiness, a tension in him that belied the casual pose.

There, Jack said to himself. *Just then, when he looked at Dite. That's it.* Randolph had said nothing, had not stared or leered or gaped. But the glance Randolph sent Dite burned the air between them.

God in heaven. He's in love with her. And he's had her.

Jack's hand fisted as he looked at Randolph placidly rocking the baby's cradle. *I could smash him for this. Beat the lying son of a bitch to a pulp*. As for Dite, what punishment would befit a whore who'd sleep with her own sister's husband?

He checked whether Theena had seen the look. She was smiling, helping Priss build her tower of blocks.

Does she know? He wished he could shield her, could protect her from the hurt to come.

Sickened by the undercurrents of lust and betrayal, Jack could no longer sit in that room. He unfolded himself from the couch and announced he needed to stretch his legs.

Dite raised her eyebrows. "You've just walked five miles to get here."

"Priss and Nat haven't though." He turned to Nat. "Did I see a red ball outside?" Nat and Priss followed close on Jack's heels.

Theena moved from her stool to sit beside Mother Chase on the settee. She sat back as the ladies carried on their conversation around her. When she'd been so ill, her family thought she'd lost her wits, not simply her joy. But she hadn't become stupid in her melancholy. She'd seen Randolph's interest in Dite quicken. Spark. Ignite.

At the time, she hardly cared. She had wanted only to yield herself to the gray shroud that threatened to entomb her. But Dite had not let her yield. Dite had bullied her into eating and walking and caring for Nat; Dite had dragged her back into life. *What would have become of me without Dite?*

Sitting next to Mother Chase, Theena felt the pull Dite had on Randolph, even now, here, in company. She saw the glances he stole, the heat in them.

He slept with her sister, but Randolph also rocked the cradle and sang to Liza. These last weeks, he'd been the one, he and Mother Chase, who noticed the first time Liza rolled over, who cooed and tickled and taught her the gladness of being alive. And Nat. He had seen he had shoes on his feet, seen he learned to mind. A better parent than she had been.

And he's been taking care of me, too. How many nights had he held her for hours in the dark when she was afraid? And all these weeks, he had never spoken an impatient word. *He's my husband, and he loves me.* What he had with Dite, that was merely physical.

Dite's and Hera's and Mrs. Chase's voices droned on. Theena's eyes were on the cradle rocking back and forth, back and forth. Randolph shifted in his chair. She saw his gaze flicker over Dite, his eyes alight with the craving of infatuation.

Theena's hands tightened on the fabric of her skirt. *Randolph is caught up with her now, but it won't last.* She forced her palms open and smoothed her skirt. *After what we've done to each other, been to each other, I can forgive him. I do forgive him.*

She rose from the settee and drifted outside where Jack and the children played. Her reawakening to the world still new, Theena lifted her face to the brilliant blue sky. That blue, that particular blue. *Never a day more perfect, nor a color more beautiful than this.*

On the shady side of the house, Jack lay on his back, both children climbing over his long legs and up his chest. He pretended to be sleeping. When Priss and Nat got within his grasp, he growled and swept them into his arms, both little ones shrieking and giggling.

Theena sat down on the ground near them, smiling at the foolishness. Jack sat up and rolled the ball for the youngsters to chase. "How are you, Theena?"

She watched Priss run for the ball, trip, pick herself up, and run on. "I feel light, Jack, like a hollow gourd. Like the wind could blow me away." Nat reached the ball first and ran back to Jack with it in triumph. "Moments like this, though," she said, smiling, "I feel myself filling up again."

Jack stretched his long arm over and waggled her foot. "You're going to be well."

"I am," she said.

Nat came barreling into her and knocked her backwards, her skirt flying above her knee. Laughing, she rolled him over onto his back and smothered his neck with kisses. He giggled and squirmed, and Theena swelled with the spirit of life returning to her.

Jack unfolded his length and rose above her, the sun behind him making a halo around his head. Extending a hand, he said, "Ready to go in?"

She raised her arm, and Jack pulled her to her feet. When she stood beside him, he kept her hand. "I'm glad you're back."

"So am I," she said. Jack's face was near, his dear face. It seemed so natural to turn her face up to his, to receive his kiss on her forehead. Like a benediction.

Dite called to them from the porch. "Dinner's ready, you two."

Dite had seen them together. But Theena didn't care. There was an innocence, a purity, in Jack's kiss that Dite would not understand. It was about love, not desire.

Holding Nat's hand, Theena strolled back to the house, Dite waiting for her. *I wonder if Daddy is the only one Dite's ever loved. And maybe me, in her way. Bless her, she'll have a hard life.*

On the porch, Theena leaned over and kissed Dite's cheek. *As of now, we're even.* She locked eyes with her sister. *The 'deal' is over.*

That night, Theena lay waiting for her husband. At last Randolph crept into the room. He pulled off his shoes and his trousers and crawled into bed. Theena shifted so that she could lie next to him, and he opened his arm for her to nestle her head against him. He smelled of sex. Musky and ripe.

Theena rolled back to her side of the bed. She didn't want him holding her, smelling like Dite, thinking of Dite. She flexed her hand, feeling the power in herself for the first time in many weeks.

This is the last time you come to my bed from another woman, Randolph Chase.

Chapter Twenty-Three

"Pierce my ears," Theena said the next morning.

Dite poured gardenia-scented water through Theena's hair. "You? I never thought you'd want your ears pierced."

"Will it hurt?"

"Yes, ninny, it'll hurt." Dite took hold of Theena's ear and examined the lobe. "I can do it though."

Theena wrapped her head in a towel and Dite fetched her jewelry box.

"You'll need a pair of earrings with a good post." Dite opened the black enameled case carelessly. A string of pearls and a diamond broach spilled onto the bed. Dite hastily scooped them up and returned them to the box.

What's that all about? Theena thought. *I thought she was penniless.* Theena looked carefully at Dite's slight flush. *Did whoever gave her those really break her heart? Is that why she's here? Or is it that her jewelry is hard-won, and she's careful of it.*

"Here they are." Dite held out a pair of dangling jet earrings on her palm. "Keep them. They match your necklace."

"Thank you. Now what do we need? A needle?"

"And turpentine. And I don't want to hear any whining about how much it hurts."

Theena endured the piercing like a Stoic. Dite inserted the jet earrings, and Theena preened in front of the mirror. *Tonight, Randolph Chase, I'm taking you back. You may be a fool, but you're my fool.*

Airing their best dresses and ironing them, arranging their hair, buffing their nails – the women spent the rest of the day preparing for the evening, for the attention of the only man in the house.

Hours later, when Randolph came in for supper, he was not admitted to the bedroom where Theena was dressing in her finery.

"At least let me have Liza," he said, and Theena opened the door just enough to hand him his sleepy baby.

Liza, if she looked like anyone at this age of pudgy cheeks and toothless gums, looked like him. Rosy and blonde, blue-eyed and broad across the forehead. Randolph adored her. He had been nervous with Nat when he was an infant, but not with Liza. He had no qualms about waking her or handling her. He possessed her entirely; with practiced hands he lifted Liza and carried her against his heart as if she were an extension of himself.

He took Liza outside to enjoy the breeze. Julie, the wet nurse, sat on the porch with her own babe. Nat played in the dirt nearby, romping his tiny horses over a fence he'd made with twigs.

"Liza," Nat piped. He reached up with grimy hands. Randolph held his babe out of reach, well aware Theena indulged the boy by letting him hold the baby. Nat asked again, insistently, "Want to hold Liza."

"Your hands are dirty, Nat." Randolph touched Nat's head as he passed by and strolled on through the evening with his treasure.

Returning to the house, Randolph turned the baby over to Julie and joined his mother in the parlor to wait for Dite and Theena. The children were to eat in the kitchen for this night of candlelight and adult conversation.

Randolph saw little of his mother these days, alone at least. He was busy, and they had a guest to entertain, after all. He was ready to be sociable, but Mrs. Chase's expression was grim.

"Randolph, I want this to stop."

Randolph's features hardened. So she knew. *Well, so what?* He left his chair and stood at the window, gazing out at Theena's rose beds.

The bedroom door opened a room away, and Mother hissed, "I mean it, Randolph. You're a disgrace to your father's memory."

At the rustle of taffeta, Randolph turned to behold his wife. Theena wore the dark blue gown he'd given her on their wedding day. Her black hair was swept up and back, revealing jet earrings and her jet necklace twinkling in the lamp light. She smiled, a little shy, he thought. *She's herself again,* he realized.

"Theena, my love. You look beautiful." He stepped over to her, took her hands, and kissed her sweetly on the lips.

He straightened, and there was Dite standing behind his wife, resplendent in a deep green silk that revealed her white bosom and caught the fire in her eyes. Even with his wife's hands in his, Randolph's heart swelled. He would give his very soul for this woman with the fiery red hair.

God help me, he prayed. *I am lost.*

To the sounds of rustling silk, the fragrance of gardenias and jasmine, Randolph seated the ladies in the dining room where crystal sparkled on white linen. When he held Dite's chair out for her, he contrived to find her elbow with his fingers. She was made of cream, of sunshine, of honey. He yearned to have her, again, and again, God help him.

He pulled out Theena's chair. Before she sat, she turned and looked into his face. "Thank you, sweetheart." She smiled at him the way she had when they were first married. She was beautiful. She was his beloved Theena, his wife. Liza's mother.

But as he pushed Theena's chair in, he sought Dite's eyes, the green gateways to his destruction. He knew it, but even now, at this moment, he longed to melt his body into hers, to lose himself in her.

Theena lifted her wine glass. *She's never looked lovelier,* she thought, her eyes on Dite. No wonder she drew Randolph to her. *Not tonight, though. Not ever again.*

Theena touched her glass to Randolph's. "To us, darling." As they drank, she read confusion in his eyes. For the first time in weeks, though, Theena herself felt no confusion. Under the table, she placed her slipper on Randolph's boot. He looked at her in surprise, and she smiled. *Yes, Randolph, I'm alive.*

Throughout dinner, Theena caught her husband's eye repeatedly, smiled at him, and laughed with him. They fell into the give and take as they used to do, and he more and more spoke to her.

After supper, Mrs. Chase crocheted while the other three played at pinochle. Finally, Theena laid her cards aside. She put her hand on Randolph's arm. "Will you come to bed?" she asked.

Dite's lowered eyes remained on her cards, but, Theena noted, Randolph could not stop himself from glancing at her.

You want her even now? Even now I'm inviting you to my bed? She squeezed Randolph's arm slightly. *You're mine, though, Randolph, and Dite doesn't want you, not really.*

Randolph put his cards down. "I'm ready to turn in, too." He stood up without another look at his sister-in-law. "Good night, Mother."

In the bedroom, Theena lit a candle, just enough light for them to undress by. "Help me with these buttons?"

In the past, he would have nuzzled her ear, kissed the back of her neck, wrapped his hands around her to cup her breasts. Tonight, he did no more than unfasten the dress.

Theena stood at the mirror and removed the pins from her hair, her eyes on Randolph behind her. The cascade of her long dark hair had always pulled him to her. He had delighted in running his hands through the heavy tresses, watching it cover her breasts. This time, his attention was on removing his boots. *It's been a long time. Patience in all things, isn't that what Daddy always said?*

Theena snuffed out the candle and climbed into bed next to her husband. A sweet-smelling breeze softly lifted the window curtains, carrying the scent of gardenias and roses, and a lusty bullfrog announced his intentions. Randolph lay on his back, staring at the dark canopy overhead.

When he didn't reach for her, Theena leaned over him, her hair spilling on his bare chest. She kissed the soft spot under his neck, and then ran her tongue over his lips. Randolph wrapped his arms around her, carefully, gently.

"I won't break, Randolph." She pressed herself against him and deepened her kisses. She stroked him and rejoiced as he swelled in response. With a deep sigh, he ran his hands down her back, caressing her curves. She straddled his body. He kissed her breasts through her nightgown, pulled the fine cotton up her leg, reaching for her, touching her.

"Take it off," he whispered.

She tossed the gown across the room and lowered herself onto him, proudly, lovingly. They found their old rhythm together, her hips returning his thrusts, his mouth pulling on her breast, her mouth open and gasping.

He's mine again. He's mine.

When Theena took Randolph off to bed, Dite remained in the parlor. *Well, I wish her well in there.* Theena looked good. Little Sister had turned into a beauty in her own right, if you liked her rather olive complexion.

Dite dealt herself a hand of solitaire.

Though he prefers my white skin. Or so he led her to believe when she bared her breasts to him in the moonlight. An unaccustomed discomfort came over Dite at the image of their last love-making. Randolph, after all, was not just any woman's husband. Even Dite felt a pang at breaking that particular ethic. Daddy would not be proud of his eldest, she knew that.

Well, she'd be on her way soon. *Theena doesn't need me any more, and it's time I looked to my own fortunes.* Randolph, she was sure, would be helpful. Or perhaps Mother Chase, if it came to that.

The old lady had been taken with her at first. What a stroke of luck that she had met the "right" people in Philadelphia. Old Ducky Fitzgerald hobnobbed with high society as often as he delved into the somewhat lower classes. He'd found Dite nursing his dear Aunt Eula. No snob, Ducky had squired her to some grand functions, where she'd met the Bakerfields. She'd had the wit to pass herself off as one of the hoity-toity. *We're not so different, Mrs. Chase and I,* Dite thought. *We both want what we want. But I know I'm selfish, and Lavonia Chase believes she's the paragon of the loving matriarch.*

Mrs. Chase moved the thread through her crochet needle; Dite played her cards. She felt Mrs. Chase's eyes on her, knowing what was to come. It was not the first time Dite had faced a lover's vindictive, possessive mother. The irrepressible Ducky's scandalized mama had eventually dragged him off to London to free him from the wiles of "that red-headed low-life," as she'd put it.

Mrs. Chase spoke her mind. "My daughter-in-law is well, Miss Theophilus. I'm sure you take gratification in her recovery after all your devoted nursing."

"Indeed, I do." Dite laid a jack against a queen, waiting for it.

Mrs. Chase set her crochet in her lap and pierced Dite with her eye. "It's time you left this house."

"Leave my sister's home?" Dite said with feigned dismay. "Where would I go?"

Mrs. Chase shrewdly narrowed her eyes. "So it's money you want, is it?"

The trees in Boston and New York must be leafy by now. Florida's winter season would soon be over, but The Peacock Inn would have a goodly share of wealthy men down for the spring.

This time I won't be a chamber maid, Dite thought. *Won't it be lovely to meet the gentlemen over dinner instead of over their reeking slop pots? Much more advantageous to chat on the verandah with them on an equal footing with their dumpy, doughy wives.* Dite touched the cameo on a velvet ribbon around her throat. *Not to appear needy when they woo you, that is essential.*

"Money?" Dite said. "Oh, I hadn't thought of money. But of course money does solve so many problems, doesn't it?" And from whom was she likely to get the most money? Randolph, or his mother?

The house slept. Randolph eased out from under Theena's arm and left the bed. He pulled on his trousers and carried his shoes to the porch door, careful to keep the latch quiet. He walked the grounds, a half moon lighting his way. An owl swooped low and hooted. He had no destination, no purpose. He only knew he could not lie in the bed next to his wife with his body and soul crying out for another woman.

He wandered the plantation, his gut on fire with guilt and self-loathing. *How can I have lost myself like this?* He did love Theena. He loved her. And the children. Their life together. They'd been so happy in the beginning, and again before Liza was born.

He walked the lane between his rows of orange trees. For once his mind didn't turn to dollars and cents, fungus, manure, pruning, weeding, rain and sun. He mourned for the man he'd been, an honorable man. Yet still he burned for Aphrodite.

Hardly knowing how he came there, Randolph stood in the hay-filled stall where he had been as much a beast as the stallion snoring gently in the next stall. The scent of leather, of straw, of horse and man – the scent of her -- filled his head.

He was consumed. He craved Dite like a drowning man craves breath.

God, help me. I don't know what to do.

Theena awoke the next morning feeling wonderful. Randolph's side of the bed already empty, she pulled his pillow to her and breathed in his scent, a musky scent from loving his wife. A new day, life renewed and affirmed by her husband's lovemaking. Maybe in the next year there would be another baby, a son this time. *Dite will be long gone by then,* she thought. Mama only had the baby sickness the one time. Dite need not ever come back to the Miami River.

Theena rolled out of the bed purposefully. *Time to reclaim my baby girl. I hardly know her, and here she is four months old.* She went in search of Julie, but Julie had only Nat and her own infant with her. Theena held her hand out to her son. "Come with me, Nat. Let's go get Liza. We haven't counted her toes for days."

Mother Chase had Liza in the parlor. The baby was focused on her Grandmother's every coo. "Who's the sweetest girl?" Mrs. Chase crooned. "Are you the sweetest baby?" Liza smiled, the drool wet on her chin.

Theena saw Mother Chase had no smile to spare for the dark child. Without looking away from Liza, she said, "Good morning, Nathanial."

"Answer your grandmother, Nat."

"Good morning, Grandmother." That over, Nat let go his mama's dress and busied himself in the toy basket behind the settee. Theena hurt for her boy. Such a loving, trusting child. When would he realize the woman he called grandmother cared nothing for him? When would he understand his skin color, hair color, eye color, his very existence displeased her?

"How is our Eliza this morning?" Theena said.

Mrs. Chase shifted the baby to her shoulder and pressed one hand against her back. Theena read the message as clearly as if Mother Chase had spoken it. *She thinks Liza is hers,* Theena thought. *She means it to be so. But that isn't going to be the way of it.*

Theena stepped over to Mother Chase's chair and held her hands out for her child. The old woman's hand moved to Liza's curly head, but Theena didn't back down. She remained standing with her hands out, and Mrs. Chase finally let Liza go.

"Come on, Nat," Theena said. "Let's take sis outside to hear the mockingbird sing." They left Mrs. Chase with empty arms.

Under a shady oak, Theena sat down with Nat between her legs. Supporting Liza's head, she placed the baby in big brother's lap. Nat stared at her, tried to touch her blue eyes, but Theena caught his fingers. "Rub her tummy, Nat. She'll like that." Liza waved her tiny fists and caught Nat in the mouth. He laughed, and Theena's world was complete.

When the dinner hour approached, Theena settled herself in the parlor with her mending to wait for the family to gather. She heard Randolph's step in the dining room, but when he didn't come through into the parlor, she put her sewing aside and went to meet him. On slippered feet, she crossed the floor and opened the door.

Randolph stood with his back to her, Dite's arms around his waist.

A few days ago, Theena might have backed out and shut the door. But no more. Theena stepped into the room. Randolph jerked away from Dite, and Dite put a hand to the buttons at her throat.

Do they really think I don't know? She gave Dite a look to tell her otherwise.

"Randolph," she said. "Come for a stroll with me down to the gate before Susan puts dinner on the table."

Theena took Randolph's arm and turned him to the door without sparing another glance for Dite. Outside, she looped her arm through Randolph's and enjoyed the feel of him held close to her side. She rubbed her face against his broadcloth, matched her steps to his and remembered the rhythm of their bodies together in the bed. Her husband.

They reached the gate and stood admiring the moon vines growing in the custard apple trees. She clasped his hand. So warm, so firm. *He'll forget her.*

"You're preoccupied tonight, Randolph."

"Am I? It's just some money matters. Nothing to it, really."

The cost of Dite's passage back North? How much does it take to sail all the way to Pennsylvania or New York? Whatever it is, Randolph can afford it, and Dite has earned her ticket.

Chapter Twenty-Four

"Lift your feet," Hera snapped.

Jack obliged as she swept under his chair. Not an hour ago she'd griped at him to get his bits of fishing gear off her table so she could put dinner on. *Time to get out of the house,* he thought. Jack wasn't proud of himself for it, but he liked being out in the grove or on the bay by himself maybe a little more than he should.

"I think I'll go down to the Peacock and see if somebody needs a hunting guide before they all head back north. Likely one or another of those Yanks will take me on."

He'd laid in a cord of firewood, made a bit of charcoal from the buttonwood trees, knitted a new fishing net for mullet. For now he had a spell of relative idleness ahead of him, and he felt about as welcome as a fly in the soup.

Hera scowled. "How long would you be gone?"

Women are so contrary. "I thought you'd be glad to get me out from underfoot."

"Well, not for days at a time."

"No more than four or five days, I promise." He took Hera's broom from her and forced her to sit on his lap, rigid as her broomstick. "Let me see right there," he said, and pushed loose ringlets away from Hera's neck. He nuzzled and kissed till she yielded, her body soft again and pliant.

"Jack Spode, you're awful," she said, but she turned her face up to be kissed.

Next morning, Jack took the beach path to Theena's skiff and found himself whistling to the wheeling gulls. Family life agreed with him, but a man needs a little breathing room sometimes.

The Peacock Inn sat beyond the Cocoanut Grove settlement, a good morning's row down the bay if the wind picked up. Jack made it in not much more than an hour, those uncommon shoulder muscles of his indifferent to the waves. He counted nine yachts of various configurations in the inlet. Likely a dozen more out in the ocean deep-sea fishing. Shouldn't be any problem finding a job.

Jack shook the sand off his feet, put his shoes on, and entered the Peacock Inn, the only resort between Fort Pierce and Key West. He found his old fishing pal Gus Grisham, now the steward. "Know anyone looking for a guide?"

"Always somebody needing a guide. Come on with me." Gus led the way to the common room with a pot of coffee in his hand. He approached a table of four men playing cards, and as he poured the coffee, he introduced Jack.

"Finest hunter in the bay country," Gus told the men, "and got more salt water in him than you'll find in a barrel of pickles."

The men looked him over through the haze of their cigar smoke. Jack stood their scrutiny with his arms crossed and one foot cocked out to the side. Not insolent, just confident.

"You know the glades?" one of the men asked him.

Jack nodded his head. "Sure."

"Think you could find us some gators to bag?" The man, corpulent but seemingly fit, fingered the gold watch chain stretched across his belly.

A better trick would be *not* finding gators once they were in the glades, but Jack simply repeated himself. "Sure."

"You got a boat?" another one asked him.

"What you need is a dugout in the glades. Mine will hold me and two more. Three, things begin to get crowded."

The big man puffed his cigar and turned to the man on his right. "What about it, Kirk? You up for some gator hunting?"

"Absolutely. I can be ready in an hour or so."

"What's your price, Spode?"

Jack named an absurdly high sum, expecting to negotiate to a lower fee, but there was no negotiation. The imposing man with the cigar simply said, "Fine. See you in an hour."

"I'll take care of the grub," Jack said. "Plan to be gone three or four days, depending on how many hides you want." *And how many skeeter bites you can stand.* Jack arranged for the provisions, then wandered over to the corral where half a dozen horses flicked their tails at the flies. He propped a foot on the bottom rail, held his closed fist out and enticed a chestnut mare over to investigate. She licked his hand opened and cleaned his empty palm. He petted her forehead, scratched her neck for her.

In a year or two, he thought, he could buy a riding horse, maybe a buckboard, too. And that sewing machine for Hera.

Jack retreated to the shade of the lower verandah and sat in one of the oak rockers with his feet on the railing. *What on earth are they doing in there? Even Hera would have been ready by now.*

The two gentlemen, Mr. Lawrence Mitchell and Mr. Alfred Kirk, emerged from the shadowy interior, ready to go. Mr. Mitchell's pack seemed about the size and heft of Jack's own; Mr. Kirk's must have weighed as much as the man himself. Mitchell, the heavy one, wore sensible canvas pants and a denim shirt. Kirk, the slender one, had bedecked himself in buckskin. His sleeves sported long leather fringe along the seams and his pants did too. Jack struggled not to smile.

"Mind if I have a look at your guns, gentlemen?" Mitchell didn't seem a man who'd take kindly to being challenged, but he handed his rifle to Jack without a word. Jack looked it over with a practiced eye. Adequate for the game they were after; in other words, the man carried a powerful rifle. The curly carving in the polished stock seemed a bit fanciful for Jack's taste, but it would do the job. "What have you shot with this?"

"A bear in Wyoming. Bighorns in Colorado. Moose in Maine. Another bear in Texas."

"Nice piece. Mr. Kirk?"

The thin man passed his weapon over and again Jack suppressed a smile. The stock's decoration included bronze inlay and J.C.K. in elaborate script, but the fanciness didn't make it a sissy gun. The vintage Sharps had been built for killing buffalo at great ranges. The octagonal barrel added additional weight, but it did keep the barrel from overheating so much; helped absorb some of the recoil too. *A man could kill an elephant with a gun like this*, Jack thought.

"What kind of action you seen with this, Mr. Kirk?"

"My father, the late Mr. Josiah Kirk, once shot a tiger with this rifle. In India. I'm sure you'll find it satisfactory."

The gun itself Jack had no doubts about. Whether Mr. Kirk could handle it, well, they'd see. "I'm sure you're right."

As the three men descended the staircase, Randolph Chase drove his wagon to the front entrance of the Peacock Inn. Aphrodite Theophilus sat on the seat next to him, her bonnet nearly hiding her face.

So Dite's time has come, Jack thought. *Wonder if Theena pushed her out, or if Dite just got tired of Chase?*

"Hello, Spode," Randolph said as he dismounted from the wagon. Dite moved the bonnet away from her eyes. She granted Jack a brilliant smile. "Jack! Imagine seeing you here."

Jack smiled back at her – how could a man not -- but he kept his distance. He watched Randolph help Dite from the wagon, then place her on her feet close enough he could have kissed her. *Possessive bastard,* Jack thought. *Though truth be, likely she's the one who possesses him. At least she's out of Theena's house. And not in mine.*

"Could you introduce us to the lady?" Mr. Kirk said at Jack's elbow.

The man's tongue might as well be hanging out like a dog's, Jack thought. *Dite will make short work of a fellow like him.*

"Dite, this is Mr. Kirk, and Mr. Mitchell. Miss Theophilus, sister-in-law to Mr. Chase and myself."

Mr. Kirk stepped forward in his fine buckskins and bowed over Dite's hand. "I hope you will be staying at the Inn? When I return, I would love to ask you to supper."

"Mr. Kirk. How very kind of you," Dite said. She had her eyes on Mr. Mitchell, however. His girth did not dissuade her. The man oozed power. Even Jack knew power was the most seductive quality a man can have, for some women.

Randolph's face was grim. He took Dite's elbow, possessive, jealous. *So it's not over yet, not for him.*

Mitchell held back, taking her measure. Dite, seemingly unaware of the man gripping her arm, granted him a brilliant smile.

Jack had seen that smile before. He turned his gaze on Randolph. *He doesn't look like a man about to put his woman on a north-bound boat. The son of a bitch. And if he doesn't, she'll make an ass of him in a week's time. My money's on Mitchell.*

Randolph escorted Dite up the stairs, and as they passed by Jack, Dite grinned at him wickedly. Yes, she conveyed, we understand the situation, you and I. *I understand, all right. If you're still here at the end of the week, Dite, I'll . . .* Jack didn't know what he'd do, but he didn't want her here fooling around with Theena's husband.

"Gentlemen?" Jack said, and led them to the beach where he'd pulled the skiff onto the sand.

By nightfall, Jack had retrieved the dugout and poled himself and his companions up the Miami River to the rapids. They portaged around the shallow rough waters and put in again just east of the marsh that heralded the glades themselves. On the big hummock where Billy had once quizzed Theena about her bearings, the men made camp.

Jack hacked mangrove branches for a smoky fire to deter the hordes of mosquitoes plaguing them. Then he built a second fire of oak and heated the ham and beans he'd brought. He pointed to the glowing eyes of a gator in the water just offshore of their little island.

"I see him," Mitchell said. "If the tales are true, we'll have to beat them away with a stick."

"Not far wrong," Jack said. "This nice weather, they'll be out sunning instead of burrowing. What are you doing, Mr. Kirk?"

Kirk sprinkled white powder from a canvas bag, circling the camp. "It's lime," he said. "It'll keep the snakes from crawling over here and wiggling into our bedrolls while we sleep."

Jack took care not to meet Mitchell's eye. "That been a problem for you in the past, Mr. Kirk?"

"No, of course not. I'm always prepared."

Jack and Mitchell each pitched a small frame to hold their mosquito nets away from their faces. Kirk had a rather elaborate folding cot with a mosquito tent over it. They let their fire go out and lay under a black sky pierced by all the stars of the galaxy.

Jack woke early and watched a snake stalking a bird's nest in the branches overhead. He toyed with the idea of waking Kirk and showing him the weakness in his lime powder defense, but resisted the impulse. Too easy to rag a greenhorn like Kirk. Besides, the man was paying him handsomely.

After a breakfast of bacon, grits, and coffee, the men broke camp and settled into the dugout. Jack poled them through the saw grass, soon regretting he hadn't warned his guests about the reason it was called saw grass. Kirk sliced his palm open on a blade he'd grabbed for no apparent reason.

"It's all right," Kirk called out. "I have bandages in my pack."

The alligators tended to congregate in pools amid the acres of saw grass, their heavy wallowing and thrashing contending with the encroaching growth. Jack headed for a smallish pool south and west from the mouth of the river. He knew of two other larger pools likely filled edge to edge with gators, but where was the fun in finding gator heaven the first day out?

They glided past turtles sunning themselves, otters busy digging crawdads, frogs so big it'd take two hands to hold one. A small hummock boasted red and yellow blooms hanging from every tree. Jack breathed in the spicy sun-warmed air. *A man can let himself be out here, just the critters and the grass, the water and the sun.*

"Mr. Spode?" Kirk called. He sat in the bow with his arms and hands and feet as near the center of the dugout as possible. He turned back to look at Jack poling from the stern of the boat.

"These snakes," Kirk said. "I mean, I knew there were snakes in the glades, but I was unprepared for their numbers. What if they try to get in the boat?"

Out of pity, Jack bent and tossed Kirk a paddle. "This'll do the trick, one tries to snuggle up to you."

Jack poled into an open area perhaps forty feet across. The water lapped around three small hummocks, too small to bother to bank the boat on. Easier to avoid the moccasins if they stayed in the boat anyway. The tufts sported a palmetto or two and an infant guava tree trying to keep its feet dry. The focus of attention, however, were the six or seven gators sunning themselves.

A mid-sized one lay on a hummock with its pink mouth wide open. Flies buzzed all around its head and collected on its slimy tongue. When it had a mouthful, it snapped its jaws shut and swallowed. "I be damned," Mitchell said. "I heard they'd eat flies, and now I've seen it with my own eyes."

Jack stilled the boat and sat down. He spoke softly to his hunters. "Trick is, stay seated so you don't rock the boat so much. Aim at the spot behind the eye if you can, or just behind the front leg."

Mitchell chose his target, a big one floating with its snout above the surface, the rest of its body visible just below the water. He aimed and fired. The monster thrashed and boiled the water, alarming the other gators far more than the sound of the rifle had.

Jack stood ready with his gaff and a lasso to haul the creature to the hummock before it gave up and sank. It was hell to get a dead gator off the bottom of a pond.

Kirk's target began to amble away into the undergrowth. He'd miss his shot if he didn't hurry. He stood up, pointed the Sharps, and fired. The kick of the huge gun knocked his shoulder back. He lost his balance, toppled out of the dugout and into the tea-colored water.

"I can't swim!" he screamed. The panicked beating of his arms against the water drew the interest of the gator he'd targeted and missed. It slid into the water and glided toward this new prey thrashing and splashing about.

"Oh, hell," Jack cursed. He measured the distances between the gator, Kirk, and the boat. Turning the cumbersome dugout between beast and man would take too long, and likely the gator would simply duck under the boat anyway.

Jack jumped over board and waded waist deep to where Kirk flailed, the man's wits completely gone without his even realizing a set of razor-sharp teeth were after him. *The fool's probably worrying about that nest of moccasins over by the hummock when he's got a pair of jaws nearly on him.*

Before Kirk could grab hold of Jack and pull him down, Jack seized the man's collar, drew him up, and slapped him across the face. "Stand up, damn it."

Jack half dragged Kirk to the boat and handed him over to Mitchell to pull aboard. Then Jack grabbed an oar and turned to face the gator. *Come on, baby, open up.*

The gator had no preference whether it chomped on Kirk or Jack, none at all. It kept coming till it was within six feet, then opened its jaws for the kill. Jack rammed the oar down its throat as far as it would go.

The oar irrevocably lodged in the gator's throat, the creature whipped its head to and fro, choking and coughing.

If the massive tail lashed the dugout, it could turn the whole thing over. Mitchell took aim, a difficult shot with the violence of the beast's thrashing, and got it under the jaw. The gator quickly sank to the bottom of the brown water where Mitchell's first kill lay.

"A damn waste," Mitchell muttered.

"Plenty more out here," Jack said as he hoisted himself into the boat. He flicked at a couple of leeches on his arms. Too late. The little blood suckers had already firmly attached themselves. "How you doing, Mr. Kirk?"

Kirk had his father's rifle across his knees, brushing off the mud it'd picked up from the bottom of the boat. The man could hardly look his companions in the eye, but he spoke with heartfelt conviction. "Thank you, Mr. Spode, I am quite well. Your timely intervention will not be forgotten, I assure you."

If Mr. Mitchell was disgusted with Kirk for causing him to lose both the gators he'd so precisely killed, he was man enough not to show it. Jack appreciated that. No need to shame Kirk any further. As for the gators, Jack thought, let the fish and the turtles take care of them. Raising a three hundred pound monster from the mucky bottom would be wasted effort when they'd see scores more before the day was out.

With a cry, Kirk yanked his sodden leather shirt off. A dozen or so leeches sucked on him, already turning liverish from his blood. Frantic, Kirk began clawing at the hateful things.

"Mr. Kirk! Don't pull at them," Jack told him. "They'll fall off by themselves when they've had their fill. Better just to wait them out."

Green in the face, Kirk rummaged in his voluminous pack and with trembling hands withdrew a silvered flask. He took a long drink and passed it back to Mitchell, who declined, and then to Jack. A man would be a fool to drink and hunt gators, keep an eye out for cottonmouths, and stay alert to where in the hell you were in the glades, but he took a sip out of curiosity. He had never drunk anything more refined than the local moonshine or the rough rum the taverns in Key West served. This was good stuff. Smooth and hot all at once. *So that's what the rich folks drink.* He passed the flask back to Kirk.

Being rich had its rewards, no doubt about it. But being in the glades on a beautiful morning, the egrets and the wood storks passing overhead, the breeze whispering through the saw grass -- who needs more than that?

In the afternoon they eased into a pond no more than eighteen inches deep. Mitchell killed an eight foot gator and Kirk bagged one just a bit longer than that. Jack enjoyed the irony of the lesser man's kill exceeding the real hunter's, but no one spoke of it. Mitchell helped Jack rope the beasts and haul them through the shallow water to the nearest large hummock. There they made camp and Jack gutted and skinned the gators.

Over a supper of gator tail steaks and canned beans, Jack asked, "How many trophies you gentlemen plan to take home?" He was thinking how much a rolled up gator hide weighed, and smelled, and how they'd be sharing the dugout with the two hides until they got back.

"I'm quite satisfied," Kirk answered. "Though I would be pleased to shoot a few otter tomorrow. I was thinking the pelts would make a lovely muff for Miss Theophilus. If she would accept them, that is."

That gun of yours, an otter will be blown to smithereens, Jack thought. *And Dite will take anything she can get from you, you poor ass.*

"How about you, Lawrence?" Kirk asked.

Mitchell slapped at a persistent mosquito. "I've no use for more than one gator hide, but certainly, I'll be glad to hunt something else tomorrow. Otters, deer, what have you."

The fourth day of the expedition, Jack poled back through the saw grass toward the Miami River, the dugout riding low in the water with the bounty of their hunt. The various hides gave off a powerful stink, inviting flies and mosquitoes to ride along with them. Both Kirk and Mitchell scratched continuously and waved at the flies and gnats trying to sip the water from their eyes.

Once they were past the rapids and floating serenely downstream, most of the flying pests deserted them. They bathed their faces in the cooler clear water of the river and revived themselves with a pull or two from Kirk's flask.

As they approached the banks of the Chase plantation, Jack considered asking the gentlemen if they'd like to stretch their legs on dry land. They could stroll up to the house, and Theena would offer them a glass of lemonade.

As if thinking of her had conjured her in the flesh, Theena appeared on the north bank of the river where Chase's men had macheted a clearing. She carried cane poles over her shoulder and Nat trailed along behind her, a black puppy trotting alongside him.

Jack whistled to them and poled the boat over to the landing.

"Uncle Jack," Nat hollered and ran for him. Jack hopped out of the dugout and swung Nat into the air. Then he turned to Theena. "Hi," he said. God, how he loved the way her face lit up when she saw him.

"Theena, this is Mr. Mitchell, Mr. Kirk," Jack said. "My sister-in-law Mrs. Chase, and this fine young fisherman is Nathanial."

"Mrs. Chase, how do you do?" Mitchell said. "I hope you can bear the scent of three men fresh from a hunting expedition."

Theena smiled at the big man. "Mr. Mitchell, you're a welcome break in a long day, smells and all."

"Mr. Spode is blessed with lovely sisters-in-law, Mrs. Chase." Kirk said. "We met a Miss Theophilus at the Inn, what, four days ago – she would be your sister?"

"Dite? Yes, she is. And did you meet my husband as well?"

"Oh, yes. The fellow driving the wagon Miss Theophilus traveled in. Fine man."

Mitchell bent over to rub the puppy's tummy, and Nat sat down to help. That left Jack at leisure to observe Theena as she bantered with the filthy, but dandified, Mr. Kirk.

She'd gained a little weight. She looked well. But not happy. It'd take time for her to get over what Randolph and Dite had been up to. Jack shook his head. How could they do that to her?

"Mr. Mitchell, Mr. Kirk, I can offer you orange juice and ham, collard greens, and cornbread if you'd care to stay for dinner."

Mitchell stood up from Nat and the puppy. "No, ma'am," he said with authority. "You're very kind, but we aren't fit company at this time. Perhaps we'll have another opportunity. If you and Mr. Chase care to travel to the Inn, I will welcome you as my guests."

Theena inclined her head. "That's very gracious, Mr. Mitchell. As it is, I'm needed here, and I believe my husband is still there."

Startled, Jack took in that information. *Randolph still there? With Dite, in a public place?* His jaw tight, he looked at Theena, but she said no more. She didn't have to. *Damn it to hell,* he thought.

Jack caught Mitchell watching the two of them. The man didn't miss much. He likely had the whole sorry mess figured out already.

The three hunters left Theena and Nat to their fishing and followed the river to the bay. By supper time, Mitchell and Kirk were soaking in their baths while Jack labored with the hides and pelts. Tom Dalkins would do the curing and tanning and shaping, but Jack had to get the messy remains to Tom's shop a mile down from the Inn.

Once he left Tom's place, Jack peeled off his clothes and plunged into the bay. Washing off four days of sweat and grime in the brackish water, Jack swam and dove with a trio of dolphins who gave every indication of enjoying his company. What must they make of the odor of gator musk he left behind him in the water?

Refreshed and clad in his change of clothes, Jack returned to the Inn for a supper. This late in the day, he'd just stay here overnight and head home in the morning. All afternoon his mind had been on Theena and Randolph, Randolph and Dite. *Maybe it's Dite I should talk to. Chase is a willing fool, but a fool just the same. Dite holds the reins in all this.*

Jack ate in the kitchen with Gus. Dark fell too early for Jack to retire to his bedroll under the banyan trees, and he strolled down to the bay in the cool evening. Guests from the Inn sat in folding chairs on the beach star-gazing and watching the ship lights bobbing out at sea.

Not far from the group of star-gazers, a young fellow carrying a lantern lit the path for a couple returning from the bay.

"Jack?" It was Dite. "I'd recognize those wonderful shoulders anywhere," she said. Embarrassed at her indiscretion, Jack wondered if she'd had too much wine.

Randolph's surly greeting indicated he'd perhaps had more than wine. "You again?" he said to Jack. Guilt and liquor made him quarrelsome. "I believe you've forgotten your way home."

That's one.

Jack had vowed long ago to roll with one insult, if he could, but he wouldn't answer for how much damage he'd do to a man who offered two.

Conscious of the guests near by, Jack said in a low voice, "I believe you're the one whose absence from home is in question."

Randolph drew back. The whiskey he'd consumed hadn't left him too drunk to feel the sting. "None of your damn business when I go home."

"You're drunk," Jack said. "We'll take this up in the morning."

Dite left Randolph's side and put her hand on Jack's arm. Too softly for Randolph to hear, she said, "Let it be, Jack. I'm leaving soon as I can. Then Randolph will go home."

"Cramping your style, is he?"

Even Dite could be hurt, and in the lantern light, Jack saw he'd hit home. Not that he was proud of it.

Randolph jerked Dite away from Jack. "Get your damn hands off her, Spode. You can't have her, and you can't have Theena either."

Jack's fist slammed into Randolph's jaw. Down he went, but he didn't stay down. The whiskey denying the pain of a cracked jaw, Randolph lunged at Jack and the two of them went at it. Jack had the superior strength and the clearer head, and after his first flash of anger, he fought defensively.

People hurried over from where they sat on the beach to congregate around the fight. From the corner of his eye, Jack saw Dite clap both hands over her face. Could the woman actually regret two men fighting over her?

Randolph crouched, panting, mouth pulled down in a snarl. Jack waited for the next onslaught. One of the figures in the crowd emerged from the dark behind Dite. He took her by the shoulders and turned her around. She buried her face in his broad chest. Too bad Jack hadn't actually put money on Mitchell.

Randolph lunged. Jack caught him a blow in the solar plexus, bringing Randolph to his knees, gasping for breath. Jack hauled him to a palm tree and propped him up.

"Stop now, Randolph. Let's stop." He turned to the crowd and told them, "It's all over. Everybody go on now."

They were alone. Randolph leaned his head back against the trunk, and the tears on his face caught the starlight. "I can't let her go, Jack." His shoulders shook and he brought his hands to his battered face.

"You can't keep her, that's for damned sure."

Randolph crawled to his feet. Reeling, he stumbled through the sand into the dark.

Jack turned back to the inn. He needed to know when Dite planned to put an end to this. Chase would pay her passage north, and she could hunt for a rich man up there. *Hell,* Jack thought, *I'll pay her passage if it comes to that.* The money from Mitchell and Kirk should cover the fare all the way to New York, if that's where she wanted to go.

Jack approached the patio at one side of the inn. A few chairs and a table shone in the light from a single lantern, and in the shadows a couple embraced. The woman stepped away, and the light caught her red hair. Lawrence Mitchell followed her into the lantern's glow, and Jack passed on silently in the dark.

Dite had found her passage north.

Chapter Twenty-Five

Theena twisted the plain gold band on her finger. After they had endured so much, why hadn't they won for themselves a more certain kind of love?

Randolph's side of the bed gaped empty for the sixth night. She knew she had no claim on higher morality. She had deceived Randolph about Nat, and that was a dreadful thing to have done. But surely she'd paid for it in suffering all those months Randolph wouldn't touch her, hardly spoke to her. Surely the blatant, willful, and now prolonged hurt he did her must nullify the guilt she'd carried since their marriage.

How do you measure hurts like these? Is one betrayal worse than another? Couldn't Randolph have kept his heart safe from her, if not his body?

Theena didn't bother heaping blame on Dite. She had always known her sister to be selfish and sometimes heartless. The letters Dite sent home to her and Hera also told a story between the lines. Dite had become an adventuress. She could make a living as a nurse, but Dite preferred the intrigue and risk of attaching herself to wealthy men for what she could get out of them. *It's sport to her*, Theena thought. *And the men, like fish on a string.*

Not Jack though. She'd never seen Jack's face take on that peculiar child-like eagerness when Dite flirted with him. Other men lost their wits under Dite's gaze – maybe Dite couldn't even help it -- but Jack would merely smile a little, and carry on.

Is Jack happy with Hera? Do he and Hera ever disappoint each other?

Next morning, Theena continued her determined efforts to reclaim her life. While she'd been ill, her mother-in-law had quietly removed Nat from family life in the dining room to eat in the kitchen with Susan. Meanwhile, Liza had reigned in the high chair at her grandmother's elbow, banged her spoon, and made as much mess and disturbance as Nat ever had, but without being fussed at or scolded.

Why on earth did I let her do that? My sweet boy. Before she sat down for breakfast, Theena marched into the kitchen. "Come on, Nat. I want you to eat your eggs with me in the dining room. I miss you in there."

She helped him into his chair and tied a napkin around his neck. "Now you can show Liza how to eat like a big boy. She's a messy baby, isn't she, Nat?"

Nat shared his biscuit with his sister and then dug into his grits.

"A gentleman doesn't eat with his elbows on the table, young man," Mother Chase said.

Nat looked at his mama, and Theena winked at him. Then he removed his elbows.

"We're going to visit Hera and Priss today, Mother Chase."

Mrs. Chase bridled. "Surely you aren't going to drag Eliza all that way. Leave her here with me."

Theena smiled. She had expected this. "Thank you, Mother Chase. But Liza is coming with us."

"But Randolph has the wagon. And he'll expect you to be here when he returns."

Theena looked at her pointedly. "And when will that be, Mother Chase?"

The old woman looked away. Her puffy eyes indicated she too had slept very little these nights Randolph had been gone. No doubt she tortured herself wondering where she'd gone wrong as a mother that her son would carry on with another woman.

"Mr. Bolton," Theena went on in a kinder tone, "has agreed to let me take one of the wagons from the orchards."

"Oh, my dear, that is too dangerous, a woman alone with two children."

Theena put her cup down. "Mother Chase, you forget I'm born and bred in this country. And with a horse and wagon, we'll be at Hera's in under an hour. You needn't worry, truly."

"Please, can't you wait for Randolph?"

Theena wiped Liza's mouth and hands, then pulled her into her lap. "No, Mother. I can't wait any longer for Randolph."

Silence hung between them for a moment, and then Mrs. Chase gathered herself. "How long will you be gone?" Her eyes were on her granddaughter's curly blond hair.

"Only a couple of nights, I think." Mother Chase would be lonely here with only Susan in the kitchen to make the house feel lived in. She already looked forlorn, in fact. "Will you hold Liza? Nat's spread honey all over his face."

Mother Chase held her hands up -- "Come to Granny, precious" -- and Liza chortled to be in her grandmother's lap.

Theena loaded the children into the wagon and set out under a cloudless blue sky. Liza napped in a box behind the seat, and Nat sat next to his mother. "Let me," he said and reached for the reins. The road was narrow and rutted; the old mule needed no guidance from its driver. "Come here, then," Theena said. She pulled Nat between her legs and let him hold the reins until he had harassed the mule long enough with his flicking and flapping of the lines.

For company, they had the myriad birds all around them. Wood storks, a parrot blown in by the last storm, mockingbirds, and even a rosy spoonbill. Theena supplied their names and told Nat where they liked to nest and how many eggs they would lay in a year. "Hear that?" she said. "That's the mockingbird singing to you."

Theena checked on Liza in the box behind her. So beautiful a child, Liza reminded Theena of a cherub she'd seen in a book. Her cheeks were pink, her skin perfect and smooth as only a child's can be. Golden ringlets tumbled over her forehead, and blond lashes curled against her cheek. Theena adjusted the light blanket and touched her finger to Liza's tiny nose. Whatever happened between Randolph and her, Theena knew God had blessed her with these two children.

Hera and Priss were in the chicken yard when Theena drove up. She left the mule under the banyan tree and took Nat and drowsy Liza to see the baby chicks.

"Couldn't have come a more welcome day. The house is just too quiet when Jack's gone."

"Where to this time?"

"Fort Pierce. He's got money in his pocket and gone to buy lemon trees."

Throughout the day, Theena let more and more of her tension go. Wading in the bay with the children, discussing colic and thumb sucking and diaper rash with her sister as they shelled peas together – life seemed so normal here. *This is how life should be,* Theena thought. *Routine and humdrum. And peaceful. Please, God.*

Once the children were down for the night, Hera and Theena put their feet up and enjoyed a glass of hard cider together.

After a day of avoiding the subject of Randolph and Dite, Hera said, "What's happening at your house?"

Theena sighed. "Randolph took Dite to the Peacock Inn so she could book a passage north. That was a week ago. I haven't seen him since."

"After what she's done, I'll never speak to her again," Hera declared.

Theena shrugged. "It isn't Dite I'm thinking about."

"What are you going to do?"

"Do?" Theena hadn't considered *doing* anything. She'd simply been waiting for Randolph to return, and then to let time and patience do their work. What was there to *do*?

"Or don't you want him back?" Hera said. "I wouldn't blame you if you kicked the bastard out."

Theena drained her cup. "I'm going to bed, Hera. Stay up if you want to; the light won't bother me."

Theena put her head down on Jack's pillow, lay on Jack's side of the bed. She felt his body's warmth, impossible as that was, and for an instant felt as if she lay in his arms.

She looked at Hera's head bent over her mending, her lovely hair shining in the lamp light. She felt closer to her sister at that moment than she ever had, and here she was, coveting her sister's husband. *Randolph and I,* Theena reproached herself. *Both of us with divided hearts. Maybe we deserve each other.*

Theena put Jack from her mind. She had had practice at that these last few years.

What if I started over with Nat and Liza on Daddy's land? She could replant the garden, hire some labor to clear a few more acres, and start a grove. Start small like Jack did. She'd teach Nat and then Liza to fish in the river, to handle the skiff on the bay. With Nat's puppy and Bertie, they'd have company and protection. Get a few pigs, some chickens. That could be Liza's first job when she was older, to gather eggs.

In the early morning, Theena woke to what she felt had been a dreamless sleep. But somehow, sometime during the night, her mind had come to a resolution. She put her feet on the cold floor and lit a candle to dress by.

"What are you doing up?" Hera whispered. "The cock hasn't even crowed yet."

"He did."

"Well. Too early for me." Hera snuggled back under the quilt.

"I'm going to wake Nat to tell him I'm going."

"What are you talking about?"

"I'm going after Randolph."

Hera sat up in the bed. Watching Theena tie her shoes, she said, "You going to be able to harness that old mule in the dark?"

"It's nearly light."

Theena roused Nat from his pallet and waited till he was awake enough to understand she was going. Then she carried him to Hera's bed and pulled the covers up to his chin. She kissed his face and smoothed his hair. "Go back to sleep, sweetheart."

Theena kissed Liza and arranged her covers.

"I'm off, then."

When Theena arrived at the Peacock Inn, they were still serving late breakfasts. A spring cold front had come through and she left the mule in a sunny patch harnessed to the wagon. She hoped she wouldn't be here long.

How should she go about this? Would Randolph and Dite be registered for one room or two? She didn't care whether she spoke with Dite or not. They'd said their goodbyes over a week ago, and Theena had nothing to add.

The man at the hotel desk was a stranger, but he likely knew all about her family's ugly secrets. She could use a little of Dite's boldness, she thought, and squared her shoulders. With a firm step, then, she approached the clerk behind the tall desk. "Can you tell me where to find Mr. Randolph Chase?"

The man looked at her oddly, but she kept her gaze steady.

"May I enquire who's asking?"

"Mrs. Randolph Chase."

He hesitated. Theena could see he had a delicate situation to handle if he knew Randolph and Dite were sleeping together. "I believe Miss Theophilus would be your sister? So sorry you've missed her." *Yes, he knows.* "She sailed north two days ago."

And yet Randolph stays on, Theena thought.

"Mr. Chase hasn't come down for breakfast this morning," he said. "Perhaps he's still sleeping."

"Then I'd like a key to his room."

The man turned to a board behind him and selected number fourteen. "Upstairs, third door on the left."

In front of number fourteen, Theena breathed deeply and knocked. No answer. She leaned her ear against the door and heard no one stirring inside. She used the key and let herself in.

Randolph lay sprawled across the bed, unconscious of her entrance. The shutters were closed against the morning sun, and the air was close and foul. Theena shut the door behind her and marched for the window. She threw up the sash and pushed the shutters aside.

When she turned around, a shaft of light hit Randolph in the face. He shielded his eyes with his arm and groaned. "God damn you, Jack. Leave me alone."

Theena studied her husband. Old bruises on his face, especially on his jaw. Two days worth of beard, red in the sunlight. Haggard. He smelled of whiskey and looked like a man with a terrible headache. Theena took some little pleasure in that.

"Jack isn't here. It's me, Randolph."

Randolph jerked his arm away. "Theena?" She might have laughed, he looked so alarmed. Stricken, guilty -- like a child caught burning ants. But Theena wasn't amused. Mixed in with the anger and resentment, what she felt was pity. To have come to this.

Randolph sat up in bed, covering his nudity with the quilt. "What are you doing here?"

"I've come to take you home."

He glanced at her, then lowered his gaze. She didn't wonder he couldn't look her in the eye.

"Home," he repeated stupidly.

Theena sat in the only chair in the room. She suspected the drink was still in him.

"I can't go home," he said.

"Why not?"

"Because I'm drunk. And I intend to stay that way."

He reached for the bottle on the nightstand, but Theena got it first. "Get dressed, Randolph. I'm going downstairs for a pot of coffee."

When she returned, Randolph sat on the edge of the bed with his pants and one shoe on. The other shoe hung loosely from his fingers.

"I need a drink," he muttered.

"I've brought coffee. And they're sending eggs and bacon and biscuits up." She poured him a cup and he accepted it with shaky hands.

"You look like you've been drunk for days," Theena said.

"I have." He gulped half a cup of coffee. "What's today?"

"Thursday."

"Only Thursday?"

"Dite's gone." Theena said.

"Yes. Dite's gone."

Theena oversaw his breakfast, watched him shave and finish dressing. "You thought I was Jack?" she said.

He found the least soiled of his shirts to put on. "You've saved me from a beating, my dear wife." He tucked his shirttail in. "Jack promised me another whupping if I was still here when he got back."

"So you got those bruises from Jack."

"None other. From your beloved Jack."

Theena took a breath and held it. What did he mean by that?

Randolph laughed. "I don't know which one of you is more transparent, you or him."

"Randolph, I'm here because I want you to come home to me, to be my husband."

"Ole rich Randolph Chase, he'll do. Might as well take him, seeing as how I'm pregnant. Seeing as Jack Spode is already taken. Seeing as Billy Yoholo is a red Indian and all."

Theena swallowed hot bitter tears. "It wasn't like that. I needed you, but I wanted you, too. You know it."

He faced her with his necktie in his hand. "I thought so once."

"And now? What about now?"

Randolph sat down heavily on the bed and leaned over his knees. "God, Theena, I'm sorry. I don't know what I'm saying."

His face hidden, so softly she had to lean to hear him, he said, "I would have gone with her, Theena, if she'd have had me. Can you forgive that?"

She touched his shoulder. "I want to, Randolph. I want us to forgive each other. I want us to be a family."

He reached his arms around her hips and held on tight. She stroked his head, only a little hope for their future keeping her from despair.

Chapter Twenty-Six

In June, Theena baked Liza's first birthday cake herself. She and Nat gathered the eggs early in the morning. While she grated cocoanut, Nat stirred the batter and licked the spoon.

After Liza's nap, Theena brushed the golden curls and put a freshly-pressed embroidered white gown on her. In the parlor Mrs. Chase sat reading one of her magazines from New York. "Will you watch them awhile, Mother Chase? I'm going to fix a tub for Randolph."

"Of course I will. Nathanial, cover your mouth when you cough. Here, Liza, come sit with Granny." Mrs. Chase pulled her lacy handkerchief from her pocket and wiped Liza's runny nose.

Theena put water on to heat and with Susan's help dragged the tub into the bedroom. She fetched towels, laid out a bar of soap and a back brush, and kept the water simmering for when Randolph came in. He used to be fastidious about his person, but since Dite, there were days he didn't even wash his face, much less shave. Sometimes at night after Randolph had gone to sleep, Theena rolled away from him to breathe from the other side of the bed.

But for Liza's birthday, she'd insist he clean up. She hoped he'd be fully sober, for once. Since she'd brought Randolph home from the Peacock Inn, he'd kept himself just shy of being drunk. Where he kept the stuff, she didn't know. It wouldn't do any good to look for it either. The men on the place had a still back in the woods somewhere.

Theena heard Randolph's steps coming through the house with that slower lumbering gait that showed he'd been drinking. He'd taken to leaving boot prints across the floors and even on the carpet in the parlor. He didn't use to do that either.

Randolph didn't fuss about getting in the tub. He pretty much did whatever Theena asked of him -- without complaint, but also without enthusiasm. While he soaked, Theena picked up the scissors. "You're beginning to look like a wild man. Let me cut your hair."

"If you want," he said and sat still while she shampooed and then trimmed his hair.

Under Theena's firm but gentle fingers, Randolph closed his eyes. He had to harden his heart against her touch. Not against Theena, not ever again. Against the kindness, the relief of being touched at all. He didn't deserve it. Remorse swirled inside him like a maelstrom. Like a drowning man, he grasped for something, anything to keep himself from going under.

He splashed water on his face so Theena wouldn't see the tears squeeze out from the corners of his eyes. He felt so empty. As if Dite had cut out his insides and left them on the beach for the gulls to pick at.

"Did you see the children when you came in?" Theena said.

Randolph shook his head, accepted the towel and wrapped himself in it. Theena picked up another towel to dry Randolph's hair, but he took her hands and stopped her. "Don't."

Theena dipped her head to catch his downcast gaze. He turned from her. She wanted to love him back to himself, to heal him with tenderness. If he'd let her. He had to help her, though. He had to try.

"Randolph." He turned his head as if to look at her over his shoulder, but his eyes avoided her face. "Randolph, you have to stop drinking."

He looked at her as if she spoke in tongues, as if she said up was down.

"For the children's sake. For Liza. For your mother. Have you seen what you're doing to your mother?"

He pulled out his small clothes from a drawer.

"Randolph, look at me. Please." He turned back to her, compliant. "You have to stop the drinking."

"No," he said. "I don't."

Theena stood by while he dressed. She wouldn't give up on him. Randolph would get through this, just as she'd come back from her own melancholia.

Randolph walked out the bedroom door onto the porch and headed for the barn. *So he keeps a jug in there,* Theena thought. *And if I found that one, he'd only have another and another in the groves somewhere.*

Is there a happy soul left in this world?

Theena seated the children at the table and Mother Chase tied a lacy embroidered bib around Liza's neck. Nat sang a little song, over and over, laughing when Liza grabbed for his hair. *There's a happy soul,* Theena thought. *But how long can he stay happy in this household?*

Randolph came in, the smell of moonshine fresh on him. Susan served dinner, and they all made the best show they could of being a family in harmony with one another.

At dinner's end, Susan brought in the coconut cake with a single candle lit in the middle. Nat's eyes grew round with excitement; Liza's seemed a little glazed. She must have not got her nap out earlier, Theena thought, but Liza focused on the flame as the cake was set in front of her.

"Make a wish for her, Nat," Theena said. He scrunched his eyes and thought. Then he opened them and said in a loud whisper, "She's going to get a pony for her birthday." Even Randolph laughed.

Theena wiped cake and frosting from the children's hands and faces. "Feel Liza's head, Mother Chase. Does she feel hot to you?"

"She is a little fevered. You can see it in her eyes," Mother Chase said.

Suddenly, Liza threw up all over Theena's dress. Nat sat quietly while the adults scrambled to deal with the mess and the sick baby. Maybe the smell got to him. In less than a minute, he heaved the contents of his stomach all over the table.

Theena put a hand to his forehead. "He's feverish, too."

Both children slept badly. Liza's fever spiked and plunged over and over, and Theena put her in bed with Nat so she could watch them both. Nat lay flat on his back, his arms and legs spread until another fever dream tossed him around.

In the morning, Liza's and Nat's mouths showed the tell-tale signs of the measles. White spots in their mouths, then the rash began. The outbreak covered their bodies, beginning on their faces and progressing downward. Theena dabbed witch hazel on their spots to relieve the itching.

In a few days, their spots faded and Nat felt well enough to play with his toy horses. What child didn't go through the measles? Thank goodness that was over, Theena thought.

Liza, though, continued to have a runny nose and a cough. She wouldn't eat. By the end of the second week, Nat was well,

Liza was sicker. It was only the measles, Theena reassured herself. It's just taking her longer to shake it.

But anxiety colored the days and nights. Theena roused every time Liza coughed, some times not sleeping at all for trying to ease her baby's chest. Liza lost weight and her face grew pale, her skin dry, her eyes distant.

Randolph hired a man with a schooner to sail directly to Fort Pierce and bring Dr. Moses back with him. If the doc was in the countryside on a call, it could mean as much as thirty-six hours before he arrived.

During the night, Theena sat in the rocker with Liza, gently patting her back. Randolph lay in the bed, stone cold sober, listening to the rocker and to Liza's tiny breaths. He got up silently and touched Theena's shoulder. "Get some sleep. I'll sit with her."

"Randolph, I'm scared. She's not getting better."

He took his baby and cradled her against his chest. "Doc Moses is on his way. Sleep, now."

Randolph held Liza upright at his shoulder and sang to her, soft and low. She put her hand on his cheek, then closed her eyes again.

Liza's little body hot against his chest, he rubbed her back, walked with her, tried to get her to drink a little water. The coughing fits when they came left her weak and gasping for breath. Theena was right. She was getting worse. His anxiety for her slipped into cold fear.

"Theena," he said, shaking her shoulder.

Theena threw off the covers. "Is she worse?"

"She can't wait for Moses. I'm going to the Inn." He passed Liza to her, her body limp and feverish.

"It's pitch dark, Randolph. I need you here."

"There may be a doctor staying at the Peacock." He ran his hands over his face. "Keep her upright. It seems to help."

Theena pressed her lips to Liza's forehead, gauging the fever. She was so very hot. "Hurry, Randolph."

She wiped Liza's small body with damp cloths and fed her willow bark tea to bring the fever down. Then Liza developed a wheeze. Theena patted her back to loosen the congestion in her chest and throat, but it didn't seem to help.

Her heart beating too fast, Theena went into Mother Chase's room without knocking. "Mother, wake up."

Mrs. Chase sat up abruptly, her gray hair in a long braid over her shoulders. “What’s happened?”

“Liza needs a steam tent.”

While Mrs. Chase roused Susan and got a pot of water boiling, Theena made a tent over the crib. Mother Chase delivered a lidded pot wrapped in a heavy tablecloth. Theena carefully placed the pot at the far end of the tent, lifted the lid, and hoped the vapor would thin the congestion.

If the damp air helped clear Liza’s chest, Theena couldn’t tell it. By mid-morning, Liza’s breathing was a rasp, and her fingernails were blue.

“Mother, what can we do?” Theena whispered, fear choking her. Mother Chase had had four children. She must know something to do.

She sought some hope from Mrs. Chase, some sign that she knew how to keep Liza safe until the doctor came. Even fear would have been better than what she saw in Mother Chase’s eyes. “What . . . What do you mean?” Theena said, though Mrs. Chase had not spoken.

Mother Chase lifted Liza from the pillows in the tent where Theena had propped her. She cradled her granddaughter gently and kissed her forehead. Then she placed the baby in Theena’s arms.

“Love her long as you can,” she said.

At noon, Theena heard horses rush into the yard. Two sets of feet pounded across the porch, into the kitchen.

“Theena! I’ve brought a doctor.”

She heard Randolph’s boots cross the kitchen floor, then the carpet in the parlor. She didn’t answer. “Theena!” She heard the panic seeping into him, his voice high and strangled.

She waited for him at the bedroom door and stood aside for him to enter. She’d dressed her baby girl, Randolph’s darling, in her white gown embroidered with yellow rosebuds. Liza’s chest was still, her face serene.

Chapter Twenty-Seven

Randolph could not come up from the depths of his grief. He doubted he ever would. He did his work, he gave Nat his attention now and then, he read. He even rolled on to Theena in the big bed, the dark hiding their faces from one another. But it was sex, not love-making.

He drifted through his days, trying to see only what was in front of him. A tree, a horse, a wagon, a plate of food. If he wasn't careful, Liza's pale face hovered, blue at the lips, looking to daddy to make her feel better. If he cut into an orange, he remembered how she'd bit into a slice, her chin and fingers sticky with juice. If the wind blew just so, it sounded like Liza's chest heaving for breath. The hole inside him gaped raw and bottomless.

So this is how Theena felt. Empty. But she'd had Dite to bring her back, and she had not lost Liza then, only her self. Dite. Before Liza died, he'd thought he would go mad with wanting Dite. Did he still want her? No. He didn't want anything. Better to be dead inside than to lose anyone, ever again.

He drew breath, month after month. He couldn't say he lived. He couldn't say he wanted to.

After a winter, spring, and summer of grieving, sometimes enveloped in a dull, gray, numbness, other times weeping herself into a wild torment, a morning came when Theena breathed in the fresh scent of fall breezes. The sky, blue again. A peach, sweet in her mouth. She took some interest in the book in her lap or the game she played with Nat. She returned to life.

Randolph and Mother Chase – for them, there seemed no relief from grieving. But Theena had Nat. He tethered her to the world, to life, and eventually, to moments of joy.

She and Nat hiked down to the river nearly every day to fish, to play in the sand, to escape the house so heavy with sorrow. He grew browner in the sun, his three year old legs sturdy and tireless. He sometimes chattered non-stop until Theena no longer listened but only smiled and nodded.

Theena wrestled with a hook embedded in the mouth of Nat's catch while he watched impatiently. "I can do it, Mama. Let me."

Neither noticed the dugout coming down stream until it slid onto their little beach. Billy Yoholo stepped onto the sand, his Rosa and two children in the boat.

Theena leaped to her feet. "Billy, my God." She ran into his open arms. He held on and rocked her back and forth. Tears spurted from Theena's eyes, the first she'd shed in weeks, but there were no sobs behind them. These were a different kind of tears, full of laughter and relief.

Rosa stood behind Billy now, her eldest already at Nat's side watching him twist the hook out of the fish's mouth. Theena hadn't seen Billy or Rosa since that awful day at the store so long ago. And now they had two children.

Had Rosa forgiven her? "Hello," Theena said.

Rosa pulled her eyes from the big boy who looked so much like her own son. She took Theena's hands in hers, then stood on tiptoe to kiss her cheek. "I am sorry about your little Elizabeth," she said. Along the river, around the bay, everyone knew everyone else's joys and sorrows.

Theena wiped her face with her apron. "Who are these beautiful children?"

"Tommy, come here," Billy said. "This is Thomas, and the little one sleeping in the boat is Rosie. Tommy, say hello to Mrs. Chase."

Theena sat on her heels. When Tommy took her outstretched hand, no shyness in him, she drew him close. "I'm very glad to meet you, Tommy. Will you call me Aunt Theena?"

"Aunt Theena," Tommy said dutifully, but his attention was on the goings on between Nat and the fish.

"That's Nat," Theena said.

Nat pulled the hook free. He reached into his can of worms and held out a fine black wiggler for Tommy. "You want to fish with me?" Tommy accepted the worm, and the boys involved themselves in their shared passion for slimy things.

The adults sat in the sand, their eyes constantly straying to the two boys. Billy, in particular, watched Nat steadily. Nat had taken up Theena's cane pole, dragging its length, so Tommy could have his.

"I want them to know each other," Theena said. She would take care to honor Randolph's feelings, his reputation, but that didn't mean the boys couldn't be together like this. Other white people and Seminoles besides herself and Billy had forged friendships up and down the bay country.

Theena looked to Rosa. Her feelings also had to be taken into account.

"Brothers should know each other," Rosa said.

Billy paused. "No." He shook his head. "Theena, this kinship shames your husband."

She watched the boys bobbing their poles over the water, alarming the fish instead of luring them to their bait. Randolph, she thought, took so little interest in Nat, or in much of anything, she doubted he'd care anymore.

"But sometimes, like this?" she said, appealing to both Rosa and Billy. "The boys could be together where no one will notice them. Now and then?"

Billy looked at his two boys. "Now and then. All right. I would not injure the man who raises Nat under his own roof, but I would have my sons know each other."

As Rosa persuaded Tommy it was time to put the pole down and say goodbye to Nat, Theena looked at the sleeping baby in the boat. Fat brown cheeks and a blissful slumber testified to Rosie's health. "She looks like her mother," Theena said.

"She's a beauty," Billy agreed.

When Billy knelt down to say goodbye to Nat, Theena pressed her hand against her nose so as not to cry. It had to hurt Billy, not seeing his child, not knowing him. Maybe that could change, if they took it slowly, didn't make a display of being together.

Theena and Billy embraced once more and Billy poled his dugout back into the current. Nat waved until the Yoholo family went round a bend in the river and out of sight.

Such lightness of heart, to have a friend in the world again. Two friends, Theena amended. Rosa had put it all behind her, the anger and the shame. Randolph did deserve protection of his name and his reputation – of his feelings, too, but somehow, she would work it out. Even if it were only to fish in the river together once in a while, she wanted Billy and Rosa and their children in Nat's life. And hers.

On the way back to the house, their poles over their shoulders and a string of fish in a bucket between them, Nat and Theena sang The Muffin Man over and over. When they reached the porch both of them fell silent. The house seemed to admit little light, and no jollity at all. *This will have to change,* Theena thought, *if only for Nat's sake. Life has to go on.*

Determined to begin now, this day, Theena began to whistle The Muffin Man and banged into Susan's kitchen with a show of noise and spirit. "Come on, Nat. Pucker up," she said. "Show Susan how you can whistle." Nat whistled, breathy and tuneless, all the way through The Muffin Man one more time.

Susan handed Nat a glass of water. "My Pa came by this morning while you were gone. He saw Hera and Jack at Brickell's last week. Said Hera looks red as a boiled lobster."

A worry line creased Theena's forehead. This pregnancy seemed awfully hard on Hera. "Maybe we'll go on over there tomorrow. See how she is." She put her hands on her hips. "And you, Nathanial Chase, need a bath."

That was Nat's cue. She loved the gleam in his eye as he slid from his chair and ran out the back door. It was Theena's pleasure to chase him down and haul him back for a soak in the big tub. He'd happily play in the water until his fingers and toes wrinkled, but the best part of it was the chase beforehand.

After supper, Nat tucked in for the night, Theena raised her head from her book when the bottle clinked against Randolph's glass. He'd left off drinking the harsh moonshine the laborers made. Now he drank imported Scotch in the evenings, and before dinner. His color had returned, but his manner was leaden.

Since Liza's death, Mother Chase had grown frail and silent. Randolph answered when he was spoken to, did his work, and sat with them in the parlor until the clock struck ten. His pall hovered over all of them, Mother Chase bent over her needlework, Theena staring at a page, not knowing what she'd read.

She needed to get Nat, and herself, out of this gloomy house for a few days.

"Nat and I are going to visit Hera tomorrow."

Randolph picked up the newspaper. "All right."

"The house will be so quiet," Mother Chase said.

This past year, Theena had forgiven her mother-in-law for all her meanness. She had become a beaten-down old woman, weighed down with grief for Liza, worry for Randolph. "We won't stay long. A day or two."

Theena went to bed. Alone. Going over the day's events, her life's events, was a poor inducement to sleep. It had nevertheless become a habit. She fingered her hair, remembering how in the early days Randolph had pressed his face into it, run his hands over it. *We were children*, she thought. *We thought we were grown up, but we weren't, either one of us*. She hardly recognized that frightened, hopeful girl she'd been when she'd married Randolph. To need someone so badly – she hardly remembered how that felt.

Neither she nor Randolph had understood how hard-won a little happiness could be. Grief for Liza thrummed in the back of Theena's mind, weighed on her heart, an ever-present ache. She didn't want that pain to go away. She wanted Liza with her always. *But, God, cannot there still be laughter and love?*

Randolph came in from the parlor, undressed in the dark, and climbed into bed quietly. Theena's head lay on her pillow, Randolph's on his. The few inches between them might have been miles.

"Randolph?" His melancholia surrounded him like a black fog. She stretched her hand out and touched him. If he'd let her, she would help him back into the world. Help him see there was yet pleasure and plans to make even after Liza, even if only in moments now and then.

She raised herself on her elbow and leaned into him. She ran her hand over his chest, caressed his face. He turned away from her. He seemed able only to rut, to engage in the physical act. Tenderness, that he could not accept.

"Randolph, won't you let me love you?"

The clock on the dresser ticked on and on. Finally, his voice flat, he answered her. "No. I don't want love. Ever again."

Once, she would have thrown herself across his body. She would have wept and kissed him and promised him that they would have another child, that he would find the courage to love again. That they could be happy together.

But she didn't believe it anymore.

If Theena wanted life, she would have to grab it for herself, by herself.

Chapter Twenty-Eight

Nat scrambled down from the wagon and ran to the banyan tree where Priss played with Gator and Daisy's latest litter of puppies. Theena helped Percy unload the things she'd brought, and by then Hera had lumbered onto the porch from inside the house.

"You've got company," Theena called to her.

"So I see. And just in time." Hera sat down heavily in the rawhide chair on the porch. "I didn't see how I was going to get dinner cooked. Now you're here, I'm turning it all over to you."

Theena waved goodbye to Percy and climbed the steps to sit with Hera. "Your feet bothering you?"

"Feet, legs, head, belly, you name it. Junior, here," she said and patted her tummy, "never stops kicking and twisting, this one."

Hera's face was flushed. Even winter along the Miami River could be god awful hot. *She's big for just six months,* Theena thought. Likely, Hera hadn't been sleeping well on top of being so uncomfortable.

"Well, Nat and I came to stay a day or two. You can sit here on the porch and watch the squirrels if you want. I'll see to Priss and the cooking."

"You are heaven sent."

"Jack out in the grove?"

"That man of mine never stops working," Hera said. "He's bought three dozen more trees from Walt Simms, so he's off that way clearing land."

Theena fixed noon dinner. Nat and Priss, who insisted on sharing a chair, whispered and giggled. Hera pushed the food around on her plate.

"You feeling okay?"

Hera passed her hand over her forehead. "You won't mind if I lie down a while?"

"Why don't you. I'll clear this away. Jack got his lunch with him out there?"

"No. I meant to take it to him."

"I'll do it. Mr. Nat and Miss Priss, time for your nap."

Theena got the children settled down, fixed a bucket lunch for Jack, and went looking for him at the new ground. The sound of Jack's machete thwacking into the undergrowth was as good a guide as the trail of slashed brush and scorched palmettos.

Theena found Jack laboring with his shirt off, the concoction he'd rubbed on keeping most of the flies and mosquitoes off him. His brown skin glistened with sweat and the muscles rippled as he swung the machete. Here was a man unbeaten, a man of heart, full of the gift of living. Pity rolled through her for Randolph, who had lost even the desire for life.

When Theena whistled, Jack turned and grinned at sight of her. "What are you doing here?"

"Heard there was a hungry man out here in the woods." She tipped the bucket so he could see the biscuits and ham.

He wiped his face and neck with his shirt before he put it on. "What's your poison?" he invited. "You want to sit in the sun so the skeeters won't want us, or in the shade where the sun won't bake our brains?"

"Sun, please."

Jack rolled a four foot chunk of palm trunk over to check for coral snakes, and the two of them sat down. Birdsong and insect whirring filled the glade.

While Jack ate, they talked about how Priss had been learning to sew buttons, how Nat could tie a fishing line on a hook. Theena was glad she'd come, Hera and Jack talking and smiling – living. She took in a glad breath, smelling the earth and the bruised bush of Jack's labor.

Theena sliced a pear for Jack and helped herself to half of it. Sweet juice dribbled from her mouth. She was about to wipe it with her apron, but Jack reached over and ran his thumb over her wet lower lip. She froze, her blood zinging through her, paralyzing her.

He shouldn't have done that. They both knew it. Caught in each other's eyes, they held back, breathless.

Slowly, as in a trance, without will or volition or thought, they drew closer. His first gentle kiss touched her very soul. Birds, insects, blinding sun – nothing existed for Theena but Jack.

After the first sweet taste of her mouth, Jack grabbed her into his arms, enveloping her, crushing her mouth with his. She clutched at him, wanting him, no other truth in the world but the wanting.

They could no more stop now than they could stop the earth's rotation. Each kiss fueled the next. Under the sun's burning eye, they yielded to the near-frenzy of touching, of tasting, of breathing in the hot scent of skin on skin.

When Jack entered her, he trembled and the air rushed into his chest. Theena thought she'd lost her breath forever. She called his name, and he stilled her voice with his mouth over hers. Passion ruled them, overwhelmed their senses, vanquished their minds. Jack pulsed inside her and exploded in groans of pain and ecstasy. Theena's cries scattered the birds, stopped the spinning of the earth.

Gasping, Theena wrapped him in her arms, his weight holding her to the earth, pressing life into her. She hugged him to her, keeping him, owning him if only for a moment. With her eyes closed, for this brief time, the world was Jack.

Recovering, he shifted his weight to his elbows. He kissed her eyes, her mouth.

Theena wiped a trickle of sweat from his forehead. "I shouldn't have come out here alone."

Jack twisted his fingers in her hair, watching the dark locks reflect white light. Then he met her eyes. "I'm not sorry, Theena."

Theena pressed her palm against his cheek, searching his face. "We can't do this again," she said.

Jack kissed her tenderly. "No, we won't." He kissed her once more, making it last.

They rose and adjusted their clothes. With slow deliberation, Jack pulled grass from Theena's hair. Theena picked up the tin bucket, found her palmetto hat, and looking at Jack a little longer, left him in the white-hot glade.

Jack watched Theena wind her way through the shadowy woods back toward the house. When he couldn't see her anymore, he picked up his machete and attacked the brush, every furious hack whittling at his confusion.

Not ordinarily a man to dwell on his feelings, Jack struggled to sort out what was in his heart. He knew what to do; that was not at issue. He would be a good husband. He'd promised himself to

Hera, and he would keep that promise, from now on. This . . . lapse . . . would not happen again.

Shame fueled every mighty thwack of the blade. He'd told Theena he had no regrets, but that didn't mean he was proud of himself. *God, hardly a year since she lost Liza. If she was herself, she wouldn't have let me do it.*

The wood rang with savage blows against the invading forest. He called himself every vulgar name he knew for an undeserving, disreputable rake. Hera didn't deserve this. Hell, Theena didn't deserve to have him rutting at her like a tom cat in heat. *Never again. Never going to risk Hera's peace again.*

Jack stopped to wipe his brow. Theena's scent on his hand came to him strong and fresh. He inhaled deeply, his hand at his nose. *Oh Jesus God.* In spite of his guilt, in spite of his vow, Jack fairly hummed with the joy of having loved Theena. He raised his face to the sky, the machete dangling at his side.

The glow from loving Jack still on her, his scent in her clothes and on her body, guilt opened up before her like a pit of quicksand. Hera. How could she have done that to her sister?

Oh, God, Hera, I'm so sorry.

With a stiffened gait, she turned off the path to the house. At the bay, she folded herself onto the beach. Her lungs felt too full of air to breathe. She wrapped her arms around her knees and bent her head.

What was wrong with her? With Dite, and Mama? Why had they no virtue? *And I am the worst of us.* Dite never pretended to be anything but self-serving. Mama read the Bible, and then sinned against both her own family and Mr. Alnot's. But at least Mama had made a clean break of it. No living with lies and half-truths.

Theena had let emotion and need carry her instead of sense and strength. Was that what happened to Mama? She hadn't controlled or denied herself? Dite never denied herself anything, but she'd always had control.

Theena covered her face with her hands. The taste of Jack in her mouth turned bitter as gall. *I forgot even my sister, my dearest friend. Is that who I am? A woman of lust and need and selfishness?*

When she deceived Randolph, she'd been frightened. She hadn't had the strength to be somebody beyond what she, and

Daddy and everyone else, imagined she would be. This time, though, she didn't even have the excuse of being too young to be wise.

"What have I done to Jack?" she murmured. He'd never have done it if she hadn't gone out there, alone, and sad. He would hate himself. And it was her fault.

Self-loathing washed over like an oily sea. She fisted her hands and opened her mouth, desperate for air.

I don't want to be that person.

Didn't the Bible promise redemption to sinners who redirected their course along a righteous path? *I don't have to be that person.* She could not undo what happened today, but she could see that she never hurt anyone again, never threatened anyone else's happiness, ever again. She was not her mother. Not her sister. She would walk that righteous path all the rest of her days.

Her spirit quieted. Her chest opened and her breath eased. She raised her face to the sky and closed her eyes. She did not ask for God's help, or for the strength to be good. Instead, she made God a promise.

I will be a good person. I will never tempt Jack again, ever. From this day forward, I will be a faithful wife, a true sister, and a good mother. In Jesus' name, Amen.

Theena breathed in the salt air. She listened to the gulls' cries, the gentle lap of shallow water on the sand. Peace descended like a zephyr. Instead of confusion and shame, clarity and certainty. She would be the person she wanted to be. She could do that now. Even if she had to do it without Randolph.

Theena had a vision of herself and Nat, just the two of them, living in a little house on Daddy's land. They'd have chickens and pigs, a garden. They'd fish and scallop, swim and walk on the beach. Life could be sweet again, and simple. She could give that to Nat.

Not a shred of cloud broke the blue expanse of sky. The bay itself shone mottled under the sun, deep blue in patches, green and gray in others. Not a soul in sight, not in a boat or on the shore. Theena slipped off her clothes and eased into the chill water and let it flow through her long hair, over her body, even into her private recesses. Taking a deep breath, she dove under the surface, her complete submersion a magic moment of green water and silver fishes.

Guilt and remorse washed away. Strength and determination took their place. Hera would never know, never be hurt, she swore it.

Shivering, Theena wrung the water from her hair and pulled on her clothes. Back in the house, Nat contentedly watched the tree-filtered sun make shadows on the wall. Theena gently moved Priss's leg so Nat could slide out from under her.

She took him onto the porch where Hera had left the basket of pears. Nat picked one up and bit into it. Sticky, sweet-smelling juice covered his chin. Theena's senses threatened to overwhelm her. The feel of Jack's thumb on her lip, then his body pressed against hers, in hers. How could it have been so wrong, just this one time? Jack had been in her heart so long, separate from Hera, it was almost as if what they'd done in the woods had nothing to do with her. But it did. It did. And it was wrong. *God, I will keep my promise. I will.*

Hera woke up feeling dopey and listless. Theena fixed her a tall glass of water with a sprig of mint in it and sent the kids to play under the trees where she could see them. Together, Theena and Hera shucked corn for supper. They watched Priss mother Nat and admired how he tolerated it.

That evening, by the light of the kerosene lamp, Jack honed his machete against his whetstone, the rasp rasp rasp accompanying the women's quiet voices. Hera taught Priss the shapes of the letters. Theena sat nearby to share the lamp while she read Nat his bedtime story.

Who could guess from this quiet domestic scene the heavy secret two of them shared? Hera did not, Theena was sure of it. She and Jack were both more concerned with protecting Hera from their selfishness than they were with the sin itself. No glances between the two of them, no guilty distance either. Tomorrow, she would go home and leave Jack and Hera to their own lives.

Hera protested the next morning. "Leave already? How are you going to get home? It's too far for Nat to walk all that way."

"I have some coins with me. We'll go into the village and find somebody to give us a lift. It'll be an adventure, won't it, Nat?"

In Lemon City, Theena did find a man and his wife taking the river road inland to their homestead north of the Chase place. Nat rode in back with the couple's big eight year old son and the two of them lay on the sacks of rice and flour, gazing at the treetops overhead, pointing out shapes in the clouds when the canopy opened.

At the gate to the plantation, Theena thanked the settlers and offered them a dime for their trouble, but they wouldn't hear of it. They rode off, and Theena and Nat opened the gate to their lane.

"We're home, Mama," Nat said.

Theena felt a pall descending. It didn't feel like a home anymore.

Chapter Twenty-Nine

The sun shone down on the white-washed house, yet somehow the stillness of the scene promised only dreary days. Grief had the Chase house in its grip, and her own mourning returned to her in full force. Liza had played here, had laughed and said Mama and Dada, had crawled and even taken her first steps in this house.

Theena took Nat's hand. Could he feel the grief in this place? He'd missed Liza, too, those first weeks after her death. How could he not suffer now from the pervasive sadness in his home?

Susan will be glad to see us. That will help, Theena thought. But it wasn't Susan who came out to meet them. Mother Chase, without even a bonnet to protect her fair skin from the sun, met them halfway down the lane.

"Come to Granny," Mother Chase said, and opened her arms to Nat. Theena stopped where she stood, amazed.

Nat hesitated, wary. His grandmother had never invited him into her arms before. Slowly, watching her face, he approached. Mother Chase gently embraced him. "I'm glad you're home," she said. She looked at her daughter-in-law. "Welcome home."

Theena grasped her hand, grateful that at last they were forging a bond. *May Randolph have missed us as much,* Theena prayed.

Susan opened the door. Nat ran straight at her and plowed into her legs. "Whoa! You get any bigger, you little bull, you'll knock me over."

Susan made a pitcher of lemonade, and another first, Mrs. Chase sat at the kitchen table with Theena and Susan to visit. They watched Nat play with Susan's white kitten as Theena gave them all the news she'd picked up from Hera.

"What is Randolph doing?" Theena asked. She hadn't heard anyone else in the house.

"Mr. Bolton persuaded him to ride through the groves this morning."

"Did he?" Theena said. Randolph had neglected the plantation since Liza died. Since before that, really. Since Dite left.

"My hope is Randolph's interest in the groves will revive him. He's so . . . . If he works again, hard, like he used to, maybe he can get through this."

Theena reached for Mother Chase's hand. "I hope so, too, Mother."

Randolph stayed among his trees through the dinner hour, which Theena took as a good sign. *The drinking and the sitting and sitting and sitting – no wonder he broods.* Maybe Bolton could draw him back into the life of the plantation.

In the hour before supper, Theena presented a scrubbed child to Mrs. Chase. "Would you like a story, Nathanial?" his granny asked him. He climbed on to the sofa next to her, always eager to be read to.

Theena returned to the bedroom to take extra care with her toilet. She wore the deep blue taffeta dress and twisted her hair into a knot on the back of her head. *I haven't been trying hard enough,* she told herself. *I, of all people, should know how a body can need help.* She dabbed on the cologne Randolph had brought her from Fort Pierce, but she left Dite's earrings in the drawer.

Randolph appeared at the table slightly sunburned across the nose. The exercise had agreed with him, and his blue eyes had lost their leaden look.

"Did you enjoy your day, Randolph?" his mother asked.

"Enjoy?" he said as he opened his napkin. "As much as one can enjoy the delights of the tropics – stinging insects, poisonous serpents, unrelenting heat and blistering sun."

Randolph's mouth had that turned-down look and his tone was devoid of any humor. Theena exchanged a look with Mother Chase. This was not the reaction either had hoped for.

Mrs. Chase tried again. "How are the groves?"

"Nat, you have a spoon. Use it," he said.

Theena touched Nat's hand to soften the rebuke from his father. Randolph spoke to Nat so seldom since he'd sunk into his grief, and when he did, it was most often like this, to scold him.

"With a manager and a few hands," Randolph continued, cutting into his meat, "the citrus grows just fine without any help from me."

Apparently being on the plantation had done nothing for Randolph's mood nor had it revived his interest in what had once been his passion. Theena changed the subject.

Several days more of Randolph riding out after breakfast did not alter his frame of mind. If anything, he brooded more without sharing his thoughts with either his wife or his mother. Saturday morning, he saddled up and rode off toward the bay without telling anyone where he was going.

The next Saturday, Randolph did the same. He came home late in the afternoon with a few purchases from Brickell's store and handed the parcels to Theena to unwrap while he washed for supper.

Theena untied the string and called Nat. *Attention is what Nat needs from you, Randolph, not presents.* "Look here, Nat, what your father has brought you."

Nat peeled the rest of the paper away to find his treasures. Five hard candies, red and green and yellow, a whistle with a pea rattling around in it, and a pea shooter! "You can have one piece of candy now, Nat. No, just one," Theena said.

At supper, Randolph told them who was marrying whom, whose baby had been born, why he'd chosen to bring home the bolt of red cloth instead of the brown. "Miss Brickell persuaded me you both needed hat trimmings, though I fail to see how any quantity of lace and ribbon will keep the sun off a lady's face."

Mrs. Chase laughed too heartily. None of them had had much practice with laughter.

He's different, Theena thought. *Not really cheerful, but not so morose. Maybe he's come to a turning point.* She reached for Randolph's hand across the table. He did not withdraw from her, yet when Theena squeezed his hand, he did not return the pressure. She hid the hurt with downcast eyes and withdrew her hand. Patience, she remembered. That's what had got her through those awful months when Nat was a baby and Randolph slept on the floor.

After supper, Mother Chase took Nat to the parlor for their new ritual of reading fables and fairy tales before bedtime. Randolph invited Theena to take a stroll with him.

Theena took his hand. She loved walking hand in hand. But after a moment, Randolph gave her hand a little squeeze and let go. She wrapped her arms around herself, suddenly cold, suddenly as lonely as a storm-tossed bird lost and solitary. When they reached the end of the long lane to the plantation gates, Randolph stopped and leaned against the fence. Theena leaned next to him with crossed arms. She waited.

"I'm leaving this place," he said finally.

Not "we," but "I," Theena noted.

"I'm selling out. That's where I've been the last two Saturdays, talking to buyers. I could probably get a better price if I went to Key West or Palm Beach for a few weeks, but I don't want to wait."

Theena still hadn't heard a "we."

"Then what?" she asked.

Randolph shrugged. "I still have the property outside of Philadelphia. I'll put it into tobacco, maybe."

Well, does he want us to come with him, or not? If Nat and I go to Philadelphia, will he be a father, and a husband?

She traced a line in the sand with the toe of her shoe. "Are you going after Dite?"

Randolph looked at the ground. "No."

He's my husband, Theena thought. *Do I just let him go? Or do I hold on and hold on?*

She stared at Randolph standing with his head turned from her. *Does he even want me to hold on?*

"Do you want me to come with you?"

She tried to see his face, but he wouldn't look at her. She saw him swallow, and then again. "Of course."

No, he didn't. Did she want to go with him?

Theena watched a flock of snowy egrets settling into a tree for the night, smelled the fragrant air. She belonged here, with her shoes off and salt on her skin. Nat belonged here, too.

She nodded, her arms crossed, her gaze on the ground. She headed back to the house, leaving Randolph behind her.

After breakfast the next morning, Nat stacked his story books on the sofa, and Mother Chase promised they'd read every one of them. He snuggled up next to her, and Theena left him with his grandmother for the day.

She set off down the lane with a day's provisions over her shoulder. Mr. Bolton had left his skiff for her at the landing, and she shoved off into the river.

The sun laid a dazzling diamond quilt over the surface of the water. At the whirring of wings, Theena looked up at a flock of brilliant flamingos flying over head. As many times as she'd seen such a sight, Theena was stunned by their beauty and grace.

Yes, here on this river, in this sun -- this is where I belong. Theena pulled off her bonnet, shook her hair loose, and let the heat penetrate to her bones.

With the unbridled growth along the bank, she nearly missed the old Theophilus landing. Next time, she'd bring a machete with her.

The homestead lay silent and still. No breeze stirred, no shadows moved across the glaring sun-lit sand. Birds warbled in the trees, else it might have been a scene from a picture book.

Daddy's cabin sprawled across the site. Wind and rain and folks helping themselves to timber had scattered the ruins. Theena walked past the roof top, now lying on the ground, to see what was left of the garden. In the four years since Daddy died, the jungle had reclaimed most of the patch. Vines draped across the edges, but hardy self-sustaining mint and tomatoes had persevered, and – what a delight, a small bed of pineapples had spread and sported a score or more of spiky-topped fruit.

Pineapples. William Wallace downriver from the Chases shipped pineapples every year and fed his family of eight on the proceeds. She and Nat could be pineapple farmers.

With growing excitement, Theena surveyed the rest of the property. All those hardy pineapples promised her the independence she intended to win in this sandy loam. Most of Daddy's 160 acres had never been cleared, but she could hire someone to help her push the jungle back.

In a gesture of resolution, Theena tossed her bonnet in the air. Let her skin turn brown as an old Cracker's, red as a Seminole's. She would not be going to Philadelphia where the whiteness of a lady's skin mattered. This place in the sun belonged to her, and she to it.

She found a hint of the path she and her sisters used to take to the bay and carried her biscuits and ham to eat on the beach. Pelicans skimmed the water as she waded through the surf, the lapping of waves through the fringe of shells like music. *Nat can collect shells and chase hermit crabs along here*, she thought.

As sudden as a windy gust, Theena's throat swelled with grief. Liza would not be here to collect eggs, to laugh with the puppies or build sand castles with Nat. She sank to her knees and sobbed, the grief as fresh this moment as it had been all those months ago.

She cried herself into a headache. Spent, she got to her feet and shook the wet tail of her dress. She leaned over to scoop water on her face, to wash the tears away. She breathed deeply, resolved to resume living, here, now, without Liza.

Back at the homesite, she looked around once more. Such peace, to have a plan, to know where she belonged. To believe in herself at last. She didn't require Randolph to make her whole. She needed only Nat, and she'd make a home for him here, on this spot.

With a lighter heart than when she'd left home in the morning, Theena headed back. By the time she reached the Chase landing, her shoulders ached from rowing the skiff .

Mother Chase had Nat in the bathtub when Theena came in. One hand propelled his toy boat, the other acted the scary alligator who sneaks up underwater, opens its jaws wide, and crunches down on the boat and everybody in it. Much growling and splashing added to the effect, and through it all, Grandmother Chase sat beaming, unmindful of the mess Nat made.

Theena stood in the doorway a moment enjoying Nat's play, and pondering the transformation in Mother Chase. For the old woman's sake, Theena was glad she had learned to love Nat. A heart needed to love in this life. And a child needed all the hearts' love he could find.

"Come sit with us," Mother Chase said.

Sweaty and disheveled as she was, Theena put off having her own wash-up and pulled a chair near the tub. "Watch this, Mama," Nat said, and demonstrated the monster's gaping jaws chomping down on the boat.

Speaking over Nat's splashing, Mother Chase asked, "How did you find your father's place, Athena?"

"Oh, it's a mess. What remains of the house is a pile of old lumber. The garden is overgrown, and the landing is, too."

But Theena knew the question had not really been about the place. Mother Chase wanted to know what Theena was going to do.

This was going to hurt her mother-in-law. She had grieved as deeply for Liza as Randolph or she had. Now she'd fallen in love with her grandson at last, she was going to lose him, too. She took Mrs. Chase's hand. "I'm staying, Mother. Nat and I are going to live on Daddy's old place."

Mother Chase nodded. "I thought you would."

"If you wanted to stay with us, with Nat and me, you'd be welcome."

"Thank you, my dear. You don't know what that means to me, that you would have me with you and Nat." She wiped her eyes. "Randolph He doesn't know it, of course, but he needs me. I can't let him go back to Philadelphia all alone."

She stood up and smoothed her skirt. "I think I'll lie down, now that you're here to finish Nat's bath." At the doorway, she turned back. "For what it's worth, Athena, I think you're doing the right thing for you and Nat."

"Thank you, Mother."

That night in bed, Theena and Randolph lay side by side in the bed, both staring at the ceiling. "I'm not going north with you, Randolph."

He turned on his side to look at her in the moonlight filtering through the gauzy curtains. Theena waited for him to say something, but he didn't. "I'm going to rebuild on Daddy's place, and Nat and I will live there."

Does he care so little, he has nothing to say? Nothing at all?

But he did care. He reached a hand out and touched her hair.

"I can't stay, Theena. It's killing me here. Everywhere, I see Liza's face, hear her laughing, remember the feel of her in my arms. And . . ." He stopped.

Was he about to say 'and Dite, too'?

"I know," Theena said.

"I'm sorry," he whispered. "I'm so sorry."

"I'm sorry, too."

She still wanted to love him, to help him, if only he'd let her. She reached for him, but Randolph took her hands, kissed them, and gave them back to her. He couldn't. His heart was broken, and he couldn't let her heal it.

The following day, Randolph asked Theena to sit with him in the parlor. There was business to discuss. "Mother and I will leave after the oranges are picked and on their way. You'll have an income, of course."

"Thank you, Randolph. Nat and I won't need much. Maybe I'll turn into a successful planter like you."

Randolph smiled at the unlikely thought. He knew the vagaries of market and weather and crop diseases. "I hope you do, but you will have everything you need, you and Nat, always."

"I need help getting the house built, first thing. Shall I ask Mr. Bolton for a crew?"

"I'll take care of it," Randolph said.

She didn't want him to go. He couldn't stay. They were no good to each other, not any more.

His face showed the ravages of his grief and dissolution. His smooth jaw line now hinted at jowls; the bags under his eyes seemed permanent. There was no joy in him anymore. She wished she could breathe spirit into his mouth, fill him with her own.

This soaring, invisible barrier he'd built imprisoned him with grief and regret. His loneliness hurt her like a hand around her throat. She touched his cheek. "Don't die of this, Randolph. Don't keep yourself in this lead box you've been living in."

"I'm not you, Theena. I'm not as strong as you are."

The clock ticked. Nat's voice came to them from the kitchen.

"I always thought you were the strong one."

"I did too. We were wrong, weren't we?"

Theena moved from her chair to stand before him. She had to make him let her in. She pushed into his lap and circled her arms around his neck. She leaned her forehead against his, and at last the wall around Randolph cracked. He held her tight, his arms squeezing her as he had not done in many months. A sob erupted from his deep chest. They cried together, at last, Theena and Randolph, their tears mingling. But it was too late. This was merely their good-bye.

Chapter Thirty

Jack's back ached every morning. He and Hera rolled toward the middle all night, both of them waking sweaty and ill-tempered. Finally he declared, "We gotta have a new mattress."

"I don't have time to make a new mattress," Hera said. "You think I don't have anything to do just because I'm not out in the woods with a machete. I have to --."

"Hera. Stop. I said no such thing."

Lord, whatever happened to the notion a pregnant woman is a happy woman? Jack thought.

Guilt tore at him. She was heavy and hot and uncomfortable. Who wouldn't be a grump? He pushed damp hair from her forehead and pecked her on the cheek. "I'll take care of the mattress."

All the while Jack gathered moss, he imagined ways to keep his side of the bed from tilting toward Hera. Maybe a cotton bolster in the middle with the moss packed higher on her side. He'd experiment. He made a buttonwood fire under the caldron and boiled masses of moss to get rid of the bugs. A chigger bite could make a man miserable for days.

As Jack went about his day's labor, he imagined the deep blue of the Gulf Stream, the whitecaps frothed up by the wind, the cool nights on deck. If he signed on with a fishing boat, he'd make enough to buy Hera her sewing machine at last. She hadn't mentioned it in, oh, five or six days.

He sat down to a hot dinner at noon time. "I made you dumplings, Jack." Hera ran her hand across his back as she set the bowl on the table.

"Love your dumplings," Jack said. December, but they were having a hot spell just the same. He'd have a hard time working off heavy fare like that in the afternoon. Priss toyed with her food. She needs a swim, Jack decided.

"How'd you like a dip after lunch?" Priss brightened and gave her daddy the smile only he could earn.

"Don't go letting her get a sunburn. Why you want to go in the full sun, I don't understand."

"Cause that's when it's warmest, Hera." He bit his tongue. He'd thought he would pay for his betrayal by being the perfect husband, but here he was, cross and irritable with her. It wasn't right, he wasn't right. He loved his wife and it wasn't her fault he was a fool.

"Put some long sleeves on her and a bonnet, honey," he said in a better tone. "She'll be fine."

"I won't burn, Mama. I promise."

Not a good time to bring up going off, Jack thought as he swatted at a fly, but it would probably do them both good if he hired out for a few days. Nearly three months till the baby was due. It'd be fine.

"I'm thinking of going over to the Inn tomorrow to see if anybody's going out for marlin."

Hera put her fork down and looked at him. "You're always going off somewhere." The last time Jack had been away over night had been more than half a year back, but he chose not to pursue that argument.

Red and blotchy with heat and pregnancy, beads of sweat dotted Hera's upper lip. Sweat-dampened golden hair curled around her face. He reached across the table and patted her hand. "Tell you what, if I get a boat job, I'll stop by Miss Brickell's and order up that sewing machine."

Hera's face cleared instantly. "Oh, Jack, really?" She left her chair and wrapped her arms around his neck. He pulled her into his lap and admired the pretty girl he'd married. *That's my Hera. Poor thing, she's just worn down.*

"How about you come down to the bay with Priss and me?" he said. "After that, we'll all need a nap, won't we?" He raised his eyebrows suggestively at Hera and she laughed.

"I don't take naps anymore," Priss announced. "I'm too big for that."

"But today," her daddy said, and goosed her in the ribs, "today is a swimming day. We'll all be tired out and water logged, and we'll all need a nap."

"Can I sleep in your bed?" Priss said.

Jack sighed and Hera smiled at him. "Sure." To start with, anyway, he thought.

Next morning, Jack kissed his wife and daughter good bye and marched down the lane with a light heart. He'd bring back a pocket full of cash, order the sewing machine, and buy something pretty for Priss.

Out on the ocean, he'd forget about women. No remembering Theena's kiss, no wishing for what he couldn't have. Just the sun and the ocean spray, and the company of men in pursuit of a great beast in the waves. He'd come home renewed, he'd come home a better husband.

Jack carried his gear on his back, but he didn't expect to do much fishing himself. He'd be assisting the Yanks with their fifty dollar rods and reels, talking them through the catch. The greenhorns were prone to jerk on the line when they should give it some slack, to let up just when they should reel in. Hauling in a marlin required more than luck.

He'd coached a beginner on a fishing trip a few years back. The Yank had hooked a magnificent sailfish, but the fellow's arms, sunburned and no bigger around than a girl's, had jerked and trembled with the exertion, so Jack had taken his chair and his rod to keep the sailfish hooked. When the beast had tired and nearly given up, Jack called the man from his bottle of scotch to reel it in. Back on shore, the Yank had posed proudly while the photographer took his picture next to the sailfish, which hung down nine feet from the cross pole. Well, Jack had had the fun.

At Daddy's old homestead, Mr. Bolton and two men stacked the new lumber while five more laborers were hard at it digging holes for the foundation posts. It was to be a bigger house than the one Daddy had built. Randolph insisted she have three rooms, a bedroom for herself and one for Nat, with actual doors, and a living area. He'd instructed Bolton to build it sturdy, as hurricane resistant as any man-made structure could be.

"I'll be in the garden, Nat," Theena said. "You stay out of the way, you hear?"

"I will, Mama."

Theena carried a hoe over her shoulder and attacked the vines and weeds that had encroached so abundantly. A flash of blue caught her eye in the loamy earth. With the blade, she sifted through the dirt to reveal her own blue velvet bag, left here by the storm, buried all this time in the garden. She shook the dirt off and caressed the worn velvet. The last time she'd opened this bag had been to put her cowrie shell inside and close it away.

She opened the bag and emptied her few keepsakes into her palm. The cowrie shell might have been freshly plucked from the bay, the sheen of the hard shell as bright as the day Jack had held it out to her in his palm. She rubbed it in her fingers, remembering, knowing he had never meant it as a gift, never meant it to have any significance when he handed it to her. But it had. He'd given it to her, and she'd worn it more than a year, still hoping he might someday see her.

Theena put the shell to her lips, memories rolling over her, images and touches.

Then she shook her head. No. No more regrets. She was about to begin a new life with Nat on this place. Determined to live in the here and now, she slipped the shell back into the bag and put the bag into her apron pocket.

Theena surveyed the rest of her garden. A stand of twenty or thirty young pineapples grew in the western corner. She weeded around them and wondered if growing pineapples were as easy as it looked. Daddy had planted a half dozen for Mama years ago, just for their own use. And now there were five times that many with no help from a farmer.

After lunch, Theena led Nat to a shady patch under the pine trees on the edge of the garden. "Time for a nap, Nathanial Chase, or you'll be a bear the rest of the day."

"I'm not sleepy, Mama. I'm never sleepy!"

"Well, just rest then. I'll sit with you." Nat resisted sleep as long as he could, but at last he closed his eyes. Through the pines, Theena watched the men working on her house. They'd be finished in a couple of weeks. Then the hammering and sawing and teasing banter of the men would stop. The silence would return.

She remembered the silence, so heavy she had trembled trying to bear its weight those weeks before the hurricane, before she'd moved in with Hera and Jack. The birdsong and rustling treetops had only emphasized the underlying quiet. She'd been frightened of so much silence, nearly undone being so alone.

Two lines deepened between her brows at the memory of those first solitary days after Hera had gone. She tore at the stiff petals of a pine cone, the prick of their spines an antidote to anxiety. She never wanted to be melancholy again, not ever. She would stay busy from dawn to dusk with getting the garden in order, with learning what she could about farming pineapples. She could spend a morning on the bay any time she wanted to. And she'd have Nat this time

So I'll be lonely, she thought. *It's been lonely living with Randolph, too.*

Nat woke as he always did, all at once, alert and ready. He sat up long enough to look around and take a breath. Then he erupted into whoops and tore across the ruined garden at a pair of squirrels scampering through the plum trees.

The silence was an illusion, Theena realized. Life was all around her. The tension across her forehead eased, the lines smoothed out at her son's joy in being alive.

Life would be good here. She was not the girl she'd been when she'd been alone after Daddy died. She'd make solitude a familiar acquaintance, and she and Nat would be content in its presence.

"They're eating our plums, Mama!" Nat yelled. He threw a pine cone at the squirrels, chittering at him, indignant at being disturbed in *their* plum tree. Theena joined him and they threw all the pinecones they could find at the thieving squirrels, finally giving up in laughter and defeat.

In the late afternoon, the crew put their tools down. Mr. Bolton offered to have one of the men row Theena's skiff back up river. She thought of the gloom pervading the house, of Randolph's impenetrable sadness, his mother's bruised heart.

"I believe Nat and I will go on down to my sister's place, Mr. Bolton. You'll tell Mr. Chase where we are?"

"Sure I will."

Nat sat down in the bottom of the skiff and Theena rowed them downstream to Lemon City. She wouldn't stay long. Just till tomorrow. She didn't want to be alone with Jack, nothing like that. She just wanted to be where there was some joy.

Once she'd pulled the boat ashore, Nat took her by the hand and tugged at her all the way up to the house. Finally, Theena broke into a trot and they raced the last twenty yards.

Priss was playing on the porch with a doll when she saw them coming. "Mama, Aunt Theena's here!"

"What's that Daddy used to say? A sight for sore eyes? That's what you two are. Priss, why don't you and Nat go play under the banyan so Aunt Theena and I can visit."

They sat on the porch, Hera in the shade. *She doesn't look good,* Theena thought. Mr. Simms was right. Her face was too red, and she'd grown so heavy you could hardly tell she was pregnant.

"How are you doing?" Theena said.

"Fine, I guess. It's just that it's so blamed hot, and here it is January." She held the stray curls off the back of her neck. "Jack always takes Priss for an hour or two every day, but he's gone off again, and I don't get a break from sunup till Priss goes to sleep."

"Where to this time?"

"He's been away two days, so I reckon he got him a couple of fishermen to go out. I think he'd rather be on the ocean than most anywhere. Don't know why he took up farming," she complained.

Then this first visit after . . . it'll just be easier without Jack and me pretending nothing ever happened. Theena relaxed into her chair. "You know you'd hate it if he was off fishing month in and month out."

Hera had to give in. She laughed. "Yes, I would. I swear, if we don't get a break from this heat soon, I'm going to start complaining about the birds in the trees. Ow!" She put her hand on her side where the baby kicked her. "This one has to be a boy with a kick like that."

"I guess Jack wants a boy."

"More than anything."

Next morning, early, Hera's complexion was already flushed. "I swear, Priss," she scolded, "if you don't settle down, I'm going set you in the corner."

Theena looked up from tying a bib on Nat. Poor Priss had simply been wiggling in her chair. "Hera, you need a break. Why don't I take Priss home with us? You can eat cold fixings and put your feet up, sleep, read, keep cool. I'll bring her back in a few days."

"I don't know," Hera said. "She's never been away from me more than a couple of hours at a time."

"Please, Mama," Priss pleaded. "Can I?"

"Well. You mind your manners and do what Aunt Theena tells you, young lady."

"Yes, ma'am." Priss bolted for the door, and could hardly be persuaded to stop long enough to finish her breakfast.

Jack and his party lazed on the deck of the sailing boat in the evening, anchored far enough off shore to be free of the mosquitoes. “I’m persuaded,” Mr. March intoned, “the best tarpon fishing is to be found in Jupiter Creek.”

“In the inlet, eh?” Mr. Bishop seemed skeptical. “All I ever caught in a creek was bass and trout.”

“What do you think, Mr. Spode?”

Jack had been woolgathering. “What’s that?”

“You willing to sail up to Jupiter? Mr. March claims the tarpon may be found there in great abundance.”

“Yep. Plenty of tarpon around Jupiter Inlet,” Jack agreed.

Next morning, they caught a favorable wind and were in the Inlet by mid-day. They left the yacht and took the rowboat to the mouth of the creek. Tarpon teemed in the clear shallows. One rose from the water, its body an elegant silver curve, then disappeared again.

“My God, look at the size of him,” Bishop cried.

“Try your wobbling spoons,” Jack advised them. Almost at once, tarpon hit both men’s lures.

Their arched backs were dark green with flashes of purple and red as the sun glinted on them; their sides flashed silver in the clear water. What great spirit they had, he thought. No greater thrill than watching a tarpon fight.

March’s catch raced away forty yards at top speed, then broke the surface, tail walked, and shook its huge head trying to dislodge the hook. Bishop’s fish zoomed high and performed a double somersault before splashing back into the water. Jack kept track of how many times each fish jumped. Back home, that was the sort of thing a sportsman needed to know if he were going to relate the tale of his fight: how many leaps and how high; how many summersaults, singles or doubles; and how long it took for the fish to exhaust itself.

The tarpon danced and feinted and raced to escape. “Let him tire himself out, March. He’ll do all the work. That’s right. Let him run,” Jack coached.

Bishop reeled his in first and Jack hooked it with the gaff. Suddenly, it rallied. With tremendous strength, the tarpon nearly dragged Jack into the water. He wrestled with it until, finally, he jerked it into the boat.

The flashing silver of March’s catch shone as Jack heaved it aboard. “My god, what a beauty,” Bishop whooped.

"How much you think this thing weighs?" March asked.

"What do you think, Spode? Must be forty pounds!"

Grinning and sun-burned, they were a happy trio that evening as the steward served them grilled tarpon steak. "My Dora positively loves fish. Should have brought her along," March said.

"You mean she'd fish with you?" Bishop asked.

"Oh, no. It's fish she loves, not fishing. You wouldn't catch her actually getting her pretty hands dirty."

"My wife declares it would ruin her complexion spending the day in a rowboat. She'd just as soon stay in Saratoga while I'm off adventuring, as she calls it."

Priss was not going to grow up to be one of those white-handed, delicate women, and Jack was proud of that. Last time he'd taken her fishing, Priss had double wrapped her hook with worms. "I want to catch a big one, Pa," she'd explained. When a good sized skip jack hit her bait, she'd fought it with all her might, but the mighty crevalle got away, nearly taking her pole with it. Priss stared at her empty, limp line, bait and hook both gone. "I think I'll just use one worm next time, Pa," she'd said. Jack had solemnly passed her the worm can.

His girl was already a fine fisherwoman. Like her Aunt Theena. Jack's thought skittered away. He had no business thinking about Theena. That was over. He was going home to his wife and child, and glad of it.

March and Bishop went on to speak of other women of their acquaintance, some intimately known. "Mitchell's got himself a firebrand, a real beauty. He's kept this one longer than most, I'll say that for her. She's from down around here somewhere, matter of fact," Bishop said.

Jack picked up on Mitchell's name. "Lawrence Mitchell?"

"Larry, yes. Do you know him?"

"He was down for gators a while back."

"You know this red-headed gal he's got with him?"

Jack looked into his gin and tonic. Dite had chosen her life, a hard life, if he had an inkling of what it meant, trying to please a man the live long day for a little security. "I know her," he said.

Marsh discreetly dropped the subject and they went on to talk about the horse racing at Saratoga.

Next morning, the yacht sailed south back to Biscayne Bay. At the Peacock Inn, Jack said goodbye to his clients and headed home with full pockets. At Brickell's he stopped in and bought Priss a fistful of hair ribbons and an assortment of jewel-toned hard candies.

For Hera, the sewing machine. Jack imagined her face when she should finally take possession of it. She'd be tickled, she sure would. He consulted with Alice Brickell about which model to order, paid the deposit, and headed home, whistling all the way. It'd feel good to sleep in his own bed tonight. It'd feel good to make love to his wife

Chapter Thirty-One

Hera had watched Priss skip along beside Theena and Nat. She had been tempted to pull Priss back, keep her home. Or maybe go with them. But she hadn't had the energy.

She found herself listening to the empty house. When had she ever had the opportunity to hear this quietness? *A body can hear herself think,* she thought. She stood in the middle of the room, feeling it, getting used to it. Not a soul to answer to, not a chore that couldn't wait. Hera spread her arms and turned slowly around, breathing deeply. This was wonderful.

There were two books in the house, Jack's Bible, and a novel Dite had left. Hera plumped up the pillows, hers and Jack's both, climbed into the bed, and opened the novel.

At dusk, Hera enjoyed a cold supper, lit a lamp, and returned to her book. *I could get used to this*, she thought. She'd not had such leisure since she was a child, and she meant to finish the story before she had to resume her roles as wife and mother.

After she fed the chickens the next morning, Hera put water on to heat. She meant to have an all-over bath and wash her hair while she was at it. Jack loved it when her hair was shiny and fresh. She'd been neglecting herself all summer. When he got back, she'd look her best.

She set the big galvanized tub in the center of the room and closed the front door in case someone happened by on the way to the bay. She filled the tub and kept a bucket of water aside for rinsing her hair. *Lord, I'm big as an old sow,* she thought as she eased her bulk into the tub.

Junior Spode kicked and rolled as Hera soaked. A bright beam of sunshine came in through the back window, lighting up her swollen breasts and her rounded belly. Unaccustomed to nudity like this, in the light of day, Hera marveled at the sight of her body moving from within. *Look at that! That must be his head, or his rear end. Jack should see this.*

She rubbed her hand over the baby, soothing him. She tickled his foot through her own skin, and crooned a sweet lullaby to him. *Can he feel me, hear me in there? Does he know how much I love him already?*

Scrubbed and clean, Hera gripped the sides of the tub to heave herself out. She barely managed to lift her weight enough to get her feet under her, and then she pushed up.

"Oh." A sharp pain ripped across Hera's forehead and she put a hand to her left eye. She stumbled out of the water, lost her balance, and fell to her knees on the hard floor. She touched her left eye again. *Did I crack my head on something? I'm so dizzy.* Everything seemed dimmer now. She crawled to the table, pulled herself up, and leaned there a moment, confused. Was it dark now?

Suddenly cold, Hera fumbled for her dress. She'd left it on this chair, hadn't she? Shivering, she reached for it on the chair back, felt it slide to the floor. She leaned over, finding it with her hand.

So dizzy. She grabbed for the table again, steadying herself. *Cold.* Struggling, she put her head through the bodice of her dress, but she couldn't manage the left sleeve. Something was wrong with her left arm, she didn't understand it.

"God, my head."

She fumbled her way across the room to the bed. *I'm so cold.* She climbed onto the new mattress, tugged at the covers, and lay back. She put her right arm across her forehead, the pain like knives slashing behind her eyes. Her benumbed left hand she lay across her belly, caressing her kicking and turning baby boy.

At Jack's whistle, Gator ran to greet him. He scratched behind the ears for him and Gator followed him up to the house. "Yoo hoo!" he called. Likely Hera and Priss were out in the garden, else they'd have come out to meet him.

Jack went on around back, but they weren't in the garden or at the chickens. *Where have they gone off to, then?*

He tromped up the back steps, disappointed they weren't home. The house had that empty, still feeling he remembered from when he'd been a bachelor. He tossed his hat on the table, then sat on the chair to pull his boots off. The tub was in the middle of the room. *Hera must have been feeling good to lug that thing in here,* he thought. When he glanced around the place, the gleam of Hera's golden hair in the alcove caught his eye.

"There you are, you lay-a-bed." Hera didn't stir. Was she sick? Jack walked over and sat next to her on the mattress. "Hey." He moved her arm from her eyes. He startled. Hera's mouth pulled down on one side, and the blue of her eyes lacked any luster, any sparkle. He stood up and stared, knowing.

"Hera," he whispered. He felt for a pulse. Nothing, no pulse, no warmth, only the dampness of her hair at the back of her neck. Still damp from her bath. "Oh my God, Hera."

Jack put his ear to her belly. He listened, he probed with his fingers. The stillness of her mounded belly, absolute. Jack's entire body shook. A low moan came from his chest. "Oh, Hera." He cupped her face in his hands, ran his fingers over her dry mouth. "Hera. Hera, don't go." He pulled her to his chest, her beautiful hair spilling over his arms. He rocked her, sobs wracking his frame.

Then, as if he'd suddenly gone mad, Jack leapt from the bed. "Priss! Where are you?"

He tore out of the house, ran to the garden, to the cook shed, to the hen house. He ran through every row of the grove, calling for her. Back to the house. Under the house. To the bay shore. No sign of her anywhere. By now Gator trailed him, anxious and upset.

Jack ran all the way into town, the dog at his heels. The first person he saw, Mrs. Place -- he grabbed her by the shoulders. "Where's Priss? Do you know where Priss is?"

"Priss is gone?" Mrs. Place said. Jack ran on. "I'll check with Laura Patterson," she called after him.

No one had seen Priss. No one knew Hera had been alone, that Hera had died alone.

Jack's frenzy nearly overwhelmed him. *Stop,* he told himself. *Stop and think.*

A small crowd trailed him to the center of town. "Somebody go sit with my wife?" he said. Two women left the group immediately, not sure what to expect when they should arrive at the Spode place.

"Bobby, you and Pat help me search along the river," Jack commanded. "Joe, take a couple of men down to the bay."

At the river, the men split up to search among the reeds and shallows. *If she tried to go for help, where would she go? She should have gone to town, but she didn't.* "Priss!" Jack shouted over and over.

Jack followed the river nearly to the bay before the word caught up with him. "She's safe!" Pat hollered as soon as he saw Jack's figure down stream. "Priss is safe!"

Jack's strength flushed away with all the fear he'd barely kept in check, and his legs went out from under him. He sat in the weedy mud on the bank of the river, his face in his hands, his shoulders shaking. Pat caught up to him and stared to see a man so undone, a man like Jack Spode.

Pat touched Jack's heaving shoulders with the tips of his fingers. "Your gal is with her aunt," he said. "A man from Chase's plantation passed by on the river. He said he seen her up there with Theena Chase and her youngun."

Jack raised himself and wiped his eyes with the back of his hand. "I'll go see to Hera, then," he said.

Back at the house Mrs. Place and Mrs. Patterson had finished dressing Hera. They'd brushed her hair and closed the sightless eyes with coins, then spread a quilt over her head. They waited under the banyan tree while Jack went in to his wife.

He climbed the porch one heavy step at a time. At the bedside, Jack pulled the quilt away and stared at his pretty Hera. Her sweet red lips were dull and dry now, but her hair, curling around her face, caught a ray of sunshine from the window. Jack pulled a curl through his fingers and watched it spring back, golden and alive.

Jack's eyes spilled over, no accompanying shudders and sobs now, just a silent steady flow of tears over his face. He ran his hand over Hera's belly, trying to feel the baby, his son, or another little girl. *We've lost our babe, Hera.*

He gripped his wife's cold hand, held it in both his own, and kissed her palm. "I love you," he murmured. He bent his head and pressed her hand to his forehead. *God, take them to you. Let them be happy at your side.*

Mrs. Place came in and found Jack leaned over the bed from his chair, his forehead on the mattress, his arm across Hera's body. She put a hand on Jack's shoulder. "Mr. Spode," she said. "I made some coffee out in the cook shed. Why don't you come on outside and have a cup?"

Jack pulled himself to his feet. He didn't look at Hera's body again. Always, whatever she felt or thought had played across her face. Now, expressionless, this wasn't Hera. She was gone.

Mrs. Patterson pulled the quilt back over the body to protect it from the flies.

The next morning, Bobby rode to the Chase place. Theena answered the door with a big smile. "Mr. Willis. Come on in."

Bobby took off his straw hat and stepped in. "Your husband to home, Theena?"

Theena tilted her head to look at him. The man twisted his hat round and round in his hands, avoiding her eyes. "He's working at the far end of the groves today."

"Maybe you could send somebody out to get him. He needs to be here."

Theena gripped Bobby's arm. "What is it? Is someone hurt?"

When Bobby shook his head, Theena's scalp drew tight. Three loved ones in Lemon City. Three ways to a broken heart. A little whimper escaped her lips.

"Tell me!"

"All right, Theena. Just sit down." Bobby led her to the settee. He let her cling to his hand and sat next to her.

"It's Hera, Theena." He looked at her now, all she needed to know in his eyes. "She's gone."

A hot poker seared through Theena's chest. "Here, now." Bobby caught her so she didn't sway off the sofa. He brought her into his arms and held her as the first wave of sobs shook her.

Leaving her family to follow in the wagon, Theena hurried away on horseback alongside Bobby.

Hera's body lay in the coffin, the lid down but unfastened. Bobby removed the lid for her and stood by, a hand at her elbow.

Theena's breath caught and scraped its way out her throat. Mrs. Patterson led Theena outside where Jack stood alone under the massive banyan tree. "I'll see to the drape, now," Mrs. Patterson said.

Shadows darkened Jack's eyes in the too pale face. His mouth, so often curved into a smile, was white and immobile. Theena reached her hands out, and he pulled her to him. They grieved, no words between them.

Theena leaned back. Jack looked lost, desolate, alone. Staring at her with swollen eyes, he stepped away, out of reach. She understood. He would not touch her again. On a shuddering breath, she nodded. For Hera's sake, they would never touch again.

They buried Hera in the little cemetery north of Lemon City before the sun set. Jack held Priss, and she kept her face against his massive shoulder so as not to see her Mama go in the ground. Theena stood between Randolph and his mother, Nat's hand in hers.

After the funeral, Randolph took Theena's arm and led her and Nat to the wagon. Theena looked back over her shoulder to see Jack take Priss' hand and trudge towards home, to an empty house.

Two weeks later, Theena rode over for Priss's birthday. She left Nat at home, but she took Percy with her so Jack could not misunderstand that the purpose of her visit was to see about Priss. Her fingers fussed with the pink ribbon tied around the wrapped bundle, Priss's present inside. If she knew Jack, he'd be thinking about Hera. He wouldn't likely be glad to see her.

Theena herself talked to Hera's spirit every day. And she prayed every day. *God, don't let Hera hate me now she's up there and knows what I did. I never wanted to hurt her. Please, God, let her forgive me.*

Percy parked the wagon in the shade of the big banyan. Jack received them formally, his arms crossed over his chest. For a moment, Theena wondered if he were going to keep them on the porch. His gaze flicked to the beribboned box in her hands.

"There's a cake, too, Jack. For Priss's birthday."

"I made a cake."

She nodded, glad she'd left hers in the wagon.

He led them inside to sit on the hard chairs around the table. He got plates and forks and brought his cake to the table. A very credible cake, Theena thought.

Theena put the present on the table in front of Priss. "Happy Birthday!"

Priss's blue eyes rounded. She reached for the pink ribbon with both chubby hands and pulled it off, opened the box, and let out a heartfelt "Ohhh." She grabbed the rag doll Theena had made and hugged it to her heart, her eyes squeezed tight.

Jack put a gentle hand on her head. "Priss, what do you say?"

"Thank you, thank you, Aunt Theena."

"What are you going to name her?"

Priss touched the eyes made of blue yarn and smoothed the pink dress. "Her name is . . . Pinky Blue."

"Pinky Blue it is, then. Are you going to feed her some of your cake?"

They ate their cake, Percy helping to keep a conversation going. While he and Jack talked about oranges and lemons, Priss climbed into Theena's lap so they could share their cake with Pinky Blue.

Jack seemed to be managing. The shadows under his eyes told her he wasn't sleeping, but Priss had on a clean dress, her face and hands were washed, her hair combed. He'd even made a cake, for goodness' sake. There was no light in his eyes, though. No hint on his face that he had ever smiled or ever would again.

Theena was glad she hadn't brought Nat. Priss needed her attention. She'd always been an affectionate child, but now she continually twisted in Theena's lap to see that her aunt was listening and watching her play. Once she'd eaten her cake, Priss wrapped her arms around Theena's neck, the doll clutched in one hand, and lay her head on Theena's shoulder.

Theena closed her throat, holding in a ragged breath, trying not to shudder or spill the tears building behind her eyes. She pressed her cheek against Priss's curls and held on.

"How's the new house coming along?" Jack said.

Theena wiped her eyes, her arm still pressing Priss close. "About done. Nat and I will move in in a few weeks."

"Before Chase leaves?"

She shook her head, neither of them really looking at each other. "No. When Randolph and his mother leave, then Nat and I will move."

Jack fiddled with the pink ribbon, wrapping it around his fingers. "He's taking care of you."

Theena frowned. "Yes, Jack. Of course he is."

He nodded, twisting the ribbon round and round.

"Listen, Jack. I think Priss might like to come home with--."

Jack's head snapped up. "We're fine. Come here, Priss."

She climbed out of Theena's lap and into her daddy's arms. "We're good buddies, aren't we?" he said, tickling her ribs. Priss giggled and squirmed, clearly the beloved child of a devoted father. And clearly the end of the discussion.

Jack did not need – or want – Theena's help. She'd have to respect that. But Priscilla belonged to her, too, and she'd need her aunt as she grew up.

"Well, we'll be going," Theena said. "Percy?'

"I'll get the wagon turned around," he said.

Theena opened her arms and Priss climbed off her daddy's lap for a hug. She kissed Priss's face, her strawberry curls and full cheeks so like Hera's.

I'll take care of her, Hera, I promise. When the time is right, I'll be back.

Chapter Thirty-Two

Theena folded a sheet and put it into one of the baskets she'd take with her to the new place. She smiled as she ran her fingers over the clumsy embroidery she'd once inflicted on a pillowcase. She didn't have to embroider anything ever again if she didn't want to. And she didn't.

Mother Chase had already sent over the settee and two parlor chairs, a rug, three lamps, and the mahogany dining table and chairs. Where Theena would find room for all that in her little cabin, she didn't know. She'd have to hang some of the chairs from the wall so she and Nat could get around.

The linen basket full, Theena leaned her knee against the bed where she and Randolph had been so wantonly happy those first months. That seemed a life time ago. Fresher were the memories of lying side by side, hurting too much to reach across the ocean of grief separating them.

"It's time," Mother Chase said from the doorway. Her eyes were red, and Theena knew she grieved to leave Nat. But she'd made her choice to be with Randolph, and Theena understood that. Mrs. Chase was too old to let her son go off a thousand miles, not knowing how or when she would see him again.

"I'm ready." She took Mother Chase's hand. "I'll write to you, Mother. I'll tell you everything Nat does. When he learns to read, when he loses his first tooth, when he kills his first bear."

Mother Chase laughed. "You keep my grandson away from the bears, Athena." Mrs. Chase picked up a basket. "This going, too?"

Theena nodded and settled the larger basket on her hip. "I will write to you, I promise."

"I know you will, dear. And as soon as I'm settled in, I'll send Nat some new story books. Be thinking what else you'll want. Shoes, maybe. Whatever you or Nat need, you'll have it, always."

"Everybody ready?" Randolph called.

The new cabin had been ready for a week, but the thought of either of them left alone in this house hurt too much. Theena had decided she and Randolph would leave together, each of them taking the first step into their new lives, together, though apart.

Theena held Nat on her lap, and Randolph and his mother sat on either side of her. Behind them, the wagon sagged with the trunks to go aboard the schooner.

At the bay, near the Peacock Inn where Dite had disembarked so long ago, they met the crew that would take Randolph and his mother out to the schooner for the trip north.

Mrs. Chase sat down on the cypress bench under the palms and pulled Nat to her. She held his hands and looked into his eyes. "I love you, Nathanial. Can you remember that?"

Nat nodded gravely. The months since Mrs. Chase had become his grandmother had been enough, Theena thought. He didn't remember the first years of cold neglect. He'd miss her, and because his granny's face was wet with tears, his eyes filled.

"When you learn to write, you and I can exchange letters. You'll like that, won't you? And I'll send you books, all the books you want." She hugged him. Nat wrapped his brown arms around her neck and held on.

Randolph took Theena's elbow and led her aside. "You'll have everything you need, you know that."

"Yes. Thank you."

A breath burst from Randolph's lungs. He tilted his head to the heavens. "God, Theena, don't thank me." He looked away until he had his voice back. "You have an allowance, an annuity really. You don't have to raise pineapples or oranges or anything else. You can do whatever you want."

"I am doing what I want, Randolph."

Randolph looked at her, more fully than he had in months. "I'm not coming back, Theena."

"I know." She stood on her tiptoes and kissed him. "Be well, Randolph." She laid her hand on his cheek. "Learn how to live again."

The trunks were stowed in the boat. Randolph knelt down. "Be a good boy, Nat. Take care of your mother. Can you do that?" Nat nodded. "When you're older, there will be money for --."

"Nat doesn't understand that now, Randolph," Mother Chase said. "Tell him you love him, son, and hug him good-bye."

"Nat." His voice came out rough, tear-choked. "I love you."

Randolph embraced him and Theena thought her heart would break. They'd all lost so much. Maybe Randolph most of all.

Randolph helped his mother into the boat, and the crew pushed off. Mother Chase waved her handkerchief at them. Nat waved back until the boat was only a speck upon the bay.

Theena lingered on shore, hating to turn her back on Randolph, her husband, Liza's father. Once she turned away, he'd truly be gone.

Nat leaned against her legs. She wasn't helping him staring after his father and his granny, tears running down her cheeks. "Come on, Nat." Theena lifted him into the wagon and then climbed up herself. She took the reins, turned the horses, and left the shore behind.

"Where are we going now, Mama?"

Theena wiped her face and put her arm around her son. No need for such a little boy to carry all that sadness home with him. This was the beginning, not the end.

"We, young man, are going to our very own little house, where you are going to find a special present waiting for you. What do you think it is?"

Nat guessed slingshot, candy, knife, fishing pole, pony. Finally he hit on it. Not one, but two kittens waited for him, ready for loving and laughing.

The new house smelled of pine and cypress. When the wind blew, the house moved not at all; when it rained, nary a drop found its way inside. Nat played with his kittens, Theena started a summer garden and read the book Mr. Wallace loaned her about raising pineapples. Percy, who'd stayed on as the new owners' stable hand, looked in on them once a week, as he'd promised, but she and Nat didn't need a thing. The days were full of labor and Nat, and Theena laid her head on her pillow every night mercifully ready for sleep.

Saturday morning, Theena and Nat sat at breakfast, still in their nightclothes, when they heard someone outside. Theena threw a large shawl over her gown and peeked out the window. Billy Yoholo and Tommy were in the yard, saying hello to the dogs and kittens. Theena quickly slipped her gown off and her dress on, didn't worry about her hair or her shoes, and met them as they climbed the porch.

"Tommy, you're so big! Have you had breakfast? Come in, come in. Nat, you remember Tommy?" Tommy, attracted to the smell of cane syrup and bacon, joined Nat at the table. They might have seen each other only the week before, as at ease as the two of them were together. Nat scooted over and they shared the same chair and the same plate.

"You got coffee?" Billy said. She did. Billy took a couple of chairs down from their hooks while Theena made a fresh pot and mixed up some more flapjacks.

The loneliness Theena had once feared was not the yawning abyss it once was. She managed well, being on her own now, just her and Nat building up the place. But lord she craved adult conversation. Billy drank coffee and let her talk.

They walked over the place, Nat and Tommy trailing along intent on their own discoveries. Theena showed Billy the new chicken house and the thriving patch of pineapples. "How many acres you think it'll take to make a profit?" Theena asked.

"I don't know the first thing about growing pineapples," Billy said.

"Well, I don't either. But I will." She cut two for him to take home to Rosa.

When it was time to go, Billy said, "Come on to the dugout, Nat. I brought you something."

At the landing, Billy reached into the dugout and held up a pair of moccasins just like the ones he and Tommy wore.

"Let's try them on," Billy said.

Theena wiped the sand off Nat's bare feet and Billy pulled the moccasins on him. Nat peered down at them, then tried them out for jumping and running.

"What do you say, Nat?" Theena prompted.

"Thank you, Uncle Billy."

"You're welcome. We better go, Tommy. You need anything, Theena?"

"Next time, bring Rosa? Plan to stay a while?"

"We will." Billy knelt down to Nat and held out his hand. They shook, and then Billy gave him a hug. Theena helped Tommy into the dugout and kissed him goodbye.

Theena bought a slate and chalk to teach Nat the alphabet. He grew obsessed with letters and drew them in the sand of the yard, on the porch floor, on the headboard of his bed. Theena didn't fuss. She just bought more chalk.

She had seen Jack and Priss just once since Priss's birthday. They'd run into each other at Brickell's. "Nat and I were headed over to your place once I'd done my shopping," Theena had said.

"Good we saved you a trip. Priss and I, we're heading out in the skiff this afternoon." Theena saw his throat working and his mouth turn down like he'd swallowed a toad. Lying didn't come easily to Jack Spode. "Right, Priss? You want to go fishing?"

Jack's lie stung. She knew she was an unwelcome reminder of probably the only thing he'd ever done wrong in his life. And before he'd made peace with himself, before either one of them had time to prove they would not repeat that sin, Hera died. No, he didn't want to see her. She understood that, but she had to do right by Priss, too. She'd give Jack a little longer, and then she would visit.

But Jack came to her first. Theena was cutting the last of the collards when Priss herself ran into the garden, joyfully hollering for Nat. She accepted Theena's hug, but she was in a hurry to see Nat's very interesting caterpillar.

Theena wiped her face with her dirty hands, wiped her hands on the apron, buttoned her top button, wiped her hands again, and went in search of Jack. He was unloading a crate out the back of the wagon.

"Hi," Theena called. *Too loud,* she thought.

"Hi, yourself," Jack said. He lifted the box to his shoulder and headed for the porch, Theena on his heels. He set it down in the living room, and then turned to find her standing right behind him. He backed up a pace.

"Don't you want to know what's in the box?"

Theena touched her chin where Jack's gaze had lit. "What's in the box?"

"Hera's sewing machine."

Rather than look at each other, they both surveyed the crate as if they might see through the slats. "Hera's sewing machine?"

"It came in today."

Theena nodded. She'd forgotten Hera had been looking forward to a sewing machine.

"She'd want you to have it." Jack cleared his throat. "I'll get my tools." He came back in with a hammer and screwdrivers.

"Supposed to be, you can put it together yourself." He set to work pulling the crate apart.

"You'll stay for dinner?" Surely he'd spend a little time with them. She wasn't going to bother him. She wouldn't touch him.

"Sure," he said, "if you got plenty."

Theena flew to the cook shed as if she wore Mercury's winged sandals. She knew she acted like a giddy girl, and she told herself to just settle down. She'd feed Jack and Priss, enjoy a little company, and they'd go home. She knew that's all there would ever be between them. *I know it, Hera.* And that was right.

She put two pots of water to boil. Next she caught a chicken. By then Nat and Priss had tired of the caterpillar and were underfoot.

"Stand back," Theena told them, and whacked the chicken's head off. It flapped out of her hands and the headless creature ran all over the yard, the children shrieking and Theena laughing with them. She ran it down and dunked it into one of the boiling pots, then let Nat and Priss help her pluck it.

She cut a bowl of okra and an eggplant, then called Nat and Priss. "Find the two biggest reddest tomatoes and I'll let you cut them up."

Okra frying in a pan of grease, eggplant simmering in a pot, the chicken dredged and crackling in the iron dutch oven, Theena ordered up some of the wild purple irises growing along the river bank. Nat and Priscilla, under Theena's watchful eye, pulled half a dozen and then put them in the crystal vase Mother Chase had left them. They'd have a pretty table for Jack and eat in the sunshine on this gorgeous day.

"Go see if your daddy can stop now and come eat," Theena told Priss. The two little ones ran – they seldom walked – into the house and came back with Jack in tow.

Avoiding eye contact, Jack seated himself on the bench and tied a napkin around Priss' neck. Last time he'd eaten at Daddy's heavy teak table was the night she found out Hera was pregnant, the first time she felt like Jack truly noticed her. Hera had had a grip on Jack that night. She always would. Theena didn't begrudge her that.

Theena was careful not to touch his hand when she passed the greens, careful not to let a glance linger. Her unease lessened when both children started talking at once and she and Jack could smile at each other as one parent to another.

Since that day in the glade with Jack, Theena had sworn to be honest with every creature under God's blue sky, including herself. She didn't miss Jack just because she was lonely. She loved him. Always had. Hera was between them, but if she was patient, maybe someday they could be friends again.

Jack put his fork down. "You any idea how a sewing machine works?"

"Never even saw one up close."

Jack sighed. "I've got it put together. It looks right. The little foot thing moves up and down when you rock the pedal. And the other little lever in the top works, too."

"Rosemary Eakins has one. She'll show me."

"Well, that's a relief. I never set myself up to be much of a seamstress."

He wiped his hands on his napkin, a hint of the old Jack in a sudden quirk of his mouth. "Did I ever tell you about the fellow in Key West used to take in sewing? Yep, a little Russian fellow." And with that Jack launched into one of his tales, this time about a secret stitch the Russian sewed into the ladies' undergarments.

What bliss, to hear one of Jack's stories. It had been too long. He caught her gaze on him, but he didn't hold her eyes. "Then what happened?" she said.

"Next thing you know, husbands all over the island got wind of this special stitch and what it meant. They tore up the undies, throwed the Russian in the sea, and that's why nary a lady on Key West wears unmentionables to this day."

"Jack, you are such a liar."

"Liar? Go down to Key West and see for yourself."

Jack and Priss cleared the table. Theena hoped Jack would sit with her on the porch, watch the children play, talk a while. But Jack coached Priss to say thank you Aunt Theena for dinner, and the two of them boarded the wagon.

She sat on the porch by herself, Nat chasing fireflies in the yard.

Jack returned the buckboard and mule to Henry at the store and carried Priss home on his shoulders. He lit the smudge pot for a few minutes to get the mosquitoes out, then closed up the house for the night. By lantern light, he rocked Priss and told her a story about pirates and buried treasure. When she was asleep, he put her in her bed and picked up the book Hera had been reading when she died. He'd already read it once, but it made him feel close to her to read it again.

Tonight he couldn't concentrate. He kept remembering the smudge on Theena's chin that afternoon. Once he'd have teased her about it, or simply reached over and wiped it off. But he didn't dare touch her, not again.

She doesn't seem to be missing Randolph, he thought. *The place looks good. She looks good.*

Won't be going back over there.

Chapter Thirty-Three

The days after Jack brought the sewing machine, Theena's gaze often drifted toward the path, to the landing. Surely Jack and Priss would stop by again. Today, surely today. But they didn't come.

She thought she knew why. *Jack enjoyed being here that day. And he isn't ready to enjoy himself.* It hurt too much. And if she could judge by her own heart, the guilt of having wronged Hera was a painful, heavy burden.

He'll get past it. Jack's not Randolph. One of these mornings, he'll feel the life flowing through him again.

In the following months, Theena made a point of going to Lemon City every few weeks. She never stayed more than half an hour, but she needed to see Priss. Priss needed to see her and Nat. Jack tolerated the visits, but he never relaxed enough to tell another yarn. Theena told herself that should tell her what she wanted to know. Jack was not the forgiving kind, either to her or to himself.

And yet, every time she saw him, she felt like a flower opening its petals for the honey bee, full of nectar, eager to be drunk from. She laughed at herself at the image that popped into her mind, aware of the sexuality of bees and flowers and men and women. Silly, funny, but real, too.

Rosemary had taught Theena to use the new sewing machine, and while Nat rested in the afternoon, Theena cut and stitched. She ruined a few pieces before she got the hang of cutting out a sleeve without a pattern, but patterns were hard to come by in the bay country. She finally got the knack of it and made Nat a red calico shirt which he refused to take off when bedtime came.

The last week in January, Theena and Nat rowed down to the store to pick out cloth. Theena meant to make Priss a dress for her fifth birthday. Miss Brickell had a new shipment in, and Theena had a grand time choosing from the blues, reds, oranges, yellows, and greens. She settled on a yellow cotton with a print of tiny orange flowers and a yard of orange ribbon for trim.

Theena and Nat lingered, had a picnic with some of the neighbors who'd come to visit and shop. She thought briefly of crossing the river and going on to Jack's house. They were more than half way there, after all. But she couldn't. She shouldn't. She'd been there just a couple of weeks ago. *Leave him alone, Theena,* she told herself. *Let him be.*

And with the next breath, she thought, *I'll make Priss her birthday dress. Then Nat and I will go to the house. And I'll make a cake. And take a basket of fried chicken.*

February fourth, Theena killed a chicken and fried it. Made biscuits, cooked a mess of winter greens. She packed it all in a basket with a pound cake, loaded the basket, Nat, and Priscilla's birthday present in the skiff, and set off downstream.

In Jack's yard, two men loaded boxes of oranges onto a wagon. A third man stood with Jack on the porch with a handful of papers. She had her eyes on him when Jack saw her and Nat coming up the path. He didn't seem to hear anything else the man said. He came down the steps and walked to meet her.

Nat ran to him and Jack caught him under the arms and raised him overhead. When he looked at her, though, he lost his smile. Theena read the lack of welcome, and wished she could sink into the sand. *Well, it's Priss' birthday. Jack will just have to put up with me.*

The wagon rolled off with the crates of oranges. Nat in one arm, Jack reached down without a word and took the basket from her. They walked back to the house in silence until Priss came running out. Theena held her arms open.

"Happy Birthday, Priscilla!"

Jack stopped where he stood. He looked so stricken, Theena knew he'd forgotten what day it was.

"It's my birthday?" Priss said.

"Yes, it is. You are five years old today, and we're going to celebrate! We're going to have a cake, and presents, and Nat and I are going to play whatever you want to play."

Nat wiggled down from Jack's arms and ran off to look for Gator. Priss held on to Theena's skirt a moment, and then followed Nat. The birthday could wait. Socks had had kittens, and Priss knew all their names.

"You forgot?" Theena said.

Jack sighed. "Yeah." He had his hands on his hips, his eyes on the ground.

"Take her to the store, let her choose something. That'll be a good present."

"I guess that's what I'll do."

He looked like he'd forgotten to feed the poor child, for heaven's sake. "It's all right, Jack. She's too little to know it's her birthday anyway. Don't take it so hard."

He smiled a little. "Thanks for coming." *Pretending,* he thought. *That's the way to get through this. Pretend it never happened, I never loved her, never touched her . . . with my wife in the house, trusting me.*

He set the basket of chicken on the table inside and then took Theena out back to admire the kittens. Jack caught Theena looking toward that patch of new ground, the acre he had been clearing when she'd brought him a bucket lunch, when she'd bit into that pear . . . . He felt the heat rise up his neck and shifted position so that both Priss and Nat were between them. How else could he prove he would have been true to Hera after that day, except by being true to her memory?

Priss attached herself to Theena. She followed her about, helped her set the table with Hera's plates and glasses and forks, all the while chattering non-stop. Jack and Nat sat on the porch stoop with two pieces of rope. Jack slowly tied a slip knot, and Nat tried to follow. By the time Priss called them in to eat turnip greens, tomatoes, and fried chicken, Nat just about had it.

Theena put her napkin in her lap, and Priss did too. Theena stirred sugar into her lemonade, and Priss did too. "She still misses her mama," Jack said quietly.

Theena nodded. "Was that the last of your crop those men were taking off?"

"They'll be back tomorrow for the last load." He watched Priss thoughtfully. He'd done the best he could since Hera died, kept Priss with him day in and day out, whether he hacked at undergrowth or picked oranges or cured a ham. But he couldn't be a mother to her. He watched her little face glowing when Theena leant over to whisper in her ear. What did women talk to each other about, anyway?

Priss helped Theena clear away dinner and reset the table for dessert. He smiled to see how grown up she was, how excited she was to have company, and a cake, and a present tied with blue ribbon. She needed more than he'd been giving her.

Priss opened her present. "It's the most beautifulest dress I ever saw!" Theena helped her put it on. A little big around the shoulders, and a lot too long. But Priss wouldn't take it off. She traced the orange ribbons banding the sleeves and the waist.

"You look like a princess," Jack told her.

"I'm going to wear it every day for ever," she said.

While the sun was warm in the middle of the day, Jack suggested they bundle up against the wind and walk down to the bay. He gave Priss and Nat buckets to collect coquina shells and strolled down the beach, Theena trailing along beside him. He kept a yard and more between them, his arms crossed over his chest. He didn't have much to say to Theena anymore. Couldn't say what was in his mind, or his heart. Didn't have much else he wanted to tell her.

Nat ran ahead, abandoning his shell collection to dig for sand crabs scurrying into their holes. Jack checked the sun. Darkness came early in February. She'd have to head home soon. Then he could relax. A flash of himself sitting in that empty house after Priss fell asleep gave him a twinge. It was nothing. A man didn't die of a quiet house.

"Jack, I'd like to see more of Priss."

He nodded. "I thought we were fine, just the two of us, but after today, I see she needs to see you."

"She could come home with me, stay a few days. I don't mind bringing her back."

Jack looked toward the house, hidden by the sea grapes and dunes, and imagined how empty it would be without Priss. But she needed to be with Theena, that seemed clear enough. And he didn't. He didn't need to be seeing Theena. It was easier to be alone than deal with all the feelings she stirred up.

"Why don't we try it overnight? I'll come by tomorrow and get her," he said.

Priss's new dress was sandy and the hem was wet, but that didn't bother Jack. He picked her and put her on his shoulders, the wet on his neck worth having Priss up there, her hands on the top of his head.

Theena bundled up Nat, and then Priss. She packed the basket aboard her skiff and picked up the oars. Jack watched as

Theena rowed away, all in the world he treasured on board that boat.

Well, he had the rest of the afternoon to pack up the oranges left on the trees. He'd better get at it.

Next day, the men came early with the wagon and loaded up the last of the crop. Jack set off for Theena's. His dugout rested on the bank of the river in town along with eight or nine others. Nobody would take another man's dugout, not in country like this, where not only did everybody know each other, they knew the peculiarities of each man's dugout.

In an hour, he poled his way upstream to Theena's. He'd made that trip a hundred times, back when he was courting Hera. Now it was Priss he went to fetch. And Theena who'd be waiting for him. He'd have to make her understand. *She shouldn't be waiting for me.*

A cheery plume of smoke indicated Theena had a fire lit in the house. Jack tapped on the door and went on in. Theena sat at a window for the light, re-hemming Priscilla's new dress. The kids played with the set of tin soldiers Mother Chase had sent from up north.

"Pa!" Priss cried. She ran to him and he swooped her up in his arms.

"Look, Uncle Jack," Nat called to him.

Jack settled Priss on his knee and discussed the arrangement of Nat's soldiers. Finally, he looked at Theena. "How'd it go?"

"Fine. Priss helped me cook breakfast this morning, and she and Nat have been busy as beavers since then." Theena bit the thread. "You all right on your own?"

Jack sat back. "What do you mean?"

Theena smiled at him. "Even men can be lonely, Jack."

"I'm fine."

Theena let it drop. But she wondered at the working of grief on the human heart. She'd come back to herself after Liza's loss when Randolph could not. She was on the way to healing after losing Hera, but she could see that Jack wasn't. Was it the difference between men and women? Or just that every one of us travels his own road at his own pace?

"You through with that dress? We need to get on."

Get on? He can't sit here ten minutes? "It's finished, but I've got a pot of stew simmering. Why don't you wait till after dinner?"

"Thank you. You've done enough. We'll be getting on."

"I want to stay, Pa," Priscilla said.

"How about we stop by Brickell's and you can pick out a birthday present?"

That persuaded her. She gathered her bundle and then held her arms up to Theena for hugs.

"I'll come get you again soon, Priss."

Jack took his girl's hand and led her out the door, down the porch steps, and back to the landing. Just like that.

A stranger would have been friendlier. Suddenly the fire didn't seem so cheery, nor the room so cozy. She pulled her shawl around her, sat in her rocker, and stared at the fire. Nat made another line of soldiers.

Chapter Thirty-Four

The evenings were hardest, after Nat had gone to sleep and Theena was alone with her thoughts. She sat in her rocker, did a little mending by the lamp light, listened to the far-off surf. She would have liked to share with someone what Nat did that day, how he caught a butterfly or coaxed a kitten with some string. She would have liked to laugh softly at someone else's talk. She would have liked to be touched.

But she meant to make every day a good one. There was the bay, the sky, there was Nat. She had learned to be happy without Randolph, even without Liza, though the ache of losing her would never go away. But she could live with it, even smile, even laugh.

It might be a long time, if ever, before Jack could let himself be happy again.

I have to make a life without Jack Spode. It's not fair to Nat, or good for me either, to put off being happy. Today and every single day -- I'm going to make every one of them a good day for Nat and me.

The morning after a rainy night, she tried to open the shed door, but it was stuck. She pulled, pushed, pounded, but it would not open. She kicked at the door and then yanked on it with all her might. *Here it comes.*

Inside, she found water in her wash bucket, rust on her hoe, and a puddle on the dirt floor. "Well, hellfire, Nat. We've got a leak."

"Well, hellfire, Mama."

Theena laughed. "You're not old enough to say 'hellfire' yet. You can say 'shucks.'"

"Well, shucks, Mama."

She stood back, trying to see the outside of the roof. A shingle had come loose and fallen off. She didn't have a ladder. Didn't have a stool. But one of Mrs. Chase's dining chairs might make her tall enough to reach it.

If Mother Chase should see me standing on her brocade chair out here in the sand!

She stood on tiptoe on her good dining chair, pounding in the last nail, when Pat O'Reilly strolled up from the landing.

"Want me to do that?" he said.

Theena flashed a proud smile at him. "It's done."

Nat stared up at him. "You remember Mr. O'Reilly, Nat."

Pat squatted so he was at eye level with Nat and stuck out his big hand.

Nat shook his hand. Pat stood up and gave Nat's head a quick caress. Theena smiled at that, liking Pat for it.

"What brings you over our way?"

"Headed to the Inn," he said, holding his hat between his hands. "Thought I'd just see how you're doing. After last night's rainstorm and all."

Is he actually blushing under that tan? What a sweet man. "Come on in, Pat. I'm always glad of an excuse to make another pot of coffee."

Theena stirred up the hearth fire and put the pot on. "Sit down, tell me what's going on in Lemon City. Mrs. Parks have her baby yet?"

Pat delivered the news and drank his coffee. Nat lined up his toy soldiers in ranks and files nearby, and Pat set his cup aside to give him some pointers. "The red shirts the good guys?" he clarified. "Then look here how you can move a half dozen of your reds over here to the left flank and keep the blue guys from getting away." He put his cup on the floor on the right flank. "See here," he said, pointing to the cup, "this mountain keeps the blues from turning that way, and so they're stuck. The reds are going to win."

Nat soaked it all up, his little face alight.

Theena had known Pat O'Reilly forever. He'd been one of those men who seemed to be intent on perpetual bachelorhood, rugged, unschooled, a good old Florida Cracker through and through. But he'd won Nat over simply and sincerely and completely. Who knew he had this gentle side?

"Would you like another cup of coffee? I have another mug. You don't have to use the mountain."

"Yes, ma'am, I would."

Pat took to stopping by every week or so. While Theena put the coffee on, he'd get on the floor with Nat and play soldiers.

"Where'd you learn about soldiering?" Theena asked.

"Wadn't always a ne'er-do-well," he said with a grin. "I was in the army for a time, in Georgia, then they sent me and my company out to West Texas."

"But you got out."

"Got no stomach for killing Indians. The poor devils still holding out and fighting off the whites, I just felt sorry for them. They lost a long time ago, just wouldn't admit it. So I come down here and turned into a fisherman."

One day, he showed up with wild flowers, blushing and shy. She asked him to stay for supper, and later she and Nat and Pat strolled on the beach. Pat knew something about most everything, and they talked about whatever came to mind. A very nice evening.

He was a good-looking fellow. Thick hair, straight and black as it could be, dark brown eyes, a rough short beard, a man with thick wrists and forearms. Black Irish, he called himself. Theena enjoyed seeing him pull his dugout onto her landing, enjoyed him sitting at her table.

But she never dreamed about Pat O'Reilly.

Theena hadn't seen Jack in weeks. He was telling her no. She understood that. But she dreamed of him, sleeping or wakeful. When she made Nat a pair of trousers on Hera's sewing machine, she thought about cutting out a blue plaid shirt for Jack. But he didn't want her to make him a shirt.

And so she let Pat come by for dinner. A week could go by without talking to another adult, and she was glad to see him. But she didn't encourage him, didn't invite his touch, didn't perform any of the coquetries that would lead him to think she was interested in more than friendship.

When Jack poled his dugout onto the bank, he saw Theena sweeping a pattern in the sand in front of the porch. Her face flushed and her mouth, that mouth, opened in a big grin. How could he not warm to that kind of welcome? Any man would. It didn't mean anything.

"Hey, you two," she called. She laughed as Gator danced around her then rushed off to find Bertie.

Jack lifted Priss onto the sand and she immediately ran for Theena. And here came Nat, hollering "Uncle Jack." Jack felt a rush of gladness as Nat plowed into his knees then held his arms up to be whirled around.

Nat took Priss inside to play with his toys. Jack stood back, his hands in his pockets.

"What is it?" Theena said.

"Let's sit on the steps."

He let Theena sit first, then took the step below hers. He wouldn't be bumping elbows with her this way, but what he hadn't anticipated was that now his face was only inches from hers. She'd been out in the garden picking tomatoes. He could smell the tomato leaves on her hands.

Jack looked at a spot just left of her ear when he spoke to her. "I've had a message from Mr. Kirk. Remember that fellow I told you about fell in the gator pond?"

"I remember."

A fly tried to light on Theena's fragrant hands. Jack waved it off. "He wants to sail down the keys, fish the Gulf Stream, end up in Havana. Likely be a five or six week trip."

Theena nodded. "Priss can stay with us. We'll be glad to have her."

"It's a lot to ask," he said.

"She belongs to me, too."

Jack stared at the worn every-day boots on Theena's feet. He liked to see her bare-footed. "I'm worried Priss will miss me too bad."

"She'll miss you, but she'll know you're coming back."

Jack worried he'd miss Priss too bad, too. He listened to her inside using her grown-up voice, negotiating with Nat over who got how many blocks.

"Well, then," he said.

"So you'll go?"

Jack picked at a splinter on the stair step. "It'd be a big paycheck. You think you can manage?"

"We'll be fine. When does he want you?"

Jack stood, brushing off the seat of his pants. "In the morning, I guess. You need anything doing while I'm here?"

Theena smiled at him. "My skiff needs a seam caulked."

"All right." *That's the prettiest mouth I ever saw on a woman*, he thought. Memory of tasting that mouth washed over him. Never again. He meant that. "Nat, come on out here. We got work to do."

Priss and Theena sat on the porch, each with a bowl of beans to snap, and talked about five year old things while they watched the men working. Nat had the tack hammer and a board to pound on while Jack mended the skiff.

Theena knew she shouldn't make plans featuring Jack Spode. But the sight of him working, Nat at his side, filled her with hope. She had everything in this world she needed. Everything she wanted, except Jack. Maybe, someday.

As Theena saw to the children and the garden, she kept track of Jack working on her boat, fixing a section of fence lazing too far out of line, showing Nat how to tie another sailor's knot. Two bright red ibis over head, scarlet against the blue sky. Theena took a breath and closed her eyes, capturing this moment, drawing it deep into her memory. This is what she wanted, everything she wanted. This sun, this sky. Her landing on the river. Most of all, Jack, Priss, Nat, and her, together.

Then Jack pulled her back to the reality behind this perfect moment. "Guess I'll get on. Come here, Priss."

She climbed into his lap and he told her he'd be gone awhile.

"How long is awhile?" Priss said.

"It's a long time, sugar. But your Aunt Theena will take care of you, and you can help her with Nat. You remember we're going to make us a boat together? When I get back, we'll do that. And what's the name of it?"

"The Priscilla," she said, very pleased.

Jack hugged and kissed his girl. With his hand on her curls, he turned to Theena. It took her breath when he let his gaze linger on her face, his own unguarded for just a moment. At the glimpse of loneliness she saw in him, she wanted to wrap her arms around him, to comfort him and tell him it was all right to be alive.

He dropped his gaze to the ground. "I hear Pat O'Reilly's been coming by."

She nodded. *Say it. Tell me you don't want him coming around here. Tell me to wait for you. Tell me . . . .*

"All right then. I'll drop Priss' bundle off in the morning on my way to the Peacock."

He was back to looking at her ear or a point on her forehead rather than at her. Her heart felt like a rock in her chest. *It's been over a year, Jack.* She wanted to say it out loud, to wail it, but it wouldn't help. He wasn't ready. He might never be ready.

"It'll be early, barely light." There was a question in his voice.

"I'll be up."

Theena got Nat and Priss settled in their bed and sat on the porch for a while. This time of year you could enjoy being out without swatting at mosquitoes every blessed minute. The night was dark as the bottom of a barrel. A front was coming, pushing clouds through, blotting out the stars. Tomorrow morning it'd be clear.

Hera was on Theena's mind. She missed her. She remembered her sunny disposition, not forgetting her jealous nature. If Dite burst through her out-grown shoes and Daddy bought her a new pair, Hera would nag and whine even if her own shoes still fit. If Mama cut Theena the first piece of cake, Hera had something to say about that, too. Most of all, though, Hera had been jealous over Jack. *It's time, Hera, to let Jack go.*

Theena laughed at herself. *As if the dead have anything to say about letting go or not letting go. Still, it's almost like Hera has a grip on Jack, and he can't get loose.* Theena closed her eyes, the tears seeping under her lids. *Let go, Hera. Let him have his life.*

Theena slept lightly that night, listening for Jack's step in the yard. Before dawn, she put on a shawl and crept onto the porch without waking the children. She heard Jack's footsteps in the dark and walked down the steps to meet him.

When he saw her outline, he stopped. "You didn't have to get up," he said.

"I wanted to tell you good-bye." Theena could barely make out his face in the predawn.

He didn't close the ten feet between them. "I told Henry Brickell I'd be away. If you need anything."

I'll wait for you. "We'll be fine. Billy and Rosa will be coming in a week or two, probably."

"Well," he said. "Priss sleep all right?"

"Not a sound out of her."

Jack set Priss' bundle down at his feet, safer than handing it to Theena. "In with her clothes, I wrote down Kirk's name. His yacht is *The Orion.*"

"All right."

"Well. I guess I'll get on." He shifted the pack on his back.

"Jack?" She took a step into the gulf between them. *Isn't he going to say anything about Pat O'Reilly? Is he just going to let me go?* She could see his bent head, looking at her feet instead of at her. She struggled to breathe through the heavy fog of disappointment filling her lungs.

"Have a good trip."

Jack walked toward the sunrise and the Peacock Inn, Theena's rooster crowing behind him. If she'd run after him, he'd have been lost. Thank God she had more sense than he did. He came close to making a fool of himself every time he saw her.

The ocean – that's what he needed. Clear his head. Sort himself out.

Hera and the baby were on his mind all the time. A boy, they'd hoped. Sometimes he could see Samuel, that's what he called him, Samuel, toddling in the sand, playing in the bay, sleeping next to his big sister. In his mind's eye, he could see Hera, the lantern light catching the gold in her hair as she bent over a slate, teaching Samuel his letters. Jack thought his heart would split in two, moments like that.

Theena's pull on him only complicated things. When Priss was older, she needed to know he'd honored her mama's memory. How did he do that with another woman in his heart? And how could he have Theena when Hera was still with him?

Pat's a good man. Jack gritted his teeth. *If she wants him, she should* --. He couldn't let himself finish that thought. He pulled out his tobacco and took a chaw, a recent nasty habit Hera would not have put up with. The tang filled his mouth and he spit. *Hell, I don't even like the stuff.*

At the Inn, Jack met up with Kirk and his friends. They boarded the sleek mahogany-trimmed yacht and set sail under a brilliant Biscayne sky. Jack gloried in the fresh gale and the deep blue of the Gulf Stream. As the ocean spray flew in his face, the muscles in his neck relaxed. He opened his lungs and breathed in the sea air.

The fishing was good. Kirk, with Jack's help, landed a spectacular sailfish, making him the envy of his associates on board. Then Jack sat in the chair while the gentlemen dined. In ten minutes, the troll line zinged and a blue marlin leapt from the sea. Jack's arms tensed, ready for the next rush.

Kirk spied the action from the cabin window and ran out with his friends behind him. "What a show!" Kirk exclaimed as Jack played the creature. "He must be eight feet. Look at that!"

The marlin's huge strength and speed noticeably pulled the yacht to starboard. Jack focused all his faculties on the giant, fought its maneuvers, guessed its next move, gave line, then reeled it back. The struggle filled him with a wild glee as every cell in his body strained to conquer the fish. God, it was good to be alive!

At last, Jack's strength all but spent, the marlin succumbed. It took three men to haul it aboard. Jack celebrated the marlin's beauty and spirit, then silently mourned its passing as the brightness of its eye, the sheen of its silvery blue scales faded and dimmed.

While the other men measured the marlin and exclaimed at its weight, Jack went forward to stand in the bow. He propped his foot on the railing and stared out to sea. *Damn it to hell. I wish it had got loose.* Seeing death, watching it happen before his eyes, brought back the vision of Hera's empty face. Incomprehensible death. Fearsome, inevitable death.

Jack ignored the to-do on deck where the sailfish and the marlin lay. Seeing the life drain from the wondrous creature back there, that had ruffled him. But before that, when the marlin had leapt and raced and charged -- lord, what a thrill.

Damn it. I'm alive. And I've been walking around like there's something wrong with that.

He took hold of the ropes and leapt onto the bowsprit. With his arms spread wide, his hands on the forestays, Jack rode the great horizontal mast as the boat lunged and lifted in the waves. Ocean spray flew into his face, wind blew through his hair. He filled his lungs and closed his eyes.

Only Jack's grip on the stays saved him from plunging into the water. Spray soaked him, wind chilled him. His arms muscles trembled as the bow cut through the sea. He felt light-headed, but something else, too, just at the edges of his being. He had a sense of life to come, of hope.

When this trip is over . . . he stopped . . . *but maybe she wants Pat.*

Jack drank that night. More than he had in a long time. The celebrating men passed the bottle of aged Scotch around and around, and finally Jack could sleep. It would be worth the hangover in the morning to have a night without dreams, he thought, but the Scotch disappointed him in that. He dreamed of huge beautiful fish wriggling free through his net. He dreamed of Theena.

The ship sailed on to Havana where tropical blooms scented the nights, pulsing music roused the animal in a man, and women beckoned with their dark eyes and swaying hips. The gentlemen of the party checked into a fine hotel. Jack preferred the other Havana and spent the evenings in a tavern near the shore. He nursed his rum and played some cards.

Every evening, a lovely, sensual senorita named Carmela leaned on his arm as he played. She wore a heavy musky scent, a bright red bodice that revealed a good four inches of bosom, and a come-hither look. He bought her all the rum she asked for. He became her chosen favorite, and he found he won at cards more often with her leaning over him. Probably because she distracted the rest of the table, he thought, grinning to himself.

Jack had no intention of bedding the girl. Not that he didn't think about taking her upstairs nearly every minute of his stay in Havana. Her soft hip leaning against him felt damned good. But he wasn't a kid anymore who couldn't resist a fine pair of breasts on a woman who beckoned to him.

Their last night in Havana, the gentlemen accepted Jack's invitation to taste the nightlife nearer the docks. The music down here suggested more. The drums penetrated deeper. The blood raced faster. The sportsmen sat around Jack's table with their rough rum, their cards, and their fine cigars, regretting they'd waited until their last night to sample this other Cuba. The women at their expensive hotel did not look like Carmela.

The dark-eyed beauty stayed close to Jack, ignoring the gamblers who tried to entice her to lean over them for a while. For luck, they said. She only smiled and rubbed her breast against Jack's shoulder, then ran her fingers down the back of his collar. Jack took her hand away and kissed it, trying to keep his attention on the cards.

A swarthy sailor at the bar had been eyeing Carmela. He raised a glass to her in silent invitation to join him. She saw his nod toward the staircase leading to the hot little rooms above, but she turned her back on the man.

Red-faced, the sailor slammed his drink on the counter, pulled his pants up at the waist, and marched through the crowd to claim the impudent whore. His money was good as anybody else's, by damn.

Carmela heard the thud of the sailor's boots approaching. At sight of his angry face, she clutched Jack's arm. "*Señor?*" she whispered to him.

Jack eyed the big-bellied man advancing on their table. Carmela dug her fingers into his shoulder.

Drunken fool, Jack thought. Carmela belonged to him for the evening whether he took her upstairs or not. The man's head nearly grazed the low smoky ceiling; he was bigger than Jack. Jack smiled. *Good. That'll make it almost fair.* He lay his cards on the table.

Jack stood up. The drunk took the challenge, threw the first punch, and the fight was on. They brawled and grappled and threw their fists at one another in a circle of raucous sailors. Jack relished every impact of his fist against flesh. It had been a long time since he'd had a good fight. A table collapsed under them, a chair splintered, half a dozen glasses spilled and broke.

Every punch, given or taken, tore through the remnants of the foggy shroud Jack had worn this last year. He took a fist to the mouth and grinned, ready for more. He threw his long right arm at the drunk and heard the man's jaw crack on impact.

The sailor sprawled flat on his back, out for the count. Disappointed – he'd been enjoying this -- Jack wiped the blood streaming from his lip.

Carmela, her black eyes alight with desire for her champion, glided to his side, clutched his arm to her breasts, and murmured something in Spanish that Jack didn't need translated. She took his hand and moved toward the staircase.

To the cheers of his fellows, Jack thought, *The hell with it*, and, grinning in spite of his lip, he followed her up the stairs for his reward.

On the yacht next morning, the gentlemen filed up the gangplank for the return to Biscayne Bay, every man of them envying Jack Spode, bruises and all. Jack welcomed them aboard, sporting a rum headache, a swollen split lip, and a sunny disposition.

Chapter Thirty-Five

Pat O'Reilly held up Nat's catch, silver and gold in the morning sun. "How about that, Nat? Think we can make a meal off this fellow?"

Back at the house, Pat scaled the bass and gutted it, then let Nat clean it in a bucket of fresh water. Priss dredged the cuts in cornmeal, and Theena fried them up in hot grease. Soon the four of them sat down to a fish and hush puppy dinner.

Nat's face was greasy and happy as he ate sitting next to Pat, his little face right next to Pat's big arm. *This is going to be hard,* Theena thought. *They've really taken to each other.* She watched Pat over her cup. *Truth is, I like him too.*

After dinner, Theena persuaded Nat and Priss to lie down for a nap. She came back to Pat in the living room and met his eyes. *He wants me. Maybe he even loves me. But he deserves to be loved back. I've let this go on too long.*

"I have to talk to you," Theena said.

Pat held his arm out to her to come sit with him. On his knee. No, she couldn't do that. It would feel so good to have a man's arms around her, but they were the wrong arms.

She took his big hand, felt the roughness of his palm. "Pat," she said. She gave his hand a gentle squeeze, then let it go.

"Pat, I'm in love with someone else."

Pat put his hands on his knees and looked down at the floor. He let his breath out and looked at her. "Jack Spode," he said, his dark eyes questioning.

"Randolph didn't leave because of Jack, if that's what you're thinking."

He shook his head. "I wadn't thinking that. But Jack . . . Theena, Jack may not . . . What I'm trying to say, Theena, Jack isn't the settling down type. He's a Conch. He spent his life wandering all over the Caribbean, 'cept for these last years Hera tied him down."

Theena's mouth tightened. She moved away from him and crossed her arms. "Jack has his grove. And Priss. He was happy with Hera." But there had been the sponging, the hunting and fishing trips. He did like to be away.

"Theena, I have money in the bank in Key West. I can make a home with you, be a father to Nat. And I won't be going off to sea and leaving you here alone."

She looked into his lovely eyes. He'd be good to her and Nat, she knew that.

"I want to marry you, Theena."

Tears wet her eyes. "I can't, Pat."

They all missed Pat, especially Nat. A few days after Pat's last visit, Nat said, "I need a matchbox, Mama. When Mr. O'Reilly comes, I'll show him my cricket."

"Sweetheart, Mr. O'Reilly isn't coming to see us anymore."

Nat gazed at her a moment, his face very grave. "He's my friend. He's coming to see me."

"No, honey. He isn't."

Nat held himself very still. Then he dropped his cricket and crushed it with his bare foot. He didn't speak to his mother or to Priss for hours, and when Theena tucked him into bed, he turned away from her kiss.

Have I done the right thing? Nat needs a father. She sat on her porch and listened to the night. *Jack's out there somewhere, under the same stars. What if Pat is right, and Jack chooses the sea?*

The next day, a little bleary eyed from an anxious sleep, Theena loaded up the kids and rowed down to the store, hoping to distract Nat.

"Good morning to you," Miss Brickell said. "Theena, I got a letter from Lavonia Chase for you, and another one from somebody I don't know."

Alice handed Theena a creamy envelope, the one from Mother Chase, but re-examined the over-stuffed white one. "It's been addressed by one of those type machines, a typewriter. From a Mr. Blakely, in Philadelphia. Who's that, you reckon?"

Theena smiled at Miss Brickell's nosy streak. "Business papers from Randolph, I imagine, Miss Alice."

Theena put the two letters in her basket along with the cloth, two spools of thread, two cans of beans and a jar of molasses. Back home, the three of them piled onto Theena's bed to read the mail. The white envelope intrigued her, but it probably was only more papers about the annuity.

They began with Mrs. Chase's letter. "Dearest Theena and my Darling Nat," it began. Grandmother described a new foal, a white filly. The brindle cow would give birth any day. "What do you think we should name the filly and the little calf, Nathanial?" she wrote.

"Cloud," Priss suggested for the foal. "Because she's white." Nat thought "Sand" would be better, so they bickered happily and wandered outside to play.

The rest of the letter was for Theena. "I've had word of Dite, my dear. I relate this to you not to be a gossip, but because I believe you would like to know how your sister does. The Bakerfields had us to supper the other day, and Bobby mentioned his friend Larry Mitchell had recently bought a townhouse in Philadelphia. Later, not knowing of our acquaintance with Dite, he told Randolph that the townhouse was for Mitchell's red-headed mistress from Florida. I doubt very much this Mr. Mitchell will marry her, but apparently the house is to be deeded in her name, so you may rest easy that she will not fear impoverishment if Mr. Mitchell tires of her. (Bobby thinks the man's in love with her, however.)"

Well, I can't say I was much worried about Dite, but I don't wish her ill, either. If she's got a little property, good for her.

"I hesitate to tell you Randolph's reaction to this news. He has been doing so well, interesting himself in the acreage up here – tobacco, he's decided – and has begun accepting invitations with me. He stayed up late drinking, like he used to, after he heard about her. But the next day, he was not so gloomy, and the Scotch decanter has not diminished unduly. He is reviving, Theena, up here away from his memories. I know you rejoice with me in this."

"P.S.," Mrs. Chase wrote. "A second letter is on its way to you. I have persuaded Randolph to make this separation legal and final. I do this not to break my ties with you and Nat, which you know I hold precious. I, and Randolph, want you to be free to live your life. You are too young to be alone. May the papers you find in the second letter make you happy, my dear. They in no way change Randolph's and my financial support nor our love for you."

Theena opened the second envelope and withdrew four sheets of official looking documents. Divorce papers. Theena, alone in her own cabin in the woods of southern Florida, blushed. She knew no one who had ever been divorced. Shameful and embarrassing, to be divorced. "Once you have signed and returned a copy of these notices," a Mr. Blakely, Attorney at Law, wrote, "the divorce will be executed."

Theena refolded the papers and returned them to the envelope. She didn't want to think about it. Right now, she needed to see what the rascals were up to and give them their supper.

Theena could hardly not think about it, however. *Divorce, such a disreputable word,* she thought as Nat and Priss ate their ham and beans. By the next day, the word shocked her less. *I feel divorced, actually. Randolph is gone forever, and though I am glad he is coming back to life, I do not miss him.* Randolph would send Nat to a good school, maybe even to a university, if that's what he wanted, with or without a divorce.

The envelope came in and out of the dresser drawer over the next two weeks. Theena read and re-read the pages, trying to inure herself to the shame of being a divorcee. Even Dite had never been divorced.

When she went to Alice Brickell's to get the mail, would the envelopes say Mrs. Athena Theophilus? Miss? The Former Mrs. Randolph Chase? How did one call oneself?

What would it mean to Jack? Would a divorce encourage him? Or embarrass him? Make him back away, feeling pushed? *I don't know!* Theena put the envelope in the drawer and slammed it shut.

Still hoping to make it up to Nat for taking Pat away from him, Theena bought two little pigs, one for Nat and one for Priss. The little white one Priss insisted was to be called Cotton. Nat named the black and white one Fish-Pie.

"Fish-Pie?" Theena asked, and Nat's explanation was a roll of delighted giggles.

After Cotton got a little size on her, Theena noticed heavy cloven hoof prints around the yard one morning. A wild boar had been sniffing around the sty during the night, and had apparently dined on Theena's corn.

The razorbacks were not domesticated creatures like Short Ribs had been. Daddy always said a wild pig was more dangerous than a panther or a bear. The boars had tusks, and they used them ferociously.

Before he left, Randolph had shown Theena how to clean her Daddy's shotgun and then taught her how to shoot it. He'd given her a new box of shells, and told her to keep the gun oiled and the shells dry. Now Theena loaded the shotgun, both barrels, and cautioned Nat and Priss they were not to touch it.

She leaned the shotgun against the fence. Nat and Priss planted twigs in the dirt to make a forest, and Theena hoed around the pineapples. She heard a rustling in the brush on the other side of the garden. The hair stood up on the back of her neck. Not a squirrel or a bird, not this rustling. And she'd moved off from the shotgun.

She heard it again, something crashing around in there. She couldn't see through the thick growth, but it came from a spot closer to the children than to her. Lifting her hoe high, she moved to put herself between them and the brush.

A boar, the biggest hog she'd ever seen, stuck its head out of the bushes forty feet away. It stared at her with glazed eyes. Theena's spine turned icy and goose bumps raised all over her skin.

Drool hung from the boar's mouth. It swayed slightly, and its head, big as a bucket, drooped like it was too heavy to hold up. It snorted and looked over the garden as if it were not sure what it saw, its eyes yellow and runny and confused.

My God, it's rabid.

Nat and Priss caught Theena's tension and looked around. "Don't move," she hissed. "Don't move!"

Theena edged toward the shotgun. The boar's rheumy eyes followed her without much interest. She took another step. Slowly. Don't scare it. *Where's Bertie?* Last time she'd seen the dogs, they'd been running after a rabbit.

Trembling, Theena wrapped her hand around the barrel and lifted the gun, never taking her eyes from the beast. *God, don't let it charge.*

The boar snuffled and stamped its foot.

Theena was shaking so, she didn't know if she could hit the boar broadside. *If it'll stand still, I can do it. I have to do it.*

"Mama?" Nat began to cry.

"Hush, Nat. Be still."

But Nat climbed to his feet and ran for his mother. Priss scrambled up to follow him.

With a grunt from deep down in its chest, the boar tracked the running little ones with its fevered eyes, pawed the ground, and charged.

"Mama!" Nat screamed. He was going to plow into her, make her miss her shot. She braced her legs for him.

Coming on behind Nat, Priss stumbled.

The boar veered and headed for Priss, lying on the ground in her red dress, an easy, helpless prey.

The instant before Nat ran into her, Theena fired, the recoil knocking her back. Too high. A few pellets had caught the fat on the ridge of its back and points of blood oozed out. The boar staggered, but it kept going, its hooves thudding into the ground, its breath labored and harsh.

Priss screamed and covered her head with her arms.

One shot left. Nat clung to her leg. Theena dragged him with her, running forward till she could not miss again. She squeezed the trigger. The blast knocked her to the ground. She scrambled up, ready to tear Priss from the beast if the shot hadn't stopped him.

But she hadn't missed. The boar lay on its side, legs thrashing. Blood arced gracefully into the air from a blasted artery.

Theena dragged the gun behind her and then dropped it as she ran to Priss. She didn't see any blood on her, or on herself, but she grabbed her up and ran for the river fifty yards away. "Come on, Nat!"

They plunged into the flowing water. Theena dunked Priss again and again, ignoring her cries and wheeling arms. She submerged Nat too until she was sure she'd washed away every trace of the perilous blood.

Shaking with fear and relief, Theena dragged Nat, Priss and herself up the low bank and collapsed. What if she hadn't had the shotgun with her? They'd probably all three be dead.

Holding each one by the hand, Theena took the children into the house and stripped off the wet clothes. Dried and dressed, she put them in her bed. "Stay here. Understand? I have to go outside, and I want to know you're in this bed."

"Yes, ma'am." Priss put her head on the same pillow with Nat's and wrapped her arm around him. "We'll stay in the bed."

Nat's eyes were huge. For once, he accepted Priss's mothering embrace.

"Nat?"

"I'll stay in bed, Mama."

Theena's legs wobbled, but she kept her feet. Ten yards from the fallen beast, she stopped. She put the back of her hand to her mouth. One sob only. There'd be no crying. She'd chosen this. There was no man on the place to help her, and maybe there never would be.

The boar stretched five feet long. Even in death, it frightened her. *Was it truly rabid? This early in the season?* She couldn't take the chance of touching it.

She gathered brush, sticks, leaves, anything that would burn, and piled it over the carcass, already aswarm with flies. Then she brought arm loads of the oak logs and pine kindling from the cook shed and shoved them over it and around it. It would take a good fire to burn this thing to ashes.

Theena went back in the house to get her lamp kerosene. Both Nat and Priss were asleep, heads together, Priss's arm over Nat, his hand in her hers. She stood in the doorway and the trembling came again. She closed her eyes and prayed. *Thank you, God.*

Outside, she poured the lamp fuel over the wood, using every bit of kerosene she had. She stood well back, struck a match, and tossed it on the pyre. The kerosene caught instantly. the fat pine spit and sizzled. Black smoke and the odor of burning hair, hide, and flesh rose into the air.

Theena retreated to the porch to watch. *I did it. With God's help, I saved us.* She shuddered and hugged her elbows, thinking of what could have happened.

The fire still burned when Pat O'Reilly ran round the corner of the house from the river. He spied the fire, saw it was not the house or the shed burning, and then spotted Theena on the porch.

She wanted to run into his open arms and have him hold her. Pat would take care of her and Nat, if she let him. She wouldn't have to be alone here, wouldn't have to do it all alone anymore. She left her chair, stepped down to the ground.

But Jack will come back. He has to come back for Priss. He'll be here in a week or two. He might -- .

"What the hell happened? I seen the smoke and smelled it a mule down the river."

Theena swallowed the tears she would not shed, the tears Pat would tenderly wipe away. *So I'm scared,* she thought, steeling herself. *Don't do this to him.*

She walked toward Pat slowly, feigning a composure she didn't feel. "An old boar came out of the woods and scared the kids. I shot it."

"And the fire?"

"Well, I couldn't move it. And I don't fancy butchering a wild hog. Too gamey for me."

"Theena, I wish to hell you'd let me--."

She shook her head. "No, Pat."

Tropical storms lashed the bay. Theena imagined that somewhere, on some island far down in the Caribbean, people were enduring another hurricane. Here, the usually clear bay turned turbid, and debris from ships wrecked out at sea over reefs and shoals washed ashore daily.

After another night of restless sleep, a high wind whistling around the house, Theena heard the jangle of harness and rushed from the house hoping to see Jack. It was Bobby Daniels, Jack's friend from Lemon City. Disappointed, she walked on out to the wagon and managed to be gracious. "Hey there, Bobby." she said. "Come on in, I'll make you some breakfast."

Bobby hopped down from the buckboard. "I got to get home, Theena, but thank you kindly." He stood there awkwardly for a moment. "I been down at the bay picking up flotsam." He nodded at the timber and the boxes in his wagon.

"So I see." *Why is he here?*

"Theena, I just come by to give you a chance to get yourself ready. We don't know nothing yet. It may not be *The Orion,* at all."

Theena put a hand to her throat, her pulse racing. Priss and Nat were inside, safe from whatever Bobby had to tell her.

He pulled a piece of planking out of the back of the wagon. In yellow paint near the ragged edge of the board, Theena read, *The Or--*.

Oh my God. The Orion. She slumped against the side of the wagon, and Bobby grabbed hold of her arm.

"Now don't go jumping to conclusions. There's an *Oread* out there, and somebody else seen a yacht named *The Oregonian.* So we got no cause to think it's from Jack's boat. Understand?"

Theena's chest felt so tight, she could hardly breathe.

"Pat said you got Jack's little gal, might want some warning," he said, "so if later on we get bad news . . . . Hell, Theena, with Jack's luck, he's likely got his feet up somewhere, enjoying a big cigar and some Havana honey." He tried to get her to smile with him. "That'd be like old Jack, wouldn't it?"

Theena pulled herself upright, nodding.

"I wouldn't say nothin' to the little one yet, I was you."

"No," she mumbled, the single word catching in her throat.

Bobby turned the wagon around and Theena ran to the back of the shed where Nat and Priss couldn't see her. She leaned against the wall, wracked by sobs. Such awful fear. The only other time she'd felt such fear was when Liza lay in her crib struggling to breathe. *Not Jack, too. God, don't take Jack.*

She cried herself dry. Feeling weak and drained, her head aching, she washed her face from the wash tub on the back stoop. No need to frighten the children. *Just keep him alive, please God. I won't ask for anything else.*

Theena straightened her shoulders and lived through the rest of the day and the next and the next as if her blood carried nettles all through her body. *God, please.* She worked hard hoeing and digging, hoping she'd fall asleep at night. But the fear kept her upright in her bed until nearly dawn when exhaustion at last brought her a few hours of relief.

After another day of minding the children, feeding them, bathing them, of breathing in one breath after another, Theena climbed into bed. She listened to the sounds of the house settling, the children snuffling in their sleep.

If she had to live here alone, raising Nat, maybe Priss, too, she could do that. She'd made a life. She didn't require a man to do that for her. She wanted more, though. She chose more, if she could have it.

She threw off her sheets, lit a candle and carried it into the parlor to light the lantern.

On the table, she spread out the papers from Mr. Blakely and read them again. If she were going to live here alone the rest of her life, the divorce would mean nothing to her. But she didn't mean to live here alone. *I want Jack. I want him mine in every way possible, heart, mind, body – and I want it legal.*

She dipped her pen and signed on the line. *There. I'm a free woman.*

She folded the papers, inserted them in the return envelope and sealed it.

Now, Jack, come home to me.

Chapter Thirty-Six

The sun shone in a cloudless sky. A sea-scented breeze blew in from the bay. Theena faced a long day, hours of waiting, of convincing herself that Jack would walk up to her door one morning soon.

She called the kids after breakfast. "Come on, you can plant cucumbers with me."

"And watermelons?" Priss asked.

"Watermelons, too. Nat, you ready?"

The ashes from the cremated boar had long since washed away in the rain, blown away on the wind. Theena no longer shivered at the sounds of squirrels or birds rustling in the brush. She built a dozen hills with her hoe and the kids poked finger holes for the seeds. With careful, gentle hands, they patted a little dirt over each seed and finally filled the row.

"Let's wash up," Theena said. Nat looked at his hands and gave them a thorough wipe on his pants. Priss, frowning, held her blackened palms out for Theena's inspection. "Sugar, that's the price we pay if we want watermelons," Theena said. "Let's go in."

Theena turned around and there was a tall, big shouldered man, the sun behind him making a halo of his sun-bleached hair, obscuring his face.

"Jack?" she whispered.

She dropped her hoe. Took a step toward him, then another. Then she broke into a run. She hit him full force, rocking him. He absorbed the shock and locked her in his arms. She had him around the neck and wouldn't let go. Skin, muscle, a two-day beard against her cheek. Solid, hard flesh. Not a dream.

Theena could hardly talk for crying. "I thought you were . . . they found a shipwreck -- ."

Jack cradled her body against his chest, holding steady against her shaking and trembling.

Priss came running, Nat right behind her. "Papa!"

Theena stepped away so Priss could have her daddy. Jack leaned over and scooped her up, kissed her a hundred times and tickled her ear. Then he reached down to Nat, who was clinging to one leg, and hauled him up, too. He kissed his cheek, and Nat wrapped his arms around Jack's neck.

Theena closed her eyes and pressed her fingers to her mouth. *Thank you, God.* The tight wire that had run through her these days of waiting suddenly let go. Her nerves softened, and the blood flowed freely again. She breathed in Jack's salty scent and gazed at him through blurred eyes.

"Guess you can tell you been missed," she said, laughing through the tears that spilled over her cheeks.

Jack kissed Priss's rosy cheek and Nat's brown one again, and they hung on tight. "I missed them too."

And me? Jack, did you miss me?

Inside the house, Jack settled in the big rocker and Nat and Priss each chose a knee to sit on.

"Nat, you must love your mama's cooking, big as you're growing." He hugged Nat to his chest. To Priss, he said she was prettier than ever, and he couldn't stop patting her middle with his big hand, caressing her head under his chin.

Theena skipped the washing of hands and faces and made coffee. The children told Jack all their adventures, climbed up and down from his lap as they showed him a blue jay feather and a particularly fine shell they had collected.

How she loved seeing him, her Nat, and Priscilla, together, happy, at peace. And how she wanted to be alone with him, to run her fingers over his chapped lips, his sun browned arms. She wanted to taste him, to inhale him if she could.

Jack admired the feather and the shell, listened and answered, all the while Theena's skirts swished around them as she made the coffee and washed the cups. Without actually watching her, he knew if she put a hand to her hair, smoothed her apron, or wiped her eye.

The cabin fragrant with the aroma of Cuban coffee, Jack held his hand out to accept his cup. His fingers touched hers and she stilled as if he had grabbed her. He took her in, the faint lines of worry in her face, the lush black hair, the eyes, her beautiful dark eyes.

Priss put her hands on his cheeks to pull his attention back to her, and he lost Theena's fingers.

"I want a story, Papa," Priss said. So Jack began to tell her about the mermaids he'd seen on his trip. Over Nat's head, he smiled at Theena. He'd told lots of mermaid stories over the years, some of them not suitable for children.

Theena watched and listened with shining eyes. She'd loved this man for so long, and somehow he had become more handsome, more . . . essential, than he'd ever been. That afternoon in the woods, when they'd allowed themselves to forget who they were, a wife, a husband – Theena's body heated through and through at that memory. Her hands had run down the deep channel along his spine, hard muscles on either side, skin smooth and warm. Her fingers had found the dimples just below his waist, dimples she'd glimpsed once long ago on the beach and never forgotten. He'd run his hands up her thighs, pushing higher, and at last -- that moment of bliss when he entered her.

And she remembered the guilt. How wrong they'd been.

Jack's glance caught her, and she blushed. What was the stronger memory for Jack? The passion, or the guilt? *God, I know I promised if Jack lived, I wouldn't ask for more, but I can't help hoping.*

Jack gave himself to the children most of the day, but he didn't let Theena out of his sight. Telling Priss "Show me how you help Aunt Theena," he followed her to the cook shed where he admired how Priss could stir the pot and pat the biscuits. But he knew too when Theena refastened a button on her dress, knew when she smudged a bit of flour on her bodice. He swore he could feel on his own skin the sway of calico against her legs.

During dinner, Jack helped Priss cut her ham and listened to her chatter, but he knew Theena's eyes were on him.

He looked up and held his knife suspended over his plate, felt himself falling into those dark eyes. *To touch those lips, to bury my face in that hair --.*

"Pa," Priss insisted. "You're not listening."

Jack kissed the top of her head. "You said you don't want your peas to touch your ham. Perfectly reasonable. We'll use your biscuit and make a wall right here."

After dinner, the children showed him the watermelon hills, the baby chicks, the new cow they'd named Milk.

Jack brushed against Theena as they both petted the cow. His arm might have been bare, so strong was the sensation through his denim shirt and her calico sleeve. He wanted more, to feel her actual skin against his, but he stepped away. *If Pat's still coming around . . . .*

Theena hardly spoke. She listened and watched, her heart full to bursting. Jack Spode, here, alive. Each contact – his fingers around the cup, his arm against hers -- kindled her body, wakened every cell. Yet Jack had stepped away from her, had not touched her again.

When she'd seen to Nat's biscuit for a moment over dinner, she'd looked up to find him watching her, his face unreadable. All his talk, all his affection was for the children. Couldn't he feel how much she yearned for his touch, for his eyes on her?

He wants to go to sea again, be a wanderer like his father and brothers. He doesn't care how much I want him.

The sun journeyed further west, and Theena grew anxious. Surely Jack wouldn't take Priss and cross the river tonight? *He must know he can stay – if he wants to.*

In the house, Theena trimmed the lamp wick. Jack picked up the scarf he'd bundled Priss's things in nearly two months back. He wrapped it around his hand, absently, his attention on the toys Nat and Priss pulled from their box. At sight of the bundling cloth, Theena couldn't hold back.

"Can't you stay here just one night? You can have my bed -- ." She stopped, embarrassed. Jack studied the floor. "I'll sleep with the children," she added.

Jack looked at the cloth in his hand, then tossed it aside. "Come on."

Priss hopped up, and he said, "Priss, you keep Nat company, all right?" She settled back with the doll Theena had made her.

Theena followed Jack toward the stand of pines not far from the house. A squirrel, angry at the intrusion, chittered and tore about in the branches overhead. They walked further into the pine-scented grove. The rush of blood in Theena's ears drowned out the birds in the trees. Her throat constricted in dread.

He's going to tell me no once and for all. He's still grieving for Hera. Or he met somebody in Cuba. He's going to ask me to keep Priss while he's at sea. He'll say he's sorry – he knows I love him – but he doesn't want me.

Trailing behind him, trying to keep from hearing any of those awful things, she said, "I didn't mean to press you, Jack. I just hate to see you go home so soon."

Jack stopped deep in the glade and turned around. The sun filtered through the pine needles, casting glints of gold in his hair. Theena gripped her hands in front of her. He looked miserable, his eyes red, and he had trouble looking at her. *He's going to tell me now.*

Jack picked up a pine cone and toyed with it. "Pat still coming 'round?"

She caught her breath. *He thinks I'm . . . that Pat and I . . . .* She shook her head. "Not any more. I sent him away." She fastened her eyes on his face. Didn't he know she wanted only him? How could he not know?

Jack dropped his gaze to the pine needles carpeting the ground, leaned his palm against a tree and let a breath out. She saw he swallowed hard before he turned back to her.

"Did you do that for me?"

Theena nodded, her throat painfully tight. She would try not to cry when he told her she shouldn't have let Pat go.

Jack leaned his face into the arm propped against the tree. He took a deep breath and let his arm fall to his side.

He took a step closer, and another. "I've been gone forty-three days, Theena, and every minute I imagined Pat here, at your place, sitting at your table, drinking your coffee. Touching you." He pressed his finger to her lower lip. "Kissing you."

"No," she breathed, shaking her head. He was looking at her now, his eyes locked on hers.

"That's good," he said. "Pat's a friend of mine. I'd hate to have to knock him in the head."

The beating of her heart made it hard to understand him. "What?"

He maneuvered her against the pine tree and smoothed the hair off her forehead. He leaned over and brushed his lips ever so gently across hers. A bright and beautiful image flashed behind her eyes at his kiss. *Yellow butterfly wings.*

She sighed. Jack stepped into the last six inches between them and kissed her mouth softly, tenderly. He ran his tongue across her upper lip, then into her mouth, touching the tip of her tongue with his.

When he broke the kiss, Theena had hardly any breath left in her. Jack put his hand under her chin to bring her eyes to his.

"Marry me, Theena."

Marry me. He said it.

She threw her arms around his neck, all the strength left to her in this embrace. He squeezed her and held on.

He kissed her eyes and cradled her head. He kissed her mouth, engulfing her, tasting, taking. Their kisses grew hotter, more intense, the long years of yearning released here in this pine grove, the trees creating a scented bower meant for this moment.

Jack opened her bodice and kissed the hollow at the base of her neck, then nosed the fabric aside, revealing the black ribbon around Theena's neck. Kissing the skin underneath the ribbon, he pulled it out of his way.

A brown cowrie shell dangled from the ribbon. He ran his thumb over it, frowning. "Is this . . . ?"

Theena's mouth crooked up on one side. "Yes. The shell you gave me."

He stared at her so long, she thought he was angry with her, thought she was still that silly girl. But no. He breathed her name and cupped his hands on either side of her face. "Theena."

His kiss was soft and slow, as if he had never kissed her before. Again, the tenderness turned into heat. Jack ran his tongue down her throat to her breast and Theena nearly lost her footing. Jack caught her up and held her so that her feet left the ground as he captured her mouth again.

She put her hands in his shaggy hair. She wanted the pine needle carpet under her, Jack on top of her, in her. She moved her knee to feel his hardness, to press into him. He groaned and set her on the ground, his hand at the hem of her skirt.

"Pa!" Priss called from the house. "Pa! Come see what I made."

With a shuddering breath, Jack laughed. He held Theena close and took several deep breaths. "You all right?" he asked her.

"No." Her body ached for him. "Not yet, I'm not."

Jack laughed and whispered in her ear. "You will be."

Together they walked through the pines, the sun dappling the shady ground, back to the house where Priss and Nat stood on the porch. "Come see," they called out, and led Jack and Theena inside to admire the dolly bed they'd made out of blocks and a scrap of cloth.

Theena fixed supper while Jack saw to the washing of faces and hands. He brought the damp cloth to her at the wash pan in the cook shed, slipped an arm around her waist and nuzzled her neck. She turned in the circle of his arms and held her face up to be kissed. She leaned him to him, letting herself sink into the kiss. *Thank you, Hera.*

She carried the food into the house to avoid sharing their dinner with the flies and the mosquitoes. Theena didn't touch the food on her plate. She wanted only to watch Jack eat. He ate a few bites, then put his spoon down. He reached a hand across the table and took Theena's.

"Marry me," he whispered.

She smiled at him. "I will."

At sunset, Theena lit the lamp and Jack patted his knees for Nat and Priss to join him in the big rocking chair. *Let them be with him as long as they can keep their eyes open,* she thought.

She sat just out of the lamp's brightest glow as Jack added to the adventure with the mermaid who wanted to give him all her treasures. "What kind of treasure?" Nat wanted to know.

Jack winked at Theena over Nat's head. "Oh, she had gold and rubies, silver and emeralds. Even diamonds."

Theena had heard other sea tales where the mermaids offered a different, more personal treasure. The kind of treasure she was going to give Jack as soon as the children were asleep. She raised a brow at him and cut her eyes toward the bedroom, a sly grin on her face. Jack threw his head back and laughed.

At last Nat, and finally Priss, nodded to the drone of Jack's voice. Theena helped him carry them to their bedroom and tuck them in. They stood together at the bedside a moment, then Theena touched his hand. She moved to the door and looked at him over her shoulder, a smile on her face.

Jack followed her into the lamplit living room. She turned at the table, waiting for him.

Slowly, he crossed the floor. With feet spread apart, his legs invading the space of her skirts, he wrapped her in his arms and buried his face against her neck. He ran his hand down to the small of her back to press her closer, the other hand following the curve of her bottom, caressing her.

Theena's chest heaved with ragged breaths as he palmed her breast. She twisted her fingers in his hair. He worked at the buttons of her bodice. Still holding her close, he reached behind her and turned the lamp out.

Theena led him to her bedroom.

In the moon's bright glow, Jack eased her arms out of her dress and let it drop. He untied the neckline of her chemise and it too fell at her feet. Intoxicated by the moonlight on her breasts, Jack's breathing deepened. He cupped her heavy fullness, touched her nipple oh so softly with his thumb, then kissed it. All those nights on the ship, he'd imagined this. Running his hands over her, tasting her, entering her slowly, loving her tenderly. *Theena, my God, Theena.*

He lay her down on the bed. Theena caressed the softness under his arm, ran her fingers over the hard biceps, licked the hollow in his neck. His hands on her thighs, her belly, her most sensitive place -- she wanted him inside. "Jack," she breathed. She took him in her hand to stroke him, to love him.

"Wait."

"No, don't wait, Jack. Do it now."

He raised himself and entered her. They yielded themselves to sensation, to passion and desperate wanting. Theena saw colored stars behind her eyes, tasted honey, smelled orange blossoms. Jack's thrusts exploded in wracking shudders, Theena's own spasms shaking her body against him.

When they knew they were in the world again, Jack rolled onto his back, carrying her with him. He held her flat against his body, ran his hand down her back, over her buttocks, pressing her into him. Even now, there was longing in his kiss.

Tenderly, he pushed the hair from her face. The moon glowed in her eyes, lit her bare shoulders, found the light in her black hair. "You're beautiful," he whispered.

Theena relaxed her body the length of his. She didn't need ever to move again. She closed her eyes for a moment, but Jack's mouth on her ear, his hand on her breast roused her once more.

The moon left the bedroom window long before Theena and Jack wore themselves out with lovemaking. Wrapped in each other's arms, they slept at last, blissful in this first night of their life together.

In the morning, they woke to the scurrying of Nat and Priss sneaking into the room. The children climbed into the bed, crawled over Theena to get to Jack, and piled on top of him. The two of them like puppies, they wallowed back over to Theena.

Jack reached past Nat for a strand of Theena's tangled hair. "Good morning."

Theena snuggled in closer and cuddled Nat, Priss, and Jack Spode, blissfully content.

The End

Bonus Section:

The first three chapters from
Gretchen Craig's novel *Tansy*

Tansy

Chapter One

For weeks, before she slept, Tansy Bouvier imagined herself dancing with an elegant, handsome man whose gaze promised love and forbidden pleasures — only to waken later in a tangle of sweaty sheets, shaken by dreams of laughing men and women whirling around her, herself in an over-lit circle, alone, isolated, and unwanted.

But this was not a dream. The dreaded moment was upon her, the moment she had prepared for all her life, and she must smile. Maman gave her elbow a pinch, a final warning to sparkle. Tansy raised her chin and followed her into the famous Blue Ribbon Ballroom.

Droplets of fear trickled down her spine as she fought both the dread and the foolish romanticizing of what was essentially an evening of business. A beginning, not an end, she whispered to herself. Time to forget girlhood dreams, time to forget Christophe Desmarais. This night, she entered the world of plaçage in which a woman's *raison d'être* was to please a man, a very wealthy man. In return, she gained everything — riches, security, status.

In spite of the fluttering in her stomach, she found herself captivated by the glamour of the ballroom. Gas lamps glowed like yellow moons between the French doors, and crystal teardrops in the chandeliers sparkled like ice in sunshine. And the music. Tansy's chest lifted at the power and fire of a full orchestra, strings and reeds and percussion propelling the dancers around the floor.

Maman chose a prominent, imminently visible position near the upper curve of the ball room to display Tansy and her charms. Tansy's task tonight was to make a splash, to outshine every other girl who'd entered the game earlier in the season. No, she thought. Not a game. Tonight, Tansy would meet her fate: luxury or destitution, security or whoredom.

What if none of the gentlemen wanted her? What if none of them even noticed her? What then?

"Smile," Maman hissed from the corner of her mouth.

"I am smiling," Tansy replied through wooden lips.

"That is not a smile. Look like you're glad to be here. Watch the dancers."

White men in stiff collars wove intricate steps and turns through the line of women, every one of whom wore a festive tignon over her hair. Tansy squinted her eyes so as to make the dancers and the chandeliers a blur of lights and swirling colors. Such a grand, beautiful sight, as if the most renowned ballroom in New Orleans were not the scene of business and barter.

She had imagined the men as leering and brash. Instead they seemed aloof and slightly bored. The young women, though, were as she expected. They wore masks with bright smiles and welcoming, deceiving eyes that promised gaiety and delight. She was meant to do the same.

"Loosen your grip on that fan," Maman whispered. "It is not a sword to be brandished at the enemy."

Tansy swallowed and opened the fan with cold, stiff fingers. She spied her friend Martine on the dance floor, vibrant in a red velvet gown. How splendid she looked in the red tignon wrapped in intricate folds around her head. She laughed, her eyes sparkling as her partner leaned in to speak into her ear. Martine had already been to several balls and had regaled Tansy with tales of handsome gentlemen who whispered love and promises as they twirled her around the ballroom. She was having a grand time waiting for the right protector to offer for her, but Martine had a boldness, a carelessness, Tansy could not match. And Martine had never been kissed by Christophe Desmarais.

Tansy glanced again at her own yellow silk, the neckline cut so deep she felt indecent. If Martine was a vibrant scarlet tanager, she felt herself to be a mere mockingbird masquerading as a canary. She touched her matching tignon, terrified it might slip on her head. "I'm too conspicuous in this dress," she whispered to her mother.

"Nonsense. No other girl here can wear yellow like you can."

A Creole gentleman, dark haired, dark eyed, no doubt very charming, bowed to Maman. "Madame Bouvier."

Tansy breathed out in relief. She might feel conspicuous, but at least she was not invisible. The gentleman was tall and handsome, his nose straight and long, his brow rather noble. For a moment, she let herself believe this handsome man would fall in love with her, and she with him, and they would dance and laugh and feel drunk with love, together, forever. She wanted to believe it.

Tansy's foolish moment passed. Maman knew every gentleman in New Orleans and the status of his bank account. If the suitor were wealthy enough, he would be encouraged.

After the merest glance at Tansy, the gentleman murmured something polite to Maman, who nodded her approval.

He bowed to Tansy. "May I have the honor of this dance, Mademoiselle?"

With a curious feeling of detachment, she accepted his arm and followed him onto the dance floor. It was only a dance. She liked to dance. She'd let the music carry her.

The gentleman wore an expertly tailored coat of deep maroon paired with gray satin knee breeches. He did look very fine, but more to the point, very prosperous. He smiled at her. "Lovely evening."

I mean you no harm she interpreted. See how nicely I smile? See how I have not once gazed at your plunging neckline, eyeing the wares?

"Yes," she managed to say. "Lovely weather."

The dance led them near the orchestra's platform. Tansy darted a glance at Christophe, sitting among the violinists. Oh God, he was watching her. Her stomach dropped and heat rushed to her face. For the rest of the dance, she focused a frozen gaze on her partner's ear, and if he said anything else, she did not note it.

At the end of the set, the gentleman returned her to Maman, tossed a bow at her and went in search of more pleasing company.

Maman scowled. "If you don't stop acting like a dry stick, I will take you home this instant."

Like the puppet she felt herself to be, she loosened her shoulders, unclenched her teeth, and obeyed. No dry sticks allowed. She would be a willow branch, graceful, pliable. Yes, that was her. Pliant Tansy Marie Bouvier, a willow to be bent to fit her destiny.

Tansy had a moment to collect herself as another Creole gentleman bent over Maman's hand and made the customary flattering remarks. He seemed pleasant, not inclined to devour young women at their first balls. He smiled. No, no fangs, no sharpened canines.

"Monsieur Valcourt, my daughter, Tansy Marie."

He was of medium height, medium build, medium dark hair and medium brown eyes. Not handsome, not ugly. Maman raised an eyebrow. Such a wealth of information in that eyebrow: this man is rich, this man is a catch, and if you know what's good for you, you'll make him fall in love with you.

"Mademoiselle, will you dance?"

Squaring her shoulders, she followed him onto the dance floor.

Tansy's resolve to ignore Christophe faltered and her eyes found him again. His focus was on the music, his brow creased in concentration. She knew men didn't set so much store in a kiss as women, but she would never forget it. She gave herself a mental shake. It was because of that kiss that her mother had dragged her here, two weeks before her seventeenth birthday, to ensure they both understood that Christophe, a mere fiddler, could not afford a beautiful canary like Tansy Marie Bouvier.

Monsieur Valcourt's attention seemed to be on the music, his gaze primarily directed over her shoulder as he moved her through the steps. He danced well. She liked the fact that he didn't try to charm her, nor did he seem to expect her to dazzle him.

They joined hands as they moved into a turn. Her cold fingers warmed in his palm, and his assumption of connection, of ease in their touch loosened her reserve. A comfortable man, this Monsieur Valcourt.

An older gentleman circled through the line to partner Tansy with a turn through the dance. He leered at her décolletage, yellow teeth on display, and he held his mouth slightly open with the tip of his tongue visible. The thought of his tobacco stained fingers in intimate contact with her skin sent a shiver of revulsion through her.

Or else, she remembered her mother's threat. Find a protector, or else face a life of penury, a few years in a brothel until your looks fade, and then what, eh?

The dance moved on and Monsieur Valcourt reappeared at her side. When he took her hand with no leer, no meaningful squeeze of her fingers, she breathed in freely for the first time all evening. The music ended. He bestowed on her an open, guileless smile that warmed his brown eyes.

Yes, she could live with this man. She didn't need to survey, and be surveyed by, a dozen or two other gentlemen. And if Maman was right, that her looks would assure her any man she chose, then she would as soon choose this one and have it done with. He seemed nice. They would likely have a family together. They would be happy enough.

She allowed herself one last glimpse of Christophe among the violinists. He met her gaze over his bow, and for a moment her vision tunneled so that all around him was hazy darkness, Christophe himself bathed in light. She closed her eyes and turned away.

Perhaps no woman could choose her own fate, but she would take control of what she could. She would be the placée of Monsieur Valere Valcourt.

Tansy opened her eyes and bestowed on Monsieur Valcourt her most dazzling smile.

Chapter Two

Five years later

ansy danced with Annabelle's Monsieur Duval, he of the yellow teeth and dandruff-dusted shoulders. Her friend had skin two shades darker than her own and her wide nose reflected her African heritage, so of course Annabelle had not been able to attract the most desirable of protectors. Even so, she reported her patron kept her in comfort, never beat her, and came to her bed no more than once a week. He'd given her two wonderful children of whom he seemed fond, and she found her life reasonably happy. For that, Tansy smiled at him as he led her around the dance floor.

The new placées-to-be danced all around her, dewy-eyed, round-chinned, and thrilled to be attended to by handsome, wealthy gentlemen. She spied one, however, who was as tense as Tansy had been at her first ball. And now, Tansy was at ease here in the Blue Ribbon ballroom, a woman more than twenty, a woman with a child.

The orchestra took a break. Monsieur Duval returned to Annabelle, and Tansy joined Christophe where he leaned against a column, the picture of languid ease. He dressed as all the musicians did, but on him the black jacket and white linen looked dangerous, the light in his roving black eyes distinctly carnal. She'd noticed more than one young woman eyeing him from behind their fans. But of course, as a man of color, however light, he was admitted here only as a musician.

Christophe handed her his glass of punch and nodded toward her dance partner. "You've made that old coot a happy man tonight."

"Maurice? He is an old coot, but a nice one." She finished his punch and handed him the glass, accidentally touching his fingers. Her breath hitched. They never touched, not since the night before her come-out in this very room. Trying to appear unfazed, she slowly fanned away the warmth in her face.

She eyed Christophe's scraped knuckles. "I see you've been brawling again."

He grinned. "Me? A shining example of virtue for all my students?"

She shook her head. "If they knew you were a brawler, they'd worship your very shadow."

"Don't tell, though. Their mamans and papas would not be well pleased. Have you noticed the Russians?"

"Is that what they are? I'd love to hear them speak."

He gestured for her to precede him. "Then allow me to introduce you."

"You've met them?"

"My legendary fame as a poker player has earned me an invitation to their table after the ball."

"I suppose you will show them no mercy."

With a wicked glint in his eye, he gave her a malicious smirk. "I will not."

They strolled toward the Russian delegation, Christophe's hands behind his back, a foot or more of space between them. She was well aware he took pains not to touch her. It was right that he do so. She belonged to Valere, after all.

"And where is your beloved paramour tonight?" he said.

Tansy stiffened at the slight curl in Christophe's lip. It was a game he played, trying to goad her into defending Valere, but she'd recently begun experimenting with goading remarks of her own.

"He's at the society ball across the alleyway, of course, with his cousins and friends. With the other *gentlemen*." She gave him a withering glance from head to toe to indicate how far he was from the status of gentleman.

Christophe chuckled. "Well done. You'll overcome your regrettable affliction yet."

She was indeed afflicted with an intransigent case of niceness, as Christophe called it. What he meant, she supposed, was that she was dull.

They split to walk around a cluster of people drinking punch. When they rejoined, Tansy fanned her face and looked about with an air of disinterest. "Valere courts a Miss Abigail, I believe."

"Miss Windsor? My fiddle and I played at her birthday ball in January. Pretty girl."

Tansy tilted her chin and looked down her nose at him.

"Forgive me. I have erred. I meant to report that the girl has buck teeth, a flat chest, and mousy hair."

"Indeed you should." Tansy drew her fan briskly through her left hand, in the age-old language of fans an indication that she detested him with all her heart.

Christophe threw his head back in a laugh. He nodded toward the arched doorway. "And here is the gentleman in question."

The slight ache of tension behind her eyes eased as Valere Valcourt leisurely made his way around the dancers, the hundreds of candles in the overhead chandeliers casting a gentle glow on his wavy brown hair. Descended from a disgraced French nobleman who'd been exiled to the wilds of Louisiana a century ago, Valere represented the quintessential Creole, privileged, entitled, at ease in his world.

Christophe slipped away. He had, as far as Tansy could remember, never actually been in Valere's presence.

Valere stopped to talk to Monsieur DuMaine, a man whom Tansy knew to be searching for his fourth placée, having tired of the others. Though he must be very rich indeed to have paid the penalties for breaking three contracts, he epitomized the most dangerous sort of protector in the world of plaçage. There could be no security in an alliance with a man of his reputation.

Martine, clad in her signature red, strolled past the two men, gently fluttering her fan in signal to Monsieur DuMaine. So Martine vied to be number four in this man's serial harem? Tansy did not like the idea of her friend allying herself with such a man. Tansy was no green girl, and the man was handsome, but really — didn't she understand he'd gone through three women in only five years?

Tansy watched Martine's little drama, worried at her friend's lack of judgment, but she was amused, too. Du Maine's eyes tracked Martine as she rolled her hips, touched a hand to her elaborate tignon to call attention to her slender neck, then made her way around the dancers toward the balcony. A scarlet tanager among wrens, she turned at the exit, raised her fan in her right hand to cover the lower part of her face, and flashed dark eyes at DuMaine. Mouth slightly open, he nodded vaguely toward Valere and strode away in pursuit. Tansy nearly laughed aloud at the man's haste.

Valere caught her eye across the room and smiled as he came to her. She put away her nagging jealousy over Miss Abigail Windsor. She had always known he would marry. He needed heirs, legitimate sons. His marriage didn't mean he would abandon her and their son. Valere's own father had raised his legitimate family with his very proper white wife, and yet had remained attached to the same placée for twenty years. She and Valere and Alain were a family now, regardless of when he married.

"Here you are," he said.

"Good evening, Valere." She smiled for him. She always smiled for him.

He stood at ease by her side, surveying the ball room, his glance falling on the group of large, bearish men in their rather rustic fashions.

"Do you see we have Russians here tonight?" she asked. "I would love to hear them speak, wouldn't you? And don't you suppose those heavy beards are hot? I don't imagine they're accustomed to our humidity."

"Russians, are they?"

And that was as much interest in Russians as she could elicit from him. So many other things she would like to talk about. Did the Society ladies dance until they glowed with perspiration? Had Valere danced all evening with Miss Abigail? But of course she could not speak of his other life.

"Shall we dance?" he said.

As Valere guided her around the dance floor, she yielded herself to the music, her mind adrift in the flowing colors of the violin, the oboe, the bassoon.

At the end of the number, Valere whispered in her ear. "Let's go home."

Tansy's lingering anxiety vanished. At least for tonight, Valere desired her, not the pale-faced Abigail Windsor.

Tansy reached for the blanket and pulled it over Valere's bare chest. In an hour or two, he'd get up to dress, then he'd leave her for his townhouse. In the morning, Alain would not even know his father had been there unless she told him. Valere took their son for granted, as he did so much in his life, but he was a good man.

Tansy lay a light kiss on his jaw and got up. She lit a candle, wrapped herself in her robe, and settled into the overstuffed chair with her book. This one was about Spaniards discovering the new world. How she would like to have been there when Columbus first made landfall, thinking he was in India. And found all those Indians! She stifled the laugh burbling up at the linguistic absurdity. She was just getting to the part where Cortés discovered the great city cut through with canals.

"Come back to bed and keep me warm." Valere's voice was muffled in his pillow. She blew out her candle and slid in beside him. "Cold feet! Woman, what have you been doing?"

She stuck one cold foot between his shins. "Reading. Did you know the Aztecs built a city very much like Venice? Canals through and around. And like New Orleans, the water table was so high, they practically lived in the marsh. I suppose it's even hotter in Mexico, though."

Valere tossed an arm over her belly. "Why is that?" he mumbled.

She moved her head to see his face on the pillow, but it was too dark to decide if he were teasing her. She suspected he was not. "It is so very much further south, you see."

"Is it?" He shifted to get comfortable. "Go to sleep, Tansy."

Chapter Three

Tansy helped Alain tie his shoes, took his hand, and set out for the Academy. She tried to do all her errands early in the day when she was sure Valere still lay abed in his townhouse and so wouldn't call while she was out. Her first task this morning, to return Christophe's History of the Americas.

She and Alain climbed the schoolhouse steps. Too early for the students yet, morning breezes wafted cool air into Christophe's schoolroom. Alain dashed for the resident cat who allowed herself to be caught and petted.

Christophe raised his head and in that one unguarded moment, revealed a depth of pleasure at seeing her that flashed through her with far too much warmth. "Good morning," he said.

"Finished the book."

He reached for it with his large, capable hand. That hand had once pressed her body against his. She'd been trimming the jasmine vine that threatened to cover the French doors and he'd stepped into the courtyard. With a gleam in his eye, a glance over his shoulder to check her mother was out of sight, he'd pulled her under the green canopy.

"What are you doing?" she'd whispered.

He caught her in his arms and dared her with his eyes. She could have backed away, like a good girl. But she'd let him pull her close. Let him lean down, the smell of jasmine and Christophe's own scent filling her head. She sighed. He kissed her. His hand traced her backbone till it rested at her waist, and then he pulled her in to his body. When he touched her tongue with his own, her breath caught. When he parted her legs with his knee and deepened the kiss, she completely lost herself in him, in the searing heat of his hand through the back of her dress.

Then Maman had stepped into the courtyard and shrieked as if a tiger mauled her only child.

Tansy jumped back, guilty and ashamed. But Christophe, all the while Maman scolded and railed, ran his thumbnail up her spine and then cupped her bottom and squeezed.

The next night, Maman had presented her at the Blue Ribbon Ball.

Tansy swallowed. She had no business remembering that stolen moment. She belonged to Valere. She was a mother. And Christophe was a respected man, a teacher, a musician. And yes, a gambler who sometimes showed up with a bruise on his chin and a busted knuckle. The two of them were no longer love sick adolescents.

"What did you think of it?" he asked.

"Very sad, the Aztecs losing everything to the Spanish, and then they died from those dreadful plagues." Did Christophe allow himself to think of that kiss? She didn't, she really didn't. She was settled now, and one long-ago kiss didn't mean so very much anyway.

"Not a happy story, no."

"Now I want a book about plagues."

Christophe laughed. "Aren't you the morbid one? Alas, my library is sorely limited." He swiveled his chair and ran his finger along the books shelved behind him. "How about this one?"

She looked at the spine. "*Candide*. What's it about?"

"Where would be the fun if I told you?" Christophe held his arm out. "Alain, come show me your letters."

Alain abandoned the tabby cat and climbed into Christophe's lap. When Alain glanced at her, a secretive smile on his face, Tansy raised her brows in collusion.

He picked up a chalk and laboriously drew an A on Christophe's slate. With his forehead scrunched in concentration, his tongue between his lips, Tansy thought him the most intelligent, handsome boy in New Orleans. He'd practiced his letters for weeks now and was about to astound his friend by writing his entire name.

"ALAIN?" Christophe exclaimed. "You wrote your name! *Tres bien*!"

Christophe hugged him and turned him around on his lap so he could look him in the eye. "You, Alain, are a great scholar."

"*Merci*." Alain slid off Christophe's lap to pursue the cat.

Tansy sat at a student table and opened *Candide*. Christophe had given her her first book, too. In her last month of pregnancy with Alain, she had lumbered across the Quarter with Maman to visit Christophe's mother. By chance, Christophe had dropped in, a book under his arm. She'd not exchanged a single word with him since that day under the jasmine, but there was no distance between them. They talked and laughed and drank his maman's punch. When he rose to leave, he handed Frankenstein, the Modern Prometheus to her and said, "Keep it." And so Tansy read her first book, staying up late into the night, frightened and fascinated.

Christophe came around his desk and sat on a corner to lean over her.

"This one is fiction."

"Is it a love story?"

When she glanced up, Christophe's eyes were on her. Sometimes he focused on her as if she were a puzzle he'd like to solve. Sometimes, like now, she felt he would lift her to her feet and take her across the desk. He wouldn't though. Christophe had never deliberately touched her since their first, their only kiss.

She couldn't meet his eyes when he forgot himself like that. It unsettled her, it hurt her. In another time, another place ... Well. She was spoken for. She was so very fortunate to have a kind, generous patron like Valere. And really, Christophe had no interest in her any more. Just now and then she let herself think he did.

Christophe removed himself to sit behind his desk again, and she breathed more easily. "Not a romance, not like you mean," he said. "But it's fun. It'll make you laugh."

"You don't need it for your students?"

"Those rascals? They're not ready for satire, the little brutes. We're reading a story about a boy and his dog at the moment."

"I want a dog!" Alain said.

"I thought you wanted a cat," Tansy said.

"Maman, I want a dog and a cat."

"We'll ask your father. Perhaps he will allow a kitten."

Alain engrossed himself in the chalk nubs he found on the desks. Christophe's lowered voice barely suppressed his impatience. "Why would Valcourt object to Alain having a pet? Surely that is of no interest to a man who is seldom in the house when Alain is awake?"

When Alain was awake? Tansy's face heated and her shoulders stiffened. She busied herself putting the book in her shopping bag. "He doesn't like surprises, that's all."

She yanked the drawstring on her bag and knotted it too tightly. Christophe thought she was a fool, a childish fool, for deferring to her patron. How could he think that of her when his own mother had been a placée at one time. And yet he made her feel she led a lamentable life. She did not need his disapproval. Maman supplied enough of that for a dozen daughters.

"Alain." She held her hand out. "It's time to go."

"Tansy." She turned toward Christophe, but she still did not look at him. "I beg your pardon."

Now she raised her eyes to his and saw only a mask, rather cold, certainly closed off. "It's nothing. *Adieu*, Christophe. I'll return your book next week."

Christophe sat, elbows on his desk, his eyes closed behind his steepled fingers. Regret scorched him. He'd upset her, again. Her visits every week to borrow a book were too important to him to risk frightening her off, and he'd hurt her. When would he learn to keep his mouth shut? He should know better than to even mention Valcourt. She almost never did.

He rubbed his face. This was an old hurt. He simply had to accept the life she'd chosen. No, that wasn't right, he thought, the bitterness edging back into his mind. She had not chosen. Her mother had done that for her. Tansy had been too young, too immersed in the plaçage culture to see other possibilities for herself.

Estelle had molded her daughter into what every white man seemed to want, a biddable woman. Christophe remembered that day at the lake when they were children. His mother and Tansy's had taken them for an outing and he and Tansy had run wild, darting in and out among the tall pines, shrieking and shouting with abandon. That Tansy had been free and bold and unafraid. She had been herself.

But Estelle suppressed all that joy and used Tansy's inherent sweetness to turn her into a nice girl, a biddable girl. Except that one afternoon when he'd caught her under the jasmine vines and kissed her. Tansy had not been sweet or biddable then. She had seized that moment, seized him in a kiss that seared him to his toes.

Christophe ran a hand through his hair. Was she that hot when Valere took her to bed? He shook his head. He had no business thinking of that. Even if Estelle's steady hand propelled her, Tansy had entered into this life with her eyes open.

What added to the bitterness, though, was that he could have supported her from the time he was twenty, a year or so after she'd been taken to the Blue Ribbon. He had already begun investing his poker winnings by then and he'd quickly become a man of property with a growing bank account. He'd never be as rich as Valcourt, but he could keep her and Alain in comfort with his pay as a musician, his salary as a teacher, and his income from the houses he owned in the Vieux Carré.

He squeezed his eyes shut. If he'd only had a little more time, been a little older when Estelle sealed Tansy's fate.

He opened his eyes to stare across the room, trying to find the resignation that sustained him. When he'd met her at his mother's that day, her belly full and round, it had been nearly two years since he'd been in the same room with her. Tansy had been radiant. But weren't all women in her condition radiant? Or had she glowed with love for her protector? He hadn't known. And now? She had her fine clothes, her own cottage, a generous allowance. All she need do in return was pretend to adore some fatuous rich man who deluded himself he could buy affection. The muscles in Christophe's jaw bunched. Valere Valcourt was empty, vain, and idle, yet he possessed Tansy Marie Bouvier.

Did she live a lie, pretending to love that ass? Or had she actually developed an affection for him? Christophe hadn't made it out, and it gnawed at him.

The thunder of feet in the hallway announced his pupils had arrived, ready to have their heads stuffed with numbers and letters and facts. He breathed in deeply. When the rascals stormed into the room, he welcomed them with a smile he didn't feel.

You have been reading the first three chapters of Gretchen Craig's novel, Tansy. *Available on Amazon in paperback and Kindle.*

ABOUT THE AUTHOR

Gretchen Craig's award-winning novels, rich in memorable characters and historical detail, are profiled on her website at **www.gretchencraig.com**.

Further details are available at her Amazon Author Page at **amazon.com/author/gretchencraig**. Gretchen also invites you to visit her blog at **glcraig.wordpress.com**.